What People Are
About This

"*I loved reading Double Deception; once I got it in my hands I could not put it down! I thoroughly recommend it to all my friends and anyone else who would enjoy an exciting 'read.'*

Some of the scenes are from a real-life lookalike's point of view i.e. how we are sometimes mistaken for the real stars and celebrities! I remember I was on a video shoot with a very well-known singer (not mentioning names here!), who continuously pursued me throughout the whole day.

I have been a Pamela Anderson lookalike for several years now and have shared many of my experiences with Barbara, both here in the UK and abroad. Barbara has successfully written an exciting crime thriller intertwined with all the pros and cons of life as a Celebrity Lookalike."

Tanya Christianssen
Pamela Anderson lookalike

"*Double Deception is an intriguing crime thriller, intertwined with the deceptive world of lookalikes and tribute artistes. If you have ever been intrigued by this surreal world, then Double Deception is your perfect read.*

The elite lookalikes and tribute artistes encounter moments of glamour, excitement, privileges, as well as occasionally some bizarre, surreal and dangerous situations.

1

During my career as a foremost Marilyn Monroe lookalike, I have worked in this capacity with the author all across the United Kingdom and Europe and can realistically pronounce that Barbara Angela Kealy has given an astute and true account of the mystifying copycat world."

Melita Morgan
Marilyn Monroe lookalike

"If ever a book lived up to its title, Double Deception does! Written by a Joan Collins lookalike who has worked at all levels in the industry in the United Kingdom and on the international stage, it weaves a gripping tale of sensual adventures crossing paths with big business, the entertainment world and the Mafia. From money laundering to passionate infidelity, jewellery heists, to Venetian Balls, moments of weakness and moments of bravery, and all in a hall of mirrors. The reader is gripped and gets to like many of the characters involved while being thankful that one has not oneself come across anyone like the baddies. Written in a visual style, one can see it would translate into an exciting film blending real movie stars with their doubles, in a story with sex, crime and glamour – what's not to like? A book to take on holiday, or enjoy reading with a whisky on winter nights with curtains drawn, finding a surprising twist on every other page, not knowing where one is being led, or what will happen next."

Stefan Lubomirski de Vaux
Distinguished Photographer

"This book is amazing. The characters you can relate to in two different ways. Firstly, their celebrity alter egos as lookalikes and secondly, the individual characters as themselves. When you read this amazing book, you imagine the people for each character! The glamorous amazing places that pop up throughout the story and the entwined love triangle that runs throughout the book. I can't wait for the sequel. This book would make an amazing film. Once I read the first chapter, I could not put it down and as I approached the end, I dreaded the last chapter because I wanted it to carry on. I want to read more. I want updates on the future lives of these characters. They are real people, looking like and playing real celebrities, entwined with fiction, crime, sex and love."

Councillor Kevin Hughes
Chairman Towednack Parish Council Cornwall Parish Councillor for Zennor Parish Council Cornwall Town Councillor for St Ives Town Council Cornwall

"A new chick-lit author has come onto the scene with her first book in the genre of Jackie Collins and Jilly Cooper. The story revolves around Belinda, a Director of a Lookalike Agency, who is also a lookalike herself. The author delves behind the scenes of the show business world of lookalikes and tribute acts, giving the reader an in-depth perspective of their lives and glamorous jobs. Combined with a host of intriguing characters, the Mafia, a powerful love theme throughout and many twists and turns along the way, this lusty, sometimes comedic book, is perfect summer reading on the beach or anytime reading with a glass of wine."

Marcia Stretch
National Secretary, British Veterans Fencing
Event Manager, Winton Cup, British Veterans Fencing

To –
David,

Happy Birthday on
27th July

Barbara Angela Healy x

About the Author

L ondon born with an Irish father and Italian mother, Barbara Angela Kealy was the fourth of seven children. Enjoying her younger years in a loving, noisy household, she remains close to her siblings and many nieces and nephews. Never a shrinking violet, Barbara, together with her sister Sandra, attended the local dance school at an early age, loving the opportunity to perform on stage whenever the teachers arranged shows for the public.

A bright student at school when she wanted to be, Barbara's first employment was as the office junior with a highly regarded travel agency in London's West End.

When still a teenager, Barbara left her home, family and friends, to follow the American dream, becoming an au pair with a wealthy American family in New York. After a few months, she left her position, and temporarily lived with her mother's relatives in Brooklyn. Soon after, she successfully found employment with a bank on Wall Street and thoroughly enjoyed working in this affluent part of the Big Apple. It was during this time that she eventually moved into an apartment on East 82nd Street with three young ladies from Scotland. Thus, the fun began!

Some time later, Barbara decided to move back to London, returning to the same company she had worked for prior to moving to New York. Always a performer at heart, Barbara joined the Lissenden Players, an Old Time Music Hall group in north London, as a performing artiste and eventually also becoming secretary. Barbara continues to be part of the very popular Lissenden Players.

Shortly after forwarding her portfolio to a prestigious agency in London, Barbara became a lookalike for the iconic actress Dame Joan Collins, and began travelling around the United Kingdom and Europe in her exciting new show business career. This has fuelled her life experiences, and certainly her first book.

Barbara is a passionate storyteller and throughout her life, people have often told her she should write a book to capture all her entertaining stories and fascinating experiences. At long last, she has now accomplished this. She lives in London, and is married, with a stepdaughter Louise, who is also a close friend.

Keep in touch with Barbara!
www.barbaraangelakealy.com
Twitter: @kealybarbara

In the thrilling world of celebrity lookalikes,
nothing is what it seems...

DOUBLE DECEPTION

by Barbara Angela Kealy

First published in Great Britain in 2021
by Book Brilliance Publishing
265A Fir Tree Road, Epsom, Surrey, KT17 3LF
+44 (0)20 8641 5090
www.bookbrilliancepublishing.com
admin@bookbrilliancepublishing.com

A CIP catalogue record for this book is available
at the British Library.

ISBN 978-1-913770-09-9.
Third Edition 2021.

First Edition publishing by Filament Publishing in 2018.
Second Edition published by Filament Publishing in 2019.

Typeset in Adobe Caslon Pro.
Printed in Great Britain by 4edge Ltd.

Dedication

To all who have suffered deception of any kind, be it love, greed or plain jealousy.

To the amazing lookalikes and tribute acts for their talent as masters of disguise and for enlightening the highs and lows of the celebrity copycat world.

Acknowledgements

Thank you to Brenda Dempsey, my publisher, for your guidance and support.

Thank you to the Book Brilliance Publishing team: Olivia Eisinger, my editor, for her encouragement and dedicated hard work for guiding me; and to Zara Thatcher, for her creative skills in typesetting and proofreading of this book.

Douglas Donaghey, my husband, who never once questioned whether I would finish writing my book.

To special friends throughout my life, for believing I could do it...

Contents

Character List.................... 14

Prologue 17

Chapter 1: Fated Encounter.................... 18

Chapter 2: Mysterious Stranger 23

Chapter 3: Passion Unleashed 31

Chapter 4: Venice Carnevale 35

Chapter 5: A Disappearance.................... 42

Chapter 6: Police Investigations 49

Chapter 7: A Ray of Sunshine.................... 59

Chapter 8: London Lovers 65

Chapter 9: Lookalikes Galore 72

Chapter 10: Passionate Rendezvous 79

Chapter 11: Spanish Liaisons.................... 87

Chapter 12: Devious Deals.................... 93

Chapter 13: Sensual Love....................101

Chapter 14: Virgin Jobs....................104

Chapter 15: Antics in Germany 108

Chapter 16: New Jersey Capers....................117

Chapter 17: The Sherlock Holmes Hotel....................122

Chapter 18: The First Lookalike Agency..................127

Chapter 19: Tanya Tales 134

Chapter 20: Diva Delights 141

Chapter 21: Ulterior Motives 152

Chapter 22: Upsets All Round 157

Chapter 23: Trouble with Kevin 168

Chapter 24: Phoenix Rising 175

Chapter 25: Christmas Celebrations 182

Chapter 26: Dominatrix 188

Chapter 27: A Wedding 196

Chapter 28: A Spy..................................203

Chapter 29: A Close Shave 212

Chapter 30: La Traviata............................220

Chapter 31: New York, New York 225

Chapter 32: Discovered 235

Chapter 33: Antwerp Diamond Heist..................242

Chapter 34: Karma Chameleon.......................252

Chapter 35: Deception and Death 263

Chapter 36: Dark Side of Fantasy 276

Chapter 37: Love Conquers All 282

Chapter 38: All Good News..........................294

Chapter 39: Monte Carlo 300

Chapter 40: Unexpected News 311

Chapter 41: Charlie Chaplin 321

Chapter 42: Web of Deceit 327

Chapter 43: Sad Turn of Events 340

Chapter 44: Mistaken Identity 349

Chapter 45: Departures and Arrivals 361

Chapter 46: New Beginnings 368

Chapter 47: Dark Clouds Gathering 379

Chapter 48: The Noose Tightens 385

Chapter 49: Venice Sparkle 397

Character List

All characters in this novel are fictitious.

Name	**Pseudonym**
Frank Lanzo	Gene Capalti

Name	**Lookalike Character**
Belinda Flynn	Joan Collins
Camp Freddie Lawlor	Liberace
Tanya	Pamela Anderson
Lady Denise Ava	Madonna
Marina Greenslade	(1st) HM Queen Elizabeth II
Louise Rickman	(2nd) HM Queen Elizabeth II
Kay Carney	(1st) Marilyn Monroe
Jane Baxter	(2nd) Marilyn Monroe
Melita	(3rd) Marilyn Monroe
Kim	Tina Turner
Vicky Sutton	Elizabeth Taylor

Gina	(1st) Victoria Beckham
Sarah	(2nd) Victoria Beckham
Glory	Britney Spears
Karen	Angelina Jolie
Julia	Helen Mirren
Kevin	Boy George
Yvonne	Theresa May
Max Rushton	HRH Prince Harry
Luke	Charlie Chaplin
Reggie Johnson	Michael Jackson
Andy	David Beckham
Mark	Brad Pitt
Adam Proctor	Johnny Depp/Jack Sparrow
Ray	Elton John
Paul	George Michael
Rob	Elvis Presley
Peter	Robert De Niro

Doug	Freddie Mercury
Danny	Neil Tennant (Pet Shop Boys)
Jack Novak	Clint Eastwood
Alfred Jones	Jack Nicholson
Hugh	Sean Connery 007
Lee	Daniel Craig 007

Prologue

She lay in his strong, tanned arms, her face resting against his broad chest, the coarse hair now turning grey. Desperately needing sleep but fighting not to allow herself that leisure, wanting only to savour every second while his tanned body lay beside hers. This amazing lover had an effect on her emotions from the very first moment they met; when those exquisite excitable feelings began to flutter somewhere deep inside her. Now becoming restless, she moved carefully, placing one of her soft, creamy legs over his sleeping body. Instantly, he stirred and became aroused…

Chapter 1
Fated Encounter

Belinda had experienced two long and serious relationships in her life but neither ended in marriage. Often, she accepted invitations from men she knew or had met through friends, but always managed to keep the relationships as platonic as possible. Married now for almost twenty years, Belinda sadly felt her marriage was becoming staid, especially during the last few months. Her husband, Matt Flynn, was a man of devious charm, possessing an extremely clever way with words. Matt had done very well for himself indeed. Now a junior partner in three successful betting offices in affluent areas of London, where Sidney Stone, the senior partner, a robust, rotund gentleman in his mid-seventies, looked on Matt as the son he and his wife never had. For some years now, Matt had been a prodigy of Sidney's and was extremely fond of the older man. These days, Sidney was forever remarking on how he wanted to retire and spend his remaining years by the sea. But for now, he was still working full-time, usually managing the flagship betting office in Victoria, the other two being located in Maida Vale and Soho. Sidney and Matt shared responsibility for the Maida Vale office, but Matt was solely in charge of the busiest and most affluent of the three, situated in the colourful and vibrant area of Soho.

Often, people remarked on Belinda's resemblance to an English actress who had appeared in an American soap. After making some enquiries with a reputable lookalike agency and forwarding her photographs on to them, Belinda was accepted and placed on their books. Almost immediately for Belinda, this new career proved very successful indeed, taking her all across the United Kingdom and Europe. How she adored portraying this inspirational actress, loving the glamour and excitement of it all; feeling beautiful when people told her she had a very strong resemblance to the star in question.

When a secretarial position became available within the agency, Belinda decided to go for an interview for the position, and again was successful, learning all there was to know about running an extremely busy company. Barely six months after starting her new position, Belinda was asked by the owner, Dawn Jarvis, if she wanted to become a junior partner. After bank managers and solicitors were consulted and legal contracts drawn up, Top Drawer Lookalike and Tribute Acts Agency had a new junior partner on board, with Dawn owning fifty-one per cent and Belinda forty-nine per cent. Being now both agent and lookalike kept Belinda extremely busy and extremely happy. Occasionally, in her role as agent, Belinda accompanied the lookalikes on certain jobs. Usually, if a particular job was in a country that interested Belinda or there were several lookalikes booked on the contract, she travelled with them as their agent, making sure everyone and everything was running smoothly. What a wonderful opportunity for her to see the world, make money and get away from her home life for a short while.

Although very fond of her husband, Belinda had gradually fallen out of love with Matt and often wondered whether she had ever really been in love at all. In the beginning, their sexual relationship was extremely passionate. Always enjoying each other's company, laughing much of the time they spent together, their relationship had now become dull. Matt's health was deteriorating slowly, mostly due to his lifestyle. Never adhering to the saying 'everything in moderation' and being a man who loved living life to the full, Matt often drank too much alcohol and smoked too many cigarettes. This caused him to cough intermittently during the day, although he was constantly announcing to anyone listening that he was giving up both bad habits shortly, or at least cutting down.

Worryingly, lately, Belinda felt that Matt hardly ever wanted her sexually; turning their relationship more akin to that of brother and sister. Of course, she reasoned with herself that his coolness was probably due to rumours she had been hearing recently. A very reliable source and a good friend of Belinda's told her that Matt had been seen in clubs and bars around the Soho area with the same woman and that they appeared to be completely wrapped up in each other. Belinda, although deep down not happy, had been reasonably satisfied with her married life until she knew of Matt's infidelity. Sadly, she knew only too well that her friend would never have mentioned this to her if it had no substance. One evening when Belinda confronted Matt about the rumour, he fervently denied everything, becoming very angry, causing Belinda to be even more suspicious because of his passionate denial. Grabbing a jacket from the coat stand and accusing Belinda of believing nasty lies about him, Matt rushed out of the house, not returning for many hours. Never mentioning anything about this again to him,

Belinda decided to bide her time and keep her distance in the bedroom from her husband for as long as possible. For the past six years, the couple had lived in a three-bedroomed semi-detached house in a smart residential area of Clapham Common, south-west London. Loving her house, Belinda didn't want to leave it.

Matt was a highly attractive man, standing almost six feet tall with wavy brown hair, now greying at the temples. His looks and enthusiasm for life belied his unhealthy lifestyle. His eyes, an unusual shade of blue, appeared at times to have a dreamy faraway look. Although slim, Matt religiously worked out in the gym several times a week, knowing this helped his occasional laboured breathing. Two years younger than his disillusioned wife, Matt was also a very slick dresser. Jealous-natured, this side of his character emerged quickly when his stunning wife was noticed and given attention by other men. Matt, although a very successful businessman himself, was beginning to feel a little resentful towards Belinda's success with Top Drawer Agency, often making sarcastic remarks about her flighty lifestyle, referring, of course, to the occasions when she had to fly off on lookalike assignments. Belinda was feeling quite trapped in her marriage, which was decaying slowly and beginning to make her feel very unhappy. Although Matt had an eye for the ladies, and as far as she knew he was still having an affair, Belinda knew her husband well enough to know he would make it very awkward for her if she decided to ask him for a divorce. Apart from his jealousy, Matt was a very controlling man and if there was to be a divorce, it would be from him, not her.

Remembering her first meeting with Matt, some twenty-two years earlier, brought the usual twang of sadness to Belinda as she remembered her beloved dog, Maxiboy, who was with her on that fated meeting. It was a beautiful, balmy summer's evening as Belinda walked Maxiboy on Clapham Common and she was completely lost in her thoughts when a striking man stooped to stroke the young dog. As the man looked up at Belinda from his crouching position, she noticed his eyes were the colour of dark cornflowers.

"Beautiful creature, just like his owner," were the first words she heard from the smiling mouth of Matt Flynn. Until he strolled into her life so confidently, Belinda had not met anyone for a long time whom she seriously wanted to be with. How could she resist this charmer, pursuing her continuously and never taking "No" for an answer? Although all her instincts warned her to be wary of this silver-tongued, handsome stranger, there followed a whirlwind romance, where Matt literally swept her off her feet and she was in love, probably for the first time in her life. But that was then, this was now, and things were not so good between them these days. Belinda knew deep in her heart that she must find the courage to ask Matt for a divorce; living this pretence was unfair for them both.

Chapter 2
Mysterious Stranger

On a dull gloomy and cold day in the middle of February, Belinda was working in the agency close to Swiss Cottage station, a very affluent area of north London. The pure and magical voice of a young Sinatra, touching her every emotion with his song of heartbreak, filled the quietness of the office when the telephone rang loudly, cutting through her daydreaming like a knife. Nonchalantly, she plucked the receiver from its cradle.

"Good morning, Top Drawer Lookalike Agency," she announced.

A male voice in broken English proceeded to explain he was the secretary of one of the agency's top Italian clients. His bosses were interested in hiring six lookalikes for two forthcoming prestigious parties at the famous Venice Mask Carnival, or Carnevale. Belinda was informed the lookalikes were to fly into Venice, attend a dress rehearsal the following morning, work at the first party that evening, and again at the main party, before flying back to London. Venice, this most magical of all cities, filled with a mass of masked partygoers, posing and preening, dancing and philandering, in a slightly surreal reinvention of a great tradition of the city; how very exciting, thought Belinda! The caller spoke quickly, explaining to her the lookalikes were required to attend both parties on two consecutive evenings and were expected to mix and mingle with guests of high standing. During the course of the evenings, they would also be required to serve canapés to the guests.

The following day, the chosen character names of the lookalikes were faxed across from the Italian client's office and Belinda excitedly went to work drawing up contracts and contacting everyone on the list and checking their availability. The chosen females included Angelina Jolie, Pamela Anderson, Helen Mirren and Sophia Loren. The males included Brad Pitt as well as Johnny Depp as the rum-loving, decidedly camp pirate, Jack Sparrow. Unfortunately, her own character, Joan Collins, was not on the client's list but Belinda hoped Dawn would agree to her accompanying the others to Venice as their agent. Smiling, she checked her lipstick in the gold ornate mirror, which covered the whole of one of the office walls. Belinda had been to Venice several times before but on each trip, she had discovered something even more special and exciting in its architecture, and Belinda was anxious to get away from the daily routine and farce of her home life. What better than to be part of the famous Venice Mask Carnevale.

After discussions with Dawn, it was agreed they would bring in a retired colleague to fill Belinda's absence, and while setting about telephoning their client in Italy about accommodation and airfares, Belinda realised how much she loved this glamorous job, even though at times it could be stressful.

That evening, full of energy and excitement for cementing this very lucrative job for the agency, Belinda arrived home to a quiet, empty house. Remembering Matt was attending a golf meeting and eating out, she ran a bath and filled the kettle for a well-deserved cup of tea, wondering who her husband was eating with.

Later, Matt arrived home from his golf meeting, slightly inebriated. Belinda had decided to sleep in one of the spare bedrooms because she knew, from experience, her husband would wake her up as he nosily moved about the master bedroom. Listening to Matt mumbling to himself as he shuffled unsteadily to the bathroom, she cringed as he called out to her.

"Are you asleep, my love?"

He then asked, slurring his words, "Why are you in the spare room, my darling?"

Belinda shuddered at his brazenness; having a good idea of where he had been after his meeting. Yet, still, he felt the need to charm his suffering wife. Feigning sleep, something she was becoming an expert at, Belinda turned over and let out a tiny soft sigh as the tears fell softly from her eyes.

The next morning, as Matt was drinking the last drop of his tea at the breakfast table, he looked closely at his wife's reaction, as he said, "Venice, eh? Very nice. Maybe I'll come with you."

Belinda was well aware of his games and showed no reaction as she replied brightly, "Why don't you take a few days off and come? You know how you love Venice."

Of course, she knew only too well he would decline her offer.

"No, not this time, darling, far too busy," swiftly came his answer. "With the Cheltenham Gold Cup coming up and, of course, the Grand National close behind, I have my work cut out here," he added, getting up from the breakfast table and wiping his mouth with a napkin. Belinda knew Matt wouldn't be accompanying her, no matter which race meeting or cup was coming up, not while he was free to spend more time with this woman she'd heard about.

Hotel Splendor, close to the famous Rialto Bridge and in the neighbourhood of San Marco, was offered as accommodation for the lookalikes and their agent. Belinda knew most of the people on the agency books, making a point of meeting them individually when they were first accepted. If their character had not been used for some time, she arranged to meet them again to make sure they were keeping up appearances and watching their weight. The agency made a point of insisting that every lookalike and tribute act updated their photographs and videos every two years for promotional reasons.

Belinda made her way to London Gatwick Airport in the heart of West Sussex, where the group were to meet at the British Airways desk in the departure lounge. Belinda held the tickets for everyone after spending much of the previous day emailing and telephoning all concerned to remember to pack their passports. Three of the lookalikes were already there, chatting happily together when Belinda arrived at the check-in desk, and they greeted her with enthusiasm. All were very excited to be working on such a prestigious job. Shortly after, two of the others arrived and almost on their heels, the sixth one joined them. With everybody present and passports in hand, they checked in with the airline and boarded the plane to Venice.

San Marco is quintessential visitors' Venice. The Piazza San Marco is famous for its pigeons, campanile, basilica, Palazzo Ducale and expensive cafés. The waterfront views are legendary and more gondolas depart from here than anywhere else in the city. In season, the piazza teems with day trippers and it is so crowded it's only possible to walk at a snail's pace, and yet a block or two away, streets are quiet and offer many museums and palaces to explore. A perfect choice of location, thought Belinda, as she and the lookalikes stepped from the plane at Marco Polo Airport, happily stepping on to Italian soil.

As was the normal procedure, a representative for the agency's Italian client was patiently waiting for them as they went through passport control. It was a sunny, warm day in Venice and Belinda noticed the streets were already crowded with tourists, although the season hadn't even started. As they were driven to their hotel in two identical cars, Belinda, taking in the passing views, marvelled at the sight of this most unique city on water.

The Hotel Splendor was perfect and everybody was extremely happy with the client's choice. Located in the heart of Venice, the hotel was within walking distance of Rialto Bridge, St Mark's Basilica and St Mark's Campanile. Nearby were the Ca' d'Oro and Basilica di San Giovanni e Paolo. In addition to a restaurant, Hotel Splendor featured a bar and lounge. Everybody had their own private room;

no sharing on this job. All rooms were close together on the second floor.

A sumptuous dinner was spent with the client's PA in the hotel restaurant. Once the PA had taken his leave, they all settled in the bar lounge, chatting excitedly about the following day's proceedings and enjoying a drink or two, when Belinda felt someone watching her. He sat on a stool at the end of the bar, his eyes were brown and they seemed full of amusement as they locked with hers and held her gaze. The very faintest of shudders swept through her body and she quickly looked away from him, continuing with the schedule for the next day's dress rehearsal, arranged especially for the client.

One by one, the lookalikes retired for the evening to get an early night. Belinda found herself alone with a glass of Chianti to finish. She had decided she would go up to her room and have a warm bath before bed, when her thoughts were interrupted by a strong American accent.

"Would you mind if I joined you?"

Belinda looked up into the brown eyes, laughter lines crinkling around them, of the man who had been sitting at the end of the bar earlier. Those eyes appeared to be dancing at her in amusement. Surprised and slightly embarrassed, Belinda answered sheepishly that she didn't mind, but that she was about to leave. Ignoring her last remark, he sat down opposite her at the little ornate drinks table, his eyes never leaving hers.

"I noticed your friends all have a resemblance to certain celebrities; you too. Are you booked to do a job here in Venice?" he asked with a grin.

"Yes, we are, how very observant of you," replied Belinda, smiling at him and letting out a nervous little laugh.

For the following hour, the conversation flowed easily between them. He told her his name was Frank Lanzo and he was a property developer working for a big organisation, known as the Society, whose headquarters were based in New York. He explained how his job took him to several countries, Italy being one of them, and because he was of Sicilian extract, his Italian was near perfect. Tomorrow, he had an important meeting near St Mark's Square and it was crucial he cemented a specific deal for the Society. Belinda noticed he didn't smile at all but his eyes took in everyone and everything around him instantly.

Feeling drawn towards this stranger for some unknown reason made her feel uneasy. Belinda liked his hair, which was iron grey and coarse, beginning to recede slightly. He was not too tall and she noticed he was thickset, with powerful shoulders and neck, yet surprisingly beautiful hands. Belinda found his accent intriguing, an accent from the streets, she decided, an authentic New York accent, a perfect voice-over for Sylvester Stallone!

They found much to chat about and Belinda completely forgot the time and the fact she was desperate for a hot bath and an early night. Everyone had to be up early and ready on time the following morning for the client's PA to drive them to the Hotel Venezia for the dress rehearsal. This particular client wanted to meet the lookalikes in person before the first party that evening. After all, they were paying a lot of money for them and the client obviously wanted to make sure the lookalikes were as good as their photographs and videos portrayed.

Belinda found it very difficult to leave the company of this stranger, who she felt she had known forever, maybe in a previous life; who knows, she thought? But Belinda had a most peculiar feeling deep within her about this man.

Frank stood up as Belinda rose to leave, taking her hand and raising it to his slim lips and kissing it, while locking her gaze to his. At that precise moment, Mark (Brad Pitt) and Adam (Johnny Depp) had come back to the bar to collect a couple of beers to take back to their rooms. The boys witnessed Frank kissing Belinda's hand and raised their eyebrows, cheekily grinning at each other. Belinda, highly embarrassed and blushing, reminded them of their early start the following morning. Blowing her kisses and smiling, they assured her they would be on time and turned quickly on their heels, strolling out of the bar, beers clasped tightly in their hands.

Belinda noticed the amusement in Frank's knowing eyes and felt a little uncomfortable under his gaze. It was as though he were laughing at her. As charming as he was, Belinda, a mature woman, took most of what Frank said with a pinch of salt. Why, she wondered, did he pick her, when there were younger women in the hotel?

Chapter 3
Passion Unleashed

U p at the crack of dawn, after a hurried coffee and croissant Belinda telephoned all the lookalikes half an hour before they were due to meet the client's representative in the lobby. All were ready except Tanya (Pamela Anderson). Tanya was one of her favourite people and she and Belinda were good friends, but she sometimes despaired of the girl. Well, hardly a girl now; she was in her late forties but as always, she was running behind time.

They arrived at the Hotel Venezia, an amazing venue, and were shown their dressing room, which was one very large area with enough space for a dozen people to change and take advantage of the make-up artists at their disposal. There was a scheduled dress rehearsal in a couple of hours and all the lookalikes, twittering and chatting, started to be transformed into their individual characters.

The day passed quickly and the client was highly satisfied with the choice of the lookalikes, noted to be some of the best in the world. As always, the Italians were perfect hosts, making sure their crew and artists were treated to the most wonderful food and drink, including wine and coffee.

Belinda and the other lookalikes were back at the Hotel Splendor close to two-thirty in the afternoon, and everybody went to their rooms knowing they were to be ready by seven-thirty to attend the first party that evening.

Belinda and Tanya decided to have one more coffee in the hotel lounge before going back to their rooms to rest. Enjoying the wonderful Italian coffee, they were surprised when a voice interrupted their conversation.

"Good afternoon, Belinda. May I join you two lovely ladies?"

Frank, full of bravado and smiles, stood beside their table looking down at them, the dancing eyes taking in everything, Tanya included. Belinda's heart fluttered as she thought disappointedly that Frank was a real ladies' man. Tanya glanced up and smiled up at Frank.

"Is that okay with you, Tanya?" Belinda asked her friend.

"Yes, of course," replied Tanya. "I shall be going up to my room shortly."

Belinda noticed the twinkle in her friend's eye. Frank was very attentive and charming to both women and was interested in how their rehearsal had gone. After a short while, Tanya left to take a rest before getting ready for the first party.

Belinda felt Frank's eyes on her as she kissed her friend and reminded Tanya to be ready on time.

"Goodbye, Frank, lovely to meet you," said Tanya, as she drifted into the lift.

Frank ordered a couple of cocktails for them and Belinda felt her heart beating much quicker than normal. Cocktails at this time of day were most unusual for her, she thought, but maybe one wouldn't hurt. This man, Frank

Lanzo, was having a very strange effect on her. He was a very mysterious man indeed, she decided.

After a while, Belinda refused another cocktail from Frank and explained she had to go soon to take a rest before getting ready for the party. His eyes bothered her; they seemed to be reading her mind. Belinda knew danger was ahead of her, yet, at the same time, she was excited about the prospect of what might happen between them. It was as if no matter how much she denied it, she fancied this man like crazy. For the first time in so long, Belinda wanted desperately to make passionate sensual love.

Frank's room was also on the second floor so they walked together to the lift. As they reached her door, Belinda swiped her card into the lock but it didn't release the door. Frank gently, yet firmly, took the card out of her hand and opened the door directly.

"What do you say to a quick coffee, Belinda? I feel as if I don't want to leave you just yet," Frank said, looking deep into her eyes questionably.

To her surprise, Belinda found herself nodding her head as he followed her into the room. She knew she would not be able to deny this man. It was too late; excitement overwhelmed her body and that intended rest would have to wait.

After having a quick check in the bathroom mirror and making sure her breath was sweet, Belinda coyly went back into the bedroom. He was standing by the minibar and pouring a couple of drinks. He handed her one as his eyes looked deeply into hers again. Accepting the glass, she took a couple of sips.

"What happened to the coffee?" she asked, laughing.

Without answering her, he took the glass out of her hand, his eyes still on her, and placed it beside his own on the nearby television table. He had removed his jacket and swiftly now he took her in his arms and kissed her lips, which made her whole body jump with excitement. Her brain was racing with the anticipation of what was about to happen between them; she was somehow a little afraid. Standing, locked in each other's arms and kissing deeply, Belinda kicked off her high heels as she feverishly helped him remove his shirt. After unzipping his trousers and stepping out of them, Frank pinched her bottom and gently pushed her backwards on the waiting king-sized bed. Shocked and taken by surprise, Belinda realised he had pushed her brassiere up to her neck, which released her ample breasts. Then expertly, her leggings and panties were pulled down, off over her feet in a flash. Becoming very excited and yet, at the same time, feeling quite vulnerable in the hands of this stranger, Belinda realised she had no idea really what kind of a person he was. Swiftly, Frank was on top of her, kissing and gently biting her nipples, which were becoming extremely hard and she knew in an instant she wanted this man more than anything else in the world. Frank moved down from her heaving breasts to her belly button and stuck his tongue into it, as a deep moan escaped her throat. Slowly and tantalisingly, his tongue and lips kissed their way down, down until he was kissing the inside of her thighs, gently biting her. Unable to control herself and burning with wild passion, Belinda climaxed, letting out a long groan as she floated in paradise.

She felt him enter her quivering body, which made her whole being feel like it was on fire. She willingly answered his every thrust as all her pent-up sexual feelings of the last years flowed from her and engulfed him.

Chapter 4
Venice Carnevale

S ensual sex in the afternoon seemed to agree with Belinda, who looked quite radiant when she met the lookalikes in the hotel lobby that evening. Although Belinda had not rested, she could not keep a smile from appearing on her lips, or a flutter in her tummy, every time she thought of him. Belinda recalled, with a faint shudder, that during their passionate lovemaking, he had huskily murmured under his breath, "Mia amore" *(My love)*; that most romantic language.

Frank had begrudgingly left her room a little while earlier, hating to leave the soft, creamy beauty lying beside him. Returning to his own room and following a long shower, Frank Lanzo made his way out of the hotel sprightly, on his way to keep his appointment with the Society's Italian associates. During dinner, hopefully, he would seal the coveted contract the Society desperately desired.

Surprisingly, Tanya had bathed, dressed and was ready on time for once.

"How did it go earlier with Mr Mysterious?" she asked walking across to Belinda with a knowing smile.

"Oh!" Belinda answered in a nervous voice. "Fine, I like him."

Tanya whispered in her friend's ear. "I know that, darling, it was written all over your body language."

Blushing and keeping her shining eyes downcast, Belinda retorted, "Oh, stop, Tanya! We were just chatting."

Tanya flashed a movie star smile as she replied, "Really? Is that what they call it nowadays?" Then she added with a laugh, "Pull the other leg, sweetie, it has bells on; ding dong!"

The party was so exciting; there were hundreds of people milling around, a mass of masked partygoers, posing and preening, dancing and philandering. Belinda noticed several well-known celebrities in the crowd and she mused to herself, what would happen if the real stars came along who the lookalikes were portraying.

Her mind recalled an incident some years ago when she was doing a lookalike job at Olympia in London. Belinda was standing with Annabel (Princess Diana) on the same podium when quietness descended the whole event. To everyone's amazement, the real Princess Diana walked right past them with an entourage of people in tow, all vying for her attention. While Belinda and Annabel stood transfixed at the vision in front of them, the Princess turned towards their podium and gave them the most beautiful warm smile, obviously acknowledging them. Sadness for the Princess overwhelmed Belinda whenever she remembered this incident.

As always, the lookalikes were a great success at the party and made a lot of money for the client's charity by having their photographs taken with the many partygoers. People remarked on Belinda's likeness to Joan Collins and insisted she was included in most of the photographs. Secretly, Belinda felt pleased for this much-needed boost.

A little after midnight, Belinda and the lookalikes were on their way back to the hotel and everybody was in high spirits. Adam (Johnny Depp) had met a young Italian woman at the party earlier and, finding her company uplifting, he decided to go out on the town with her and her friends. Knowing that Belinda as his agent did not approve of this, Adam promised he would be back at the hotel in a few hours.

"Isn't it a little late to be going out on a date? You should be resting for tomorrow's party, and besides, you hardly know this young woman," said Belinda, a frown of worry crossing her brow fleetingly.

"No, not really, Belinda," he answered reassuringly. "I know all I need to know about her and her friends, and please don't worry. I will be back at the hotel later to catch up with my beauty sleep, I promise," he added, beaming one of his famous Jack Sparrow smiles at her.

For all his reassurances, Belinda was worried. The final and most important party was scheduled for the next day and she wanted to make very sure all her lookalikes were rested and fresh for the next event. Belinda reiterated this fact to Adam, but he promised her profusely he would be back soon.

Having returned to the Hotel Splendor, Belinda thanked the lookalikes for their professionalism and wished them goodnight, as they wearily made their way to their individual rooms.

When she was looking in her handbag for her room key, she jumped as she felt a hand lightly touch her arm.

Turning with a smile, her heart leapt as she looked up into those brown, dancing eyes.

"How did the party go, Belinda?" he asked, as she blushed like a schoolgirl under his stare.

"Oh, wonderful, Frank! We all thoroughly enjoyed it, thank you," she managed to reply, although her voice sounded wobbly and nervous.

Frank told her his meeting earlier in the day for the Society had gone smoothly and according to plan. He said his superiors were again extremely happy with his progress, convincing the people concerned that the Society was the only organisation they should contemplate awarding the contract to. Belinda said how happy she was for him and the Society while desperately trying to appear relaxed in his presence, but she knew she was not convincing. Realising Frank had the ability to make her feel embarrassed, more like a schoolgirl than a mature woman, Belinda wondered whether he thought her to be in need of love and affection. Of course, where Matt was concerned, this was true but Belinda often received attention from men, some who were several years younger than her.

Looking directly into her eyes, Frank told her she had been amazing when they had made love and he hoped he had brought her as much pleasure as well. Belinda could hardly speak; she was feeling ashamed of how she had acted: like a slut with this complete stranger. Yet, she desired to do it all over again with him; quivering deep down as she remembered his touch and mouth on her body.

Frank said he was leaving the following evening, flying back to New York to personally hand over the coveted contract to his bosses. At these words, Belinda's heart shattered into a million pieces; this stranger had stolen her heart. The heart she had always protected so well, hiding it away from most men vying for her favours.

Frank, sadness showing in those eyes, put his arm around Belinda's shoulders and gave her his mobile number and email address so they could keep in contact. Occasionally, he said, his job required him to fly to London on business for the Society and he would love to meet her again and hoped she would too. Belinda knew her disappointment at his leaving the next day showed on her face. She had been telling herself ever since their first meeting that this was only a five-minute fling and he would soon forget all about her. As far as she was concerned, this was her swansong and she knew deep down in her soul that, like the swan in the fable, her heart would sing before it died when she parted from him. Frank, she thought, seemed to be able to read her every thought and she blushed charmingly, as she wished him a happy and healthy future.

"Are you free some time tomorrow, Belinda?" came his husky voice, but she hardly heard what he was asking as her heart was heavy with grief at his imminent departure.

Snapping herself out of her sad thoughts, Belinda quickly answered, "Yes, I can be, Frank, but I must sleep now before I drop. Tomorrow, believe me, I shall stay in bed until lunchtime."

Smiling down at her, Frank uttered, with a sexy throaty laugh, "I shall knock gently and bring you your breakfast."

Belinda blushed as her green eyes sparkled and shone when she smiled up at him.

"Adorable," he whispered in her ear. "Now, madam, permit me to walk you to your room."

Later, and on her own, after taking a much-desired warm shower, Belinda fell exhausted onto her king-sized bed, falling into a deep sleep almost immediately. But as night faded into dawn, Belinda thought she heard someone tapping on her door. Although still in a state of drowsiness, she woke immediately.

"Frank?" she called out secretively, but there was no reply apart from the continuous tapping on her door.

Hurriedly jumping out of bed and checking her appearance in the full-length mirror, Belinda slowly opened her door a crack and peered out. It was just after six in the morning. Suddenly, excitement erupted within her as his eyes danced into hers.

Grinning broadly, Frank whispered, "Buongiorno, signora, la prima colazione e arrivato." *(Good morning, madam, your breakfast has arrived.)*

Tantalisingly, Belinda crawled on top of Frank as he lay naked on the large bed. She loved his skin, the feel and the colour; a natural, light tan associated with some Italians, Sicilians and people from the Mediterranean. Frank let out a deep moan as she used her lips and tongue to slowly kiss her way up his body, while he lay, eyes closed, thrilling at her touch. Slowly, he reached for her ample breasts and cupped them in his hands as she deep kissed his mouth then, little by little, moved down his tingling body before covering her full lips over his manhood, causing her lover to let out a loud moan of passion. Now crawling cat-like up his body until her lips were level with his, she softly kissed him, then lay in his tanned arms and closed her eyes.

Wow, this is definitely my kind of breakfast, was the last thought she remembered before drifting off with a satisfied smile on her flushed face.

Stretching out her arm to touch her lover, Belinda found herself alone in the large bed. Sadly, she realised Frank had already left after their morning of amazing passion.

With one eye half-open, Belinda checked the time on her alarm clock beside the bed. It showed nearly two in the afternoon; she had slept through lunch and was feeling quite famished after also missing breakfast. Well, the usual kind of breakfast, that is! Belinda remembered that Frank was flying back to New York that afternoon and would already be on his way to Marco Polo Airport.

She reminisced about their lovemaking, slowly going over every single detail in her mind, wanting to savour it forever. Her body tingled at the very thought of him, but feelings of jealousy rose immediately in her throat, thoughts of Frank with other women. She knew she had to quash these thoughts as quickly as they came because she must be realistic. This was probably just a fling for him; after all, she told herself, there were many younger women available out there who would jump at the chance to be with a man like him. Belinda felt deep sadness and loneliness at the thought of never seeing Frank again. How could any other man live up to her mysterious lover now?

Chapter 5
A Disappearance

Sharp at six o'clock that evening, Belinda rang each lookalike to make sure they were almost ready for their last party appearance of the Venice Carnevale. Everybody was dressed and ready; everyone, that was, apart from Adam. Alarmed at getting no answer from Adam's room, Belinda called Mark and asked him if he would go and knock at Adam's door, while she checked with the reception downstairs to see whether Adam had returned from the previous evening. Mark called Belinda back to disclose the worrying news that he had banged on Adam's door but to no avail. They decided to ask the reception desk to bring up the pass key to Adam's room.

A little less than fifteen minutes later, Belinda knew that Adam had not returned after last night's party; his bed had not been slept in. Absolutely fuming with him, Belinda was seriously thinking about taking him off the agency's books. This line of action would be unfortunate because Adam was the top Johnny Depp lookalike and he had perfected the character of Jack Sparrow to a fine art, but Belinda reminded herself unreliability was never tolerated in this industry.

Taking a deep breath, Belinda called the Italian client to inform them Adam was unwell and unable to work that evening. Hearing the irritation in the deep intake of breath coming down the telephone from the client, Belinda quickly offered her services as the Joan Collins lookalike to replace Jack Sparrow. Letting out a sigh of relief, she was thankful the client liked the idea of having La Collins on the platform for a change.

Jubilantly, Belinda strode into the bathroom with the knowledge that the reputation of the agency had been saved.

'Frank, my darling, I will miss you forever,' was the prevailing thought in her mind, as she expertly transformed herself into the diva La Collins.

The fireworks display at the end of the last party of the Carnevale was simply amazing. The crowds seemed even louder and crazier than those at the previous party. Belinda and the other lookalikes had so many photographs taken with revellers, their feet were aching and on fire. The food was excellent, as was the wine that flowed all through the spectacular Venetian Carnevale. Belinda marvelled at the luck of being well paid to attend such a wonderful party.

Everybody had consumed a few drinks by the end of the evening and were celebrating the satisfactory completion of the contract. Together, they walked slowly back to their hotel, tired and weary, but happy and enjoying the warm spring-like night.

Alone in her hotel room, as she was about to fall into a much-needed sleep, Belinda's thoughts flew to Frank; positive now that no other man ever had a chance with her, her body and soul belonged completely to him now. But no one remembered Adam.

The following morning, Belinda was having breakfast in her room. They were to be at Marco Polo Airport by one o'clock that afternoon. The client telephoned Belinda, complimenting her on the lookalikes and, of course, La Collins. Drinking down the last of her tea, Belinda telephoned the lookalikes to make sure they were up, having breakfast and packing, ready to leave for the airport. Adam! She had forgotten to check on him last night when they had arrived back from the party.

Trying not to panic, Belinda quickly called Adam's room: no answer. He was probably in the shower, she told herself. She'll call again in twenty minutes. Belinda was still angry with him for missing the last party and not honouring his contract. When she saw him later, she would read him the Riot Act about his appalling behaviour.

Half an hour later, Belinda tried Adam's number again: no answer. Worry seized her body, causing troubling thoughts to flash through her mind. Calling Mark again, he agreed to go to Adam's room, but when he knocked and knocked, there was no response. They decided to call reception and have the pass key brought up again to get into Adam's room. Maybe he was a deep sleeper and did not hear Mark knocking. Maybe he came back to the hotel the evening before and, finding they had all gone to the last party, had gone out again with his new-found lady friend. These were some of the worrying thoughts flooding Belinda's mind as the bellboy clicked open Adam's door.

The room was empty, exactly as it was the night before.

"Where is he? What has happened to him? He knows we are flying back to London today," cried Belinda as she and the others stared at Adam's empty room.

Checking the drawers and wardrobe, they found some of Adam's personal belongings still there.

"Oh, my God. Where is he?" whispered a frenzied Belinda to Mark, her voice becoming increasingly louder. "He will miss the flight. I am so angry with him. That is it. He is finished with this agency. I don't care how good he is in character; this is the last straw."

Mark tried to calm her down.

"Do we call the police? I mean, something could have happened to him?" he asked Belinda, worriedly looking out of the window, willing Adam to come walking along towards the hotel.

Belinda agreed the police should be called, although at the back of her mind, she recalled hearing that a person had to be missing for at least forty-eight hours before the police can do anything. Belinda silently prayed that Adam would walk into the hotel at any moment, but to her despair she knew she was wrong and the local police *(Polizia di Stato)* were called.

They explained to Belinda and Mark they could do nothing until forty-eight hours had elapsed from the last time the person in question had been seen. In Adam's case, it was only about thirty-four hours ago. After calling Dawn at the agency in London to let her know what had happened, it was agreed Belinda would stay and take a later plane. Dawn asked Belinda to wait a few hours before rescheduling the flights, by which time Adam would have hopefully shown up.

At midday, the other lookalikes were ready to leave for Marco Polo Airport. Tanya (Pam Anderson) offered to stay with her, but Belinda wouldn't hear of it. Julia (Helen

Mirren) also offered to stay with Belinda; being a single woman, she told Belinda she was happy to stay and give her support. Belinda was touched by their concern for her and Adam's welfare, but she assured them she'd be perfectly fine alone.

An alternative room was found for her in the hotel as her original one had already been cleaned for previously booked incoming guests. Alone in her new room, sitting thoughtfully on the king-sized bed, Belinda's mind flew, as always, to Frank. Her body ached for his touch and the way his eyes seductively caressed her.

Into a troubled sleep she fell, her dreams of dark and frightening faceless people.

Suddenly awaking, Belinda noticed that it was already four in the afternoon. Calling the reception again, Belinda was informed that Adam had not, as yet, returned to the hotel. His belongings were now waiting for him in the small alcove beside the front desk in the foyer because his room was booked out to other guests. Belinda decided to leave the task of booking their plane tickets home until the following morning, remembering that the police would not start searching for Adam until midnight, when the forty-eight-hour policy was up.

Refreshing herself, Belinda decided to take in some air; sitting alone was beginning to make her tense, nervous and sullen. Slowly, she walked to Piazza San Marco, past the Basilica and St Mark's Campanile. Not for the first time, she marvelled at this amazing city. Hundreds of pigeons filled the blue skies as she reached the Ca' d'Oro and Basilica di San Giovanni e Paolo. A huge brick edifice built in the Italian Gothic style, being the principal Dominican church of Venice, its opulence and beautiful interior engulfed her and she entered quietly to light a candle for Adam's safety. The peacefulness of the Basilica di San Giovanni e Paolo inspired her to kneel and pray.

Wandering through the interesting alleyways, Belinda admired the many little, but expensive, boutiques. Stopping for real Italian coffee, the way she loved it, she sat outside the little café, watching the throng of people passing by. Again, her thoughts were full of Frank. Venice, she sadly realised, was a very lonely city when your love had gone away.

It was already dark when Belinda made her way back towards the Hotel Splendor. Having not eaten anything all day, she was beginning to feel very hungry and decided to have an early dinner before resting for the evening while she waited for the remaining few hours to pass. Of course, she must call Matt; he had tried to reach her on her mobile earlier, but she had missed the call. Dawn had told her she'd let Matt know what had happened and Belinda knew he'd want to make quite sure she was safe. Although Matt was having an affair behind Belinda's back, he nevertheless loved his wife.

As Belinda had almost reached the entrance of the Hotel Splendor, her eyes fleetingly caught the sight of a grey-haired man's shadowy figure in the busy crowds.

"Frank," she called out without thinking, but the figure had disappeared around a nearby corner. With her heart racing alarmingly, she pushed through the crowds of people to try to catch the person up. As she reached the corner, to her disappointment there was nobody around who looked anything like Frank and she begun to wonder whether it was her imagination.

Slowly, entering the hotel, Belinda went straight to reception and enquired whether there was any sign of Adam; but there was not. Worried, she thanked the commissionaire and took the lift to her floor. Following a quick shower and retouching of her make-up, Belinda wandered down to the hotel restaurant for dinner, becoming increasingly worried about Adam's disappearance. One or two men sitting alone made eye contact with her and smiled; she ignored them.

Belinda poured herself a glass of Chianti from the half bottle she ordered with her dinner as her thoughts were of Frank.

"Oh, Frank," she whispered lowly. "I miss you so very much, my love."

Chapter 6
Police Investigations

Although finishing the food on her plate, Belinda had hardly tasted it. Forlornly, returning to her room to await the police to contact her, Belinda called Dawn at home to keep her updated. Dawn agreed Belinda should stay for a further one or two nights, if necessary. Business was a little quiet at the moment and Dawn assured her she could manage alone until Belinda returned.

Kicking off her red high-heeled shoes and slipping off her navy two-piece suit, Belinda sat on the bed and lay back to relax, drifting into a state of drowsiness.

The loud ring of the telephone made her jump. She rushed off the bed to answer its urgent peel, her heart in her throat as she answered.

"Pronto."

"Belinda, it's me, Frank. I'm downstairs in the lobby. I took a chance to enquire with the reception whether or not you had checked out already. Can I come up?"

Feeling confused, she uttered, "But, Frank, I thought you flew home a couple of days ago."

Letting out a deep sigh, Frank replied, "Yes, I know. I'll explain everything in a few minutes. Can I come up, please?"

Quickly, Belinda checked her appearance in the beautiful ornate mirror surrounded with Botticelli cherubs, grabbed her black lacy dressing gown from the armchair, and managing to pull it on as Frank tapped lightly on her door. Her heart fluttered excitedly at the prospect of being with him again so soon as she unlocked the door.

He looked tired, she thought, as Frank kissed her briefly on her mouth, causing her body to quiver at this touch. He said he needed a stiff drink as she gazed up at him questioningly. Frank explained to Belinda that on his way to Marco Polo Airport a couple of days before, he received a call from his superiors, instructing him to stay in Italy a little longer because an urgent problem had arisen and it was imperative that he took care of it immediately. The problem had now been dealt with satisfactorily and he was due to fly back to New York the following evening.

Belinda asked Frank where he had been staying for the last couple of days and he explained that one of the Society's Italian associates, and a very good friend of his, had insisted Frank stay at his home in Venice. Frank said he had been extremely busy during the last few days and had no time to see her again until now. Hoping she was still at the Hotel Splendor, he had returned.

Belinda poured Frank a Jack Daniels on the rocks and handed it to him. Sipping her sweet white wine, Belinda told Frank how Adam had not been seen for almost two days and how everybody was worried about him. She added that the Polizia di Stato had promised to notify her as soon as they had any information regarding Adam, but only after the forty-eight-hour missing person policy came into effect.

Frank, noticing how worried Belinda was, tried to console her. Seeing she was close to tears, he tried to reassure her that Adam, being a young man, was probably enjoying himself with his new lady friend and had forgotten the time.

"He will show up, I am certain of it," said Frank, putting his arm around Belinda's slumped shoulders and pulling her gently towards him.

"Look, it's almost ten. We have two hours before the missing persons policy is up; care for a cocktail in the bar?" he asked, looking deeply into her worried face.

Looking up at Frank, Belinda noticed, yet again, the amusement in his eyes that danced into her soul. As she was about to answer him, Frank brought his head down and kissed her lips, hungrily tasting her as he slipped his tongue suggestively into her waiting mouth.

Sounds of pleasure and fulfilment escaped from Belinda's throat during their passionate sensual lovemaking. With breath labouring, Frank fell backwards on the bed as Belinda kissed his mouth again and again.

"I adore you," she whispered to him, but his eyes were now closed as he rested with a smile on his mouth.

Leaving Frank to slumber on the bed, Belinda ran a quick shower, retouched her make-up, put fresh underwear on and slipped into her dressing gown once more. Swallowing the remainder of her wine, she sat on the bed to watch in awe, this stranger, now sleeping peacefully, whom she adored. Carefully so as not to waken him, she pulled the silk counterpane over his manly body. Opening a book laying on her side table that she had been reading, Belinda curled her legs under herself and tried to concentrate on the story unravelling before her eyes, but found she could not concentrate. Every few minutes, she checked the clock.

For a short while Belinda dozed off, falling into a worried sleep about Adam, but was woken by the sound of light tapping on her door. Jumping up, she reached it within seconds. Her throat felt restricted as though she'd suffocate; a bad feeling engulfed her very being.

Slipping the lock on the door and gingerly opening it, Belinda looked up into the handsome face of the hotel manager, apologetically smiling down at her. At once, she saw he was accompanied by two polizia. Quickly, she unfastened the lock and allowed them to enter. The colour left her cheeks when the more senior polizia told her in broken English that Adam had been traced to the local hospital. He had been taken to the main civic hospital in Venice that occupies a fifteenth century monastery.

Due to the special circumstances and being accompanied by the Polizia di Stato, Belinda, accompanied by Frank, was allowed to visit the hospital straightaway. She had the strange feeling she was walking into an art gallery rather than a hospital as they were escorted through the large, brightly coloured corridors. The many paintings on the massive high walls were some of the most beautiful she had ever seen.

In contrast, Adam's face was ashen with tubes coming out of his nose and mouth. He was lying on a high bed with spotless white sheets.

"My God, what happened to him?" cried Belinda as they were shown into Adam's room. The elder polizia explained he had been brought in by a young Italian woman and a gay man the previous evening. The day of the final party, thought Belinda to herself. Apparently, the doctors were informed that Adam had been drinking heavily and certain soft drugs were found in his body. The young woman and her friend had brought him to the hospital because they were fearful for his life, not being sure which drugs Adam had taken during the evening and, of course, he had also been drinking heavily. Belinda was told how the young woman told the doctors she kept pleading with Adam to stop drinking, but he was too far gone to take any notice. The polizia had taken her and her friend's names, addresses and contact numbers for further investigation.

Frank kept his arm around Belinda's shoulders as she quietly cried. In her position as agent, she was responsible for all the lookalikes, although they were mature enough to take care of themselves. Frank noticed remarkably that Belinda's tears turned her eyes the colour of emerald grass.

The doctor on night duty explained to all of them about the injuries Adam had sustained internally due to his lethal cocktail of drugs and alcohol, and that he was being kept in an induced coma for the time being. Reassuring them that everything possible was being done for the young man, the doctor added that they were hopeful Adam would make a full recovery. The hospital needed to contact Adam's next of kin as soon as possible. Belinda gave them the details and told them she would also call Adam's parents. The polizia explained that they had to interview Adam as soon as he was out of his induced coma in order to verify the young woman's statement.

As they were leaving the hospital, the elder of the two polizia was scratching his bald head with a puzzled expression on his rotund face.

"You know, Mario, names I forget, but I never ever forget a face, and that American, he seems very familiar to me for some unknown reason, but I cannot for the life of me think where I know him from," he said thoughtfully.

"Probably resembles someone from the past, Andrea," replied his partner.

"Yes, of course," agreed Andrea. "Must be my suspicious mind rearing its ugly head again," he added, and they both laughed.

Dawn was beginning to break over the Piazza San Marco as Belinda and Frank strolled back to the hotel. Walking her to the entrance, he kissed her gently on her mouth.

"I have things to do before I fly later, Belinda, so sadly I must say goodbye right now and hope we will meet up again soon," Frank uttered as his arm tightened around her waist.

"Frank, I don't expect anything from you," answered Belinda, eyes downcast with sadness. "You know how to contact me if you want to," she added, hardly looking at him, fearful of what she might read in those dancing eyes.

"Yes, I know and I want to," he reiterated. "Very much so, but it will take time. Believe me, I will contact you whenever I can."

Bringing his strong head, with its wiry, grey hair, down to hers, Frank Lanzo again kissed her long and tenderly. As always, excitable tremors shot through her body. When at last she opened her eyes, he was already walking away, turning around to blow her a kiss.

"Goodbye, my love," she whispered under her breath, as the tears started to cascade down her sad face.

Slowly, Belinda entered her room, kicking off her shoes and throwing her coat on the nearest armchair. She flung herself on the large bed and sobbed uncontrollably until she was completely exhausted.

A few hours later, she called Matt and told him what had happened and that she would be flying home as soon as Adam's family had arrived to support him. Deciding to wait a few hours before calling Dawn, who was also very concerned about Adam's welfare, Belinda slipped out of her clothes and crept into the bed, the fragrance of Frank's eau de toilette on the counterpane filling her senses. Her heart leapt with excitement as her mind remembered his every caress and kiss.

"Oh, Frank, how can I possibly live without you now?"

Belinda slept for four hours before reaching for her mobile. She found Adam's contact numbers. Shaking slightly, hating to be the bearer of bad news, she forced herself to dial his parents' number. Almost immediately, a female voice answered: it was Adam's sister, Caroline. As Belinda began to tell Caroline what had happened, Caroline interrupted her and told her the Polizia di Stato had already telephoned them an hour before and that she had booked three open return tickets to Marco Polo Airport that afternoon. Belinda tried to sound optimistic about Adam, but she could not prevent her voice sounding a little shaky.

Adam's family had booked into a little motel not far from the Hotel Splendor. They arranged to meet Belinda at her hotel after they had visited the hospital with the Polizia di Stato, who were escorting them to see Adam and meet with the respective doctors.

Calling the airline, Belinda booked her flight home for the following day; there was no reason for her to delay her flight home any longer; Adam was being supported by his family now.

Later, Belinda walked down to the bar and ordered a glass of red wine. Having eaten dinner in her room earlier, she was now ready to meet Adam's family.

Less than thirty minutes later, three people walked into the hotel lounge. Although Belinda had never met any of them before, the younger woman waved to her. Belinda jumped up from the bar stool and walked briskly across to them, holding out her hand and asking if they were indeed Adam's family.

"As soon as I saw you, I knew who you were," said Caroline, smiling. "You really do look like Joan Collins," she added, looking closely at Belinda.

Graciously smiling, Belinda ordered drinks for them and listened intently as they told her how Adam was doing. When everybody was sitting comfortably on the soft leather sofas, Belinda explained what had happened, and Mr and Mrs Proctor were very sweet and thanked her for staying behind in Venice to support their son. Mr Proctor, a worried look etched on his face, confided to Belinda that Adam had been such a quiet and studious young boy, always top of the class but as he grew older, he became more gregarious and even a little wild at times. Caroline explained to Belinda that the doctors were much more positive regarding Adam's condition since yesterday and suggested the family spend as much time as possible at his bedside. Tears welled up in Belinda's eyes on hearing this. No matter how angry she had been with Adam, she was nevertheless fond of the young man. Ever since he had joined Top Drawer Agency,

Adam and she had been good friends. After warm wishes of farewell to Belinda, the Proctor family left the bar and returned to their motel.

After a continental breakfast the following morning, Belinda decided to take a leisurely walk through Piazza San Marco and treat herself to a coffee in the Caffè Floria while the music played by the café musicians drifted soothingly over the magical square. Venice, so beautiful and romantic, and yet so empty and soulful when your love is no longer there. Walking slowly from the Bridge of Sighs to the Rialto Bridge, Belinda stood to daydream as she gazed at the gondoliers expertly rowing their gondolas, loudly joking among themselves as they passed each other on the lagoon. Occasionally, one of them broke out into a classical rendition of *O Sole Mio*, which quickly brought tears to Belinda's sad eyes.

The remainder of the day was spent relaxing and reading, until it was time for Belinda to leave the hotel and make her way to Marco Polo Airport for her flight home to London.

Belinda's thoughts for the duration of the flight were of Frank, wondering whether he was really divorced or if indeed married. For the last half hour of the flight, she closed her eyes and slumbered until the seat belt sign came on as the pilot announced they were now descending into Gatwick Airport.

Looking out of the side window, Belinda marvelled at the intricate and beautiful patchwork of the English countryside from the air. The winter sun was shining as the plane's wheels touched down smoothly. Some passengers clapped their appreciation for the pilots' expertise and Belinda felt the usual twang of excitement travellers experience when arriving back home.

Much to her surprise, Matt was waiting and waved to her as she came out of the arrivals entrance. Trying not to show her shock, Belinda, smiling warmly, waved back and walked quickly across to greet him. Matt took her small suitcase and kissed her briefly on her mouth: she felt nothing. Again, her thoughts were full of Frank. Matt explained that Sidney had offered to manage the Soho betting shop for the rest of the afternoon, enabling Matt to collect her.

On the drive home, the two chatted easily about the Venetian Carnevale and, of course, Adam Proctor. Belinda had always felt relaxed in Matt's company. Knowing him for so long now, she always imagined their marriage would last forever, but since she found out about his long affair with another woman and now, of course, since her affair with Frank Lanzo had begun, Belinda was convinced that one day, she would eventually leave her husband.

Chapter 7
A Ray of Sunshine

It was Thursday, and Belinda woke reasonably early and set off for the agency, happy to find Dawn already there. Most of the morning, they spent discussing the Venice Carnevale, the Italian client and Adam. His sister had promised to call Belinda later that afternoon after she and her parents had visited Adam again in the hospital.

Settling back into the routine of her life, Belinda constantly wondered whether she would ever hear from Frank again. Although they had exchanged contact numbers, Belinda vowed not to call him but wait to see if he contacted her. This morning, as she was telephoning and texting certain lookalikes and tribute acts with potential jobs, Mark (Brad Pitt) arrived with paperwork and a cheque entrusted to him by Belinda when he and the other lookalikes flew home from Venice a few days earlier. Mark stayed for a while, downing cups of coffee as he chatted with Belinda and Dawn. Now standing up, ready to leave, Mark quickly read and signed a new contract for another viable job, this time without Karen (Angelina Jolie). On reaching the door, he turned and asked his agents to keep him informed of Adam's progress.

Approximately three weeks earlier, the agency had put an advert in *The Stage* magazine hoping to recruit more lookalikes and tribute acts. It was always good for business to have at least a couple of people portraying the same character. This was necessary for the agency to cover themselves in the event that the client's number one choice was either busy or unavailable.

Dawn was in her office drumming up business while Belinda, photographs of wannabe lookalikes and tribute acts covering her desk, chatted in depth on the telephone. Finishing her call, Belinda smiled at the man and beckoned him in, immediately taking an instant liking to him. This flamboyant man introduced himself to her. His name was Freddie Lawlor and Queenie was his pet poodle. Belinda noticed he was very gay, very camp, to say the least. His mannerisms were extremely feminine, but he came across as very likeable and charming. Belinda was finding it increasingly difficult to keep a straight face as Freddie explained to her that after reading their advertisement in *The Stage* magazine, he had decided to give it a go and come along personally to meet the agent. By this time, Dawn had come out of her office and joined them, a quizzical look on her pretty face.

Bowing slightly to Dawn, Freddie told them he was forever being told he had a strong resemblance to Liberace, hence his hope now to become a lookalike. Rushing on before anybody could stop him, Freddie apologised for the fact that, unfortunately, he could not play the piano but he could sing and dance. Before either of the ladies had a chance to answer, Freddie immediately broke into a rendition of a famous old-time music hall song called *Nobody Loves A Fairy When She's 40*. Belinda and Dawn began to laugh so much, the tears ran down their faces, completely ruining their carefully applied make-up. Freddie liked the fact they laughed so much because it was supposed to be a funny little song. Mesmerised while watching Freddie perform the funny little ditty, Dawn and her younger partner agreed he did have a kind of resemblance to the late, great pianist Liberace.

Dawn enquired whether Freddie had brought any photographs with him, portraying Liberace. Yes, he had and looking through them, Dawn decided they could possibly find work for this charismatic gentleman. Freddie was asked to complete a four-page application form and Belinda asked him if she could take his photograph for their records.

"Oh, please do," answered Freddie, his smile beaming from ear to ear. "May I put Queenie down for a few moments please?" he asked.

"As long as she is house-trained," quipped Belinda, smiling.

"Oh, he's a boy, not a girlie," corrected Freddie. "And yes, of course, my little Queenie is house-trained," he added, looking quite aghast at Belinda's suggestion.

Finding her depressed mood had lightened since Freddie had walked through the door, Belinda made her mind up that she would definitely put him on the agency's books as a Liberace lookalike. As Freddie gushingly thanked both ladies several times before turning to leave, he mentioned he was also looking for a part-time job and he was a whiz with administrative work and quite the expert on the computer. If they were to hear of anything in the future regarding a vacancy, he'd appreciate it if they informed him. Belinda promised to do so, and as the door closed gently behind Freddie and little Queenie, Belinda agreed with Dawn that he would be very useful whenever they needed help in the agency. Far more economical, reminded Dawn, to hire him direct rather than go through the expensive temporary employment agencies.

"I love him already, don't you?" asked Belinda, as Dawn turned to go back into her office.

"He is a ray of sunshine and has the perfect temperament to portray Liberace," replied Dawn, still smiling.

"He is so camp, he made me laugh, Camp Freddie," added Belinda, collecting the empty coffee cups from her desk and taking them into the little kitchenette.

Later that afternoon, Adam's sister Caroline called Belinda and gave her the good news that Adam had been taken off the induced coma and was gradually coming round. Caroline was returning to her job in the UK in a couple of days and her parents were staying until Adam was ready to fly home, which looked much closer now than originally thought.

After appearing in another successful Old Time Music Hall show with Lissenden Players in a venue out of London, Belinda began the long drive home, with only her Sinatra CDs for company. Surprisingly, the journey took much less time than Belinda had imagined. Thankfully, at this late hour, the roads were quiet.

It was almost one in the morning when Belinda quietly opened her front door and started to make her way up the stairs to her spare bedroom. Matt was sleeping in front of the television in the lounge. Quietly switching off the television and lamps, Belinda gently tiptoed out of the room. Collecting a heavy duvet from her bedroom cupboard and slipping off her shoes, Belinda crept downstairs and gently covered Matt with it, as the coldness of the early hours settled in the house.

Taking her mobile out of her handbag, she peered at her text messages. 'Hey, Belinda, how are you? I hope everything worked out okay for Adam in Venice. Let me know please, Babe. It is early evening here in New York and I am relaxing and thinking about you.'

Belinda's heart didn't just skip a beat, it did a complete somersault. Excitedly, she tried to remain calm and answer his message. Her fingers were shaking and it took several attempts before she eventually sent her reply to Frank.

The lovers messaged each other for the following fifteen minutes or so, neither wanting to say goodnight. Frank's text said he was contemplating flying into London for a couple of days quite soon; not for work commitments, but because he missed her so much. He added that since they last saw each other in Venice, she was continuously in his thoughts. When reading these words, Belinda's heart leapt.

Memories of their sensual passionate lovemaking came flooding back to her but she cautioned Frank, explaining they would have to be extra vigilant if she were to meet him in London because her husband seemed to be known by many people. No matter where he went in London or further afield, it was guaranteed Matt would cross paths with somebody who knew him. Frank assured her they would be careful and he was planning to arrive in a couple of weeks' time, suggesting she told her husband she was booked on a lookalike job outside of London and would have to stay the night. Frank said he would text her as soon as his ticket to London was booked. Even though Belinda knew about Matt's dalliance with another woman, she was well aware all hell would break loose if she were to be caught with another man.

Unfair indeed, but not wanting to rock the boat, Belinda knew if she wanted to be with her lover, they would have to be as discreet as possible. Before she fell asleep, Belinda knew, deep in her heart, she would risk anything at all, if necessary, to spend time with Frank Lanzo, anything. But she remembered to delete his messages, so there was no trace of them.

Chapter 8
London Lovers

After much discussion with Belinda, Dawn had decided to interview Freddie for a job with the agency for three days a week, with the option to work extra days when things were busy, or if Belinda was away working on a lookalike job.

After further discussion, the lady agents agreed that Freddie be offered a part-time administrative position. They felt Freddie would be perfect for the office and found he was exceptionally educated once they had begun to interview him. It was finally agreed, due to the fact that Queenie, his poodle, was completely house-trained, Freddie could bring him on his work days. Both ladies found Freddie amusing and uplifting. With blue eyes shining, he flamboyantly kissed Belinda and Dawn, thanking them profusely for giving him a chance to prove himself. Freddie reminded them he was also waiting excitedly for his first lookalike job.

Shortly after employing Freddie, Belinda received another text from Frank. His flight was booked and he had made a reservation at the Phoenix Hotel, London Heathrow Airport, which Frank had decided was a discreet venue for them to meet. Although obviously very excited, Belinda was also a little apprehensive and knew she must take Dawn into her confidence, hoping her partner and good friend would understand about this imminent rendezvous of hers. Dawn, six years Belinda's senior, was an attractive blonde with large brown eyes that did not miss a trick. Happily married, she told anyone who listened she had luckily married her soulmate.

A keen businesswoman, Dawn thrived on owning the best lookalike agency, not only in London and the UK but also in Europe. Often interviewed by television stations, Dawn made sure her agency was at the very top of the list. Aware of Belinda's less-than-happy marriage and of Matt's 'bit on the side', Dawn had told Belinda many times that she should seriously think about filing for divorce, especially now that Belinda was a partner in the agency and much more self-sufficient.

To Belinda's shock and surprise, Dawn was very happy and a little excited when she heard about Belinda's affair with Frank Lanzo, a Sicilian American from New York. Although happy for her younger partner, Dawn also warned Belinda to be careful and not to get hurt by this new love of hers, because she didn't really know anything about him. Agreeing to give Belinda an alibi in the event that Matt might call the agency to check Belinda's whereabouts when she was with Frank at the Phoenix Hotel, Dawn assured her that she and Freddie would verify Belinda's story that she was on a job in Paris for three days. This would not appear suspicious to Matt because he knew travelling abroad was part and parcel of the glamorous life his wife led in her role as a lookalike.

Returning home later that evening, and feeling far more confident, Belinda decided to tell Matt immediately about her fabricated forthcoming job in the romantic city of Paris.

The following couple of weeks seemed to drag slowly for Belinda, but they became more excitable for her too, as each day brought her closer to Frank.

Freddie had worked with the agency for a short time and was proving to be a real asset. He was computer literate, but he was also funny and generous, fussing and mothering Belinda and Dawn, and of course little Queenie; a real mother hen. They loved having Freddie working with them and everyone appeared to be in high spirits on the days he was in the agency with them.

On a warm sunny day at the end of May, Adam unexpectedly strolled into the agency. Dawn and Belinda stared at him with opened mouths. Not only was he looking tremendously well with his hair now a little longer than usual, but he would give Johnny Depp himself a run for his money in the looks department. Adam explained that he decided to surprise them and decided not to call before arriving. His parents had bought them a beautiful transparent lampshade with four curved arms, handcrafted by Murano glass masters. They wanted Belinda and Dawn to have the gift for the agency's office because of their kindness and understanding while Adam was in hospital in Venice. His Italian girlfriend had visited him in hospital and the Polizia di Stato were at last satisfied with her explanation of what actually happened that night. Adam apologised profusely for his behaviour and promised he would never let them, or the agency, down again. Dawn and Belinda glanced at each other, both knowing they would forgive him. In his usual flamboyant way, Freddie fussed with the beautiful lampshade and Adam, who looked uneasy the whole time he was in the office, which made the two agents giggle.

When Belinda arrived at the Phoenix Hotel, it had been a beautiful summer's day. Belinda wore an off-white skirt suit with a burnt orange vest and gold sandals, with matching handbag. As she entered the hotel and walked towards reception, several people looked her way with admiring glances. Belinda felt confident about how attractive she looked, and satisfactorily smiled to herself.

The receptionist, holding Belinda's gaze and politely smiling, called Room 314 for her and informed Belinda she could go up. With her heart beating so fast she could barely trust her legs to carry her along the corridor, she was conscious of the sound of rushing in her ears, caused by her excitement. Her hands were shaking as she tapped lightly on the door which, to her surprise, opened immediately and there he stood, as handsome as ever: her lover. As they looked at each other, she was reminded of how his dancing brown eyes, full of amusement, appeared to look deep into her soul.

Frank reached out and gently pulled her to him and kissed her so passionately on the mouth that she had to catch her breath. Once inside the room, Frank pressed her up against the wall and she could feel his hardened manhood pressing against her quivering body. Expertly and swiftly, he pulled her panties down, off her legs, then a little roughly, which added to Belinda's excitement, Frank shoved her skirt up around her waist and as he bent his knees, she jumped up and wrapped her legs around him. Entering her feverishly after several unsuccessful attempts, Frank groaned as Belinda felt him inside her and she imagined her heart was about to burst with so much love and passion for this man, she found it difficult to breath.

With their passions spent, Frank kissed Belinda's lips as she withdrew her legs from around his waist. With his arms still wrapped around his lover, Frank ushered Belinda to the king-sized bed and as she lay encircled by his manliness, she was overwhelmed by the strongest feelings of love and adoration, which filled the depth of her soul for this stranger.

The following day, having hired a car at the airport, Frank drove Belinda out past Windsor into the opulent countryside, where they arrived at an inviting Italian restaurant. Frank had been recommended by a friend, who had eaten there recently, to try this particular place. For the next two hours, the lovers chatted and laughed together, ordering sumptuous Italian fare with the best Italian wine available. Frank Lanzo spoke fluent Italian to the manager and was treated most respectfully by all staff, which greatly impressed his adoring companion.

During their lavish lunch, Frank enquired about Belinda's husband's line of business, and she told him, smiling brightly, that Matt had become a junior partner in the betting shop where he had worked for several years. There were three shops in total and Matt spent most of his time in the latest one to open, which was situated in Soho. Belinda proudly emphasised to Frank that his business was flourishing. Frank enquired about the other two betting shops and where they were in London. It struck Belinda fleetingly that Frank seemed a little too interested in her husband's businesses after he questioned her about Matt's senior partner but, she reasoned, he was probably making polite conversation. After all, Frank was a businessman himself and would naturally be interested and curious.

Afraid to know the answer, but nevertheless needing to know, Belinda candidly asked Frank if he were married, as she herself was; but he assured her he had been divorced for some years now and had one grown-up son whom he was very close to. Seeing the relief in her eyes, Frank flippantly told her that these days he was a free agent and although there was nobody special back in New York, he added quickly that he did have a life there. Being of a jealous nature, this revelation made Belinda feel uneasy and she began to wonder how many other women Frank was seeing.

On returning to the hotel room, Frank fell asleep almost immediately as he threw himself across the bed and reached out for Belinda, who childishly went to him and lay beside him, feeling extremely tired but ecstatically happy in the knowledge that this amazing man had feelings for her.

After a short rest, Belinda eased herself gently out of Frank's arms and ran a shower, taking off her make-up and slipping into her new black negligee. Carefully, she removed Frank's loafers and unzipped his trousers, gently easing them off his legs, which caused Frank to stir but he continued in his deep sleep. Finding an extra blanket in the closet, Belinda pulled it over them and switching off the lights, falling into a deep sleep lying contentedly beside her lover.

Early the following morning, Frank woke and went into the bathroom as Belinda slept soundly. Quietly returning to the bed, Frank climbed in beside her sleeping body and was immediately aware that deep in the pit of his stomach, something stirred. Wrapping his arms around the slumbering Belinda, she woke and turned towards him, ready and excited to have her passion exalted. Their lips came together and their tongues found each other in wanton abandonment as the lovers reached paradise together.

On the Friday - the thirteenth - they put superstitions aside and decided to take a long drive out of the airport complex. The day was sunny and warm and Frank wanted to see as much of the English countryside as he could; he was beginning to love Merry Ole England, its traditions, its people and its character. That night they stayed in the beautiful town of Marlborough in a wonderful seventeenth century Coach Inn. Frank was very taken with the Inn, especially when he saw the four-poster canopy bed they were to share that night. The lovers made full use of that romantic looking bed.

All too soon, Saturday night turned into Sunday morning. Frank held Belinda close to him as she quietly wept in his strong, tanned arms. The thought of being without him filled her with deep sadness. How quickly the last few days had flown by; how could she possibly live without him now? They had grown so close during their time spent together, but now he had to leave her and she had no idea when they would be together again. Frank took a small cream box out of his jacket pocket and placed it in Belinda's hands. On opening the box, to her surprise she found a beautiful diamond brooch in the shape of a bell, sitting on a soft pink cushion. How she loved it! She threw her arms around Frank's strong neck and told him she loved him so much. Smiling, he silenced her with his kisses. All too soon, as she watched the man she loved turn and walk away from her, Belinda prayed that time would pass quickly so they could be together again soon.

Hopefully, she could take a trip to New York for the agency to meet up with Frank, without arousing her husband's suspicions.

Chapter 9
Lookalikes Galore

On Monday morning, with a heavy heart Belinda arrived at the agency to find Freddie already there, busy tidying the office. Queenie gave out a little bark in greeting and Belinda had to fight to hold back the tears that were threatening to spill over.

"Belinda, darling, you are back. How are you, sweetheart? Tell Freddie all your news. We missed you, didn't we, Queenie?"

Little Queenie reacted to his master by yapping in agreement. Freddie always had the power to enlighten Belinda's mood, causing her to laugh and instantly feel happier and enabling her to hold back her hot tears as she felt her spirits lighten.

Encouraging her to sit down, Freddie poured them both a cup of coffee from the percolator, chatting excitedly as he told her all about his new lover, an Italian Opera singer, a wonderfully talented artiste of the stage, who worked not only in Milan but all over the world, including London. Freddie, swooning, confided to Belinda that he was madly in love for the first time in his life. All his other relationships had just been crushes, but, although smiling happily at Freddie, Belinda doubted that because Freddie was always falling in and out of love with one gorgeous guy or another, each time announcing this was the real love of his life.

Hurrying into the agency, Dawn apologised for being late, causing Freddie to jump up as he fussed around, pouring her a cup of coffee before she had time to take her jacket off.

Belinda greeted Dawn with a kiss and followed her friend and partner into her office. After telling Dawn all about her time with Frank, she confided to her that Frank had seemed a little too interested in Matt's businesses. Dawn, not wanting to worry Belinda, assured her that Frank was probably just making polite conversation when he questioned her about Matt, but deep inside Dawn Jarvis had a feeling that something was not quite right, and she decided to keep her eyes and ears open as far as Frank was concerned. Being a woman with strong insight, Dawn knew that Belinda was besotted with Mr Lanzo and she would never say anything untoward about him.

Making a vow to watch out for Belinda, Dawn finished her coffee and started to work through the pile of emails and letters sitting on her desk. Freddie went off to the post office, taking Queenie with him. Dawn spent the latter part of the morning drumming up new clients, while Belinda tried hard to concentrate on completing the contract for the Rat Pack tribute act that were about to fly to Germany for a week of shows at the Starlight Nightclub in Berlin.

Almost two agonising weeks passed before Belinda received a text message from Frank, explaining that he was hoping to be back in London within the next couple of months, this time for his company. It would be a very short business trip, but, nevertheless, it gave them another opportunity to meet again. Belinda's heart leapt as she read the message, happy that she would be in her lover's arms again soon, no matter how short his stay might be.

During the next few days, Belinda and Dawn worked on the agency's accounts. They had several wannabe lookalikes coming in for registration and to have photographs taken, hoping to join the agency. Close to midday, a short bald man rang the agency's doorbell and was greeted by Freddie with his usual flamboyant flourish of arms. Freddie, eyes widening, could not for the life of him think whom this man was supposed to look like.

As the bald man entered the office, he said, "Bruce Willis."

"Where?" asked Freddie, quickly looking around the room with excitement.

"Me. I am a Bruce Willis lookalike," announced the bald man, looking quite crestfallen after Freddie's impertinent question.

"Oh, sorry. Yes, of course, Bruce Willis," stuttered Freddie, trying to keep a straight face as he handed the man a registration form to complete.

Freddie swanned into Dawn's office and announced Bruce Willis' arrival.

"Does he look like him?" asked Dawn, her voice dropping to a whisper then glancing at Belinda, raising her eyebrows in anticipation.

"Well," replied Freddie, placing his hands on his hips, "let's put it this way, he has the same shoes!"

"What?" asked Dawn, as the two partners dropped their jaws in shock.

All day, a stream of wannabe lookalikes came into the agency, each expecting to be taken on but at least half left disappointed at not being given a chance to fulfil their dreams. As Dawn continuously reminded anyone who would listen, Top Drawer Lookalike and Tribute Acts Agency were only interested in the very best. Camp Freddie was kept extremely busy, handing out registration forms and showing each artiste into Dawn's office to be auditioned by both partners. The Bruce Willis wannabe had left rather disappointed at not being taken on by the agency.

Lady Denise Ava, the agency's top Madonna lookalike and tribute act, was passing by in her new white BMW when she decided to pop in to see Belinda and Dawn, wanting to explain to them exactly what happened during her tribute act in Istanbul the week before. Lady Denise was far better at spreading the news than any tabloid newspaper on the streets. Her title bought with her affluent parents' money, Lady Denise was a beautiful woman of Maltese descent, now in her early forties, with the most perfect skin, dyed blonde hair and large green eyes, rivalling Madonna's own.

Colour was the key word for the Lady, wearing the very brightest beautifully, turning the heads of many eligible men. When Freddie answered the door, there was an immediate chemistry between them and Freddie began gushing and fussing over her, which Lady Denise gladly encouraged. Freddie, as flamboyant as ever, felt amazing as Lady Denise laughed at all his silly jokes and feminine mannerisms.

A couple of years earlier, Lady Denise, known then as plain Diana King, was sent on a tribute job as a Madonna tribute act to the Wild Wind Nightclub in the lively Turkish city. During the interval of her act, the client came into her dressing room and told her, quite bluntly, that he didn't think she was a good enough tribute act for Madonna, then went on to say that, in his opinion and the opinion of his staff, she did not sing well at all. Because of this, he had decided to pay her off right there and then, replacing her with their resident female singer for the second part of her act.

The Top Drawer Agency had no option but to send Lady Denise to the Wild Wind Nightclub in Istanbul again recently, due to the fact that their only other tribute act was unwell and could not fulfil her contract. Dawn's mind raced back almost two years to the telephone call she had received from the Turkish client, demanding most of his fee back due to the inadequacies of their Madonna tribute act. Lady Denise had promised Dawn she had completed several singing lessons since that incident two years earlier and assured Dawn that the Turkish client would be more than satisfied once he heard her sing again.

When Lady Denise had arrived at the nightclub the previous week, the client was shocked to see the agency had sent Diana King again after he had specifically asked them not to.

"Oh, but I am not Diana King. I am Lady Denise Ava. I can understand your confusion, because Diana King is my identical twin sister, but she is not a good singer or dancer, I agree. Please give me a chance to prove this to you now I am here. Although we look exactly alike, we sing and dance completely differently."

Still looking shocked, the client fell for her story. Finding Lady Denise Ava immensely charming, he granted her a chance to sing for him before agreeing to her performing in the evening show.

Luckily, she told her agents, her lessons had paid off as she had improved her singing two-fold and the client liked her tribute act very much this time.

"I was so proud of myself," boosted Lady Denise. "I actually pulled it off and proved what an amazing Madonna tribute act I am, when I put my mind to it, of course."

"You are incorrigible," laughed Dawn. "We had a fax from the Turkish client a couple of days ago, congratulating us on our excellent tribute acts. Thank you, Lady Ava, for your efforts," added Dawn, still smiling.

"I can honestly say, the client actually believed my twin sister story and he assured me that if he ever required another Madonna tribute act again, he would ask for me personally," smiled Lady Denise as she leant across to place her coffee cup on the desk.

Before leaving the agency, Belinda asked for her availability for the following Saturday evening; a mix and mingle with four other lookalikes at the London Hilton. Digging into her bright orange handbag and consulting her tablet, she agreed, before swanning out of the agency followed closely by Freddie, who before opening the door for their visitor kissed her on both cheeks.

Time seemed to drag for Belinda, her mind lingered continuously on Frank. She could almost smell him when she closed her eyes. Life had lost its sparkle for her. Usually of a happy and optimistic nature, Belinda found when she was not with Frank, nothing made her feel really happy and she wondered why love hurt so much. Quietly, she decided to take one day at a time until she was in Frank's arms again.

Matt went about his business as usual, sometimes arriving home early for dinner and sometimes staying out until the early hours of the morning, explaining to Belinda he was with the boys having a late drink at one club or another in Soho. Of course, Belinda knew he lied to her most of the time, and although she now felt indifferent about her husband's escapades, she feigned anger with him, complaining about his late hours to make him think she still cared.

Chapter 10
Passionate Rendezvous

More than a month passed before Belinda received another text message from Frank. Again, he was travelling to London, this time on business for his company but only for a couple of days. Frank told her where he would be staying and asked her to meet him there the following Friday. With her heart beating quickly with excitement at the very thought of being with Frank again, Belinda couldn't keep her inner happiness shining out of her eyes.

All too slowly, Friday came around and Belinda found herself in the foyer of the Sherlock Holmes Hotel, off Baker Street close to Regent's Park. Frank was already waiting to meet her.

"Belinda," he murmured when he saw her, "I've missed you."

Into his strong arms she ran, ignoring the glances of other people in the foyer. Frank took her arm and walked her towards the swing doors and down the steps of the hotel, into the summer sunshine.

"Let's take a little walk; I need some air," he uttered quietly, his lips close to her hair. "We can then go up to my suite and say hello properly," he added with a twinkle in his dancing brown eyes.

Wanting him so badly, Belinda found she could not be in this man's presence and not hunger for him again and again. They walked to Regent's Park, glorious in its summer colours, strolling quietly by the Regent's Canal, watching the swans and ducks diving for bread thrown by two elderly ladies. Frank had his arm around Belinda's shoulder as they chatted and walked contentedly for some time before heading back to the hotel.

As soon as they entered Frank's room, he covered her mouth with his ardent kisses; he wanted her now. They stripped each other quickly, both pulling off each other's garments as quickly as they could, so urgent was their need to make love. Kissing and touching each other, Belinda was desperate to please her lover.

After their sensual passion had been exalted, a smile danced at the corners of Frank's mouth as he rolled over and lay on his back. Belinda snuggled under his right arm. They lay there, the lovers, in slumber, holding each other for a long time.

Suddenly waking, Belinda drowsily glanced at the digital clock on the television set and became wide awake immediately because it showed it was almost midnight. Earlier, Belinda had called Matt and told him she was going to have dinner with Tanya and would be home late. Gently, she shook Frank, who grunted and opened his eyes. Tenderly, he kissed her mouth, but she pulled away from him, knowing if she returned his kisses, she would never get home and the nasty arguments would erupt with Matt.

"Tell him you are staying with Tanya because you don't want to travel home at this late hour," suggested Frank sleepily to her as he fondled her breasts.

More than anything, Belinda wanted to stay the night with her lover, so she quickly called Tanya, who agreed readily to be her alibi. Nervously, Belinda tapped out her home number on her mobile phone but there was no answer. Knowing how possessive Matt was, Belinda was relieved she did not have to speak to him directly but left a message explaining where she was. Entering the bathroom for a shower, she rinsed her panties, hoping they would dry by the morning, Belinda returned to the bedroom again. Frank was in a deep sleep and the sight of this man never failed to fill her soul with love for him. Hanging up their scattered clothes, she pulled an extra blanket over them both and contentedly fell asleep, wrapped in his strong tanned arms.

All too soon, the first glimmer of dawn began to light up the skies and to Belinda's dismay, she noticed it was already seven in the morning. Grabbing her mobile, she dialled her home number and listened for several minutes as it continued to ring out. No answer again; she knew only too well where Matt had probably spent the night. Quickly, she left another message for him and explained she would be home within a few hours. Matt, she knew, would be on his way to the Soho betting office to make sure everything was in order for the busiest day of the week. Climbing back onto the bed where her lover lay, she seductively kissed his mouth. Dancing brown eyes opened as he smiled and pulled her to him.

"Buongiorno, dolce Belinda," *(Good morning, sweet Belinda)* he uttered in his husky New York accent.

"Good morning, Mr Lanzo. I hope you are awake now because I have to leave very soon," answered Belinda, her lips still touching his. Almost abruptly, Frank sat up in bed and rolled her over on her back. After what seemed like no time at all, they reached the place between heaven and earth simultaneously. Belinda knew only too well she could never get enough of this man; she was completely his; no other man now could ever come close to how she felt for Frank Lanzo.

Dear God, she prayed. Please let him love me.

The lovers remained together in Frank's hotel room until she had to leave and return home. The sun was now shining over a blue-skied London. On such a beautiful warm sunny day, it would be impossible not to feel happy, but not so for Belinda. Flying back to New York later that afternoon, Frank had told her he did not know when he would next be in London, but suggested maybe she visited him in New York later in the year. Frank promised he would keep in touch until they could be together again.

Heavy-hearted, despair filling her soul, Belinda arrived home and kept herself busy, tidying her already tidy home.

Just after seven that evening, Matt arrived. Kissing his wife lightly on her mouth, he explained, apologetically, that he'd had one too many vodkas the night before and had gone home with Jason, who lived close to the club where they had been drinking. Of course, Belinda did not believe him for one moment, knowing it was all lies, but she had to remind herself that she too was lying, explaining to Matt again why she had decided to stay with Tanya. Both outwardly accepted the other's explanation, simply because both were guilty.

Unbeknown to Belinda, Frank had visited all three of Matt's betting offices on the previous Thursday. Frank had actually arrived in London late Wednesday evening and spent all of Thursday checking out different venues he wanted to see, the betting shops among them. In the business world of Frank Lanzo, men did not discuss business with women; they expected the women to accept what they were told and enjoy the benefits that business brought.

Frank knew much of Matt's whereabouts, listening intently when Belinda had mentioned, during one of their many conversations, that Matt had recently taken over the running of the latest and most viable of the shops, the one situated in the heart of Soho where Matt, she explained to Frank, spent most of his working week.

Frank had casually walked into the Soho betting office, which was busy with customers with their eyes focused on the large television screens, each vying their chosen horse to win. Checking the list of horses on the boards, Frank browsed through the many available newspapers, strategically placed on the little round tables for the customers' convenience. There were three men behind the long, curved counter and a young blonde woman. After selecting his choice of horse for the one o'clock race at Doncaster, Frank had walked up to the counter and asked for Matt Flynn.

A tall, dark-haired man checking the tills looked up and said, "Yes, I'm Matt Flynn. How can I help you?"

Frank introduced himself as Gene Capalti, one of his pseudonyms. As he shook hands with Matt, he explained that a gambling friend of his from New York, who had recently stayed in the Soho area, told him Matt had a great knowledge of the race game and assured Gene that Matt would point him in the right direction when making a bet. Obviously, this glowing praise appealed to Matt's conceited nature and he beamed at Gene with all his boyish charm.

The two strangers spent some time discussing bookmakers in the UK, the rest of Europe, the gambling licences, the horses, and how the business had changed during the last few years. Matt asked Gene if he was in the gambling business himself, but Gene told him he was a property developer for a big corporate company in New York and was looking for properties in London to invest or buy. The two men were getting along very well and Frank sensed in Matt a real gambling man, one who would take risks in life because he was so conceited with a big ego.

After placing his bets, Frank left the shop, arranging to meet up with Matt later that day. Matt, taking an instant liking to the American, had suggested they met at Gerry's Club, after Gene had explained to him he had a lucrative proposition that could possibly be of interest to Matt.

Gerry's Club was an actors' club, and a true institution. Set up in 1955 by Gerry Campion, the actor who was famous for playing Billy Bunter, his private members' club and drinking joint was a popular haunt for actors, writers, directors, producers, artists, musicians, dancers and other creative and theatrical types. Gerry's was also one of the last places keeping the Soho Boho tradition alive.

A dimly lit basement with an eclectic playlist and walls adorned with actors' headshots and theatre posters, Gerry's was a place of character and colour. Matt knew without doubt that Gene would appreciate Gerry's Club and he was not disappointed when Gene agreed with him how impressed he was with the famous club. Gene made it clear to Matt straightaway that under no circumstances was he to mention their meeting or their possible business plans with anybody: no wives; no girlfriends; nobody. Matt, being streetwise and secretive by nature, understood perfectly what Gene was saying to him.

In the darkest corner of the club where they shared a bottle of fine Italian red wine, Gene laid out a plan. He explained that he knew Matt liked to gamble and went on to say some of the best gambling opportunities did not present themselves to ordinary members of the public. He called this type of gambling professional. It carried a premium risk and a premium reward. To illustrate his point, Gene laid a £20 note on the table.

"If you guess correctly which country this note is from, you win it," said Gene. "Get it wrong, and you have to give me one of your twenties."

Matt took one look at the money and replied, "It's British, of course."

"Is it now?" asked Gene. "Give me one of your British twenties."

Matt took one from his wallet and Gene placed the two bank notes down side by side on the table.

"I brought this one with me from America," he said, pointing to the first note. "We have a man who makes them there. Good, aren't they?"

Matt held it up and examined it. It looked perfectly real to him. Gene knew it would be a little bit inconvenient and might feel strange to start with. It would mean some double bookkeeping. But he encouraged Matt to give it a go, just with a little money to start with. Of course, he conceded, Matt would be offered a remuneration arrangement, which suited this increased level of responsibility.

"It'll give the business a boost and a new identity," promised Gene.

Here was the plan. The Society bought fake British notes across from the States. Matt shuffled them in with real money at the bookmakers and the punters would take the fake notes away as prizes. The Society, which supplied the notes, wanted to ensure the American pounds gradually disappeared and were replaced with real British pounds. After Matt listened intently to Gene's proposition, he said he needed a couple of days to think things over before giving his answer, although he had already made up his mind to take advantage of this lucrative proposition, despite the risks involved.

Belinda knew absolutely nothing about her Frank meeting Matt. To make sure Belinda did not find out about their meetings and their possible future business together, Frank used his pseudonym to ensure there were no slip-ups. Frank Lanzo becomes Gene Capalti when in London dealing with Matt and the other bookmakers. But to Belinda, he was Frank Lanzo; a double deception.

Chapter 11
Spanish Liaisons

Freddie was not working on Monday – it was his day off – and Dawn was away until Wednesday, so Belinda opened up the agency and tried to keep her mind off Frank and on the business in hand. The following weeks were extremely busy for the agency; many of the lookalikes and tribute acts were working at the London Docklands for *Ciao Magazine*; four of them were hired for a photo shoot; one of the Marilyn Monroe impersonators had been flown to Copenhagen for a small part on a television show; and the Royal Family lookalikes were as busy as ever – so much so the agency had as many as six lookalikes of the Duchess of Cambridge, all working on different jobs at the same time in different parts of the world! Dawn had remarked many times that it was imperative for the agency to have several people on their books portraying the same character, making sure their clients would never be disappointed.

Unbeknown to the foreign clients and even some of the British ones, many of the top lookalikes and tribute acts were signed up to all the leading agencies and so when a client booked the top lookalike of any one character, they were presented with the same impersonator from all agencies. There were times when lesser-known agencies undercut the more renowned ones, winning the contract. When Dawn learnt of this, she gave her top lookalikes and tribute acts a clear ultimatum. If they wanted to be represented by any other agency, she would take them off her books. Knowing she owned the very best agency in the country, and possibly in Europe, this ultimatum paid off for Dawn, with almost all of the acts remaining on her books exclusively.

A prestigious Spanish client from Madrid had been doing the rounds of all the lookalike agencies in the UK, trying to find the best people for the lowest cost. Because news travels fast, all the agencies were aware that a very viable Spanish contract was up for grabs. As Belinda got up from her chair to make herself another cup of coffee, the telephone rang in Dawn's office. Moving quickly so as not to lose the call, Belinda picked up the receiver.

"Good morning, Top Drawer Agency."

The telephone call lasted ten minutes and as she replaced the receiver, Belinda's spirits had heightened. The Spanish client had decided to award their prestigious job to Top Drawer Agency, pending photographs and DVDs. Ten of the top lookalikes were required for a television show. They were to be seated around the audience so the cameras could pick them out during the programme. They wanted lookalikes for: HRH Queen Elizabeth II; Theresa May; the Duchess of Cambridge; Prince William; Joan Collins; Simon Cowell; Adele; Harry Styles of One Direction; and David and Victoria Beckham. After telephoning Dawn at her home to discuss the finer detail, Belinda felt excitement building up in her at the prospect of getting away and spending time in the very modern and lively Spanish capital.

The rest of the day was spent telephoning the chosen lookalikes, checking their availability for the job. When all information was to hand, Belinda sent it to the client in Madrid with the necessary photographs and DVDs. By the end of the working day, there had been no further news from the Spanish client, but Belinda knew only too well it would be at least a couple of days before Top Drawer Agency received firm confirmation they were to win the contract. Closing the agency after six that evening, her mind, as always, focused on Frank.

The next morning, Freddie, along with Queenie, were in the office when Belinda arrived. Freddie kissed her on both cheeks and immediately poured her a hot cup of coffee. Queenie excitedly wagged his little tail as Belinda tickled him under his white furry chin. After lunch, when Freddie and Queenie were out for a visit to the post office, a message came through from Madrid, confirming that Top Drawer Agency had been awarded the Spanish television contract. Feeling very excited about this forthcoming job, Belinda set about drawing up contracts for each of the lookalikes. Marina Greenslade (Queen Elizabeth II lookalike) called later in the afternoon, expressing how much she was looking forward to working professionally with Belinda again.

Madrid turned out to be a very enjoyable job. All the lookalikes, Belinda included, flew into Madrid Airport and were taken to lunch by the clients as soon as they checked into the Hotel Maria. Their first evening was free, and some of them went for dinner to a family-run Spanish restaurant, a couple of streets away from their hotel. Belinda's room was sandwiched between Marina (Queen Elizabeth II) and Yvonne Grant (Theresa May), and she giggled to herself about her noble neighbours. Marina Greenslade was one of the most famous lookalikes in the UK, and well known all across the world as the best lookalike of Queen Elizabeth II. Belinda liked and admired Marina, and enjoyed listening to her many interesting stories of her escapades as one of the world's most admired lookalikes.

The television show was being recorded the following morning and the lookalikes were due at the studios early where they were given breakfast on set along with the crew working on the show. There was the usual rehearsal, and then straight into make-up. Belinda always did her own make-up, only needing a little powder from the professional artists to make sure her skin was not shiny. While waiting in the make-up room, Marina and Sarah (Victoria Beckham) were discussing another job they had worked on recently, but Marina found Sarah far too opinionated and told her so. Sarah, full of the cockiness of youth, retaliated and stood her ground, refusing to allow the older woman to have the last word. Quickly stepping in to calm the situation before it got out of hand, Belinda gently ushered Marina away from Sarah, sitting her down in a comfortable armchair and pouring her friend a cup of tea.

When everybody had been wonderfully transposed into their characters, the Spanish producers and director, who were extremely pleased with their UK lookalikes, placed them in seats around the theatre along with the public, enabling the cameras to easily pick them out during the show, hoping the viewer would think they were looking at the real celebrities. Belinda was seated cosily next to a very handsome young man, who was supposed to be her toy boy! As the cameras picked her out, the toy boy was shown holding her hand, all tongue-in-cheek fun; an easy and enjoyable job.

Everybody was in good spirits by the end of the recording, and later that evening they were taken by the clients to a restaurant that featured a Flamenco floor show, which was quite spectacular. After wonderful food and plenty of vino, the evening came to a close, and everyone arrived back at the Hotel Maria, exhilarated after such an amazing day.

Due to fly back to the UK the following day, Marina and Belinda rose early because they had decided to visit Madrid's Museo Reina Sofia, where they marvelled at Picasso's *Guernica*. This painting was created in response to the bombing of Guernica, a Basque country village in northern Spain, by German and Italian war planes at the behest of the Spanish Nationalist forces in April 1937 during the Spanish Civil War. The Guernica showed the tragedies of war and the suffering it inflicts on individuals, particularly innocent civilians and animals.

Everything was running smoothly under the hot Spanish sun as their flight from Madrid to London Gatwick took off, carrying the excited lookalikes. Belinda had a close friend, Marcia, who lived less than a mile from Gatwick Airport. Marcia had insisted Belinda park her car in her driveway whenever she flew from there. Meeting Belinda at the arrivals lounge of Terminal Three, Marcia drove her friend half a mile to her home where they had a quick coffee and chat. Thanking her friend and kissing her, Belinda drove herself home.

To her surprise, Matt was at home and lying on the couch in front of the television, sleeping as usual. Immediately taking a hot bath, Belinda got herself ready for bed, tiredness overwhelming her now. Before leaving for Spain, Dawn had told her to take the Friday off and have a good rest, and Belinda was very grateful for an extra day to herself.

Chapter 12
Devious Deals

L ife for Belinda was very full, but still nothing seemed to make her truly happy, not since meeting Frank. He dominated her every waking thought and always her dreams. How she missed him: his strength of character, his sense of humour and his sensual passion, which she longed for continuously.

Early one rainy morning while Matt and Belinda were hurriedly having breakfast before driving to their respective jobs, Matt told her he was attending a bookmakers' seminar in Belgium the following week. It was a one-day conference and he would stay the night in the hotel where the seminar was being held.

"Is Sidney going with you?" asked Belinda.

"No, there's no reason for him to go really. I have a gut feeling he will be retiring soon," replied Matt, as he kissed her quickly on the side of her face.

Not having heard from Frank in a while now, Belinda's heart grew anxious, although she remembered he'd told her he couldn't contact her for a few weeks. However, checking her mobile for text messages and emails, Belinda could not help but worry.

Matt's seminar in Belgium was in fact a meeting with Gene Capalti and another American gentleman, who was a solicitor for the Society. The business was dealt with amicably in the famous restaurant, Alexandre, where there was remarkable cuisine, together with the best wine in Brussels. When all the business avenues were satisfactorily completed, and all three men had much fine food and wine, Gene stood up and paid the bill with a card. Gene and the solicitor shook hands with Matt, who was feeling ecstatic and excited now; happy that this lucrative proposition had been cemented legally with the Society, thanks to Gene Capalti.

Freddie was late for work on Wednesday morning, after a lovers' tiff with his Italian opera singer, Claudio. Poor Freddie; his eyes were red and puffy from crying, and his lips were turned down in sorrow. Belinda tried to cheer him up, but Freddie was inconsolable. Queenie sensed Freddie's sadness and was very anxious, as dogs are when bonded with their master or mistress.

"I am sure Claudio will cool down, Freddie, and call you. Please cheer up. Poor Queenie is upset too," encouraged Belinda, handing Freddie a cup of coffee.

"He takes me for granted, Belinda. He never says thank you when I do something nice for him. He acts as though I should be honoured to do these things for him."

Walking up to Freddie, Belinda gave him a cuddle. "Don't worry, darling. The course of true love never ran smooth; look at my love life!" she said, smiling at him.

After a little coaxing from his friend, Freddie pulled himself together and, opening the computer, began to answer the many emails cluttering up the inbox.

The day somehow seemed to drag and Belinda offered to take Queenie outside to cock his leg. As she and Queenie returned to the office, a message came through on her mobile; a message from Frank – at last. Very excited, she anticipated where in the world the Society would be sending him but, unfortunately, Frank explained he was still waiting to find out, although he was thinking about her. Belinda's disappointment now matched Freddie's sadness. Why, she thought, did love hurt so much?

The following day, it was as if Freddie's lovers' tiff had never happened. It turned out that he and Claudio had made up the previous evening and spent a wonderful night together. Freddie was back to his chirpy self and little Queenie reacted favourably to his beloved master's new high spirits.

After taking a telephone call, Dawn shouted out to Belinda and Freddie.

"I can't believe it! Glory (Britney Spears) has fallen in love with Andy (David Beckham) and has decided to become a Victoria Beckham lookalike!"

"Pardon?" laughed Belinda. "Victoria Beckham? Glory looks nothing like her."

"Maybe not, but she does not want to be Britney Spears anymore because she wants to work with Andy from now on!" replied Dawn, raising her eyes to the ceiling.

"We have Gina as our top Victoria Beckham, who always works with Andy," reasoned Belinda. "We also have Sarah and she is an excellent cover for Gina. Did you explain to Glory that we will not accept her on our books as Victoria Beckham?" she added, getting up from her chair and walking into Dawn's office.

"Yes, of course I did, but she said Andy wants to work with her too. Apparently, they want to be together," replied Dawn, looking quite worried.

"In this case then, we lose our best Victoria Beckham and our best Britney Spears," Belinda said, now also looking worried.

"I will call Andy and try to reason with him this afternoon," said Dawn, glancing out of the window at the dull cloudy day. "I will make it clear to him that Top Drawer Agency will not accept Glory as yet another Victoria Beckham, and that is final."

Belinda knew only too well that when Dawn made up her mind about something, there was no reasoning with her at all.

Life without Frank was unfulfilled for Belinda. She missed him desperately. Lately, she and Matt hardly had much to say to each other, and he was spending more and more time in his Soho betting shop. He explained to Belinda he was in the middle of training new recruits, which in fact he was.

A couple of weeks into a warm and pleasant June, Freddie became extremely excited, having been accepted as Liberace in a photo shoot for a gay calendar to be shot in Germany. The calendar was to portray a different gay star for each month of the year: Elton John for January; Freddie Mercury for February, and so on. Camp Freddie as Liberace would be the celebrity for September. Freddie was over the moon: he felt as if he had just proved himself to the world. To have the honour to portray the amazingly talented Liberace, Freddie assured Belinda and Dawn he would make a wonderful job of it. Both agents were really happy for Freddie; they were both fond of him and knew he would do justice to the memory of Liberace.

"New York?" exclaimed Belinda. "I thought you were busy with the betting shops and yet right now you want to go to New York?"

She was becoming a little angry.

"Yes, but only for three days. A couple of the lads are going for a break and asked me to join them. You know how much I have always wanted to visit the Big Apple, so I told them I would join them," answered Matt, playing with the TV remote control.

"What about the Soho shop? Who will run that while you are swanning around New York?" retorted Belinda.

"Sidney will cover me and Oliver will cover Sidney at the Victoria shop. John will take care of Mayfair during Oliver's time at Victoria," replied Matt.

"Well, you seem to have everything already sorted out. When are you leaving?" Belinda asked, slipping off her shoes and replacing them with her bedroom slippers.

"Sunday morning, flying from Heathrow. Back first thing Thursday morning. You will be okay, won't you?" enquired Matt, turning to look at his wife.

"Yes, of course I will, you will be back in the blink of an eye. Besides, we are very busy at the agency right now, so I'll probably work late most days," she added, entering the kitchen to cook their evening meal.

Matt enjoyed the flight to New York with his friends. When they had passed through customs at JFK Airport, they took a cab and were driven to their four-star hotel, close to Carnegie Hall and two blocks from Rockefeller Center at 50th Street and Fifth Avenue, a classy part of town. Matt told his friends he was meeting an American acquaintance on Monday evening and could not go with them to the theatre, as previously arranged.

The following day, Matt and his friends visited Ground Zero, which they found very beautiful, yet sad and eerie. The whole area was crowded with tourists from all over the world, which was to be expected.

Early on Monday evening, Matt's two friends left the hotel on their way to the theatre while Matt waited in the foyer of the Wainwright Hotel for Gene to meet him there. Gene arrived and parked his car outside the main entrance of the hotel, immediately waving the doorman over. He swiftly thrust a large dollar bill into the man's hand, asking him to check if a Matt Flynn was waiting in the lounge.

Within minutes, Matt appeared and Gene called out to him. Once inside the car, the two men drove towards West 56th Street to Patsy's, a family-run Italian restaurant, famous for being the favourite eating place of the late Frank Sinatra. When Gene and Matt were shown to their table in the very plush restaurant, Matt noticed, as they followed the maître d', that the restaurant was packed with diners. Quite unusual for a Monday evening, he thought, but then Patsy's had a very famous reputation.

On taking their seats, Matt saw the table was laid out with four place settings. Gene handed Matt the wine list and explained to him that two of his work colleagues were joining them for dinner. Within less than ten minutes, two burly, Italian looking gentlemen were sitting opposite Gene and Matt. After the introductions, Matt learned that Aldo Lamarina and Sergie Belladoni, being of Sicilian heritage, were made men of the Society and in the future, either one or both of these gentlemen would be flying into London when Gene was unavailable to oversee all three betting shops. The four men had a wonderful evening of fine conversation, fine Italian cuisine, even finer Italian wines, and the setting up of a very successful business deal between Matt and the Society through Gene.

In the following few days, while Matt and his friends were still in New York, Gene telephoned him several times. Matt was feeling extremely excited, although somewhat sceptical about his new venture. Gene had explained to him the Society were willing to give Matt enough money to buy out his senior partner Sidney's fifty per cent share of the three highly successful betting shops, thus securing the Society with fifty per cent of the entire businesses. Matt was learning fast that Gene had a unique art of hiding money.

Completely confident his partner would accept a lucrative offer for his fifty per cent share of the businesses, Matt knew that Sidney, who had been contemplating retirement, could not refuse such a generous offer. Gene would fly into London at least once every six weeks to primarily oversee the Society's interests. In exchange for the offer awarded to Matt, the Society would require Matt to launder some of their illegal money through his betting offices. The Society had to show a legitimate source for their illicit monies and one of the ways in which they were able to do this was by owning or part owning outwardly legitimate businesses and mixing their illicit earnings with the legitimate earnings received from these businesses. Matt was now well and truly involved in this money laundering double deception.

Gene knew from his many conversations with her that Belinda never visited her husband's betting shops and he felt safe in the knowledge that it was highly unlikely he would run into her when he was working with her husband. Matt's desire to make as much money as possible, coupled with his greediness, made it easy for him to sign on the dotted line in Patsy's on that Monday evening. Becoming an outside Associate of the Society, his three betting shops were now fifty per cent owned by them. In the interim, making Matt a very rich man indeed. However, he was fully aware that Belinda must never know about his dealings with the Society; in fact, no one could know. It was not possible for Matt, being neither Sicilian nor Italian, to take omertà; a cultural expression and code of honour that placed legitimate importance on a deep-rooted family sense of a code of silence. Nevertheless, he was made fully aware of the consequences if he discussed their deal with anyone. This also applied to other outside Associates.

Flying back into London on Thursday, chatting happily with his good friends, Matt waved to one of his employees who had met them at the arrivals lounge to drive Matt straight to the Soho betting office. As the car speed towards London, Matt telephoned Belinda, letting her know he had arrived safely. Happy to hear her husband had a good time in New York, Belinda agreed with him that next time he was to visit the Big Apple, she might accompany him.

Chapter 13
Sensual Love

Arriving at the agency, Belinda was all smiles as she had received a text from Frank. Frank said he was missing her terribly and he may be in London again within a month or so on business for the Society. His text said he would stay at the same airport hotel as last time so she could visit him without causing suspicion. As she took her lightweight jacket off, Freddie arrived with Queenie, who was sporting a blue, velvet collar with diamanté.

Freddie, thought Belinda, seemed very highly strung and she enquired whether he was okay. With hands flailing about in exasperation, Freddie explained that Big Hands Harry had tried to ravage him at a party on Saturday night and he had trouble trying to defend his honour, which really upset him because he couldn't fancy Big Hands Harry in a million years! Freddie went on to explain he also had trouble with Rammer Bill at the same party, and he was even more repulsive than Big Hands Harry!

"I'm just grateful that Claudio was working on Saturday evening and wasn't with me at the party, otherwise all hell would have broken loose," tutted Freddie, putting Queenie down gently on the carpeted floor.

"Thank God for that, Freddie," replied Belinda, trying desperately to keep a straight face. "You do not want to upset Claudio, that's for sure," she added, walking across to Freddie and giving him a hug.

The following few weeks were deliriously exciting for Belinda as she waited in anticipation of being with Frank again. Missing him so badly every minute of every day, she noticed she was beginning to live for their rendezvous. Needing to find an excuse to give Matt for the two nights she would be away from home, Belinda spoke with Dawn who agreed to cover her friend's alibi, which was that Belinda (as Joan Collins) and Vicky (as Elizabeth Taylor) were booked for two evenings at a fashion show in Leeds. Dawn assured Belinda that Freddie would be made aware of this fact.

With her heart in her mouth, Belinda lightly tapped on Room 158. Slowly, the door was opened and there he stood as handsome as ever, naked but for a large white towel wrapped around his waist. She felt her heart jump with excitement as he gently pulled her towards him and kissed her passionately on her mouth. Her eyes filled with tears as emotions became too strong to control. How she adored this man and everything about him.

"Cara Belinda, Mi sei mancato," *(Darling Belinda, I have missed you)* Frank whispered in her ear and led her into the room, where he expertly removed her clothes, leaving only her black lacy panties. His mouth found her heaving breasts, as he gently bit and rubbed her hardened nipples. Groaning with ecstasy, Belinda opened her legs and wrapped them around his waist.

He could not get enough of this sensual woman.

For the very first time in her life, Belinda felt completely fulfilled sexually. They lay in each other's arms, both so happy to be together again, both quickly falling into slumber.

When they awoke a few hours later, it was already dark. Frank, now feeling hungry, decided to take Belinda to the hotel restaurant for dinner. He told her they would go back to his room and relax, talk, watch the television, have a nightcap and make sensual love, again and again.

All too soon, their love-filled days had passed, and Frank had to leave to return to New York.

Two days prior to meeting Belinda, and unbeknown to her, Frank, with more American-made twenty-pound notes securely hidden in his luggage, had arrived in London to distribute more fake money to all three betting shops.

Gene (Frank) was satisfied that the older senior partner had indeed taken Matt's very lucrative offer to buy out his fifty per cent share of the businesses. This amounted to a massive amount of money, and Sidney was more than happy with the extremely generous offer Matt had made him. Certainly, he would not have to worry about money ever again, not for the remainder of his life. Now both in their mid-seventies, he and his wife, Judith, were ready for that home by the sea.

"How on earth did the bank lend you so much money, Matt?" asked Sidney early one morning while they were having breakfast in a café close to the Soho betting office.

"I have winning ways, Sidney, my friend, as well you know," replied the younger man, grinning and tapping the side of his perfectly-shaped aquiline nose.

Chapter 14
Virgin Jobs

Freddie was almost in tears as he kissed Queenie goodbye and told him to be a good boy for Aunties Belinda and Dawn until Daddy was back home in three days' time. The date for the gay calendar shoot in Düsseldorf had arrived, and Dawn and Belinda had been delighted with this excellent booking. The agency had supplied eight of the required twelve tribute acts booked by the German client. The other four were famous gay European singers and the client had already booked them through an agent in the Netherlands. Freddie looked very smart in his cherry red leather bomber jacket and tight black jeans. After kissing Belinda and Dawn goodbye, and once more cuddling Queenie, who was already whining, Freddie picked up his small blue suitcase on wheels and headed to the door. Belinda had readily agreed to look after Queenie in Freddie's absence. It would be nice to have a dog back in her life after all this time, she mused as she stroked the sad little Queenie.

Freddie met Ray (Elton John) and Paul (George Michael) at the British Airways desk and discovered the two knew each other well because they had worked together many times before. Freddie was surprised when he found neither of them were homosexual. After the usual introductions, Paul suggested having a quick drink in one of the lounge bars in the airport before they went through to duty-free. Freddie noticed that people were beginning to stare at the three of them as they walked into the bar. How he was going to enjoy this fascinating, exciting life as a lookalike; somehow, it made him feel like a real celebrity. Relaxing with their drinks, Freddie was thoroughly enjoying hearing all about the many experiences of his new friends, when suddenly he was aware that a hush had descended on the airport lounge. Noticing all eyes were looking in one direction, Freddie turned to see what had caught everybody's attention when Ray let out a loud laugh and announced.

"It's The Boy, I knew it was him. Only The Boy could cause such havoc."

A little gasp escaped from his taunt throat as Freddie's amused eyes took in the apparition that was mincing along, heading straight towards them. Here was Kevin (Boy George lookalike and tribute act), referred to as The Boy, but Freddie could have sworn it was the real star.

Hurrying along, pulling both suitcases on wheels, Wayne, The Boy's bodyguard and partner, huffed and puffed as he tried to keep up; his handsome face turning an embarrassing shade of red. Kevin would never dream of travelling anywhere abroad without his bodyguard and lover. Freddie learned that although Wayne was of very slight build, he was in fact a black belt in aikido. The Boy was dressed as flamboyantly as ever: tartan trousers, a long black silk tunic top, covered in crusted bling stones, a brown fake fur waistcoat thrown over his shoulders, with six-inch heeled boots in silver leather, and to top it all, a green felt hat! Freddie quickly decided that out of the whole planet, Kevin was indeed the most flamboyant of all.

The Boy's make-up had been expertly applied to his neat features, including bright green eyeshadow to match the colour of his eyes and, of course, his hat.

"Wow, he's really good! He fooled me, that's for sure," uttered Freddie, under his breath as Ray stood up and laughed as he slapped The Boy on the shoulder.

Paul laughed even louder and shook hands with Kevin, who pouted and asked impertinently, as only he could, "Well, where are our drinks, ladies?"

The green eyes then turned and looked directly at Freddie, whose mouth had dropped open.

"Boy, meet Liberace," mused Paul. "You two girls should have lots to talk about," he giggled.

As Freddie stood up politely, a big grin spread across The Boy's amused face, as he uttered, "Well, hello, Liberace, I am indeed a big fan. I hope you can tickle those ivories good and proper."

Freddie was speechless, like everyone who had ever met Kevin.

The British Airways plane later landed smoothly at Düsseldorf Airport. Freddie had now met the lookalikes and tribute acts from the UK who were booked on the photo shoot through Top Drawer Agency and he was determined to be a success for Dawn and Belinda on his virgin job.

The agency seemed empty without Freddie. Dawn had taken advantage of the quiet phase they were going through by taking a day off. Belinda was happy to deal with the telephone enquiries and other tasks alone. Little Queenie lay around all day looking sad until Belinda took him for his walkies; only then did he become lively. This was for her benefit as well as Queenie's, finding a brisk walk helped clear her head as she became increasingly melancholy without Frank. Life these days felt completely empty for her once Frank had returned home to New York. Just one lonely day without him felt like a year to her.

Her mind continually relived moments of their amazing sexual lovemaking. The way he fulfilled her very being and how, in return, she loved him unconditionally. These thoughts flooded her mind continuously.

Matt appeared to be busier than ever now that Sidney had actually retired, employing two extra experienced bookmakers to help with the growing volume of clientele during the busy race season, placing one at the Victoria shop and the other with him at the Soho shop.

As the Society had instructed, Matt had never mentioned Gene to his wife, or to anyone at all who were not employees of the betting shops. They were merely informed that Gene was contracted by Matt to oversee the business when needed. Matt agreed it was best Belinda knew nothing about his American friend; that way, she would not become curious. Being confident his wife would not visit him at his place of work, Matt knew this would make it very unlikely for her and Gene to bump into each other in the foreseeable future. His secret business dealings with the Society would be kept secret, not only from Belinda but from everyone, just as Gene had strongly advised him. Matt knew he was now deeply involved with shady characters but his gambling nature and the prospect of making unbelievable amounts of money helped make his decision easier to take the risks.

Chapter 15
Antics in Germany

A t Düsseldorf Airport's arrivals lounge, Freddie and the others were met by the client's representative, who had driven a ten-seater Mercedes A-Class with enough space for all the guests and their suitcases. Arriving at Hotel Adler, Freddie felt better when they were each dedicated their own en-suite rooms: he really didn't want to share with anybody.

The photo shoot was scheduled for the following day and they had the evening to themselves. Kevin had decided to hit the high life of Düsseldorf and suggested they go to the famous Altstadt, which he said was a wondrous square kilometre that had more to offer than any other district in the whole of Düsseldorf. This is where the waiters were diamonds in the rough and the next beer comes without being ordered.

"That suits me, ladies," laughed Kevin. "It is the major nightlife centre of Düsseldorf with the trendiest shops in town and numerous bars and dance clubs. Let's go; what are we waiting for?" He coaxed them, beaming from cheek to cheek.

"Not tonight, Boy," said Paul. "We have an early start tomorrow. We'll go to the Altstadt after the photo shoot tomorrow evening. A nice dinner and a couple of drinks will do me tonight; what do you say, guys?"

The others agreed with Paul, and The Boy had to contend with a quieter evening than anticipated. Freddie would have gladly accompanied Kevin and Wayne, but decided it was better to go with the majority vote because this was his first lookalike job and he wanted desperately to make a good impression.

Danny (Neil Tennant of the Pet Shops Boys) was very chatty and quite pompous; Freddie liked him very much. Doug (Freddie Mercury) was also very flamboyant and friendly, but Kevin was the most flamboyant of all and he had the wickedest sense of humour, keeping everybody in fits of laughter all evening. Freddie could only imagine what havoc a night out on the town with Kevin could bring.

It was almost three o'clock the following day before the director called Freddie for his turn to be photographed as Liberace, which would grace the month of September of the Gay Icon Calendar.

When Freddie came out of make-up, he looked amazingly like Liberace. Absolutely everyone complimented him. How he loved the photo shoot, although it took quite some time before the photographer was completely happy with the images he had taken. The wardrobe department dressed Freddie in a pink satin suit, together with a white-feathered cape, which was draped across his shoulders. Four enormous diamond rings were put on his fingers and several heavy gold chains placed around his neck. A beautiful white grand piano and matching stool were hired, and Freddie was photographed seated at the piano where the most elaborate candelabra had been placed. For the gay tribute calendar, the photograph of Freddie as Liberace was moved from the month of September to December because the producers decided it was more fitting for Christmas time.

Just after eight-thirty, the producers called it a wrap, extremely satisfied with the chosen photographs. It had been a long and tiring day but the clients were very impressed with all the lookalikes and tribute acts, and promised to send them each a copy of the calendar via their agents.

"Okay, ladies," pouted The Boy. "Let's get ready for our night in Altstadt."

Kevin was the only tribute act to leave his make-up on for their evening on the town. The others went straight back to their hotel rooms to cleanse their faces from powder, eyeshadow and lipstick, which had been applied thickly to accommodate the bright cameras used on the photo shoot. Freddie stayed close to Ray and Paul; for some reason, he felt safe with his two new friends.

The Boy, closely chaperoned by Wayne, flamboyantly swanned outside the hotel to ask the commissionaire to call a taxi. As he swayed towards the swing doors of the hotel, all eyes, as usual, were fixed on him. How he thrived on all the attention, continuously getting a kick out of keeping people guessing, wondering whether or not he was the real thing.

As Ray stepped out of the taxi, followed by Paul then Freddie, a large crowd surrounded them, people trying to get a good look at the lookalikes. Some people ran up for autographs and almost everyone took photographs of them. As soon as Kevin appeared, the noise from the growing crowd was ear-splitting and people started to dangerously crowd him, chanting *Karma Chameleon*. As flamboyantly as ever, he blew kisses to everyone as he kept close to Wayne, who impatiently waved the excited crowd away.

With a twinkle in his eye, Kevin uttered, "Hey, please, one at a time, and please do not tread on my new stilettos," which set the unruly crowd cheering even louder.

Within minutes, three police cars arrived but had difficulties dispelling the unruly mass, strongly advising the lookalikes to leave the area. After all the excitement, signing of autographs and posing for photographs, the police managed to push the group of lookalikes through the cheering crowds and back to safety.

Once away from the trouble, the lookalikes headed towards a group of enticing restaurants. It had been a long and tiring day, hours spent under bright lights, patiently hanging around until their character was required by the producer and photographers. Now, they were ready to have a good meal with some famous German beer and fine wines. They entered a very elaborate restaurant called Die Fledermaus.

Looking around the restaurant as they stood in the doorway, Paul announced, "I doubt if we will all get in here, boys. It looks pretty busy to me."

As the lookalikes turned to leave, the maître d' came rushing up to them, smiling, arms outstretched. A very short man of slight build, hair which was obviously dyed, sleeked down tight to his small head, a thick black moustache covering his thin lips, and light grey eyes that did not miss a trick.

"Gentlemen, gentlemen!" he called out to them in a thick Germanic accent. "A very warm welcome from the famous Die Fledermaus. Please do not leave. We have plenty of room for all of you. Please, give me a few minutes, and your table will be ready."

The bemused lookalikes watched intently as, snapping his fingers in the direction of two tall, slim waiters already serving other tables, the maître d' gave them orders to bring an extra table and prepare it immediately for nine people.

"What a character! He would make a great Groucho Marx," laughed Freddie, as the others agreed with him.

Everybody in the restaurant was staring at the newcomers, whom being used to the attention, just chatted and laughed among themselves as they waited for their table to be laid. Obviously, The Boy played to the crowd, breaking into one of his hit songs, while Wayne, in his role as bodyguard, stood close by.

As the beers were later downed and the wine bottles emptied, the lookalikes became very noisy, laughing loudly and talking above each other. The Boy, true to character, became more and more flamboyant and started making fun of the other diners, who were not amused and were now beginning to get angry with these outrageous 'doppelgängers', or lookalikes.

"Must go splash me boots, well, stilettos in my case," quipped Kevin as he clumsily got up from the table, almost toppling over after his high consumption of wine. Swiftly, Wayne jumped up and managed to steady him. "Oh, don't fuss, I'm fine. Now, I must go pee," he hissed as he made his way to the toilets at the back of the restaurant, waving and blowing kisses to the other diners, as he gingerly minced his way through the crowded tables, dangerously wobbling on his six-inch killer heels.

Laughing at their flamboyant friend's antics, the other lookalikes started to egg him on, knowing that The Boy would play up even more. Freddie was so tipsy by this time, he could not stop the tears of laughter running down his flushed face as he watched Kevin disappear into the ladies' powder room. Unfortunately for Kevin, the maître d' had also witnessed him entering the ladies' and was completely shocked at such disgusting behaviour. After a short while, Kevin strolled out again, the little maître d' waiting at the entrance for him with a very stormy look on his face.

Stopping Kevin directly, he asked him angrily why he had used the ladies' instead of the men's room.

"Oh, please," retorted Kevin. "I have to powder my nose, darling, and I can't be doing that in the men's room now, can I?" He flamboyantly turned on his heels and swanned back towards his table, leaving the maître d' staring after him, dumbfounded and open-mouthed in disbelief.

Making his way quickly through the busy tables towards the other lookalikes, all of a sudden The Boy accidentally tripped and crashed into one of the tables where four diners were being served their entrée. All hell broke loose with plates of food thrown into the air as The Boy crashed into both waiters, landing heavily, face down, onto the table. Screams from the two females eerily filled the restaurant as all four diners jumped up from their seats, chairs crashing to the floor. Glasses shattered into tiny fragments as the wine turned the pure white tablecloth bright red. Plates of hot food crashed to the floor as a diner, sitting at a table close by, had a plate land on his arm, food splattering his light blue suit.

The restaurant was in turmoil. The maître d's face had turned ashen and he looked as if he was about to pass out. Tall, slim waiters from all sides of the restaurant frantically tried to pull The Boy off the table, although Wayne had already reached him and was trying his hardest not to laugh as he also tried to help Kevin. Stunned at the sight in front of them, the table of lookalikes, together with the rest of the diners, watched fascinated as they witnessed Kevin strewn across the table with his solid legs in the air, minus one of his killer heels and as if on cue, probably out of shock, every one of them began to laugh uncontrollably. Out came their mobile phones, excitedly taking photos and videos of this unbelievable incident.

"Only The Boy," uttered Paul, wiping his eyes with an orange, silk pocket handkerchief. The maître d' was jumping about as two burly men, both built like tanks and both bald, security written all over them, came hurrying through the tables towards the chaos happening on the restaurant floor.

By this time, Kevin was back on his feet again after retrieving his other stiletto. Wayne was busily brushing him down, but it was making the stains on Kevin's elaborate clothes worse and he angrily knocked Wayne's hand away quite roughly.

Watching with amusement, the lookalikes suddenly sobered up as the two security baldies abruptly asked Kevin to accompany them to the manager's office. Having no option but to agree, Kevin followed security to the back of the restaurant and into the manager's plush offices with Wayne in tow. At least half a dozen waiters scurried about helping to clear up the mess, hoping to bring some normality back to their startled diners. Speedily dressing another table for the stunned customers, on whose original table The Boy had landed face down on, the waiters were instructed to offer complimentary drinks as a goodwill gesture. The maître d' assured them their bill would be taken care of by Die Fledermaus.

The lookalikes, including Freddie, had finished their entrée and were waiting for their dessert which arrived almost immediately.

"I will never forget this night; it will stay with me forever," quipped Freddie, wiping his mouth effeminately with his serviette.

"Yes, me also," replied Ray. "One minute The Boy was strutting his stuff, and the next, he was spreadeagled across a table, head first in a bowl of pea green soup!"

At this remark, an uproar went up but the other diners were not amused and looked disgusted as they turned their angry eyes at the table of die Englisch Doppelgängers *(the English Lookalikes)*. Some fifteen minutes later, the maître d', security, Kevin and Wayne came slowly out of the manager's office. The two bald security officers each held one of The Boy's arms as they marched him towards the exit of the restaurant together with Wayne, who tried to look professional but was made insignificant by the two burly security men.

Having paid their bills and swallowing the last of the beers and wine, the table of lookalikes jumped to their feet and followed Kevin and Wayne out of the restaurant. All eyes were on them as Freddie took a sneaky backward glance and, quite tipsy, waved to the fuming diners then, giggling to himself, left the Die Fledermaus.

"What a night!" he mumbled, a wide smile fixed on his handsome face as he joined the rest of the lookalikes outside in the coolness of the evening air.

The following morning saw the lookalikes' plane take off on schedule from Düsseldorf Airport en route to London Gatwick. Kevin had been given a life ban from Die Fledermaus restaurant, not because he caused such havoc through crashing into the waiters and ruining other people's evening, but primarily because he had used the ladies' room instead of the men's. Apart from the life ban, Kevin had to pay all damages to the restaurant immediately, otherwise be threatened with the Polizei.

On the plane, Kevin acted as though the previous night's crisis had not bothered him at all, even though his antics had cost him a pretty penny. Seated comfortably on the plane, Wayne beside him, Kevin giggled and squealed as he reminisced about their evening.

As was normal practice, most of the lookalikes, after arriving back in the UK, had telephoned the agency to let Dawn and Belinda know how the job had gone in Germany. Obviously, the client would also be in contact with the agency, giving their opinions on the lookalikes and how successful they felt the photo shoot had been. Ray had insisted the night before that the incident at Die Fledermaus must not, under any circumstances, be mentioned to Dawn or Belinda. It was better to forget all about it, he had reasoned, and everybody agreed this was the most sensible thing to do. Yet none of them would ever forget the unbelievably hilarious evening when they witnessed Kevin made up as The Boy sprawled across a dining table, legs in the air, minus one stiletto, lying face down in a bowl of pea green soup.

Chapter 16
New Jersey Capers

Frank had been instructed by the Society to arrange for Matt to make another trip to the United States – this time to New Jersey – to attend an important meeting. Matt was to be accompanied by James Swift, one of his latest recruits.

James, a tall, attractive man in his mid-forties, with floppy, sandy hair and a quick, boyish grin, was of the same devious, greedy nature as Matt. Like his new boss, James had one aim in life: to get rich quick, no matter what he had to do to achieve it.

Recognising this quality in James' character at the interview had confirmed to Matt that this young man had the perfect credentials he was looking for. Someone he knew would be open to try almost anything for money; someone who would be completely discreet and who would stop at nothing to realise his get-rich-quick dream. Someone who thought the way he himself thought. The perfect junior partner.

At dinner the following evening, Matt told Belinda that he and James were flying to New Jersey to attend a casino convention. Matt explained to her that he was going to take a work colleague with him and, after much thought and deliberation, he had decided on James because he felt his new recruit was the brightest and, at the same time, James would benefit greatly from the experience. The truth, of course, was that James was to be interviewed by Gene and other members of the Society, as Matt had been previously.

The meeting and interview between James and the Society ran surprisingly smoothly. Gene complimented Matt on his insight in choosing James as his junior partner to work closely with Matt and the Society, overseeing the betting shops. The Society, in turn, complimented Gene on his choice of recommending both Matt and James. A highly respectable, smooth running London business partnership was of the highest importance in which to launder their dirty money without detection. The Society were well aware London was one of the most important cities in the world.

Every day, as Belinda drove to the agency, her thoughts, as always, were full of Frank, wondering how he was and, with jealousy almost choking her, if he was dating other women while they were apart. The long silences between their text messages and the many weeks between their meetings were beginning to depress her. Every time Frank left her to return home to New York, Belinda became more and more morose; finding his departures increasingly depressing for her and difficult to bear. Making up her mind to speak to Frank about her feelings when they next met, Belinda desperately needed to know from him whether they would ever be sharing a future together. Only too aware that life was short, especially now that they were both growing older, Belinda's dream was to spend the remainder of her years with Frank.

In the past, Belinda was always very excited to be flying abroad and portraying the beautiful Joan Collins, but lately, even with this exciting lifestyle, she was finding little satisfaction in it all. Nothing really made her heart sing anymore, only Frank's dancing brown eyes that seemed to look deep within her soul.

Meanwhile, Freddie was still deeply in love with Claudio, the talented Italian opera singer, but unfortunately for Freddie, Claudio's temperament left much to be desired. One day he would kiss him to death, and the next, berate him with violent outbursts. Poor Freddie; he became more and more stressed, and more and more weepy. Dawn and Belinda begged him to finish this fiery relationship with Claudio, telling him they felt the Italian was disloyal and he would dump Freddie as soon as he met someone he liked better. Of course, Freddie politely listened to their concerns for his welfare; after all, they were only looking out for him as good friends do. But Freddie knew in his heart and soul he could never give up Claudio, not for anything in the world. He simply adored the opera singer.

Frank texted Belinda to explain he had urgent business in Venice. However, the good news was, he would fly direct to London after that to attend a meeting and they could be together again very soon.

A really nice job for the Michael Jackson lookalike was confirmed with Top Drawer Agency, and Reggie Johnson excitedly flew to Finland to perform at a special tribute concert in memory of the superstar. Reggie not only possessed an amazing resemblance to the late star, but he could dance and sing exactly like his hero. Even with the scandal surrounding the life and death of Michael Jackson, there was still great demand for his lookalikes, and Reggie was kept extremely busy portraying the late King of Pop in his inimitable style. The Finish music magazine *Rumbala* had arranged for one of their reporters to interview Reggie regarding his experiences as a tribute act and lookalike for Michael Jackson.

Their choice of reporter was an English girl of French and Swedish extraction, a dark-eyed woman in her late thirties named Freya. Reggie was always very polite and courteous to everybody; he was a real gentleman. His family came to London from Guyana when he was a child. As soon as he and Freya met, the chemistry was apparent. They were strongly drawn to each other immediately.

The interview between Reggie and Freya went very smoothly indeed, and they were happy with the outcome. Reggie invited Freya to have coffee with him and she accepted his kind invitation readily.

Three days later, when it was time for Reggie to fly back to London, they were besotted lovers. Within a few weeks, Freya had made arrangements to follow Reggie to London, where they found a small flat in the affluent vicinity of St John's Wood, north London. Reggie worried that the flat was too expensive for them, but Freya, being used to the best in life, assured him they could afford to live there, obviously with help from her adoring parents, and so they settled in together, enjoying the magnetic chemistry between them.

One evening, whilst out with girlfriends, shortly after setting up home with Reggie, Freya heard from one of her friends that a very rich, mature Australian woman was willing to pay ten thousand pounds to have a good Michael

Jackson lookalike make love to her. Apparently, the woman had a real fetish for everything Michael Jackson and was serious about the amount she was willing to pay for her own pleasure.

Freya's ears pricked up! "Really? Do you happen to have her name and number?" she nonchalantly enquired.

That same evening, Freya mentioned the rich Australian woman to Reggie, gently putting out feelers to see how he felt about it. Immediately, he flatly refused the proposition Freya was suggesting to him. A shocked Reggie could not believe she would contemplate him making love to another woman for money; even for a lot of money. Poor Reggie was very upset, but, cleverly, Freya pacified him by pointing out how that much money would help make their lives more comfortable and they should really think seriously about taking up such a lucrative offer.

By the next morning, Reggie had agreed to meet with the rich Australian woman. Of course, conniving Freya was thrilled that Reggie had come around to her way of thinking, although she pretended not to like the idea at all. The deal was set; the rich Australian lady met with Ronnie and instantly adored him, and she thought he was so very much like her idol. Of course, Freya reasoned, Reggie must make the lady happy. No matter what she wanted from him, he should do it; anything and everything for her pleasure. After all, she was paying a lot of money for one session with the lookalike of Michael Jackson.

Deep down, Reggie hated the very idea of what was expected of him, and he had to down a couple of stiff whiskies, focusing solely on the money before undertaking this most distasteful lookalike job.

Chapter 17
The Sherlock Holmes Hotel

With butterflies in her stomach, her hand slightly shook as Belinda tapped on Room 17 of the Sherlock Holmes Hotel on the agreed Wednesday. There was no answer. Fear gripping her heart, Belinda tapped louder: still no response. With both hands, she gently pushed the door; panic beginning to engulf her. Immediately, the door opened and surprised, she walked in and called for Frank. No answer. Belinda was beginning to feel very worried and called out his name again. The bathroom door opened slowly and there he stood, naked apart from a pair of white briefs, a bottle of champagne and two glasses in his hand. Those dancing brown eyes penetrated her soul, making her feel a little embarrassed. His smile reached from one side of his handsome face to the other, showing off his slightly uneven, yet attractive, teeth. That smile – she would remember it, she knew, until the day she died – shone like the sun. How she loved this man with all her heart.

"Belinda, mia cara, mi sei mancata così tanto," *(Belinda, my darling, I have missed you so much)* uttered Frank, his voice hoarse with emotion.

Like a child, she ran to him and with his hands still full with the bottle and glasses, he wrapped them around her and they stayed there filling each other with their love.

Later, after a few drinks and much chattering, Belinda disappeared into the bathroom.

Within a few minutes, she emerged wearing black lacy crotchless panties and a matching black brassiere. Frank, relaxing on the king-sized bed having removed his briefs, held out his arms to her and she went to him, unable to take her gaze away from those dancing brown eyes that still seemed to mock her.

After the most amazing sex together, they climaxed both in their own private ecstasy and yet deeply entwined with each other. Elated, Belinda collapsed onto the bed as Frank lay gently on top of her, his limp manhood resting on the luscious moulds of her bottom.

Within minutes, they fell into a deep sleep. London was sheathed in semi-darkness by the time Belinda stirred, needing to use the bathroom. Frank was still sleeping soundly as slowly she slid her legs from under his tanned body, being careful not to waken him. He looked tired, she had thought when she first arrived earlier.

As she emerged, freshened from the bathroom, Frank, snoring loudly, turned over on his back and slowly opened his eyes as if his own snoring had wakened him. Climbing back onto the large bed, Belinda nestled up close to his side and he stretched out his right arm and wrapped it around her as if he were protecting her from the world. Because Frank was due to fly back to New York the following morning, Belinda had decided she would stay with him for the night, telling Matt she would be staying with Tanya, the Pam Anderson lookalike. Often having stayed with Tanya in the past when they'd had girlie nights out, there was no reason for Matt to be suspicious.

As was usual, Frank had arrived in London a couple of days earlier than he had led Belinda to believe. His business was overseeing the three betting shops and checking on how Matt and James were managing the Society's interests. Frank was keen to ensure that nothing appeared strange to the customers. Provided the customers walked out of the shops as winners, they were happy, and in turn the Society was happy. Being completely satisfied with the way things were going and how well the businesses were doing, he had made his report, ready to hand over to the Society once back in New York.

As for Belinda, although she was deliriously happy having Frank in her life as her lover, lately she was beginning to feel dissatisfied and now wanted more from their relationship. Her love was so strong for Frank, she was ready to ask Matt for a divorce so she and Frank could spend more time together and bring their love for each other out in the open for the whole world to see. How she hated being so deceitful. Now she needed Frank to commit.

Later that evening, over a very lavish dinner in The Club at The Ivy restaurant, situated in West Street, near Cambridge Circus, Frank and Belinda toasted each other. The Club at The Ivy is for private members only with a hidden entrance via an adjacent flower shop. It was opened on the three floors above the restaurant, with membership drawn primarily from creative industries and the arts and, of course, the affluent. Obviously, Belinda mused, Frank could afford to be a member. The Club at the Ivy boasted a piano lounge, a dining room and the drawing room, open for breakfast, lunch and supper, and a wood-panelled library of books, reflecting many of the members' interests in art, literature, film, theatre, architecture and design. It also contained a film screening room and entertainment space known as The Loft, a further private dining room seating up to fourteen people, and a cigar terrace. Belinda had been to The Ivy Restaurant before with Matt and friends, but she had never been in The Club at The Ivy, and was extremely excited and impressed with everything; she couldn't wait to tell Dawn and Freddie about it on Friday.

During dinner, Belinda mentioned to Frank that she was ready to face the consequences and ask Matt for a divorce, enabling her to spend more time with Frank. To her dismay, the dancing brown eyes became dull and serious as they looked intently at her. Suddenly, she felt an alarm bell go off deep inside her.

"Bad timing, my darling," said Frank, taking one of her hands in his over the silk tablecloth.

"But, Frank, I feel confident enough now to ask for a divorce," whispered Belinda, beginning to feel a little afraid.

"The time is not right, Belinda," stressed a frowning Frank. "Especially for me. I am running around across the globe right now and even if you were with me in New York, we would hardly see each other. You know what my job entails, darling. I am sorry, but we will have to be patient and see each other whenever we can for the time being. Please, darling, don't make this any harder for me than it is."

Struggling desperately to hold back her hot tears, Frank squeezed Belinda's hand tightly and mouthed, "Ti amo, amore mio," *(I love you, my love)* to her, gazing lovingly into her tear-filled eyes.

Belinda pulled herself together and replied quietly, "I love you so much."

Arriving back at the Sherlock Holmes Hotel a little after midnight, they slept in each other's arms until the dawn crept gently through the drawn curtains.

Waking a little groggily, Belinda gazed lovingly at her lover, peacefully sleeping. Gently pushing her tongue into Frank's slightly parted mouth, suddenly their lips entwined and in a lover's reply, he pushed his hot tongue into her eager, pouting mouth. His hands quickly found her breasts, heaving with arousal and passion. Expertly, his mouth and tongue licked and sucked her nipples, causing them to become hard and erect, begging for more. Softly, his hand moved down to her thighs – those thighs, how he loved them – creamy and white. As Frank stroked them urgently, a breathy gasp escaped Belinda's throat. In a flash, Frank was deep inside her, sounds of pleasure, fulfilled. How she loved the taste of him, he now owned her heart and soul.

But on that same day, Frank was on his way back home again to New York.

Chapter 18
The First Lookalike Agency

When Belinda arrived at the agency, a little downhearted, Dawn was already at her desk, busily checking the many emails and messages scattered there. As Belinda entered, Dawn looked up, then slowly took off her gold-rimmed glasses.

"Belinda, darling, please cheer up. He will be back, you know that. Come along now, darling, we have the *Daily Mail* newspaper coming in today. They want to do an article on Marina Greenslade and her long association with the agency as HM Queen Elizabeth II."

"That's great news. Forgive me, just feeling a little low, but I'll play to the cameras as always. Don't worry, I won't let you or the agency down," replied Belinda, trying to sound light-hearted as she switched on her computer.

At that moment, Freddie came hurrying through the door, carrying Queenie under his arm as usual. "Good morning, ladies! How about a nice hot cup of tea to get this party started?" he sang as he gently put Queenie down on the thick carpet.

Freddie turned his knowing eyes on Belinda. "How's the love affair going, darling?" he asked with a grin.

"Oh! Wonderful as ever, thank you," replied Belinda, keeping the lightness in her voice, but Freddie had already noticed the sadness in her eyes.

Sharp at noon, the *Daily Mail* team arrived with their heavy cameras and lighting. Freddie, desperately trying not to trip over the many wires scattered about the agency floor, fussed around the crew, making sure they had everything they needed. What an asset he was, thought Dawn, as she and Belinda were being interviewed for the article.

About half an hour later, the door opened and in rushed Marina Greenslade as Her Majesty. When Marina Greenslade first appeared on the scene, there were stand-ins and doubles, but never lookalikes as they are known today. At the time, there were no lookalike agencies, only theatrical agents who were not interested in anybody who happened to resemble a famous celebrity or member of the Royal Family. The theatrical agents only required talented people on their books, actors who had worked hard and learned their craft through the ranks. As fate would have it, there was a young, bright, go-ahead woman working for Ugly Bugs Agency, and when she first noticed how some people actually did look like famous celebrities, the term lookalike was born. This inspired the young woman to leave her lucrative job at Ugly Bugs and open her own agency. Hence, the birth of Top Drawer Lookalike and Tribute Acts Agency.

Everybody had stopped what they were doing when Marina Greenslade swooped into the office and demanded complete attention from the whole room. The journalist and photographers from the *Daily Mail* stood to attention and found it difficult to keep their eyes off Marina, who waved her gloved hand in the air, announcing in her true

Queen Elizabeth II voice, "Sorry to be late, darlings, awful traffic. But, firstly, I must use the throne room."

Freddie fussed around excitedly, bowing profusely as he walked Marina to the bathroom, offering her a cup of tea at the same time.

Marina had several photographs taken and gave the journalist an amazing insight into her life as a HM Queen lookalike. Such wonderful stories she had to tell about the many famous celebrities and aristocrats of English society she had met over the years. One of her memories was meeting several prominent TV celebrities at a Red Cross Charity Gala. Everybody was amazed at how much Marina looked like the Queen and made so much fuss of her. Of course, there were some artistes and celebrities who strongly objected to lookalikes, complaining that they had worked hard all their lives to be successful and then along came people with a slight resemblance to someone famous and they were shot to fame and fortune without an ounce of talent. Of course, they had misjudged Marina Greenslade. She was an extremely talented woman in her own right and a wonderful soprano.

After almost two hours of interviews and photographs, the extremely satisfied *Daily Mail* crew called it a wrap and left. Staying to chat for a good hour after the *Daily Mail* crew had left, Marina thoroughly enjoyed catching up with Dawn, her close friend and agent.

Eventually, after kissing everybody goodbye more than once, including little Queenie, who wagged his furry little tail, Marina Greenslade made her way towards the door ready to take her leave. Belinda offered to walk with Marina to her waiting car, reminding the number one lookalike that she would be forwarding a contract to her the following day for signature in respect of an imminent job in Dubai.

When Belinda arrived back at the agency, Dawn was pulling on a cashmere cardigan over her spotted summer dress.

"I'd almost forgotten my appointment with the bank in half an hour, Belinda," she said, quickly picking up her handbag and car keys off her desk. "I will go straight home from there. Please check the incoming emails and deal with them, and I'll see you tomorrow," she added.

Turning back as she reached the door, Dawn looked directly at her partner.

"Before I go, please remember, darling, he will be back shortly. Chin up now," and then she was gone.

Belinda threw Dawn a kiss and suddenly felt her spirits rise. Freddie was busy clearing up after the photo shoot so Belinda decided to take Queenie downstairs to cock his leg.

After locking up for the evening, Freddie and Belinda decided to go for a quick drink at a nearby pub and managed to find seats at a round table outside. Queenie sat at his master's feet and watched as the world strolled by. The weather had been very clement and everyone was out and about taking advantage of it while it lasted.

Freddie was telling Belinda how things were going for him with Claudio. Although still madly in love with the handsome Italian opera singer, Freddie feared Claudio was indeed something of a 'player'. Belinda, being close to Freddie, tried to tell him gently that she felt it would be better for him to leave Claudio and find somebody who would treat him with respect. Agreeing with what Belinda said, Freddie assured her that he would probably leave Claudio someday, but definitely not today!

Arriving home a little later than usual, Belinda found Matt was mowing the little square lawn in their back garden, taking advantage of the warm weather. Belinda called to him from the kitchen window and as he turned, he smiled at her.

"Just finishing up, darling. Put the kettle on, would you? I could kill a cuppa," he called back at her.

As she filled the kettle, Belinda thought how lately Matt had been more attentive to her and, much to her dismay, he was also becoming more amorous again. Matt was, after all, her husband, but because of the amount of water that had gone under the bridge, Belinda felt their marriage had become something of a farce. Perhaps, she reasoned, his affair with the other woman had run its course and Matt was looking for Belinda's affections once again. She knew, for the time being, she must carry out her marital duties so as not to cause Matt to be suspicious of her, but no man, including her handsome husband, would ever touch her heart and soul the way Frank had done. She was now his woman, his and only his.

During the following week, while Belinda was busy in the agency, she received a telephone call from Frank. Fighting to keep back hot tears of emotion, Belinda's heart sank as she listened with earnest to what Frank was saying to her.

Unfortunately, he would not be back in London for at least three months because an unforeseen major problem had arisen for the Society at their Costa Rica concern. Frank, together with another Associate, had been elected to fly to Central America to deal with this major problem. They were expected to stay as long as it would take to make sure that everything was back on track and, more importantly, until the Society was completely satisfied that their expertise and presence was no longer required in Costa Rica. Only then would Frank and his colleague be able to return to New York. Frank was scheduled to leave within the week.

Belinda was completely devastated as he tried to console her, stressing gently that he too was devastated at having to wait so long before they could be together again. Trying to cheer his lover, Frank suggested that when he was back again in New York, he would arrange for her to meet him, possibly in Florida, because he would be due a vacation himself by then and he had always loved Florida and was sure she would too. The weather in New York, he explained to her, could be turning a little chilly by then, so Florida would be the best option in late autumn.

Belinda tried to cheer up, but how could she possibly live without him for three long months? Her life now seemed to have no meaning without him; he had become her entire world. Frank promised to text her as often as possible while he was in Costa Rica and he would also call her from time to time, when it was safe for him to do so. She must try to look forward to their next meeting when they could spend real time together, he reasoned with her, as though he were reassuring a child.

Having no option but to throw herself back into her life, Belinda kept herself busier than ever. The agency was ticking over very nicely indeed, which always kept a huge smile on Dawn's pretty face. Almost every date in the calendar for the forthcoming weeks were booked with lookalikes and tribute acts travelling up north to Manchester, Liverpool and Newcastle, with others on their way to Swansea, Llandudno, Cardiff and other cities in the

UK. Many European jobs were confirmed and booked, with the agency sending their lookalikes and tribute acts to Germany, Spain, France, Italy and further afield.

This was an exciting time and the morale in the agency was running extremely high. The very ambitious Dawn was extremely light-hearted and happy as the jobs continuously came in, one after the other.

Although Belinda was happily caught up in the buzz, deep down she continued to feel lost and lonely without Frank.

Chapter 19
Tanya Tales

Tanya, the Pam Anderson lookalike, arrived back from a job in Athens and immediately called Belinda to arrange to meet for dinner at the end of the week. Always pleased to see Tanya, Belinda readily agreed, although she thought she heard Tanya's voice faulted slightly, as her friend replied she had a lot to tell her about.

On Saturday, Tanya was already waiting outside Le Café du Jardin in Covent Garden as Belinda arrived a little later than arranged. Rushing up to Tanya and apologising for her lateness, they embraced each other. Tanya looked lovely as always, but a little tired. Arm in arm, they entered the restaurant and were soon seated.

"What an unusual menu," remarked Belinda, as her eye took in ostrich, wild rabbit, swordfish, but also chicken and rump of lamb.

"Yes, it is, but there is something for everyone here," replied Tanya.

The friends ordered swordfish with vegetables of the day and a carafe of French wine between them.

During dinner, Tanya wanted to know how Belinda's relationship with Frank was going and grinned broadly while Belinda told her about their sensual meetings in London. With a worried frown settling on her forehead, Tanya advised Belinda that she should tell Matt as soon as possible because it could get very nasty if he were to find out about her affair from someone else.

"Remember, Belinda, the devil makes the pot, but not the lid," quoted Tanya, looking knowingly into her friend's eyes.

As the evening progressed, Tanya told Belinda she'd had some trouble with their client's representative in Athens. Silently, Belinda listened as Tanya explained in detail what had happened in her dressing room after her mix and mingle lookalike job had finished for the evening. Apparently, the representative, a burly, short, strong boned Greek, whose eyes had insolently studied Tanya's body previously, had knocked at her dressing room door and entered without invitation, carrying a bottle of champagne. Tanya continued with her story, explaining to Belinda that for the sake of the agency, she had decided to be polite and had accepted one small glass.

"You know, his eyes never left my face while he filled the glass, until I placed my hand over it, indicating that was sufficient for me," said Tanya, dropping her voice to a whisper, not wanting the other diners to hear what she was saying. Continuing, she told Belinda that his menacing eyes slowly flickered down to her breasts, and continued further down.

"This man was a proper creep," she hissed, her voice rising above her normal breathy whisper. Flushed with the wine and indignation, Belinda was angry at what had been relayed to her. As was the agency's policy, there had been long discussions with the client's representatives regarding the welfare of all lookalikes working alone in any foreign country. They had been assured that all artists would be safe and well looked after during their stay.

"He insisted I drank more champagne and took my glass from my hand to refill it, an insolent smirk spreading across his ugly face," added Tanya, slowly taking a sip of her wine. "When I refused to drink any more, he placed both glasses on the nearby table and, without any hesitation, he made a grab for me. I was shocked! His hands slipped arrogantly down the front of my low-cut dress, and before I knew what was going on, those vile thick hands shot swiftly up my skirt as he tried to finger me."

With eyes open wide in disbelief at what she was being told, Belinda reached across the dusty pink tablecloth and touched Tanya's arm with concern for her friend.

"I was sickened," whispered Tanya, the emotion sounding in her voice. "I lashed out and slapped him so hard across his swarthy face that his bull head sprung backwards. Instantly, the hands were withdrawn and I quickly pushed him towards the door, shouting and threatening to call the police."

Belinda told Tanya that she would discuss this incident with Dawn, who would speak directly to the client first thing on Monday morning.

"The pig then tried to blame me, saying that I had encouraged him and had been trying all evening to entice him," continued a tearful Tanya as Belinda listened, a worried expression crossing her forehead. "You know, he said he was sure I wanted him sexually because I had been friendly to him and he had been more than happy to oblige," added Tanya. "But luckily, he started to apologise profusely, begging me not to call the police in because he would lose his job, and he had a wife and three young children at home to feed."

"What a nerve!" murmured Belinda. "I'm so sorry, Tanya, but why didn't you call the agency right away?"

Shrugging her shoulders, Tanya replied, "There was no point in calling; it was very late in the evening, and I knew I wouldn't have any more trouble from this idiot after I had threatened him with the police. Besides, that was not the first incident of this nature I have had to deal with in my life, and it probably will not be the last," swiftly added Tanya.

Tanya and Belinda had become very good friends and confidantes. Now in Covent Garden, their evening was over far too early as Belinda and Tanya, chatting about how their individual lives were going, confided in each other about their lovers. After ordering coffee, they eventually left the restaurant, promising to meet up and eat there again very soon.

It was past midnight when Belinda quietly turned her key in the front door lock. Almost immediately, she realised that Matt was in the lounge with his favourite music playing low.

"How was your evening, darling?" he asked, rising from the elaborate, wine-coloured couch to greet his wife. "Oh, by the way, Belinda, I have told James he can stay over this evening. We had a few drinks and he can't drive home now," added Matt quickly.

"James?" asked Belinda.

"Yes, he fell asleep in the armchair, we have no option, but to let him stay," answered Matt, closely watching her reaction.

"Fine, of course. If he has been drinking, obviously he can't drive home," agreed Belinda, entering the lounge and gazing down on a handsome, fair-haired young man, lightly snoring.

"Matt, why don't you wake your friend and show him into the spare room? He can't possibly sleep there; he still has his shoes on," remarked Belinda, turning to look directly at her husband.

"No, no, I'll take his shoes off, but he is too far gone to wake now, darling," suggested Matt, pulling James' suede loafers gently off his feet and covering his friend with a warm overthrow. "I'll introduce you to him in the morning, darling," said Matt, turning the lamps down low after switching off the music centre.

"I am completely bushed, so tired, I'm off to bed, pronto," he whispered quietly so as not to waken James.

Walking up to Belinda, he pecked her lightly on her lips then turned and left the cosy lounge, carrying his own shoes with him.

James woke with a dull ache in his back, obviously through sleeping in the armchair. Quickly, his mind recollected the night before as he realised he must have fallen asleep after he and Matt had drunk a couple of bottles of wine between them when they had arrived back from the pub. Stiffly, he got up and moved slowly, becoming aware of a dull pain in his head also. Gingerly, he headed for the bathroom.

As James came back into the lounge, Matt appeared with a pained expression on his face.

"Never again, mate," he murmured as he noticed James looked even worse than he did. "You look as bad as I feel," he laughed as James tried to slip his feet into his loafers.

"Definitely never again," replied James, his voice slightly shaky. "Until the next time, of course!" he quipped. "We had a great evening though, and thanks for letting me stay the night."

"No problem. Come on, let's find something for breakfast," urged Matt, heading towards the kitchen, followed closely by a hungry James. They decided boiled eggs with buttered toast would be best for their delicate stomachs this morning.

As they were eating their breakfast, prepared expertly by Matt, Belinda entered the kitchen, having left some of her make-up on from the night before due to her tiredness.

Glancing up, Matt smiled. "Belinda, my sweet, meet James, my number one boy," he announced, taking a mouthful of hot black coffee.

James got up from his chair and shook Belinda's hand gently. "Good to meet you, Mrs Flynn. I have heard so much about you," he said, smiling down at her.

"All good, I hope?" quipped Belinda, smiling back at him.

"But of course," came James' quick answer. "All very good indeed, but Matt didn't tell me how beautiful you are."

"Flattery will get you everywhere," joked Belinda as she poured herself some coffee. "Oh, please call me Belinda," she added, sitting down at the breakfast bar beside them.

Within the hour, James took his leave, telling Belinda he hoped they would meet again soon.

"Well, what do you think of James?" asked Matt when he returned to the kitchen.

"Yes, a very presentable young man, and a handsome one too," smiled Belinda. "Although I sense some sort of an undercurrent, as if there is much more to him than meets the eye," she added, looking thoughtful.

"Really?" queried Matt, pouring himself another cup of black coffee. "Oh, James is okay, I trust him explicitly," he added. "You know what a good judge of character I am. After all, I picked you, darling," he continued, smiling to himself.

Belinda let out a throaty laugh. "Now who swallowed the Blarney Stone this morning?" she asked but her face clouded over as she added, "Seriously, Matt. Be careful where James is concerned; just a feeling I get," she warned, taking the shell off the top of her soft boiled egg.

Slowly, the days passed for Belinda. Several times she heard from Frank, expressing his love and saying how much he missed her. Unfortunately, he was still unsure exactly when he would be returning to the United States, although the problem in Costa Rica had been solved. Assuring her it would not be too long now before the Society would be happy for him to leave, Frank told her he was finding it uncomfortably hot and unpleasant in the South American country and how he could not wait to return to New York.

Chapter 20
Diva Delights

Gene's replacement was due to arrive in London any day now. The only explanation Gene had given Matt was that the Society were sending him to another country to sort out major problems that had arisen there, but he had not disclosed which country he would be going to.

Apparently, Gene's replacement to oversee the betting shops would be Sergie Belladoni. Matt had met this particular Associate of the Society when he had first attended the meeting in New York with Gene. Matt was happy with the replacement as he liked Sergie very much, this very robust and jovial American-Sicilian, who seemed to equally enjoy eating good Italian food and laughing at his own jokes. James would also get along well with Sergie, Matt was very confident about that.

As Sergie, tall, thickset and suave, walked purposely through Heathrow Airport, he had fake money cleverly hidden in a black leather briefcase held tightly under his left arm, as he dragged his pulley trolley behind him. A feeling of sheer relief swept across him as his eyes darted everywhere, until they landed on a man holding up a board with his name boldly written on it. Matt had booked a chauffeur company to collect Sergie because he and James were extremely busy.

As James was helping out at the Victoria betting shop, Matt had arranged for him to leave early enough to be at the Soho betting shop so they could take Sergie for a couple of drinks at Gerry's Club before dinner at San Carlo Cicchetti, a new experience in Italian restaurants set in the midst of Piccadilly. When Sergie arrived, Matt escorted him into the back room for them to go through the latest developments regarding the Society's interests, and later Sergie was favourably impressed as he walked with Matt and James through the doors of San Carlo Cicchetti. Set in sophisticated yet relaxing interiors, using light colours alongside huge expanses of light grey Italian marble, San Carlo Cicchetti reinterpreted the delightful Venetian culinary custom of Cicchetti – delicious, small plate dishes to share or eat alone – enjoyed with a beer or glass of wine.

"The attention to detail is astonishing," remarked Sergie, as he slowly ate his way through several different dishes. "I love it here; delicious food in immaculate surroundings; great choice, guys!" added Sergie, drinking down his third glass of Valpolicella. Enthusiastically, Matt and James agreed with him, and were happy that Sergie approved.

The three men had a thoroughly enjoyable evening, but eventually fatigue overtook Sergie, and after a little while he was ready to return to his hotel and sleep.

While they were waiting for the bill, Sergie, a little tipsy, asked with a big grin spreading across his round face, "Have you ever taken Frank here?"

Matt and James looked at each other and both answered the question with a question simultaneously.

"Frank?"

For a fleeting moment, James caught a look in Sergie's eyes, which he could not quite make out.

"Sorry, guys," said Sergie quickly, "I mean, Gene. You know, some of us guys call him Frank because he eats and sleeps Sinatra, so much so that we have nicknamed him Frank," he explained, giggling to himself. "Yeah, Gene is truly obsessed with Frank," muttered Sergie, more or less to himself as he checked his Cartier wristwatch for the time. "Well, guys," he said, getting his heavy bulk up out of his chair, "thanks for a great evening, and even greater Italian food."

Jumping into a waiting taxi, Sergie congratulated himself on his clever cover-up explanation he had given Matt and James.

The next morning, when Belinda arrived a little late at the agency, Freddie had made Dawn and himself toast and coffee, and as Belinda came through the door, he asked her if she would like some. Refusing the toast but accepting a much-needed cup of hot coffee, she hung her wool jacket on the coat stand and turned her computer on.

"Good morning, Belinda, darling. I have something here that could very well cheer you up. A nice job has come in for yourself and the Liz Taylor lookalike," announced Dawn, looking up and smiling at Belinda.

"Oh! Excellent, Dawn, anything to keep my mind busy," replied Belinda, walking across to Dawn's desk and reading the email. "Nice, a photo shoot for Joan and Liz to advertise the new range of sunglasses from Daring Diva in Brighton. Be lovely if we get to keep a pair of them!"

remarked Belinda, accepting the hot coffee handed to her by Freddie.

"I would like another lookalike job," he said, looking in the gold ornate mirror and playing with his immaculate hair.

"One will come up soon for you, I am certain," encouraged Belinda. Freddie winked and crossed his fingers in the mirror at her.

The day, although bathed in bright sunshine, dragged by slowly for Belinda, just like all other days now that Frank was so far away; every one of them seemed to drag. Dawn had left early to attend a doctor's appointment, Freddie had taken Queenie out for walkies, and Belinda was reading through the incoming emails when the doorbell rang. Half-expecting to see Freddie and Queenie back from their walk, she got a surprise. It was Adam, their Johnny Depp lookalike.

"Adam, how lovely to see you! To what do we owe this pleasure?" enthused Belinda, kissing Adam lightly on both cheeks as he walked in.

"Dawn recently called me about a potential job in Dubai early next month, so as I was in the locality I thought I would pop in to see you all and find out how the job is progressing," replied Adam, sitting down on the dark red chaise longue and grinning broadly at Belinda.

"Oh, yes, it looks like it will go ahead. As soon as we hear, we will let you know immediately," offered Belinda, flicking through the provisional jobs in the diary.

"That's great. I have never been to Dubai and would love to go," replied Adam, watching Belinda closely. "By the way, how are you these days? Still seeing the Yank?" he added, lying back and slyly smiling.

"Adam, please, it is supposed to be a secret. Do you want to get me hung or something? Please be more discreet," retorted Belinda, sitting down at her desk and angrily staring at him.

"Of course not, sorry, darling," came Adam's answer. "Just being nosey; you know you can trust me completely."

Belinda spoke quietly under her breath to Adam. "Yes, I am still seeing the Yank, as you call him, but his company have sent him away for a few months and I will not see him again for quite a while, so I am not happy at all. Usually he flies to London every few weeks and we manage to meet up."

Adam sat up quickly. "It must be love or something, Belinda. I have never seen you so smitten before. I hope you do not get hurt, my darling," he said, looking at her worriedly.

"Thank you for your concern, Adam, but I have a good feeling about this Yank," Belinda replied, smiling as she handed him a contract for his signature. "You will be pleased to know this job is London based. The venue is the Oscar Wilde suite at the Hotel Café Royal on Regent Street," explained Belinda.

"Excellent stuff," smiled Adam. "Not too far for me to travel, but please let me know as soon as you hear anything about Dubai. Now that job I definitely must have."

As Adam handed her back the signed contract, his eye caught the diamond brooch in the shape of a bell, pinned on Belinda's dark blue jacket: a gift from Frank.

"Very nice! Are they real diamonds, darling?" he asked, studying the way the brooch sparkled and noticing how big the middle diamond was.

"Of course they are, silly!" laughed Belinda. "My Yank, don't you know, has superb taste."

"Very nice indeed. Must have cost him a pretty penny," said Adam, thoughtfully.

After Adam had left the agency, his mind was working overtime. He recalled when, still in the Venetian hospital, how the elder polizia had asked him if he knew who Frank was. Adam had told him that as far as he knew, Frank was a friend of Belinda's who she had only met since arriving in the amazing Italian city. Although Adam was not feeling well at the time, he remembered that the polizia, called Andrea, kept muttering that he was positive he knew Frank's face but could not remember from where. Adam learned that the polizia decided it must have been years ago but that he would check back in the records to see if anything came to light. Andrea was insistent that there was something very familiar about this gentleman that kept nagging at the back of his mind. Adam was also asked if he knew Frank's surname, of which he did not. He remembered that Andrea had handed him a card and told him if he were to find anything out about the American, no matter how minuscule, he would be very grateful to hear about it immediately. Adam had kept Andrea's card.

At Matt's Soho betting shop, Sergie had spent the entire morning and part of the afternoon on the computer, deep in accounts and paperwork, before the accounts and documents of the other two betting shops in Victoria and Mayfair arrived. Matt had popped out to the other stores to discreetly put fake money into their systems before he spent the afternoon together with Sergie, going through every invoice and account with a fine-tooth comb.

"Good work, Matt. Everything's in order, just like the Society expects," beamed Sergie, finishing his sixth cup of coffee of the day.

Approximately two weeks after Sergie flew back to New York, Belinda was full of joy once again, so much so that she could not keep the beaming smile off her face. Frank had telephoned her with the good news that he had flown back to the United States the previous day from Costa Rica. The Society were extremely pleased with Frank's expertise of dealing with the troublesome Costa Rica businesses, which were now all running smoothly once again. Frank had told her he hoped to be back in London, for his company, within a few weeks, but he wanted to see her so badly he was hoping she could fly to Spring Lake, New Jersey for a few days to be with him, possibly the following week.

Belinda's very existence took on a completely different dimension now. How she adored him, but sadly she had to let him know that she was booked for a lookalike job advertising Swedish sunglasses, to be shown on television and in cinemas throughout the UK and Europe. This was quite a prestigious job and she had already signed the contract. A very disappointed Frank assured her he understood and agreed they would meet in a few weeks' time when he was again in London on business.

The job for Daring Diva sunglasses was scheduled to take place in the popular and buzzing seaside town of Brighton. It would be a nice day by the sea for Belinda as Joan Collins and Vicky Sutton as Elizabeth Taylor, posing for photographs, wearing the latest and most amazing sunglasses from the very upmarket Swedish company, Freja. If the changeable English weather permitted, the photo shoot would take place directly outside the entrance of the Grand Hotel, the first exclusive hotel in Brighton, built in 1864, ostensibly for the upper classes who visited the fashionable resort. Its imposing fascia of grandiose Italian renaissance and classic Victorian architecture proved perfect for the photo shoot.

Luckily, the day turned out to be a sunny day and Belinda dressed accordingly in a long flowing chiffon dress of the most beautiful pastel colours. Vicky Sutton travelled down from Manchester by train. Meeting at Brighton Station, the two ladies were greeting each other and chatting happily together when the Swedish client's chauffeur-driven car pulled up alongside them and a female alighted and walked briskly towards Belinda and Vicky, recognising them immediately as the booked lookalikes. Within minutes, they were standing outside the famous Grand Hotel, which looked even more radiant in the early morning sunshine.

Many photographs were taken of the lookalikes wearing the glamorous new range of sunglasses, but they were relieved when the team stopped for a well-deserved lunch break. Sadly, Belinda noticed that during lunch, Vicky had a couple of glasses of wine with her salad. Every lookalike and tribute act on the agency's books was well aware of the 'no alcohol' restriction while working and Belinda was surprised that Vicky had completely disregarded this fact. Lately, there had been several stories from other lookalikes about Vicky's drinking, and sadly now Belinda had witnessed this for herself.

Deciding to have a quiet but firm word with Vicky about this when their job had completed, Belinda realised that over the past few years she had grown fond of her and they had become good friends while working together on many lookalike jobs. Although Vicky, now in her mid-sixties, had a strong resemblance to the beautiful late Elizabeth Taylor, she was beginning to show signs of her overindulgence with alcohol, and this was beginning to ruin her looks.

Belinda recalled a mix and mingle job in the affluent city of Oxford. Several lookalikes were booked, herself and Vicky included. When Vicky arrived from Manchester, again by train, it was quite obvious that she had already had 'one too many' and was beginning to slur her words. Jack Novak (the Clint Eastwood lookalike) was not happy at all about Vicky being on this particular job. Many guests at the party were starting to notice that Vicky was not only slurring her words, but also spraying everybody with her saliva. Jack, a perfectionist and hard taskmaster, was outraged when Vicky slid down one of the walls in the crowded cream and gold ballroom and started to laugh uncontrollably. Belinda, together with the Sophia Loren lookalike, tried desperately to get Vicky back on her feet again, but she kept sliding back down the wall. Some of the guests actually thought Vicky was play-acting at being an inebriated Elizabeth Taylor and they began to laugh at her, not realising that Vicky was in fact very drunk indeed. Belinda remembered Jack striding up beside her, looking very anxious.

"Belinda, we have to get her out of here. She will give the agency a bad name and we will all have to suffer," he said, his voice dropping to a whisper.

With a worried look on her face and nodding in full agreement, Belinda replied, "Yes, of course. I will tell her the job ended earlier than expected. We can then get her out of here and up to her room, well away from the guests and the festivities."

Within minutes, Belinda and Jack escorted Vicky to her room where Belinda helped to take off her beautiful violet evening dress and climb safely into bed. Vicky, oblivious to everything, kept kissing Belinda and saying how much she loved her before almost immediately falling fast asleep. Returning downstairs to the ballroom, Jack and Belinda continued for the remainder of the evening, alongside the other lookalikes, with the job they were booked for – to mix and mingle with the party guests, have photographs taken, and dance the night away with admirers.

When the Brighton film crew called it a wrap, Belinda and Vicky were delighted because they were allowed to keep a pair of sunglasses of their choice. After selecting their favourites, the chauffeur-driven car arrived to take them back to the train station. While they were walking down the platform, a number of Japanese tourists started calling out to them.

"Hello, Elizabeth Taylor, Joan Collins, we love you!"

Belinda and Vicky looked at each other and started to laugh when, suddenly, one of the tourists from the group began running towards them. Then another, and another, until the whole party were running down the platform after the startled lookalikes, waving notepaper in the air, pens at the ready, wanting Elizabeth and Joan's autographs. The two friends ran now, faster and faster, the adrenalin gushing through their veins, but the Japanese tourists soon caught up and surrounded them. Belinda and Vicky obligingly signed on behalf of Joan Collins and Elizabeth Taylor in their roles as professional lookalikes as the Japanese tourists excitedly chatted and giggled, pointing their mobile phones and cameras at Belinda and Vicky.

Chapter 21
Ulterior Motives

F rank had booked a spacious, elaborate double room, again at the Phoenix Hotel in the complex of London Heathrow Airport, and asked Belinda to meet him there on the day of his arrival. In case Frank's meeting ran past the scheduled time, he had left the spare key to his room at the hotel reception and asked Belinda to go straight to the room where he would meet her as soon as possible.

Shaking with excitement, butterflies fluttering around inside her, Belinda let herself quietly into Frank's room. Belinda noticed a dark oak table bearing a wonderful bowl of several fruits and a bottle of champagne on ice. Walking across to the table, she saw there was a gold-edged pink card laying on the bowl of fruit.

'Belinda, darling,' it read. 'Please relax until I get back. Why not take a shower and chill?'

Smiling to herself, Belinda took a handful of black grapes from the fruit bowl and decided to take that recommended shower. Humming to herself, eyes closed, she stood under the deliciously warm waterfall, allowing it to drench her hair as she threw her head back and her hair hung down past her shoulders. Suddenly, her eyes opened as she heard his voice uttering, thick and emotional.

"Il mio amore." *(My love.)*

Frank had quietly let himself into the suite with the other key and had deftly discarded his clothes as soon as he arrived. At the sound of his voice, Belinda's knees went weak as her eyes, blurred by water, took in the shape of Frank as he stood in the doorway of the steamy shower room.

Smiling at her, she came face to face with those dancing brown eyes. With emotion catching his breath as his eyes roamed over her naked body, Frank slowly, and without taking his eyes off of hers, began to soap her and caress her, starting with her neck and working his manly hands down to her breasts, the pink nipples becoming hard, begging for his caress. Belinda felt his erection pressing against her bottom as he gently turned her around and cupped her heaving breasts, soft and soapy, in his hands. Slowly, she threw her head backwards in ecstasy on Frank's chest and he brought his head down and softly kissed her throat as Belinda groaned with deep passion, turning around to face him. Slowly, Frank's hands moved down her back towards her bottom and continued to caress her. She felt his hands between her legs, which she instinctively opened.

Gently yet strongly, he caressed her while their mouths locked together, tongues slipping in and out, and as she savoured every second with him, she climaxed, her juices flowing from her, answering his caresses. His mouth found her hardened nipples and licked, sucked and bit them gently, fulfilling her sensual need. Suddenly, she felt herself being lifted off her feet as Frank swooped her up, spreading her legs wide and positioned them around his waist, her back leaning heavily on the wet shower wall, hair damp and curling untidily around her head. Soapy arms were wrapped around his thick neck as her fingers played with his greying hair. His manhood stood erect and proud and he moaned deeply in his throat as he slowly, yet urgently, entered her, wanting to savour every movement and moment.

A breathy sound escaped from Belinda as Frank thrust into her as she writhed in ecstasy.

Frank had told Belinda he was scheduled to leave London early the following morning, when in fact he was to visit the betting shops on that day then fly back the next day. For the time she was to spend with Frank, Belinda had arranged her usual alibi with Tanya, telling Matt she would stay with Tanya because they were having dinner with a couple of other friends and she would go straight to the agency in the morning. Matt had indeed agreed this was a safer option for her, instead of making her way home late at night.

Having no intentions of leaving the hotel room at all, Frank and Belinda found they had so much to talk about and catch up on. Frank had ordered a wonderful dinner for them, which was brought up to his room on silver platters by two young bellboys whom Frank rewarded with a very generous tip. Belinda was very impressed with everything, and she and Frank enjoyed the fine cuisine and wine the hotel had to offer. The remainder of the evening was spent cosily together in the king-sized bed, talking, laughing, eating, drinking and making sensual, sexy love. Belinda knew only too well that she was deeply in love with Frank. But this long-distance affair was beginning to take its toll on her, hating it so much when he had to fly back home and leave her yet again.

It was during the following afternoon that Matt telephoned Belinda, letting her know that he would be home late that evening, explaining that a meeting with James Swift had been arranged and this would take place after work over dinner at one of the many Soho restaurants.

"Don't wait up, Belinda. I will probably be quite late," concluded Matt.

Of course, Gene, as well as James, was joining Matt for the meeting and dinner. Gene, as always, was completely satisfied with the way the businesses were being run in all of the betting shops. Sergie had warned Frank that he had mistakenly used Frank's real name instead of his pseudonym of Gene when chatting to Matt and James on his last visit but he had covered himself with Frank's obsession of Sinatra. Frank agreed with Sergie that a slip-up like that was easily done, but congratulated Sergie on his astute sharp thinking.

On the following day, Saturday, Frank flew back home to New York, sweet memories of Belinda ever present in his mind.

"We should send all Marilyn Monroe lookalikes to the casting, Belinda, but I would rather not waste the client's time. We are all aware there are only two or three who will have a chance of getting this job," said Dawn as she tore the fax off the machine and handed it to her partner to read.

"Yes, I agree completely, Dawn, but apart from Jane and the new girlie, Kay, who else did you have in mind?" Belinda asked, glancing through the contract that had arrived from the television company.

"Oh, it has to be Melita," replied Dawn. "She will go down extremely well, I am sure."

After checking through the many other Marilyn Monroe lookalikes on the agency's books, Belinda had to agree with Dawn and, without wasting further time, she got to work, telephoning their three top Marilyn Monroe impersonators for their availability. The client had also requested to see other lookalike characters, but Belinda was a little disappointed that the name of her character was not included this time. This was indeed a very prestigious job because it was for a television commercial advertising the new dramas and films to be aired throughout the autumn. Jane Baxter had been the reigning Marilyn Monroe lookalike with Top Drawer Agency for some years now. A professional woman in her mid-forties, extremely elegant and quite a few inches taller than the real Marilyn, Jane's skin was white and creamy, and her hair was fashioned in exactly the same Marilyn style. With her large eyes and small features, she was certainly very impressive and had been extremely successful in her chosen role as a lookalike. The agency had several Monroe lookalikes on their books, mainly because this was one of the most popular characters.

The agency was experiencing one of its busy periods and Belinda had the most revered television client to manage. As well as the three top Monroe lookalikes attending the casting, the clients were interested in seeing the Humphrey Bogart, Sir Winston Churchill, James Dean, Elvis Presley and Audrey Hepburn lookalikes.

Chapter 22
Upsets All Round

L ady Denise Ava telephoned the agency and Dawn answered her call. For most of the night, she had been worrying whether or not she should tell Dawn and Belinda about the trouble from the previous evening at the Grosvenor House Hotel in Park Lane. Apparently, Kim (the top Tina Turner lookalike) had upset the clients and guests while performing *River Deep, Mountain High* on stage during the cabaret, wearing an extremely short dress with nothing on under her dress at all. The female guests were shocked and disgusted because there were many men present, who were obviously enjoying this wild woman shimmering in front of them. Angry women of all ages complained to the organisers of the evening. They were determined that the Tina Turner tribute act must be reprimanded; her antics had completely shocked and embarrassed them. Lady Ava felt it was time for Dawn and Belinda to speak to the lookalike because ever since her father had sadly passed away, Lady Ava had found her friend Kim had been getting out of hand and quite outrageous. Many times she had tried to speak to and help her friend, but Kim seemed to be on a downward spiral.

Dawn listened intently as her informer explained exactly what had occurred during the job. Dawn was as shocked as the ladies who had witnessed Kim's performance, and thanking the Lady, she told her she would let Belinda know what had happened. Hopefully, between them they could get to the bottom of the problem and try to help Kim.

"I told him, in no uncertain terms, to go to hell," said Freddie that morning as he was handing Belinda her coffee.

Belinda's eyes opened widely as she accepted the cup and saucer. "I hope you mean it this time, Freddie. You know Claudio will never be faithful to you. He will break your heart good and proper if you stay much longer in this unsavoury relationship," she said, looking at him closely.

"Oh, don't you worry, darling," replied Freddie. "I am sick and tired of his philandering and continuous lies. Of course, I am still madly in love with him. But it doesn't hurt as much anymore, probably because I have met someone else recently, whom I quite fancy."

Belinda was surprised at Freddie's words.

"That was quick, wasn't it? I hope you know what you are doing," she added, a worried look fleetingly showing in her eyes.

"Oh please, I will be very careful, darling. Don't you worry about little old me," said Freddie, placing a saucer of milk on the floor for Queenie.

"What is he called, this new fancy man of yours?" Belinda asked.

Freddie's handsome face broke into a very wide grin as he clasped his long slim hands together, dreamily looking into space, and replied, "Dodgy Rodger."

Almost choking on her coffee as she fell into hysterical laughter, Belinda exclaimed, "Dodgy Rodger! Oh, please don't tell me Dodgy Rodger is your new lodger?" she asked, which made the two friends laugh so much, tears ran down their faces.

"How did you guess, sweetie?"asked Freddie sarcastically, beginning to hiccup uncontrollably. Poor Queenie cocked his little furry head to one side as he watched his beloved master falling all over the carpeted floor laughing hysterically.

"Seriously, Freddie, you really fancy him?" asked Belinda, wiping her streaming eyes with a handkerchief.

"Yes, I think I do, darling. He is sexy in a dodgy kind of way," came Freddie's quick reply.

"Honestly, Freddie, you have a terrible taste in men, you really do," laughed Belinda.

Freddie, sobering up now and getting up off the floor slowly, looked deep into Belinda's blue-green eyes and replied, "Touché."

Matt appeared to be spending longer hours at the betting shops these days, which made Belinda think this affair was back on, or maybe he had met somebody new. Feeling no jealousy anymore about her husband's sordid flings, Belinda secretly hoped this was indeed the case because she was well aware Matt would not normally seek sexual favours from her if there was another woman in his life. Ever since she had met Frank, Belinda was no longer attracted to her husband, but she was completely wrong about him this time. There was no other woman or affair in his life at the moment. Matt was far too busy making sure the Society's money was completely safe in all three betting shops. The extra money coming into his private account was well worth the negative, and sometimes worrying, thoughts he had of his becoming an outside Associate of the Society.

Both Matt and James were making more money now than either would have believed possible. Matt had noticed how complacent James appeared to be about his own involvement and wished he himself could be more like his younger colleague.

Some days later, just before closing time, Gene telephoned Matt at the Soho betting shop. There was an important business seminar in two weeks in Venice for the new European Outside Associates who were now tied closely in with the Society. When Belinda learned of her husband's forthcoming trip to Venice, her heart lurched with the memories of her time spent there with Frank. Matt had to rearrange the truth, telling his wife he and James were to attend a bookmakers' seminar. With the way things were changing so quickly these days regarding the UK and European markets, Matt told Belinda this particular seminar would be of great benefit to his businesses in the future.

On a chilly autumn morning, Matt kissed Belinda goodbye before placing his case into the boot of his dark blue BMW. Gene had arranged for a chauffeur-driven car to meet the two Londoners at the Marco Polo Airport, ready to drive them to their hotel, the Locanda Ca' Amadi, a five-minute walk from the Rialto Bridge.

When Matt saw that the rooms were furnished in typical Venetian style, he was indeed impressed. Set in a historic thirteenth century palace, the Ca' Amadi featured beams and paintings dating back to the 1400s with its main saloon overlooking a Venetian canal. The House of Marco Polo was built between the thirteenth and fourteenth century, and the Ca' Amadi was situated in the area where the family of the famous merchant and explorer owned several buildings. In the fifteenth century, the palace was the residence of the Count Francesco Amadi, from whom Ca' Amadi derives its name. This amazing hotel was very close to Saint Mark's Square. From here, they could also catch a Vaporetto water bus. James was also completely in awe of everything his eyes were witnessing.

While Matt and James were unpacking their cases, Matt's telephone rang out startlingly, rudely interrupting his thoughts.

"Ciao, Matt, I hope everything is to your liking, my friend," came the deep tones of Gene's voice.

"Ciao, Gene," responded Matt into the mouthpiece. "Yes, thank you, everything is wonderful, just wonderful. The hotel is magnificent," he added, smiling into the telephone.

"The seminar is to be held here at Ca' Amadi so we do not have to travel," added Gene, letting out a deep laugh at his own joke. "As I mentioned when I called you last week, tomorrow there is to be a dinner-dance gala evening here. I think you and James will approve: magnificent rooms; plenty of fine Italian foods; a free open bar; and, my friend, luscious women to keep you sweet. I trust you have both brought a tuxedo with you?" he added as an afterthought.

"Yes, of course; James and I will be suited and booted, as we say in London," replied Matt, light-heartedly. "Looking forward to it."

"Excellent," replied Gene. "I will pick you guys up at reception, promptly at four o'clock sharp."

"Okay, thanks, Gene, we will be ready and waiting," came Matt's answer.

The seminar was full of many European members, who, like Matt and James, were now in cohorts with the Society in one way or another. There were several speakers and both Matt and James were intrigued by the many topics, which enlightened them immensely in cost-effective ways of how to run certain aspects of businesses more successfully.

Everyone present was given a dark red embossed folder containing copies of every topic covered by the many speakers and lecturers during the afternoon. Canapés and cocktails were served as the seminar finished. Gene introduced Matt and James to several business people from practically every major European city; most spoke fluent English, much to Matt and James' relief.

The next day, the dinner-dance was held in the Leonardo da Vinci Rooms at the hotel, which were magnificent. The ceiling frescos were created by students under Tiepolo's tutelage, and everybody attending the gala remarked that it was a real pleasure to be in these breathtaking surroundings. Massive gold ornate mirrors covered practically every inch of the amazing silk covered walls. Images of Botticelli angels adorned every corner of the rooms.

When Matt and James, together with other members, arrived at these wonderful rooms, their eyes took in the classical beauty before them. Round tables, exquisitely laden with pure silk tablecloths, lead crystal wine glasses and gold cutlery, covered three-quarters of the floor area, leaving a small area which appeared to be for dancing. On a small raised stage sat seven handsome musicians, playing a compilation of Beatles songs. *Can't Buy Me Love* rang out above the noise of the many guests arriving, everyone chatting excitedly as their eyes openly admired the venue. Attractive leggy women, all heavily made-up, dark eyes flashing, red coloured lips smiling, strolled around the rooms carrying silver platters, offering flutes of champagne. Matt and James sat at the same table as three very distinguished German gentlemen, each with an impressive command of the English language. Sergie made up the sixth place. Gene sat on a table close by and came to enquire how they were enjoying themselves.

"I'll be back to London in a couple of weeks, guys," he told them, shaking their hands. "Sorry not to have had more time to spend with you, but as you can see, I am stretched."

"No problem, Gene," replied Matt. "James and I are having a wonderful time."

At these words, James grinned broadly and gave him the thumbs-up sign.

Smiling, Gene walked across to Sergie and spoke quietly to him in Italian. Whatever Gene had said, Sergie nodded his head solemnly in agreement, keeping his eyes downcast.

The evening proved to be magnificent, as all the Society's events were. The choice of menu could not be faltered and the finest Italian wines flowed continuously. Halfway through dinner, several glamorous ladies entered the rooms and mingled through the tables, asking the gentlemen if everything was to their satisfaction. These ladies were hand-picked and booked to be 'nice' to the gentlemen, to dance with them, drink with them and do whatever it was the gentlemen required. James' eyes lit up as he silently watched one lady in particular circling the rooms; she was wearing a flowing green dress. Her skin was fairer than the others and not so tanned, more ivory; he liked that. She stood out. Her shoulder-length, dark auburn hair caught the light as she weaved in between the tables with the other ladies. James noticed her lips; they were a beautiful shape and not too full; perfect, he thought.

Slowly, he whispered to Matt quietly that he had seen the woman of his dreams. Placing his knife and fork down on the porcelain plate, Matt looked up and followed James' eyes. As he studied the lady in question, he smiled and whispered back, "Oh yes, classy lady. Your taste has improved, my good fellow," and they laughed together.

Sometime later, Matt noticed the classy lady whom James fancied was deep in conversation with Gene as they stood at the entrance of the rooms. When finding the right opportunity, Matt made James aware of the fact that the 'classy lady' seemed to be a good friend of Gene's and warned James to be careful if he had any intentions of trying to meet her. James readily agreed with Matt but later James asked her to dance with him and, of course, being a handsome young man, full of boyish charm, the classy lady accepted his invitation immediately. How he loved the way her body swayed in tune with Adele's *Someone Like You* as she melted in his arms. James learned that the lady was of Italian and Russian ancestry and was born in northern Italy, which explained her ivory skin tone, auburn hair and green eyes. She told him her name was Isabelle, she was divorced and had no children. Chatting and laughing, they were thoroughly enjoying each other's company when James asked Isabelle if she knew Gene well.

"Signor Capalti is a colleague of mine. We have worked together for the Society many times," she explained.

Isabelle liked James very much indeed, but shortly afterwards, and much to his disappointment, she gently made her excuses and joined the other ladies on the far side of the room. When James arrived back at his table, he noticed Matt was dancing with a very beautiful brunette, almost as tall as he was. Although Matt was older than James, he was equally as handsome but with his mesmerising blue Irish eyes, many people remarked that he had film star looks. After a couple of dances, Matt returned to the table to find James drinking champagne.

"Well, how was the woman of your dreams, my friend?" he asked James, smiling and pouring himself a glass of fruity red Valpolicella Classico.

"Amazing. You were right, she is very classy; half-Italian and half-Russian, very sexy indeed," replied James, raising his eyebrows and grinning. "By the way, I asked her how well she knew Gene and she told me they were colleagues, having worked together many times for the Society in the past," he added, watching for Matt's reaction.

"Okay, so they are work colleagues. I should think Gene more or less knows everyone in this ballroom. He is a master at what he does," said Matt, looking around the room as he sipped his wine, slowly allowing it to run down his throat, savouring every drop.

Sergie got up from his chair and came around the table, sitting beside Matt and James.

"Everything okay, guys?" he asked loudly.

"Absolutely marvellous. We are having a whale of a time, thanks, Sergie," replied Matt.

"Aldo and I are going to the casino later. You are both welcome to join us," Sergie said winking at them.

"We would love to join you, my friend," replied Matt, "but unfortunately we have a very early flight tomorrow morning and have decided to call it a night, but thank you for the kind invite. When you next come to London, we'll take you to The Sporting Man's Club in Edgware Road. I suspect you will really appreciate it there."

"Okay, it's a deal, Matt. I look forward to it," replied Sergie.

The end of the banquet came all too soon but Matt and James had drunk their fill and were feeling extremely tired. It had been a long day, and an even longer evening, although indeed magical. They had met several influential people from all across Europe and were handed many business cards, now safely tucked inside their wallets. James had asked Isabelle again to dance during the evening, but she politely declined, although she told him she had enjoyed meeting him. James was sad, but as Matt pointed out, she was probably booked with another man for the rest of the night.

When Matt and James reached their hotel rooms, Matt suggested James joined him for a nightcap to help them unwind after an unforgettable day and evening.

"Actually, Matt, that is a splendid idea, my friend. Lead the way," responded James. Matt poured black coffee and handed James a sambuca. They sipped their pleasingly warm liqueur and chatted about the events of the day.

After an hour, Matt got up and said, "Sweet dreams, my friend, time to go. We have an early flight, remember?"

"Yes, of course. I am shattered and will sleep like a baby," responded James, also yawning, getting up from the soft plush armchair. Swiping his card to enter his hotel room, James' eye caught movement at the far end of the corridor. Straining his eyes to make sure they were not lying to him, James saw Isabelle tapping quietly at one of the hotel room doors. Her high-heeled red shoes were slipped off and she was carrying them with her evening purse; she appeared to sway slightly. James was rooted to the spot as he noted the person who answered her discreet tapping had stepped out of the door and circling her in his arms, gently pulling her into the room with him. Immediately, James sobered up, probably with shock, he mused to himself. Matt was right: Isabelle did know Gene very well indeed! Now James knew why she had given him the brush off earlier when he had asked her for another dance. James felt both jealousy and hatred for Gene Capalti in that moment.

On their way home the following day, James told Matt everything he had seen at the other end of the corridor from their hotel rooms.

Matt's eyes opened wide as he listened. "The lucky old dog."

"Dog is right," hissed James through his gleaming straight teeth. "The dog spoilt my chances, that's for sure. Isabelle fancied me, I guarantee it," he added angrily.

"She obviously had a prior engagement with Gene, and let's face it, he is a real top dog, don't you think?" answered Matt, teasing the younger man. "Besides, you have many lovely ladies all vying for your attention right here on your doorstep, so let poor old Gene have a little fun too," he added sarcastically, and the two friends laughed.

Chapter 23
Trouble with Kevin

Freddie and Queenie arrived early at the agency on a grey, nippy Monday morning. How sad it was, he thought, now that autumn was in full swing, winter would soon arrive, bringing with it the short dull days and long dark nights prevailing for the next few months. Freddie, like most people, disliked the winter in London. Of course, he told himself, Christmas was invented purely to help pull everyone out of the doldrums, being it was the only excitement there was to help boost the morale during the dark, cold months. Dodgy Rodger and he were hoping to go away somewhere warm during the Christmas period.

Dawn had told him she and her family were staying at home this year and would happily look after Queenie if he and his current partner wanted to go away. Freddie was more than happy to accept Dawn's very kind offer, having already asked Belinda, but she and Matt were going away to stay with her sister Carole and family who lived in Devon. Belinda did not think it wise to take Queenie all the way down to Devon because it would be a very long journey by car and Queenie was not a very good traveller. Glorious Devon would be a refreshing escape from London, and hopefully with everyone and everything to distract her attention there, Belinda hoped she would not pine so much for her lover.

Belinda walked briskly through the agency's large oak doors smiling. Frank had texted her late the night before while she was almost asleep. Knowing instinctively it was him, and with excitement exploding in her tummy, she had grabbed the mobile and read his words, telling her he was hoping to be back in London on business in a week's time. The message ended with the words, 'Tu sei il milo unico amore.' *(You are my only love.)*

"Well, good morning, Belinda, you look happy. Don't tell me, I suppose lover boy has been in touch again?" asked Freddie, looking up from Dawn's desk where he was printing emails.

"That is the only thing that makes me happy, Freddie, my darling. You know me too well," replied Belinda smiling as a blush touched her warm cheeks. Together, they enjoyed a cup of hot coffee while Queenie lapped up his saucer of milk that Freddie placed carefully on the floor for him.

"Darling, I have to go to the post office and buy stamps for Dawn," announced Freddie, jumping up and clearing away the coffee cups. "Come on, Queenie, my poppet, walkies."

"Okay, Freddie," replied Belinda.

Many requests were now coming in across the UK and Europe for tribute acts and lookalikes. With the imminent Christmas period, the agency was extremely busy, not only during December but also into the beginning of January. However, Kevin (their Boy George lookalike) had caused more pandemonium for the agency. A job had come in for Helen Mirren, Kylie Minogue, Jack Nicholson and Clint

Eastwood lookalikes, together with Boy George. They were booked to attend a very prestigious charity function at the Savoy Hotel in the Strand, London. The lookalikes were to mix and mingle with the glamorous guests before dinner and afterwards to have photographs taken with them, if requested. Most lookalikes were gregarious, possessing the need for attention, but Kevin always managed to upstage everyone. Most people loved the way he strutted around the place but there were people who could not tolerate him: the way he dressed; the way he walked; and, in particular, his big ego.

One such person was Marty Paul, a well-known and highly regarded blues singer. Marty Paul was the booked entertainment at this event. After entertaining the guests and during dinner, the lookalikes were asked to leave the banquet room and go into the huge kitchen area to have something to eat along with the waiters and waitresses. After the dinner was over, they returned and Helen Mirren and Kylie Minogue were in big demand with the gentlemen. Jack Nicholson and Clint Eastwood were always top favourites and were photographed many times, mostly with adoring females, although there were also many men vying to have their photograph taken with these two tough guy film stars. Kevin, being so flamboyant and amusing, was number one choice with the younger guests, and they all wanted to stand beside him to be photographed, laughing at his very witty one-liners.

Walking across the dance floor on his way to the stage, one of the younger guests asked Marty Paul if he would kindly have his photograph taken with some of them. The singer immediately agreed and, smiling his famous smile, he stood in line with some of the guests to be photographed.

As the photographer was about to take the picture, Kevin sauntered quickly across to the waiting group and slid in beside them. Seeing this, Marty Paul frowned angrily and walked away from the group, apologising to them that under no circumstances would he be photographed with this ridiculous Boy George lookalike.

Hearing these cutting words, Kevin threw back at the furious singer, "What's your problem, Mr Paul? Can't take being upstaged?"

Ignoring this remark, like a true professional Marty Paul immediately made his way to the stage to begin the opening of his act. Kevin, shrugging his shoulders effeminately and in true Boy George fashion mouthed, "Up yours," to the singer and sauntered off to mix and mingle with the noisy crowds.

Overall, the evening was a great success. Jack Novak, as Clint Eastwood, was a big hit with the ladies; he was an exceptionally handsome man, with a tanned, toned body, fair hair, expertly bleached by his hairdresser, and mischievous soft green eyes. Men as well as women were drawn to him, yet he was never flash or big-headed. Belinda had always had a soft spot for Jack, admiring his talent. He could also imitate celebrities from all walks of life; pop stars, film stars, politicians. He was also an extremely talented singer and when not earning big money wooing the ladies as a Clint Eastwood lookalike, he was part of a successful Rat Pack show.

Alfred Jones was their number one Jack Nicholson double, and he and Jack had a very special chemistry. Alfred, a thorough gentleman from Cardiff, could equal Jack's charm. He was also another great favourite with the ladies. Both men were not only handsome and charming, but they had wit and sophistication too and were a great asset to any function.

As the evening wore on, the lookalikes were mixing and mingling professionally with the guests while Marty Paul crooned in the background. Kevin strutted around the cream and gold room as if he was the most marvellous person on the planet. His earlier conflict with Marty Paul now forgotten, Kevin was working the room extremely well, thoroughly enjoying the lively banter. Surrounded by other celebrities, a prominent television actor was talking to the other guests. Sitting quietly beside him, a blonde woman listened and smiled as he chatted on.

From time to time, in the middle of his conversation, the actor would turn to her and romantically kiss her lips. The suave English actor, Eton educated, was Nicholas Hart and the reason for his show of affection towards the blonde woman was because he had married her only one month before. The high society wedding was all over the media. As Kevin sauntered across to the table, he immediately interrupted Nicholas Hart's conversation and started to banter with some of the celebrities. Appalled by such behaviour, Nicholas Hart became enraged and, fidgeting uncomfortably in his chair, looked Kevin straight in the eye and in no uncertain terms, told him not to be so bloody rude interrupting his conversation.

Kevin, in true Boy George fashion, turned around immediately and looking directly at the actor and pointing to the blonde woman, replied, "Oh, why don't you take your mother home. I think it must be past her bedtime!"

With this, Nicholas Hart jumped up from his chair and raising his beautifully cultured voice, roared, "How dare you! This is my wife, I'll have you know!"

Like quick silver came Kevin's reply. "Well, there is certainly no accounting for taste, is there?" And flamboyantly turning on those famous stilettos, Kevin minced his way through the other tables, leaving Nicholas Hart, his wife and the other celebrities on the table staring after him, open-mouthed in disbelief.

By the end of the evening, it was evident that Nicholas Hart and Marty Paul had complained about Kevin and, in turn, the clients had spoken with Alfred and Jack about Kevin's outrageous behaviour. Alfred, being a very talented advocate, apologised to the clients on behalf of the agency and gave his word he would talk to Kevin immediately. Obviously, the clients would be issuing a complaint to the agency and there was talk of withdrawing Kevin's fee due to defamation of contract.

At the end of the evening, while the lookalikes were in the changing area preparing to leave the venue, Alfred and Jack spoke to Kevin and told him quietly exactly what the clients had said. Kevin shrugged his shoulders as he slipped out of his stilettos and answered in his defence that he felt Nicholas Hart and Marty Paul were rude to him first and he would not tolerate anyone, no matter who they were, speaking down to him. Alfred reminded him that the clients were calling the agency first thing in the morning regarding these unfortunate incidents.

"I too will call them and explain what really happened," said Kevin, becoming agitated. "Who do some of these people think they are?" he added, taking off his emerald green top hat and handing it to his bodyguard, driver and lover, Wayne, who stood quietly nearby, hoping this would not trigger one of Kevin's horrible black moods.

Dawn and Belinda were horrified to hear about the incidents involving Kevin, although neither were surprised because they were well aware of his bizarre behaviour at times. The client's representative had indeed telephoned the agency the following morning, and Dawn had answered the call in her inimitable manner and managed to sort everything out satisfactorily. Of course, she was angry with Kevin and told Belinda she was seriously contemplating taking him off the books. Dawn agreed with the client that the agency would withdraw the fee for the Boy George lookalike due to his unacceptable behaviour towards two of their prominent guests.

Later that morning, when Kevin eventually called the agency, Dawn told him in no uncertain terms that his fee had been forfeited as a goodwill gesture to the clients from Top Drawer Agency due to his seriously outrageous behaviour the night before. There was nothing Kevin could say to Dawn in his defence; she would not listen to any excuses and threatened to take him off the agency's books. This was his very last chance. If anything remotely like this happened again on a booked job, Dawn warned him, he would be banned from the agency forever.

For once in his life, Kevin kept quiet and ate humble pie while his agent did all the talking. After all, he reminded himself, Top Drawer was the number one tribute and lookalike agency, not only in the UK and Europe, but possibly in the whole world.

Chapter 24
Phoenix Rising

Arriving again in London with more fake money, Gene (Frank) spent two days with Matt at the Soho betting shop, going through the accounts and invoices until he was satisfied yet again that everything was running smoothly regarding the Society's money. Gene had decided to take Matt and James to Claridge's for dinner on the last evening, explaining to them he had felt bad about not spending time with them recently at the seminar in Venice. James smirked to himself and glanced fleetingly at Matt, remembering what James had witnessed in the hotel after the wonderful dinner and dance.

Arriving at the famous Claridge's for dinner, where Gene had booked in the Foyer and Reading Room restaurant, the huge sparkling light sculpture and grand art deco of the foyer transformed the restaurant into a magical dining space. Frequented by famous faces for more than a hundred years, it was the perfect venue for dinner and sipping cocktails in London. Neither Matt nor James had been to this particular restaurant in Claridge's before.

"You know, Gene, Claridge's is Mayfair's art deco jewel apparently, so I compliment you on your impeccable taste, my friend," smiled Matt, holding up his glass of burgundy in a toast.

"Thank you, Matt. I guess I'm turning into a true Brit," offered Gene, and they laughed.

As the evening unfolded, Frank secretly became excited about his meeting with his beautiful Belinda the following day.

Belinda was so looking forward to being with Frank again. To her, it felt like months and months had passed since they were last together. Frank had booked a room at the Phoenix Hotel, which suited him for a day and night while he entertained Belinda, feeling safer out there, away from prying eyes. Belinda checked with the receptionist for Frank's room number and, alighting from the large lift when she reached his floor, Frank, wearing nothing but a pair of boxer shorts, was standing at his door waiting for her. On seeing him, Belinda's heart leapt in her breast and without thinking, she ran the remainder of the way into his strong waiting arms. Emotions of love and sadness welled up inside her, unable to hold back the hot tears that began to stream down her flushed face.

"Darling, Belinda, I thought you would be happy to see me," teased Frank as he held her at arm's length and looked at her tear-stained face.

Through her tears, Belinda glanced childishly up at him and they laughed; his dancing brown eyes, mocking her in a loving way. Guiding her gently into the room, Frank closed and locked the door behind them. Seductively, he pushed his tongue into her eager mouth, their lips entwined. Belinda became more aroused as Frank began opening her blouse to reveal her luscious breasts, heaving with arousal and passion. Gently, he pushed her against the side wall, cupping her breast in his strong hands while bringing his head down to lick and suck her nipple. Slowly and tantalisingly, he moved his hand inside her wrap-over skirt.

Belinda moaned softly to herself as she leaned sensually against the wall, her whole being begging for him. She caught her breath as he masterly wrapped her in his arms then carried her to the king-sized bed. As she answered his every movement, Frank whispered, "Tu sei la mia gioia e amore." *(You are my joy and my love.)*

The day was spent in Frank's hotel suite. Dinner with champagne was ordered and brought up for them by the bellboy. Frank was always happy and relaxed to be in Belinda's company, feeling he could be himself when with her, knowing she adored him and would never judge him. Sadly for Belinda, Frank had told her this was just a lightning visit for him this time to London. Unfortunately, he explained to her, he had to return to New York later that evening, ready for an important meeting the following morning. Seeing how upset and sad she looked, he held her close to him and promised his lover he would make it up to her. Christmas was barely three weeks away, and he and his son would be flying to Bermuda to spend some bonding time together during the holidays. For too long now, Frank had hardly spent time with his only child, due to his high-profile job with the Society, which often took him away from New York and home.

The agency was extremely busy in late November, and for the more popular characters, Dawn and Belinda had to use their second and third choices because their number ones were already heavily booked. Kay (the new Marilyn

Monroe) was booked on a job in West London together with Vicky (Liz Taylor), Hugh (Sean Connery 007), Adam (Jack Sparrow), as well as Belinda as Joan Collins. Eager as her agent to get to know Kay better, Belinda was looking forward to working with her for the first time.

Vicky had been informed that on her contract, a clause had been inserted referring to a 'no drinks' policy and this would be inserted on all tribute acts' and lookalikes' future contracts. The wonderful Hugh was always a pleasure to work with and Belinda liked him very much. The feeling was mutual and they had worked together many times in the past. As far as Belinda was concerned, Hugh was the perfect gentleman. Of course, everyone had a soft spot for Adam, especially when he strutted about in the guise of Captain Jack Sparrow.

All in all, this job had cheered Belinda up immensely and an added bonus was that there was very little travelling involved being in London, apart from Vicky, of course, who would travel down from Manchester. The job went wonderfully well. It was another popular 'mix and mingle'. The clients were launching a new mobile phone franchise and money seemed to be no object. After being welcomed warmly by the client's representative, they were shown to their changing area where refreshments were laid on for them.

Kay seemed at home with the others; Hugh and Adam hung around Kay, happily listening to her girlish chatter. Belinda and Vicky, being good friends, found space together at the back of the changing area to have a good chat. After a short while, walking across to Kay, Belinda asked her how she was finding her new role as a Marilyn Monroe lookalike. Kay appeared to be enthusiastic about everything and Belinda found her friendly and cheerful; someone who came over as very confident indeed, which, of course, helped a great deal in this type of show business.

Adam chatted with Belinda a little asking how her romance was going with Frank. Belinda told him things were going slowly but very well. Knowing her marriage was not a happy one, Adam reassured Belinda that her little secret was safe with him and winked. But he could see sadness in her eyes and uttered in her ear, "Don't worry, sweetie. What will be, will be."

"Just look at the men, Belinda," whispered Vicky, raising her eyes, the pupils now the colour of lilac due to her new contact lenses. Belinda followed Vicky's gaze and noticed many of the male guests were surrounding Kay, vying for her attention.

"Oh yes, she's definitely got Marilyn down to a fine art," said Belinda, turning away and continuing to mix and mingle with the guests.

Some time later, Hugh strolled across to her and announced she looked as ravishing as ever this evening. Giggling, Belinda thanked him. Hugh always managed to make her giggle like a teenager; she put it down to his Welsh charm. Like the debonair gentleman he was, Hugh took her left hand gently and planted a kiss on it.

Halfway through the evening, Belinda found herself beside Adam who was entertaining several guests, especially the ladies, every one of them wanting their photographs taken with him.

Belinda knew her Joan Collins character attracted male and female fans of all ages. They all adored La Collins, but Belinda was aware, as were every tribute act and lookalike, that you had to have a thick skin to survive in this business, training yourself to hear only the positive remarks and learning to ignore the negative. As she smiled and preened for the flashing cameras, Belinda recalled how she had learned long ago one had to build a shield around oneself in this copycat world.

Vicky appeared to be thoroughly enjoying the evening and was always at her best when mixing and mingling among a large audience. To be the top Elizabeth Taylor lookalike was a great honour for any woman. She often told the other lookalikes that, after all, Liz Taylor had often been referred to as the most beautiful woman in the world and even now, after her sad demise, there was nobody who could match her beauty. Vicky had controlled her drinking habits and her good behaviour was paying off.

At the end of the very successful job, the client's representative spoke to Belinda and complimented Top Drawer Agency on their Class A lookalikes.

"We have several more functions coming up and will most definitely be calling you for more of your wonderful lookalikes," beamed the woman to a smiling Belinda. "I must say, you were all amazing this evening, especially Marilyn Monroe. We will definitely book her again. By the way, is she also a tribute act, able to perform Marilyn's famous songs?"

Always happy to hear good positive remarks, Belinda assured the woman Kay was even more amazing on stage and she did sing live. Later, telling everyone how happy the client's representative had been with all of them, Belinda took Kay to one side and quietly told her that everyone was extremely impressed with her. Beaming from ear to ear and with excitement shining in her eyes, Kay told Belinda how much she was looking forward to the kind of jobs where she would be expected to sing as Marilyn Monroe.

The women left the Thistle Marble Arch Hotel together and said their goodbyes in the bustle of the crowds on Oxford Street where Belinda and Vicky watched in disbelief as Kay Carney, dressed in a very tight, black Monroe-style dress and looking exactly like the famous blonde icon, high heels clicking on the busy pavement, wiggled her way down Oxford Street towards Oxford Circus tube station. Pulling her small silver case behind her, nose in the air, ignoring the appreciative wolf whistles from several grinning men in the crowds, Kay caused the usual heavy London traffic to come to a standstill. Camera phones focused on her every step as tourists from across the globe excitedly snapped this apparition of Marilyn Monroe before them.

"I guarantee your new girlie is going straight to the top," exclaimed Vicky as she and Belinda finally lost sight of Kay in the throng of Oxford Street.

"Oh, that is an understatement, my friend," replied Belinda, and the two ladies laughed out loud as, arms linked, they turned towards the car park.

Chapter 25
Christmas Celebrations

C hristmas was welcomed with open arms by everyone after the busiest season for the Top Drawer Agency. On checking the books, the early part of January already looked quite hectic, much to Dawn's delight. Freddie and Dodgy Rodger were flying out to Skiathos, one of the beautiful Greek islands and considered the next big thing for gay and lesbian holidaymakers. Belinda and Matt enjoyed a trip to Devon in the picturesque West Country to visit Belinda's youngest sister, Carole, her husband, Mick, and their daughter, Fleur. Belinda had felt she had two different personas: the one who adored and wanted to spend the rest of her life with Frank, and the other one who pretended to be content with her life as Matt's wife.

Early on Christmas morning, while everybody was leaving for the Christmas Mass at the local Roman Catholic Church, Belinda received a text from Frank which read, 'Buon Natale amore mio, mi manchi.' *(Merry Christmas my love, I miss you.)*

A warm glow filled her inside and shone through her eyes, making them sparkle with happiness, rivalling the brightest Christmas candles.

Following a crisp, dry and pleasantly sunny December, January came, bombastically blowing and whirling the dead leaves off the ground and into the frosty air. January had arrived with a rare arrogance this year, as if making sure everyone knew he had taken over, proud in the fact that everybody had been dreading his arrival. In the UK, winter had finally found its resting place for the following few months. Coats, hats, scarves, boots, warm gloves and watery eyes were on show everywhere as people covered up to keep out the icy coldness of the first month of the year, and dreading even more his successor, February.

Freddie and Dodgy Rodger had a marvellous time on the island of Skiathos, and came back looking tanned and rested. Little Queenie squealed loudly when he saw his beloved master. Gently taking Queenie from Dawn's arms and with tears rolling down his handsome face, Freddie allowed the little dog to lick him, while at the same time Queenie yelped excitedly. When Belinda finally arrived, they all sat around sipping hot coffee and reminisced about their enjoyable Christmas holidays.

Adam had now learned, while chatting with Belinda on the telephone a few days earlier, that she was still very much in contact and smitten with Frank. Adam and Belinda had been good friends ever since they had met and she tended to confide in him.

"His surname isn't Sinatra, is it?" joked Adam, knowing she adored the late great singer.

"Unfortunately, no," giggled Belinda. "It is very Italian though, Lanzo, and this is the only surname I want now," she added frivolously.

"Lanzo?" repeated Adam. "Belinda Lanzo," he teased. "Sounds like a film star's name."

However, Adam's friendly banter with Belinda was purely to find out Frank's surname without her becoming suspicious, so he could relay it to the polizia in Venice.

Apparently, there was a very strong possibility that Frank, probably using a pseudonym at the time, had been involved in a famous diamond heist in Venice many years before when he was much younger. It was apparently reported that there were three known international master thieves operating together, but before the polizia could get permission to bring them in for questioning, they disappeared from the streets of Venice, taking with them the very valuable diamonds. As the years passed, the famous diamond robbery case had eventually been placed in Piazzale Roma's police files marked 'Unsolved'.

Belinda, together with one of her girlfriends, Eileen, a member of The Lissenden Players Old Tyme Music Hall group, arranged to meet at Victoria Station on a chilly Friday evening in the middle of January. They were to have dinner with Simon and Bryanne, two of Belinda's favourite people, who were wonderfully gay, and Belinda adored them both. Simon was English, tall, well-built and very handsome. About forty-five years of age, Simon possessed an unusual laid-back charm, coupled with his Gemini mercury wit. He wore his head shaved, giving him a very butch appearance, which attracted many a member of the opposite sex, much to his dismay. Bryanne, on the other hand, was a proud Scot, some ten years older than Simon. Of medium height and slim build, Bryanne, wonderfully flamboyant, was also very handsome, sporting a marvellous Elvis quiff, even though his hair had turned pure white during the last few years.

Proud not only of his quiff, Bryanne was also extremely proud of his piercing blue eyes and accepted graciously the many compliments from the world. The couple had an amazingly flamboyant dress sense and both were blessed with charisma. Practically every evening found Simon and Bryanne out somewhere in London, often frequenting the Covent Garden and Soho areas. There was not a show worth seeing that these boys had not seen. How they loved the theatre! Belinda recalled fondly when she had first been introduced to them. The Lissenden Players had been booked to perform for a Red Flannel show somewhere in Waterloo. Red Flannel were an organisation of Labour Party supporters, hence the name. Many Labour politicians attended the show, and Simon and Bryanne had been invited by a friend, who was a member of the Party. It was Belinda who caught Simon and Bryanne's eye during the show when she performed the very funny tongue-in-cheek number *Please Don't Touch Me Plums*. With her rendition of this very amusing ditty, Belinda knew she had brought the house down.

Having been extremely impressed with the show, Simon and Bryanne felt they had to congratulate her and the rest of the cast personally for a very enjoyable evening of entertainment. That was the beginning of a wonderful friendship between Belinda and the two beautiful boys.

The beautiful boys had invited Belinda and Eileen for dinner on the Tapestry Castle, a floating, albeit moored, ship on the Thames at the Embankment. Since the early 1980s, the Tapestry Castle has been run as a bar and restaurant and is considered one of the capital's best. The ship offered a comfortable interior, a wide range of beers and wines, and some of the finest cuisine in London. Simon had told them he and Bryanne thought the Tapestry Castle outshone most of the other floating pub-restaurants on the Thames, partly because her central position offered great views of some of the greatest sights in London. The Tapestry Castle was a real favourite with tourists and Londoners alike. Belinda was well aware she and Eileen were in for a fun evening with the boys, and the ladies were already impressed with the chosen venue.

The friends ordered their aperitifs and chatted and laughed, with Simon and Bryanne telling one funny story after another about their escapades on their latest holiday in San Francisco. Dinner was surprisingly good and plenty of beer and wine was consumed by everybody, which had them feeling wonderfully happy and relaxed.

Halfway through the evening, Simon told his dinner guests that they were soon to be invited to a wedding. Looking at each other quizzically, Belinda and Eileen wondered who of their friends were getting married.

"A wedding?" queried Eileen, leaning towards Simon and giggling.

"Yes, a big flashy wedding, Eileen, my darling," replied Simon, winking at Bryanne who sat with his elbows on the table, resting his face in his hands, beginning to feel the effects of the amount of beer and wine he had drunk during dinner.

"Whose wedding?" enquired Belinda, breaking out into giggles.

"Mine and Bryanne's, of course," Simon replied, putting a loving arm around his beloved partner, whose grin reached from ear to ear. The ladies roared with laughter and Belinda's bluey green eyes widened with awe while Eileen's jaw dropped open as they stared in disbelief at their two friends, who were now hugging each other and laughing.

"Wow, that's fabulous news!" squealed Belinda, getting up unsteadily and wrapping her arms around Simon and Bryanne.

"Wow, yes, fabulous," agreed Eileen, rushing out of her seat and joining in with the group hug.

"When will this happen?" asked Belinda, sentimental now due to the four glasses of red wine she had already consumed. Tears of happiness welled up in her eyes as she kissed the beautiful boys continuously.

"On Valentine's Day, which we think is very appropriate," offered Bryanne, still smiling broadly. "And this lucky boy gets me as his Valentine," he laughed, pinching Simon fondly on his smooth cheek.

The next day, Frank called Belinda on her mobile as she was about to leave the agency. As Frank's distinctive New York accent flowed to her through the phone, Belinda's heart skipped wildly in her bosom and she quickly left the agency to speak privately with her lover while she walked towards her parked car. Frank told her he had thoroughly enjoyed Christmas and New Year with his son, quickly adding he had missed her beautiful face and sexy body and thought about her constantly. Frank said he hoped to be in London in February and, as she reached her car, he whispered to her, "Arrivederci, bella, a presto." *(Goodbye, beautiful, see you soon.)*

Chapter 26
Dominatrix

"You must be joking!" gasped Belinda as she listened with disbelief to what Dawn was saying to her.

"I wish I was joking, but unfortunately this is not a silly rumour," replied Dawn, walking across to Belinda's desk and handing her a cutting from a magazine. Belinda's eyes passed quickly over the article with the headline *Tina Turner Lookalike's Secret Life as a Dominatrix*, and smiling up at her from the shiny page was Kim, dressed in a black busk, lacy stockings and holding something called a tawse, a strong leather belt split into two or three tongues at the end; obviously a tool of the trade.

"OMG!" exclaimed Belinda loudly. "What on earth possessed her to resort to this kind of decadence?" she asked, looking up at Dawn for some kind of an answer. Dawn gently took the cutting from her partner's hand and studied it again.

"Money, fame, the usual, I suppose," she replied. "We know what Kim is capable of, so we really should not be so surprised," she added, glancing at Belinda and shaking her head.

"Well, yes, I know, Dawn, but this will not do the reputation of the agency any good at all," reminded Belinda, looking worried.

"Quite," replied Dawn. "I really think the best option is to take her off our books once and for all. This agency cannot afford to be associated with this kind of sordid publicity. I will deal with it immediately," added Dawn, walking quickly back to her desk to telephone Kim.

Kim had no idea that her agents had seen her article in the magazine; after all, these types of magazines had ninety-five per cent male readers. Although her curiosity was aroused, Kim did not think there was anything to worry about. She imagined Dawn would probably ask her to have new photographs and videos done as Tina Turner because her present ones were now quite out of date. During the last few months, she had meant to update her publicity photographs and videos but found she was so busy with her new dominatrix career that she had found it difficult to put even one day aside to accomplish this task for her lookalike character. Arranging with Dawn to go into the agency in a couple of days' time, Kim had to telephone two of her regular clients to reschedule their appointments.

Smiling to herself, she reminisced about some of the men who visited her home where she had one large room kitted out like a dungeon and where she wore latex outfits to fulfil their fantasies, each one eager to have her dish out the pain to them and pay her handsomely for doing so. Kim knew, for some of them, this was a form of escapism, but for most of them it was about reliving the past; maybe from being caned at school by an attractive female teacher, evolving into a desire to be spanked in adulthood. The vast majority of her clientele were upper-middle-class men in their fifties to late seventies. From good advertising and word of mouth, Kim now had a slew of doctors, lawyers, professors, business executives, and even a minister or two, all of who had elaborate fantasy worlds they seemed to use as a kind of relief valve to alleviate the stress of their high-power positions. Kim guided them through their weird kinks, which was a very satisfactory job for her, and she made much more money being a dominatrix than being a Tina Turner lookalike.

As soon as she arrived at the agency and saw the frosty looks on her agents' faces, Kim knew they had seen the magazine article. Uncomfortably for Kim, both sets of eyes looked directly at her questioningly. Dawn purposely handed the magazine to Kim, which was opened at her article. Embarrassed, Kim shifted on her chair and placed the magazine on Dawn's desk.

"Well? Did you think your seedy little secret would not get out once you published this article?" Dawn said coldly.

A hot flush coloured Kim's cheeks as her eyes met Dawn's icy cold stare. Quickly getting up from her chair, she answered in her defence.

"This does not interfere with my lookalike work. I reschedule my clients if a lookalike job comes up on the same day, even if their appointments had already been booked with me."

Dawn glanced with despair at Belinda then, leaning towards Kim, lowered her voice and said, "That is neither here nor there, Kim. You have definitely crossed the line this time, bringing the good name of this agency into disrepute by the mere fact that you are associated with us." Sitting back in her chair, Dawn shook her head.

"Kim," said Belinda softly, "we have all been worried about your behaviour of late; you seem to be sinking very low just to attract attention. We all know how much you grieved when your father passed, but you must understand the position this puts the agency in. This is going too far and the agency cannot, and will not, stand for it," added Belinda, looking directly at Kim, who muttered something about being desperately short of money and needing to make some quickly to pay her mortgage.

Dawn reminded her that all tribute acts and lookalikes sign a contract when they are first taken on, agreeing not to do anything untoward that would bring the agency's good name into disrepute. The agents said they had no alternative now but to take Kim off their books. Both ladies were saddened by having to take this path of action with Kim, but they had discussed it thoroughly and felt they could no longer trust her.

At these words, Kim angrily retorted, "Fine, take me off the books if that is what you want to do. I belong to some of the other agencies anyway, so I will still be portraying Tina Turner along with my dominatrix career."

Then swiftly, she strode to the door and was gone. Glancing sadly at each other, Dawn and Belinda were worried because they were losing their top Tina Turner lookalike and tribute act. At the same time, they felt a sense of relief knowing Kim would no longer have the chance to bring the good name of Top Drawer Agency into dispute.

Although the month of January was cold and at times snowy, the sun shone strongly almost every day, which made things much more bearable, especially for the millions of people who rose early during the dark mornings of winter and had to rely on the London transport service to get them to work on time.

Recently, Belinda noticed that Matt was back to his bad old ways, staying out very late some nights and occasionally not coming home at all until the following day, telling Belinda he had stayed with James Swift. Belinda decided either his old affair was back on, or he had met another barmaid. Belinda felt relieved he no longer bothered her again for sex and although married to Matt, Belinda for some reason felt guilty she had cheated on Frank.

The hectic time at the agency had now quietened down. Dawn booked a last-minute holiday and went off for two weeks with her family for a winter break to the beautiful ski slopes of Switzerland. Belinda and Freddie were happy to cover for her. On most days, they took a leisurely lunch together, choosing one of the many fashionable public houses in the area so that Queenie was allowed inside to sit at their feet while they dined on a hearty pub lunch. Belinda was happy that Freddie seemed to be settled at last with Dodgy Rodger. She often mused to herself how men were such silly creatures and little boys at heart.

"How dodgy is Rodger these days?" she suddenly asked.

"Aw, quite dodgy, my darling," came Freddie's reply, grinning and winking at her.

"Seriously, Freddie, I hope he doesn't get too dodgy with you," replied Belinda, looking for Freddie's reaction.

"Of course he doesn't, darling. He acquired his nickname because he is known to have light fingers, so watch your diamonds, darling, when the Dodge is about," giggled Freddie, swallowing down the last drop of his lager.

"Honestly!" exclaimed Belinda, also giggling. "You certainly know how to pick them."

After a pleasant lunch and on their walk back to the agency, little Queenie trotting beside them on his new blue studded leash, Freddie questioned Belinda about Frank.

"I am really worried about your safety in case Matt finds out about your affair," he told her, a frown descending on his forehead.

Belinda assured him everything was fine because she was always very careful with her alibis. "Frank will be in London again in February," Belinda mentioned excitedly to him. "I just pray it won't clash with Simon and Bryanne's wedding on Valentine's Day, which falls on a Friday this year," she added, a worried look in her eyes.

Glancing at his friend sideways, Freddie had an uneasy sense of tragedy about Belinda, which he tried to push out of his mind.

Stooping down to swoop Queenie up in his arms, he uttered to her gently, "Just be careful, darling."

Gently kissing Freddie on the cheek, Belinda slipped her arm into his and they returned to the office.

A couple of days later, while Freddie and Queenie were at the post office, Belinda received a fax from one of the agency's clients in the Netherlands. The clients were requesting to see photographs and videos of certain lookalikes for a big corporate dinner and dance to be held in Sofitel Legend The Grand Amsterdam, one of the Netherlands' top luxury hotels. All chosen lookalikes would be flown out of London on Friday late morning, ready for the job that same evening, then they would fly back late the following day. The lookalikes would have their own rooms in the hotel and the client had requested they should all be on the same floor. Belinda had hoped the Joan Collins character would be asked for, but unfortunately it was not to be this time. The final line-up of lookalikes included Marilyn Monroe, Charlie Chaplin, Laurel and Hardy, Elvis Presley, and Liberace.

"Wonderful!" exclaimed Belinda aloud when she read the last name on the client's list. Darling Freddie, she knew, would be over the moon.

As Freddie returned, Belinda noticed a sullen look on his handsome face, and enquired why this was. She was told that Dodgy Rodger had called Freddie on his mobile, informing him he had to go visit his elderly father in West Glamorgan at the end of the week and would be away for anything up to a fortnight. Dodgy Rodger's father had been taken ill three days earlier and Rodger's sister had telephoned him to please think seriously about going as soon as possible because their father was very poorly and at his grand old age, they could not afford to be complacent.

"I know the Dodge has to go, Belinda, but I will miss him terribly," whined Freddie, gently lowering Queenie down onto the floor. .

"Come on, Freddie. Of course he has to visit his father. You will be fine and before you know it, he will be back again. Besides, my darling, I have a little surprise for you that I think will make you feel much happier," encouraged Belinda, giving him a cuddle and grinning up at him.

"No, no, nothing will make me feel better. I can't bear to be away from the Dodge for so long," groaned Freddie, wiping his eyes as tears threatened.

Picking up the fax off her desk, Belinda handed it to Freddie, who curiously read the request for lookalikes in Amsterdam. As his eyes fell on the name of Liberace, he jumped up from his chair and let out a very loud, "Yahoo!" which made little Queenie bark and wag his curly little tail ferociously, sensing that his beloved master was feeling happy again.

"Oh, so you have already forgotten about Dodgy Rodger?" teased Belinda, and they laughed and giggled while Queenie rolled over on his furry back and insisted on having his tummy rubbed by anyone who would oblige.

Chapter 27
A Wedding

Within just a few days, the client in the Netherlands had made their choice for the lookalikes. Freddie was over the moon because the Liberace character was chosen, along with Charlie Chaplin, one set of Laurel and Hardy, Elvis and Marilyn Monroe. As everyone suspected, Kay Carney was the chosen Monroe. The fee to be paid was exceedingly higher than most other European jobs, and Belinda knew Dawn would be very pleased because this one job would help keep the agency running smoothly for some time during the slower months.

Freddie, feeling very smug indeed, sat next to Kay on the flight out of Gatwick Airport. Freddie thought her an amazing Monroe lookalike. As far as he was concerned, Kay <u>was</u> Marilyn Monroe. The Charlie Chaplin and Elvis lookalikes sat beside each other, and the Laurel and Hardy lookalikes were across the aisle together at the front of the plane. For the time being, Freddie had completely forgotten about Dodgy Rodger. Freddie had never met any of these particular lookalikes before, but found them very friendly and fun to be with.

After causing quite a flutter in the airport lounge while going through customs, the lookalikes were driven to the Sofitel Legend The Grand Amsterdam. History and elegance defined this luxury hotel, standing close to the city centre attractions: the Royal Palace, Hermitage Museum and Amsterdam's best shopping streets. Unfortunately, this was a whistle-stop visit for the lookalikes, not staying long enough to take in the iconic sights of the famous Dutch city.

They were given a private room each situated on the same floor, as Belinda had stipulated in the contract for the clients. Apart from Kay and Freddie, the others had worked together several times, but Kay being Kay, had the boys eating out of her hand in no time. As for Freddie, everybody liked him instantly.

Later, the lookalikes had assembled in a side room close to the ballroom of the hotel where the evening was to be held. Freddie looked uncannily like Liberace wearing a white tuxedo with a silver sequinned waistcoat, which sparkled with his every movement.

"Hey, Liberace, you planning on stealing my thunder?" laughed the Elvis lookalike as his eyes took in Freddie's flamboyant appearance.

"I'd be hard pressed to do that, Mr Presley," replied Freddie, laughing. "You make me look positively demure in your bright red one-piece."

Rob, the agency's top Elvis lookalike, had an amazing sense of humour, which everyone appreciated, Freddie included.

The evening was a great success. This was another mix and mingle job, and Freddie, much to his surprise, proved very popular and was asked time and again during the evening whether he could tickle the ivories like Liberace.

"But of course I can, darling," was his tongue-in-cheek reply, as he waved his long arms in the air flamboyantly, causing everybody to laugh at his antics.

After a few hours, the lookalikes were given a break to eat and relax before returning to the ballroom to complete their contracted hours. They were seated at a round table in a small side room waiting to be served dinner, when Kay came rushing in looking excited yet embarrassed, her bright red lipstick quite smudged. As she reached the table, she threw herself into a vacant chair and exclaimed how famished she was. Luke, the amazing Charlie Chaplin lookalike, put his arm around her protectively and explained dinner would be served directly.

Freddie looked around the room and asked, "Where's Rob?"

Kay blushed slightly, before Rob came hurrying into the room, a big smile spreading across his handsome face, showing off his beautiful white teeth.

"I'm starving, where's dinner?" he asked, taking the last vacant seat at the table, beside Freddie.

"Where have you been, Elvie, baby?" Freddie asked.

"Oh, I got caught up in the heavy brocade drapes in the ballroom with a very lovely lady. We were wrapped up together for a little while there," laughed Rob, impersonating Elvis' Memphis accent perfectly and stealing a fleeting glance at Kay, who kept her eyes downcast.

Freddie, never one to miss a trick, noticed a bright red lipstick smudge on the side of Rob's mouth. He winked knowingly, and remarked slyly to the King, "Sounds like a lot of fun, Elvis. I see your lovely lady wears red lipstick," which made everybody on the table laugh, Kay included.

The following day, Freddie received a call from Dodgy Rodger with the sad news that his father had passed away the night before and that he was staying in West Glamorgan until after the funeral the following week.

It was Saturday morning and Belinda was sleeping in the spare bedroom, which she had been doing so for some time now. For a short while at Christmas in Devon, she and Matt had shared the same bedroom, both trying to keep up normal appearances in front of her sister, Carole. What a farce her marriage had become, she thought, as she turned over sleepily, fighting desperately to remember the wonderful dream she was having before being awoken by Matt's loud snoring, which reached her from the other bedroom. On the brink of falling back to sleep again, Belinda's mobile, laying on her dressing table, whistled out loudly. Now immediately awake, Belinda knew before reaching for the phone and reading the text message that it was from Frank, and her eyes sparkled. Frank had texted to let her know he would be in London for one day in early March and staying at one of the hotels close to London Heathrow Airport and hoped she would be able to meet him. On reading this, she felt herself blush with sexual desire for her lover.

Before she knew it, Valentine's Day had arrived. Simon and Bryanne had extended their wedding invitation to Matt, as well as to Eileen's partner. Matt graciously declined the kind invitation because, apart from the busy schedule of race meetings being held, he had arranged for decorators to start refurbishing the Soho shop. They were contracted to work in the evenings so Matt would not have to close the shop during the day while the decorating was in progress. Matt being Matt had decided to oversee this operation, wanting to be on hand in case the decorators came across any problems, no matter how trivial. Eileen's partner had also declined the invitation, so Belinda and Eileen met and travelled together to the Deck, situated on the roof of the iconic National Theatre where the ceremony was to take place.

Once the wedding vows were taken, the guests could step out onto the Deck's private outdoor terrace and enjoy champagne, high above London's vibrant South Bank. This stunning venue, with its spectacular panoramic views across London and the River Thames, excited every one of Simon and Bryanne's guests, and each of them were mesmerised.

As if Saint Valentine had personally taken control of the wedding, the sun shone, albeit weakly. As Simon and Bryanne stood in front of the female registrar who was to marry them, Belinda noticed how extremely handsome and happy they both looked. The bridegrooms wore identical silver-grey, three-piece suits with purple coloured shirts, together with matching tie and handkerchiefs, and grey suede shoes. Pinned to their lapels was a cluster of dusty purple velvet flowers. Belinda's eyes filled with emotional tears as she witnessed her first same-sex marriage. There were one hundred and twenty invited guests.

Simon was the youngest child of a large family and all his siblings and their offspring were present, together with Bryanne's mother, only brother and two elderly aunts. There were so many other colourful guests, mostly homosexual men, each one trying to be the most flamboyant and the most beautiful; everyone looked wonderful. Several lady friends, some escorted by male partners and some escorted by female partners, watched with wide eyes as their two fabulous friends were united in matrimony, while the female photographer professionally recorded this wonderful occasion.

Round ebony tables, dressed beautifully in rose pink, were placed in the large hall with seating for eight guests each. Simon had requested soft pink lighting to complement the rose-coloured tablecloths.

The wedding feast was tastefully prepared together with champagne and wine, which flowed freely. The shining eyes of the guests confirmed everybody was having the most wonderful time. After amusing speeches from the best man and family members, the party moved to the Terrace Bar, also at the National Theatre, because unfortunately dancing was not permitted on the Deck. Simon and Bryanne had hired the Terrace Bar until midnight where the drinks and dancing were aplenty, late into the chilly February evening. Belinda danced for most of the evening with several charming gentlemen.

During one of these dances, a tall, dark-haired man made it clear that he was interested in getting to know Belinda better. Smelling the alcohol on his breath as his lips brushed insolently against her ear, Belinda politely but firmly pulled away from his grasp and told him that she was married and not interested in anything other than dancing. Abruptly, she turned and made her way back to her table, continuing to enjoy herself for the rest of the evening with Eileen and some of the other guests.

When midnight arrived, far too quickly, the two bridegrooms kissed each other as everybody clapped with excitement for them and their future happiness. The happy newly-married couple had always wanted a city chic wedding venue with a difference and, as everybody agreed, this was certainly City Chic!

A few days after Simon and Bryanne's wonderful wedding, Belinda received a text from Frank, explaining that his visit to London had unfortunately been postponed for at least another few weeks. Disappointment flooded Belinda's senses but she desperately tried to reason with herself that it was only a short delay, and besides, she would gladly wait for her lover forever.

Chapter 28
A Spy

Some weeks later, again laden with the Society's fake money, Gene (Frank) flew into London to spend two days going through the usual procedures of business for the Society with Matt and James. Frank had booked into the Sherlock Holmes Hotel in London for this trip, where many fellow Americans frequented, because it was an iconic hotel off Baker Street and Frank always enjoyed walking in Regent's Park close by.

Satisfied yet again with the way all the betting shops were continuing to operate, Gene took Matt and James to dinner at the Ritz Hotel as a thank you for their continued good work. As far as Matt and James were concerned, Gene was scheduled to fly back to New York early the following morning, when in fact he was staying an extra day and night, transferring to the Rainbow Blue Edwardian Hotel near Heathrow Airport, making it possible for him to spend some precious time with the lovely Belinda, well away from prying eyes.

Belinda, heart racing, raised her right hand to tap quietly on Room 15 of the Rainbow Blue Edwardian Hotel. Instantly, the door opened wide, revealing her handsome lover, wearing a burgundy silk dressing gown as he stood there smiling down at her. Their eyes locked, Belinda feeling a flush on her cheeks as his dancing brown eyes laughed at her shyness. Catching her breath, she rushed into his outstretched arms as tears of happiness spilled from her eyes. Frank brought his strong head down and kissed her emotional tears and then her waiting mouth.

As always, those wonderful feelings, deep down within her, stirred and the butterflies began to flutter and flutter, almost taking her breath away.

"Quanto mi sei mancato, tesoro," *(How I missed you, my darling)* he uttered huskily into her ear, and she moaned softly as his lips brushed lightly on her neck. With experienced hands, Frank undressed his lover sensually and slowly, unbuttoning her scarlet blouse and revealing a black lacy brassiere beneath. His fingers expertly unzipped her dark grey pencil skirt, which slid to the floor around her feet, leaving her standing in her black underwear. Swiftly, he pushed her brassiere upwards towards her neck, allowing her ample breasts to fall out. A groan of passion escaped from Frank's throat as his mouth and tongue caressed her breasts. Belinda instantly threw her head back and moaned quietly as her body was set on fire with love for him. Laying on his back across the bed, Frank closed his eyes as Belinda straddled his thick manly body. Seductively, working her way stealthy up his tingling body, she kiss-licked him until her lips found his mouth, tongues entwined together in wild passion.

Squeals of passion filled the room as they climaxed together in fabulous sexual abandonment and lay in each other's arms, peaceful and contented before falling into a drowsy sleep.

Stirring, Belinda opened her eyes and looked at the digital clock on the bedside cabinet. Darkness had taken over from the day's light outside.

"Darling," she whispered in Frank's ear as he lay softly snoring, "I'm famished."

Frank grunted loudly as he slowly opened his eyes, smiling broadly as his gaze rested on Belinda's face, anxiously looking down at him. "Okay, babe, go take a shower and then we can go eat. Can't let my best girl go hungry now, can I?" he uttered, turning those dancing brown eyes on her, and again, she could feel herself blushing like a schoolgirl.

Frank and Belinda took the lift down to the splendid decor of the hotel's lobby. There were several men mingling around and chatting in small groups. Frank ushered Belinda towards the Purple Sky Restaurant with its subtle art deco styling, a striking centrepiece bar and a menu that celebrated the best of all worldwide foods. This too was extremely busy. The maître d' came directly up to them and offered a choice of three tables that were unoccupied. Frank decided on a table secluded at the back of the restaurant; nice and private for them, he thought. Soft, relaxing music filled the air, but there was quite a lot of noise coming from the lobby where more gentlemen had gathered, laughing loudly and calling out to each other.

"There must be a party taking place this evening," remarked Belinda as she sat down on the dining chair the maître d' held out for her.

"Certainly sounds like it," agreed Frank. "I hope they quieten down by the time we want to sleep," he added, turning around and looking in the direction of the laughter.

Looking at him slyly, Belinda asked demurely, "Sleep, you and I?"

Understanding her meaning instantly, Frank threw back his strong head and laughed out loud, appreciating her sense of humour, then looking deep into her eyes, he murmured, "Come ti amo." *(How I love you.)*

"Sorry I'm late, guys," offered a fair-haired young man as he rushed into the lobby, going up to one of the men who was chatting in a group.

"No problem," answered Jonathan Bartlett, shaking hands with the latecomer and thanking him for coming. "We are waiting to take over the bar lounge any minute now. Besides, it is my fault for changing the venue at the last minute, but I seriously think everyone will really appreciate this place," he added confidently.

"Yes, I heard that from other people. I am really looking forward to it," replied the fair-haired young man. "I think this will prove to be a very interesting stag party indeed," he said as an afterthought.

A few minutes later, the group of noisy gentlemen began to slowly make their way into the bar lounge to celebrate Jonathan Bartlett's last week of freedom, the fair-haired young man, James Swift, among them.

During their sumptuous dinner of seasoned and marinaded salmon fillets, Belinda and Frank caught up on how each of them had spent the last few months. Frank held her hand while she chatted openly to him as the red wine loosened her inhibitions.

"Frank, when do you expect to make an honest woman of me?" whispered Belinda, keeping her eyes downcast for fear of what she might see in his.

Stiffening in his chair, Frank gently took his hand away from hers. Looking at his lover deeply in her eyes, he half-whispered to her, "Please don't bring this up now, Belinda. How many times must I tell you, darling? This is definitely not the right time for us to make future plans together. You know I want nothing more, but you will have to be patient for some time yet. I am sorry, but my hands are tied with the Society for the foreseeable future, and I cannot offer you anything permanent right now."

Belinda noticed his dancing eyes had lost their twinkle.

"At this rate, we will both be past it before you are ready," she retorted, looking unhappy and downcast.

"Darling Belinda, you have no faith in me at all. I have told you again and again that one day we will be together. I want this as much as you do. Please believe me," responded Frank quickly, taking her hand again.

Looking up and weakly smiling at him, Belinda answered quietly, "I do believe you, darling. I just feel that time is passing us by so quickly and neither of us are getting any younger."

Squeezing her hand, Frank, gazing at her, assured her, "Have patience, darling, I promise you; our time will come."

Smiling brighter now, Belinda replied, "Yes, of course, darling. I will not ask you again, I shall wait until you are ready."

"Tu sei il mio dolce bella," *(You are my sweet beautiful)* said Frank, smiling at her.

Excusing herself, Belinda got up from her chair and went in search of the ladies' powder room, situated in the hotel lobby.

James was thoroughly enjoying Jonathan's stag party. There were several people he knew, which made it all the more enjoyable. Beer and spirits flowed freely the whole evening, and he particularly loved the scantily dressed waitresses who expertly weaved their way through the noisy groups of men as they became more and more gregarious with the large amounts of alcohol they consumed.

After using the gentlemen's room in the hotel lobby, James felt hungry when he spotted the restaurant. A delicious smell of food filled his senses and he decided to have something to eat before drinking any more alcohol. Stepping into the Purple Sky Restaurant, James noticed how charming it was as the maître d' escorted him to a table for two, close to the back of the restaurant.

After ordering himself a medium rare fillet steak with French fries, James glanced around the restaurant, admiring the art deco theme. Raising a glass of cold water to his mouth, he almost dropped it. Blinking his eyes repeatedly, not believing what they were telling him, James thought he was seeing things, because partly hidden from view, at another small table, sat Gene Capalti. James reasoned with himself that Gene's flight must have been postponed as he distinctly remembered Gene telling him and Matt that he was flying back to New York early that morning.

Rising from his chair to make his presence known to the American, James stopped rigid in his tracks. Shocked and furiously blinking his eyes again in the dimness of the room, he saw entering the Purple Sky Restaurant, and making her way directly to Gene's table, Matt's wife, Belinda. With his mind working overtime and sinking back again into his chair, James held the menu in front of his face so as not to be discovered. Slowly pulling his smartphone from the inside breast pocket of his navy cashmere suit, he gingerly pointed it in the direction of the unsuspecting couple and stealthily he took a video of them as they gazed lovingly into each other's eyes. James was extremely excited about this bombshell that had fallen into his lap, although not quite sure what he should do about it. Deciding this would be his private secret for the time being, he knew he could use it to his advantage sometime in the future.

Belinda sat down opposite Gene. James, still hiding behind his menu, noticed the American reach across the table and take her hand, sensually pressing it to his mouth and kissing it.

"My God," muttered James to himself. "These two are besotted with each other." Racking his brain, he tried to fathom out how they had met when a waiter arrived with his main course. At almost the same time, Gene and Belinda got up from their seats and walked slowly out of the restaurant together, Gene with his arm protectively around Belinda's waist. With his eyes following their every movement, James could not help but think what a perfectly matched couple they made and how much they complemented each other.

As they disappeared from view, James' mind was racing. He knew for certain Matt had never mentioned Gene to Belinda. He himself could vouch for that. The

Society had sworn their Outer Circle Associates to complete secrecy. He could not tell Matt about what he had witnessed, even though he knew Matt had a lady friend tucked away somewhere in Putney. Although James felt he would be betraying Matt if he decided not to tell his partner and friend, an inner voice warned him to keep it to himself for now. He must have time to think about this when he was sober. The betting shops' turnover had immensely increased since they were in league with the Society; more like in league with the devil, he mused. But he did not want to bite the hand that fed him. Gene had to be treated with kid gloves if James and Matt were to continue making more money than either of them ever knew was possible.

James had almost forgotten about Jonathan Bartlett's stag party, but after paying for his dinner, which he hardly recalled eating, he returned to the bar lounge and joined in his friend's celebrations. As James threw himself into the fun surrounding him, he wondered what it was that Gene possessed that made women want to be with him. His mind flew fleetingly back to Isabelle and Venice, remembering how she sunk into Gene's outstretched arms at the open door of his hotel room.

I wonder whether Mrs Flynn is aware of what her boyfriend gets up to behind her back, sniggered James to himself as he swallowed down another pint of beer.

At the end of a rather rowdy stag party, the guests took their leave. James managed to get a lift back into London with a couple of Jonathan's work colleagues.

The next day, Matt was in the Soho betting shop when James came through the door late the following morning, looking tired and a little pale.

"Good morning, James. I can see you enjoyed yourself last night," said Matt, grinning.

"You missed a great stag last night, Matt; in more ways than one, I can tell you," uttered James, checking his appearance in the full-length wooden-framed mirror, which hang on the wall beside the gentleman's toilet.

"Yes, I would like to have gone, but you know I had a prior engagement," replied Matt, winking at James.

As James got into the swing of the busy day, Matt said to him, "So, what did I miss?"

James whistling under his breath and grinning, answered, "Oh, you would be surprised, my friend. It was a great stag party with plenty of luscious waitresses flittering about everywhere, serving champagne."

"Pity I couldn't make it; sounds like my kind of party," said Matt, taking his mobile phone out of his jacket pocket as it rang.

"Okay, Belinda, glad you had a good time with Tanya, see you later, babe," he said quietly, finishing the call.

James sniggered to himself, knowing now that Belinda had spent the night at the hotel with Gene Capalti.

Chapter 29
A Close Shave

On Monday morning, as Belinda arrived at the agency, Dawn and Freddie were already drinking hot coffee. Freddie jumped up as she came through the door and planted a kiss on both cheeks. Queenie wagged his little tail and ran towards Belinda, and she bent down to rub his furry tummy.

"Well, how did it go, darling?" Freddie asked, referring to her night with Frank on Friday.

"Amazing as always, thanks, Freddie," replied Belinda, slipping off her fake fur jacket and walking across to Dawn, who was busy reading emails at her desk. Belinda kissed Dawn on the cheek and asked how her weekend had gone with her lovely family. Belinda envied Dawn in many ways; her life was so organised and uncomplicated, her marriage so solid, and she knew Dawn was still in love with her husband Maurice and, of course, she adored her teenagers.

"I had a wonderful weekend, thank you, darling, but more to the point, how was Friday?" she questioned, looking into Belinda's eyes, as if searching for the truth.

Revealing all her girlie secrets about her night with Frank, Belinda giggled as Dawn uttered, "Yummy," and raised her eyes to the ceiling as a big smile spread across her pretty face. "You really must give him an ultimatum, Belinda, otherwise this affair will only ever be an affair," Dawn added quietly to Belinda as Freddie refilled their coffee cups.

"Oh, believe me, Dawn, I have tried and tried but he has told me again and again that I must be more patient. Frank's hands are tied at the moment with his job and it is not a good time for me to push him too much right now," she explained quickly, her eyes showing her true disappointment.

"Okay, darling, but please do be careful. I would not want to see you get hurt," said her friend, looking at her with concern before returning to the list of email messages waiting to be dealt with in her inbox.

During the course of the day, several lookalikes came into the agency to have their portfolios updated. Dawn had arranged for a highly recommended photographer to spend some days in the adjoining studio to encourage many of the lookalike and tribute acts to update their photographs and DVDs. Reggie Johnson, the number one Michael Jackson tribute act, had been the first to be photographed by Stefan Dufort, an amazing photographer who boasted royalty among his sitters.

The Helen Mirren lookalike was very happy to have the opportunity of getting her photographs updated and excitedly sat for Stefan directly after lunch. Tanya, looking amazingly like Pam Anderson, also arrived for her session with Stefan, and Lady Denise Ava, the Madonna tribute act, came rushing through the agency's door, apologising for her lateness due to the heavy London traffic. Stefan Dufort would most certainly enjoy photographing her, mused Belinda to herself.

In the middle of the afternoon, Jane, the agency's original top Marilyn Monroe lookalike, arrived chatting to Frank Parsons, the only really workable Sir Anthony Hopkins lookalike. Jane had been good friends with Dawn for some years since the first day she had been signed up by the agency as a lookalike.

Nowadays, she was also good friends with Belinda and probably confided more in her than Dawn, possibly because Belinda was also a lookalike and had worked with Jane many times. However, since the arrival of Kay Carney, the new top Marilyn Monroe lookalike, Jane had found her work opportunities had dwindled considerably and lately she was finding it difficult to live comfortably on her few lookalike jobs. Jane confided in Belinda that her mother, Brenda, was suffering with breast cancer and although she had been in remission, the consultant at the hospital had revealed that the cancer had returned and Brenda was to have more chemotherapy. Belinda's heart went out to Jane: she knew how close she and Brenda were; more like sisters than mother and daughter, possibly because Brenda had been barely seventeen years old when she had given birth as a single mother to her only child, Jane.

"Your mother is a real fighter, darling. After this next bout of chemotherapy, I am sure she will go into remission again," said Belinda gently to Jane, hoping to make her feel less anxious.

"I really hope so, Belinda," she replied crestfallen. "I really could not bear it if anything happened to her."

Placing her arm around Jane's shoulder, Belinda insisted the younger woman must try to be more positive and, of course, more than anything else, to pray. Jane gave Belinda a weak smile and nodded her head with its wonderful bleached blonde hair, as always, the replica of the real Ms Monroe.

Apart from her concerns and worries for her mother's health, Jane also confided to Belinda that her partner, Rick, seemed offish with her lately. She had decided he must be tired because he worked long hours as a croupier in one of London's most famous casinos on the Edgware Road. Belinda was already aware how disgruntled Rick was because Jane refused to take any holidays at all in case she missed a lookalike job. Jane told Belinda that Rick had threatened to go on holiday alone if she kept this nonsense up. "After all," he had spitefully sniggered to her, "most of the Marilyn jobs these days are going to the new girl, so there's no excuse to restrict yourself from taking a break every now and then." It had been a few years since they'd had a proper holiday and by hook or by crook, he would be having one, with or without her. There was a more serious problem brewing in Jane and Rick's relationship, which was making Rick more and more unhappy. Apparently, he wanted to start a family immediately and told Jane she should seriously think about it, considering her age. Jane had tearfully confided to Belinda that Rick's words had made her freeze because starting a family was the last thing on her mind right now, and for the foreseeable future.

After her photo shoot with the amazing Stefan Dufort, Jane left the agency and Belinda's fear that Rick would actually leave her friend if she continued to ignore his wishes seemed to be imminent.

Recently, Frank was missing Belinda more after each meeting with her, finding she was continually on his mind.

In the Venice arrivals lounge at Marco Polo Airport, Frank found his suitcase was one of the first to arrive on the baggage carousel. Within minutes, he was standing with his passport, ready to hand it to the serious looking female clerk behind the foreign arrivals desk. As he handed the clerk his passport, she appeared to react. Looking up to meet Frank's eyes, she spoke to him in broken English, while at the same time pressing a button under the desk.

"Would you kindly wait here for a moment please, Signor Lanzo? There are some people who are interested in speaking with you."

With his mind racing wildly through reasons why anybody in Venice would want to speak to him, Frank endeavoured unsuccessfully to get some information from the flustered young woman, when two men arrived, both looking very professional in dark suits.

"Good day, Signor Lanzo," greeted the shorter man of the two. "Would you please accompany us to the manager's office for a few minutes; just routine stuff, nothing to worry about, Signor" he added reassuringly.

Frank was completely taken aback and demanded to know what exactly this was all about.

The taller of the two men looked Frank squarely in the eye and answered, "All in good time, Signor Lanzo. This will only take a short while."

Frank was led into a small side room a short distance away.

"Please take a seat. We will try not to detain you for more than a few minutes," said the shorter man, pointing to a wooden chair beside a round, highly polished table.

Sitting down grudgingly, Frank took his wristwatch off and changed the hands to European time.

"Listen, I have no idea what this cloak and dagger stuff is all about, but I have somebody meeting me outside the airport imminently," demanded Frank, putting his watch back on his right wrist.

Almost immediately, the door opened and two airport officials entered: a rotund, bald man, probably in his sixties, accompanied by a younger fair-haired man.

"Good day, Signor Lanzo, I am Pietro Gabrini, Manager of Airport Security," he said, looking down at Frank, who was becoming very agitated about this intrusion of his plans.

Pietro continued, not taking his eyes off Frank. "Please allow me to apologise for this inconvenience to you, but we need to check your fingerprints once more."

"Why? What is wrong with my fingerprints?" demanded Frank, beginning to feel hot under the collar. "I have been visiting this part of Italy for many years and have never had anything like this happen before. I have very influential friends in this city, Signor Gabrini. Now, what is this all about?" Frank's voice rose in anger as he jumped up from the wooden chair.

"Signor Lanzo, please calm down and answer my questions. The sooner you do, the sooner we will be able to let you go about your business," soothed Pietro as if patronizing an unruly child.

Frank was beginning to get worried. Surely, he thought, this could have nothing to do with the diamond heist many years ago, but of course not. He had been taught as a young man how to temporarily make his fingerprints disappear for up to approximately thirty days, and he had kept to this procedure whenever he visited Venice, knowing that it was possible that somewhere recorded in the 'Unsolved' crime files, his original fingerprints were being kept.

"Okay, but can we get on with this, pronto? I have Count Luigi Boggia waiting for me outside," demanded Frank, sitting back down on the uncomfortable little chair.

Once the fingerprint task was completed, they were taken out of the office to be studied further. Pietro made a call on his mobile phone and gave orders to his security team for Count Luigi Boggia to be brought to the VIP lounge and given refreshments while he waited for Signor Lanzo. Smiling at Frank, who was by now feeling extremely hot under the collar, the Manager of Airport Security seemed to enjoy questioning Frank about his visits to Venice and whether he had ever been there in the early 1980s. Much to Frank's annoyance, this was all done in a smiling, patronising way and although this was not quite an interrogation, Frank felt that it was the next best thing.

"Well, Signor Lanzo," he smiled, "you are now free to go. Your fingerprints are, I am informed, non-existent. I suppose this was due to an accident of some kind?" he asked, eyebrows raised questioningly.

Looking directly at the manager, Frank dropped his voice menacingly. "Yes, a very bad accident, many years ago."

Pouting his lips, Pietro suddenly announced, "We apologise for any inconvenience caused to you, but of course you will understand we are doing our job."

On hearing this, Frank retorted angrily, "I have never been so humiliated in all my life! You will be hearing from my solicitor, Signor Gabrini, believe me!"

Still smiling as he shrugged his shoulders, Pietro placed a chubby hand on Frank's shoulder. "Oh, before you go, Signor Lanzo, do you know of, or have you ever heard of, an American gentleman by the name of Gene Capalti?"

Already halfway out of his wooden chair, Frank sat back down again and, without flickering an eyelash, he looked Pietro Gabrini squarely in the face and asked brazenly, "Gene who?" Then, getting up and strolling confidently to the door, he turned and added, "Sorry, Signor Gabrini, can't help you, never heard of the guy."

Then he was gone.

As Frank closed the door of the manager's office behind him, he was unaware of three sets of eyes who had been watching and listening to his encounter with Pietro Gabrini. They were safely hidden behind a one-way mirror. The three men turned and looked at each other quizzically. Two of them were the polizia, Andrea and Mario, who had accompanied Belinda and Frank to the Main Civic Hospital some months before. The third man was Adam.

"Okay, boss," said Mario, touching Andrea on the shoulder. "This American is definitely not your diamond thief of years ago. His fingerprints, or lack thereof, have just proved his innocence, even if they have been tampered with!"

Andrea shrugged his shoulders, and frowning, replied. "He is a sly one, Signor Lanzo."

Secretly, Adam was happy about the outcome of this situation, because being extremely fond of Belinda and genuinely wanting only the best for his dear friend, he also knew that Frank was now her only real chance of happiness.

Chapter 30
La Traviata

Count Luigi Boggia smiled while he listened intently as Frank relayed to him exactly what happened at Marco Polo Airport.

"Of course, Signor Gabrini must be aware that it is possible you had messed about with your fingerprints for obvious reasons," offered the Count, as Frank finished talking.

"I guess most people know this is possible," Frank said nonchalantly. "The point is, my present fingerprints do not belong to Gene Capalti," which made the two friends laugh together.

"Come, my dear friend. It is time for us to eat," said the Count, taking Frank's arm and guiding him towards a quiet Venetian square. "I have booked us at Osteria Farfalla. I know how you love this restaurant."

Frank smiled appreciatively. "Ah, Butterfly Tavern, wonderful choice. You are a man of taste."

Count Luigi Boggia did not have to prove to the world that he was indeed a real titled Count. You need only to glance at this elegant gentleman to know he had the great fortune of being born into Italian notability. The nobility of Italy comprised individuals and their families recognised by sovereigns, such as the Holy Roman Emperor, the Holy See, kings of Italy or certain other Italian kings and sovereigns, as members of a class of persons officially enjoying hereditary privileges, which distinguished them from other persons and families. Count Luigi Francesco Umberto Boggia arrived to his privileged position in life some sixty-nine years before.

An extremely handsome and tall man of slim build, it was his black hair, now turning grey at the temples, that gave him such a distinguished look, together with his Van Dyke goatee. His eyes were of the palest blue-grey, rivalling the Venetian winter skies. Class and style oozed from his every pore and his choice in cologne was breathtaking. Single again now at this time in his life, having divorced three wives during the last thirty years, the Count had two daughters and one son, all from his union with his first wife, Alessa. His children were now in their early to late thirties and adored their charismatic and charming Papa.

The Count and Frank enjoyed a wonderful dinner at Osteria Farfalla, a typical Venetian restaurant, offering traditional dishes, giving diners the chance to savour the authentic and natural flavours. The atmosphere of the restaurant was simple and elegant, and there was a small private dining room for business lunches or more intimate gatherings. The Count had booked this room of privacy for himself and Frank. If Osteria Farfalla was good enough for a former Italian Prime Minister and the Secretary of the Treasury, then it was good enough for Count Luigi Francesco Umberto Boggia and his dining partner, Signor Frank Lanzo.

After long business discussions and a delicious dinner, the Count told Frank he had secured four tickets for this evening's performance of La Traviata at the Teatro La Fenice. Frank raised his eyebrows again in appreciation when the Count informed him he had asked Isabelle and another beautiful woman to join them.

"I know how you love Isabelle's company, my friend, so I took the liberty of calling her. She agreed immediately," smiled Count Luigi Boggia, leaning towards Frank and winking at him knowingly. "I myself will have the pleasure of escorting Countess Sophia Adessi. We will collect the ladies for pre-theatre drinks," added the Count, still smiling.

Frank slightly stiffened in his chair. Yes, he liked the beautiful Isabelle and they had known each other intimately in the past, but in the last few months his only sexual thoughts and longings had been for Belinda. Frank had always been a womaniser and often had more than one affair going on at the same time in different parts of the world, but lately, he reasoned with himself, either he was getting old or he was definitely in love because he felt happy to wait for his lovely Belinda.

The Count looked puzzled at Frank's reaction. "Is everything acceptable to you, my friend?" he asked, looking at Frank questionably.

"Yes, yes, of course. I look forward to seeing the wonderful La Traviata and, of course, the beautiful ladies," replied Frank, not wanting to appear ungrateful or to upset his very dear friend.

Teatro La Fenice, the Phoenix Opera House, is one of the most famous and renowned landmarks in the history of Italian theatre, as well as those in Europe. The evening was simply amazing. Frank had always adored La Traviata and it was always wonderful to see Isabelle. The Countess

Sophia Adessi, a stunningly beautiful woman in her early sixties, and Count Luigi Boggia were very close friends and spent much of the evening giggling together.

Frank was staying with the Count at his impressive Secondo Piano Nobile apartment in one of the best Grand Canal Palazzi in the city, which was not only luxurious but also coupled with absolutely mesmerising Grand Canal views. The Count's private rooms were exquisite and his guests slept in luxurious bedrooms further down the hall. While the ladies accompanied each other to the powder room in the interval, Frank explained to the Count that he would rather not entertain Isabelle for the rest of the night once back at the Count's apartments.

"Are you unwell, Frank?" asked Count Luigi Boggia, looking concerned at his friend.

"No, not unwell, but extremely exhausted, and I need to sleep alone this evening, if you don't mind," replied Frank, feeling embarrassed like a child under the Count's curious gaze.

"Oh, but of course, Frank, you are your own man. You must follow your own heart, my friend," said the Count, smiling understandingly.

By the end of the evening, Frank had made his excuses to Isabelle, who was notably upset at not spending the night with her oldest but very sensual lover. Count Luigi Boggia decided he too would not invite Countess Sophia Adessi back to his apartments this time but insisted on having a nightcap with Frank. When the ladies had been escorted safely to their individual homes, Count Luigi Boggia poured two glasses of sambuca and asked Frank quietly, "My dear friend, tell me, are you sick or in love?"

Frank almost choked on his first sip of sambuca.

"Where the hell did that come from?" he shot at the Count.

"Now, now, Frank, this is me, Luigi, your best friend in all the world. I know you, and I know it must be one of two things: either you are very sick, or you are in love with another woman, for you to turn the beautiful Isabelle down. My dear friend, which one is it?" asked the Count soothingly, sitting down and taking a sip of his sambuca, as he stretched out his long legs and allowed his taste buds to savour the aniseed as it slid slowly down his throat.

Frank tried to blame his lack of interest in Isabelle on tiredness but in the end he had to confide in the Count and relay to him how he had fallen deeply in love with a married woman.

"Oh, my God! A married woman, Frank! Be very careful, my friend, this can only bring you trouble," exclaimed Count Luigi, sitting up straight and shaking his elegant head solemnly at Frank. "Soon, you must reveal to me who this love of your life is. But now I must explain to you a business proposition you might find very interesting," added the Count, tapping the side of his fine Roman nose.

Frank's curiosity was swiftly aroused and, leaning closer to his aristocratic friend, he looked him directly in the eye as he whispered, "I am all ears."

Count Luigi Boggia graced Frank with one of his beguiling smiles and whispered back, "Pensa diamanti, amico mio." *(Think diamonds, my friend.)*

Chapter 31
New York, New York

"I love this lady," announced Dawn as she replaced the telephone on its cradle. "Another prestigious job for Kay; she is certainly making her mark as the top Monroe. New York this time, lucky girl."

Belinda looked up from her computer and whistled. "How fabulous; I am jealous. I would give anything to go to New York," she sighed.

"Yes, I bet you would," replied Dawn, letting out a knowing giggle. "You could pay an unexpected visit to Mr Lanzo," she suggestively added.

Belinda let out a throaty laugh. "Oh, what a great idea! Maybe I could chaperone Ms Monroe on this trip?"

Dawn, with a twinkle in her eye, retorted, "Ms Monroe would have to chaperone you, my darling, more like."

Belinda giggled, but deep down she envied Kay, and she was not the only one, simply because the Marilyn Monroe character was in great demand all over the world, unlike many other lookalikes. How Belinda would love to visit New York and surprise Frank, although she had no idea where he lived, apart from that it was close to Central Park. They had never discussed exactly where he did live in the Big Apple, and as far as she knew he was divorced and living alone, although his son would occasionally stay with him.

Dawn's voice interrupted Belinda's thoughts. "I really do wish that Jane secures a Monroe job soon. Fingers crossed another one will come up while Kay is away in New York so that it can definitely go to Jane," she said, picking up the telephone and dialling Kay's number to relay the exciting news to her.

Belinda was becoming exceedingly worried about Jane. The girl had so many problems and worries to contend with at the moment: her mother's health; her troubled love life; and now, to top it all off, Kay coming along and winning most of the Marilyn Monroe tribute and lookalike jobs. Kay had always enjoyed life; the attention she received every day, purely because she looked like the amazing Marilyn Monroe. It was like a drug to her.

Kay had been to New York many times in her life. Her father was in fact a native New Yorker, although he had married a Scottish woman and lived in London. Even though the marriage had broken down a long time before, the couple stayed together, possibly for the sake of their three young children and partly through financial convenience. In time, as the children became adults, Kay's parents had divorced and both had remarried simultaneously. Kay always tried to get along with both couples.

Kay thought this latest lookalike job in New York was just amazing. A supersized version of the famous image of Marilyn, her skirt billowing atop of the New York City subway grate, was on display outside the Times Square subway station. This was part of an exhibit that featured many other Monroe photographs on view inside the 42nd Street station. Kay's contract stipulated she was to stand alongside the famous image for three hours every day for one week. Kay had several friends who lived in New York; most of them were homosexual and she adored being in their company. They in turn adored being seen out with the finest Monroe lookalike on both sides of the pond.

The New Yorkers, and indeed the many tourists, were very impressed with Kay as she stood proudly and very professionally beside the giant billboard of the greatest icon who ever lived. Many of them told Kay she looked exactly like Marilyn while the mobiles clicked at her continuously, taking photograph after photograph, each snapper wanting to keep this fabulous apparition in front of them to show friends and family. On the first day of Kay's job, as her white dress, the replica of Marilyn's, billowed in unison with the famous icon's billboard situated over the subway grate, several men of all ages asked to take her to dinner, either after she finished her job for the day or later that same evening. Kay accepted two of her admirers' invitations; although still married to Charles Cooper, Kay occasionally acted as if she were a single woman.

"What the eyes do not see, the heart does not grieve over," she reasoned with herself. As far as she was concerned, she had given Charles the best years of her younger life but now she intended to taste some of the other pleasures that were awaiting her and, of course, the world was her oyster.

As the second day of her contracted lookalike job came to an end, Kay was collected by the client's representative and driven back to her hotel. The female representative offered to show Kay around Manhattan that evening but

Kay politely declined the offer, explaining that she had already accepted an invitation from a friend for dinner. This, of course, was not true. The invitation had not come from one of her friends, but from one of her admirers she had met only the day before while working. Kay felt quite confident to spend the evening with this particular gentleman; she found him very exciting. Not only was he handsome, exquisitely dressed and well mannered, but he was wealthy; having a great nose for money, Kate could certainly smell it on Paul Shay.

After her lengthy pampering, Kay decided to call Charles and tell him she would be out late that evening with her gay friends and that he should not call her until the following evening. Charles knew most of Kay's homosexual friends in London and New York, and felt confident they would look after her and make sure she arrived back at the hotel safely at the end of the night.

As the receptionist's voice informed her that Mr Paul Shay had arrived and was waiting for her in the foyer, Kay picked up her white mohair jacket and checked her appearance in the full-length mirror. Always confident and having a high opinion of herself, Kay knew this evening she looked even more fabulous in her tight, low-cut black dress, the hemline several inches above her knees, with black lacy tights encasing her slim legs, teamed with black suede high-heeled shoes. Wiping red lipstick off one of her white porcelain teeth, Kay whispered to her reflection, "Move over, Marilyn; tonight you have strong competition."

Paul could not take his grey eyes off the beautiful apparition walking towards him; this creature was amazing, he decided, and almost as fabulous as the real Marilyn Monroe. Kay, with her usual flamboyancy, strutted straight to her dinner date as he got up from the reproduction Queen Anne chair he had been sitting in, patiently waiting for her in the hotel foyer.

As Kay reached him, Paul smiled down at her, showing white, even teeth. "You look amazing," he said to Kay as he placed a hand under her right elbow and led her out of the hotel entrance and into the warm, spring evening air on Fifth Avenue. Paul had booked dinner at one of New York's trendiest restaurants, where they could also dance the night away if they so desired. The Silver Unicorn proved the perfect venue to entertain Kay for an evening. This club livens up the mood with the talented all-female bartender staff, who not only hula hoop and dance on the bar, but also spend a good part of the evening swinging around above the bar, scantily dressed for the enjoyment of the customers, especially the gentlemen.

Kay loved this venue as soon as she strutted in on Paul's arm, whom she noticed was well known here. The whole place went suddenly quiet; all eyes were on the couple as they were shown to a dimly lit corner of the restaurant by the maître d', to a highly polished, small square table set for two.

Being a real gentleman, Paul read the menu out for Kay and she graciously allowed him to order for her. Along with Paul's choice of dinner, he ordered a bottle of the best champagne and after four glasses, Kay became very tipsy and flirty with Paul.

While busy in the agency, Belinda received a text message on her mobile from Frank, letting her know he was back home again in New York. Freddie came swanning into the office and broke Belinda's train of thought.

"Morning darling," greeted Freddie as he allowed Queenie to jump from his arms onto the floor.

"Oh! Good morning, Freddie, and of course, little Queenie," replied Belinda, grinning from ear to ear, eyes sparkling. Freddie and Queenie had always been able to make Belinda feel happy, and once again she silently praised Dawn for making the decision to employ Freddie.

"Are you okay? You look flushed, sweetheart?" remarked Freddie, closely watching Belinda. "Not coming down with the flu, I hope?" he added, reaching out and touching her forehead.

Smiling secretly, Belinda assured him she was fine. To Belinda's relief, Freddie seemed to have settled down with Dodgy Rodger again. It had been quite a few months since the two men had moved in together and they still seemed besotted with each other. Continuing to deal with the incoming emails, Belinda mused to herself that it looked like there could be another invitation to a same-sex marriage in the near future.

In New York, Kay's mouth felt like sawdust, her head throbbed and she felt quite dizzy, having to force her heavy eyes to open, as she gradually took in her surroundings. Where was she? This was not her hotel suite. Kay started to panic, becoming frightened. Moving gingerly, she slipped off the king-sized bed, and slowly her brain remembered.

Paul practically begged her to have a nightcap with him in his very fashionable penthouse after they had left the Silver Unicorn. Scattered about the floor, Kay noticed her black dress and satin underwear. Gradually, her foggy memory begun to clear and she recalled the night before, feeling quite tipsy but agreeing to have just one last drink with him. This was Paul's penthouse, but where was he? What time was it? So many questions were running through her bewildered mind. Then she realised with horror that, try as she may, she could not remember anything at all after having that last drink with Paul. Glancing around, her hand automatically went to her private parts; she felt a little sore there and she stumbled towards the bathroom to check herself. Taking a quick glance in the mirror, which covered the whole side of one of the bathroom walls, Kay was alarmed to see she had what looked like love bites on her neck, trailing down to her breasts. Rushing out of the bathroom, she checked the time on the bedside clock; it was almost midday and she was due at work in a couple of hours. Kay grabbed her handbag, which lay on the floor beside the dishevelled bed, and was relieved to find all her personal belongings were still there: her money, her hotel key and her mobile phone. As she returned to the bathroom, her eye caught sight of a sheet of paper taped to the screen of the large television set in the corner of this beautiful room with its Queen Anne-style furniture. Paul certainly had taste, she thought, reading the short note, which he had left for her.

It read: 'Wonderful evening, Ms Monroe. We must do it again soon. I will be in contact, Paul.'

Kay took a quick shower, again noticing how red the love bites were on her neck and breasts. She hoped she could cover them with make-up ready for her lookalike job. As Kay showered, she again became aware of the soreness in her vagina, and on checking she found the area was quite raw looking. Fear gripped her throat as she could not remember having had sex last night but then she could not remember anything after that last drink. She promised to herself to get some answers from Paul when she spoke to him later.

When Kay was satisfied with the way she looked, doing her best to cover up the marks on her neck and breasts, she let herself out of the penthouse and called a yellow cab to take her to her hotel to prepare properly for the next part of her contract.

The hours of work that day seemed to drag on and on, and her head was still causing her pain. When at last her contracted hours for the day were complete, Kay was very relieved indeed. Checking the messages on her mobile phone, Kay wanted to see whether Paul had tried to contact her. He had not.

Kay returned to her hotel to sleep and recover. Sleeping fitfully for some hours, it was already dark outside as Kay opened her tired eyes. She felt quite famished as she climbed out of bed and checked her mobile for missed calls. She was relieved to see Paul had left her a text message stating that he was hoping she would be free to have dinner with him the following evening and he would call her later to make arrangements. Kay was desperate to find out exactly what happened the night before and she decided to call him back straightaway.

After a couple of rings, Paul answered. Although he was happy to hear from Kay, she felt he sounded a little nervous. Questions about the night before came spilling out of her mouth. Still in his office, Paul explained to Kay he could not talk at the moment but assured her nothing untoward happened apart from her driving him crazy with desire. Swiftly ending the conversation, he told her he would collect her from her hotel the following evening and they could have a long chat over dinner. Having no option but to agree with what he proposed, Kay rang reception to order dinner for one in her room. This evening, she would take a long hot bath, relax and have an early night.

The following evening, Paul arrived at Kay's hotel reception as she walked out of the lift. Paul, already standing, walked towards her, arms outstretched, a big smile on his handsome face. On seeing him, Kay caught her breath, partly attraction and partly fear; she could not quite make out what she was feeling about this person. Paul did most of the talking while he drove Kay to another very fashionable restaurant, Bobo, a very glamorous East Midtown eatery, where the gorgeous setting and beautiful crowd are in keeping with its pricey and high-quality catch. Paul particularly appreciated the bar scene in this upmarket restaurant and he hoped the beautiful Kay would appreciate it too.

During the car ride to the restaurant, Kay asked Paul what he had given her to drink the evening before last because she could not remember a single thing after drinking it. Paul assured her she was indeed tipsy but she was more than willing to be extra nice to him and he also assured her she made a real play for him. Kay told him she was very upset about the love bites on her body and she was shocked a grown man would act like a teenager. Paul apologised profusely but added he found her so sexy, he could not help himself. Kay's inflated ego accepted his explanation but she had decided not to drink any alcohol whatsoever this evening.

As the couple enjoyed each other's company at Bobo, little did Kay realise that Paul Shay had indeed surreptitiously drugged her alcoholic drink two nights before. As Paul had kissed her neck and began to remove her tight black dress, she did not hear the front door open, nor had she been aware that one of Paul's friends tiptoed quietly into the room, video camera at the ready.

Chapter 32
Discovered

Sergie arrived in London early one April morning to replace Gene (Frank), who had taken some time off for a well-deserved rest. Frank had been informed by the Society that within a couple of weeks, he would be assigned to deal with high-powered delicate business in Antwerp and he was to be accompanied by Count Luigi Boggia. Frank was already aware of this as he and the Count had discussed it while he was last in Venice, but neither had any idea exactly when they would be expected to undertake this delicate mission. In one way, Frank was pleased to be busy as it would help keep his mind from continually thinking of Belinda and how miserable he felt without her. He reminisced often about their exotic lovemaking and how, after all this time, they were still crazy about each other. This was a most unusual sentiment for Frank, and deep down inside, he knew he had fallen in love with Belinda. He had been waiting for her all his life.

Matt and James were happy to have Sergie back again to oversee the accounts of all the betting shops. The businesses had been doing extremely well, especially last month during Cheltenham week; life was, indeed, very good. They found Sergie's jovial manner uplifting and amusing. They were earlier informed that Gene could not visit London due to unforeseen commitments elsewhere but that Sergie would replace him, as he had successfully done in the past.

After collecting Sergie from London Airport, James stopped for dinner with the American on their way back to the Soho shop. Sergie explained to James that Gene was due to fly to an undisclosed destination within the following week or so to deal with very high-powered business for the Society and they were adamant that Gene was well rested before he left New York, hence his cancelled visit to London.

"Mind you," offered Sergie, more to himself than to his companion, "he is forever flying here, there and everywhere for the Society, and let's face it, James, none of us are getting any younger. All this jet-setting takes its toll in the end, buddy boy, that's for sure."

"Gene is indeed a lucky man," said James, winking slyly at Sergie. "He certainly gets about," he added, grinning widely, which had Sergie nodding in agreement as they continued to enjoy their fillet steak dinners, washed down by Sergie's favourite vino.

Freddie sensed Belinda's despair. She had confided in him of how she could not bear to wait so long before seeing Frank again. Freddie sympathised with her and decided to cheer his friend up, arranging to take her out to dinner the following evening, inviting Tanya along too.

Freddie, Tanya and Belinda arrived at Joe Allen in Covent Garden. All had dined there before and thoroughly enjoyed the whole buzzing experience. Unfortunately, Freddie's lover, Dodgy Rodger, had to work late and could not make up the foursome.

"Never mind. All the more attention from the ladies for me," quipped Freddie. Joe Allen was forever busy, no matter what time one arrived. This stylish American dining venue opened in 1977 in the heart of Covent Garden, and was always fully booked with theatregoers, artists, journalists and performers alike. Everyone seemed to enjoy the relaxed, casual feel throughout. Rumour had it that a big movie star had bought the site where Joe Allen stood to build a hotel, and the famous American dining venue would have to find another home.

"I love the atmosphere here," remarked Tanya, as they were shown to their table in the middle of the large dining area. "No wonder it attracts an eclectic clientele of the West End's young and trendy crowd," she added, glancing around at the full, buzzing restaurant.

"Well, we are young and trendy, are we not?" asked Freddie, waving his arms dramatically about in the air, causing his two lady companions to giggle out loud.

As the evening wore on, Tanya and Freddie listened intently as Belinda brought them up to date on her relationship with Frank. They were concerned for her, not only because she knew little about Frank's life in New York, but also because they knew if Matt ever found out about Belinda's affair, he would never accept it. Matt was a real controller and would never allow another man to take his woman away from him, even though he had the occasional affair or fling behind her back.

During dinner, Tanya complained about how the demand for her lookalike character, Pam Anderson, was very slow these days and that, unfortunately, she would not be able to give up her pole dancing job just yet until demand for her character picked up again. Of course, she knew this was unlikely to happen as Pam Anderson was not topical at the moment, and had not been so for a little while now. Both Freddie and Belinda sympathised with her but they too, as lookalikes, had similar worries. It was a well-known fact in the business that to earn enough money to live comfortably on the proceeds, you had to portray the most iconic of characters and even then, it was not definite the work would come in regularly.

"Hey, Belinda, darling! Lovely to see you, sweetheart!" Belinda heard the familiar voice of her friend, Simon, his attire amazing as always, as he came up to her table and stood there grinning down at them.

"Simon, I didn't realise you were here. Where is Bryanne?" exclaimed Belinda excitedly, looking around the vast restaurant.

Simon bent down and planted a kiss on Belinda's cheek and pointed across the room to a large table where a smiling Bryanne sat, white quiff bouncing as he waved profusely at her. Belinda introduced Simon to Tanya and Freddie, who raised his eyebrows in approval.

Asking after Eileen, Belinda's friend from the Olde Tyme Music Hall who had attended his and Bryanne's wedding in February, Simon suggested, "We really must make arrangements to meet up with you and Eileen soon, darling. Tonight, Bryanne and I are out celebrating with some old friends." Bending down and kissing her once again, Simon turned to Tanya and Freddie and, grinning broadly said, "Nice to meet you both. Have a lovely evening," and he strolled back to his waiting dining companions.

Freddie watched Simon walk back to his table and whistled quietly under his breath.

"What a gorgeous hunk. I could easily fall in love with him," he whispered to the ladies.

"Please!" gasped Belinda. "You are supposed to be head over heels in love with Dodgy Rodger!"

"Well, of course I am," retorted Freddie, fidgeting in his chair. "But no harm in window shopping, is there, darling?" He looked longingly at Simon and Bryanne's table. Raising her eyebrow, Tanya glanced at Belinda and the two women burst out laughing.

During the evening, while making her way back from the ladies room, Belinda stopped at Simon and Bryanne's table.

"Here she is!" announced the effervescent Bryanne as he jumped up from his chair. "The most glamorous female in London, well, apart from me, that is!" Everyone around the table burst out laughing at his remark and, giggling, Belinda kissed Bryanne on both cheeks. Wishing them all a wonderful evening, she made her way back through the crowded restaurant towards Freddie and Tanya, who were busy chatting together.

Meanwhile back in New York, Paul and Kay had enjoyed their evening at Bobo, and Paul had tried several times, unsuccessfully, during the evening to persuade Kay to have champagne. But she was not feeling her best and, much to his disappointment, Kay stubbornly refused to drink alcohol all evening. Paul Shay was an opportunist and had already seen the DVD his conspirator had taken of himself and Kay having sex a few nights before, unbeknown to Kay who had been completely spaced out due to the laced nightcap he had given her earlier. Paul had decided to sell this special DVD to the highest bidder; one in particular at the top of his list was a famous German company. Paul reasoned that once Kay had returned to London, she would be none the wiser, and besides, he decided the DVD did not show her face completely. Kay had been cleverly filmed from sideways on, or with her eyes closed and part of her face hidden. Paul could still see a strong resemblance to Marilyn Monroe and he knew only too well that, eventually, fingers would point at Kay Carney due to the fact that she was becoming quite a celebrity worldwide.

Her last evening in New York saw the client's representatives escort Kay to dinner at a very exciting restaurant. The clients were so impressed with Kay that she had been informed they would most definitely book her again and it was highly likely it would be quite soon because they had a big function coming up and her presence there, as Marilyn Monroe, would delight and enthral their many high-quality guests. Kay was becoming used to everyone vying for her presence portraying the iconic star that it was no surprise to her at all that this major New York client would want to use her services again. After all, she was indeed the number one Marilyn Monroe lookalike, not only in the UK and Europe, but now also in the USA.

After a sleepless night flight, the following morning saw Kay arriving back in London, and that afternoon she telephoned Dawn to report back on the New York job. Dawn adored Kay. She was her biggest earner and most celebrated lookalike of all time now. Having always loved a winner, Dawn especially loved one who was making big money for her beloved agency and who, in her opinion and many others, was the most amazing Marilyn Monroe lookalike ever. The whole world seemed to want a piece of Kay Carney, just like they had wanted a piece of Marilyn Monroe all those years ago.

Touching briefly on her experience with Paul when she popped into the agency a few days later, Kay was not surprised that both Dawn and Belinda lectured her on the perils of drinking alone with strangers. Belinda sensed Kay was worrying about something, so when Kay was ready to leave Belinda offered to walk with her to her car. As the two women descended the agency's stairs and stepped onto the busy London streets, Belinda asked Kay if there was anything troubling her.

"Of course not," giggled Kay nervously, but Belinda could see in the younger woman's eyes there was something on her mind.

"Kay, you know Dawn and I are not just your agents. We are also your friends, and want to make sure you are completely safe at all times," said Belinda gently, trying not to lecture the girl as they reached Kay's parked car. "Please remember, you can always talk to either of us about anything, anything at all. We are here to help, and are both very broad minded indeed," she added.

"Yes, of course, Belinda, thank you. I do know that and appreciate it," replied Kay, clicking open her car door. They kissed each other on the cheek and said their goodbyes.

Chapter 33
Antwerp Diamond Heist

awn had taken a week's holiday from the agency as her parents, who lived in Cornwall, were to spend some time with Dawn and her family in London. Freddie agreed to work every day to cover Dawn's absence, which helped Belinda and earned him extra money. But the week seemed to drag and Belinda found herself becoming more and more depressed, continually thinking of Frank and wondering what he was doing. Her body longed for his caress and she found herself daydreaming about their sensual lovemaking. Freddie and little Queenie were a source of comfort for Belinda during these sad times, and she thanked Freddie several times for working the whole week to help her out and to keep her company.

"Think nothing of it, my beauty," said Freddie, winking at her. "Queenie and I love being here with you, and besides, I am always happy to make extra money," he added, filling the kettle.

Requests for tribute acts and lookalikes were trickling in slowly, but by the end of the morning Belinda was encouraged to see several possible jobs had been received.

"Anything for the illustrious Liberace?" Freddie asked nonchalantly.

"Sorry, darling, not this time, but hey, chin up! You know how fickle and unpredictable this business is," soothed Belinda, knowing perfectly well how Freddie was feeling because she too was hoping for more work.

"Yes, I know," agreed Freddie. "I really must be more patient. Something will come up shortly, I am sure," he added, clipping the pale blue leash onto Queenie's diamanté collar. "Lunch time, Belinda, come along, let us go cheer ourselves up at the Red Bull."

"Great idea, Freddie, I am famished, let's go," replied Belinda, following Freddie and Queenie out of the agency's heavy door.

Later, back at the agency and halfway through the afternoon, they heard a tap on the door, and as Belinda and Freddie looked up simultaneously, Kevin, the Boy George tribute act, swanned into the office, followed closely by his black belt karate bodyguard and lover, Wayne.

"Kevin!" squealed Belinda, which made little Queenie jump up and run across to Kevin.

"Hi guys! Just popped in as we were in the neighbourhood," giggled Kevin, taking off his sunglasses and eyeing Freddie up and down as Freddie smiled shyly at him, pouting his lips.

"Kevin, you must have a crystal ball or something," joked Belinda, getting up from her chair and planting a kiss on his highly painted cheeks.

"Well, of course I have, silly girl," answered Kevin, bending down and rubbing little Queenie's furry tummy.

"We have a request for you that has literally just come in, and here you are, turning up out of the blue," enthused Belinda.

"Yes, I was about to telephone you for your availability," added Freddie shyly.

"Well, I saved you the price of a phone call, darling," laughed Kevin, pursing his lips at Freddie, who blushed under the gaze of the notorious Boy George lookalike.

"Okay, spill the beans, old girl, where is this job?" he asked, walking to Belinda's desk.

"It sounds like fun, actually," offered Belinda. "The client is asking for a George Michael tribute act and yourself for an AIDS gala to be held at The Grosvenor Hotel, Park Lane next month. They have requested that you sing a couple of numbers each straight after the dinner and speeches before the disco starts," she added, handing Kevin the email.

"Check my diary, Wayne, am I available?" Kevin asked, looking at Wayne who had been stroking Queenie again, now laying on his back with his little legs in the air.

"You are free that day, Kevin, but you have a tribute show the following evening in Birmingham, remember?" stressed Wayne, looking up from the diary.

"That is close," exclaimed Kevin. "Never mind, we will drive up to Birmingham the following afternoon and I can sleep in the back of the car," he reasoned, looking around the room for approval.

"Excellent, I will inform the client you are available," said a delighted Belinda.

"Hey, Freddie, why don't you come with us to the gala? I can pass you off as my dresser. That would be okay with the agency, wouldn't it, Belinda?" asked Kevin, turning his small blue eyes questioningly at her.

"I can't see why not," replied Belinda. "But it is up to Freddie whether he would like to join you or not," she answered, looking at Freddie who had a big grin on his face.

Nodding his head, he uttered huskily, "Oh, yes please, I would love to."

"Right, that is settled then. Must go, have things to do and people to see," exclaimed Kevin, striding towards the door with Wayne following him, and little Queenie following Wayne. "See you soon, Belinda, darling, be happy. Freddie, we will meet you there. Make sure you dress flamboyantly; can't have you letting the side down now, can we?" giggled Kevin, raising an eyebrow as he put his sunglasses back on. "See ya," he called out, and he and Wayne were gone.

Freddie, clapping his hands gleefully, yelled out, "Yes!"

Frank flew from New York direct to Malpensa International Airport in Milan, Italy. On arrival, he was met by Count Luigi Boggia's bodyguard and chauffeur Alessandro Longo. Alessandro, now in his late fifties, had become the Count's closest confidant after his services were awarded to the Count by the Society, who had recommended Signor Longo very highly to Count Luigi Boggia. Alessandro was of short and stocky build, typical of his Sicilian heritage. He had lived most of his life in southern Italy, apart from the year he spent in New York as a young man. His dark brown eyes missed nothing, taking in everything and anyone in their focus. His hands were the size of shovels. In his younger days, he had the potential to become a talented boxer and dabbled in the vicious boxing world until he had become an Associate of the Society. A divorced father of four, Alessandro had now made it his life's work looking out for, and keeping safe, Count Luigi Boggia, whom he held in very high regard.

Frank had never met Alessandro before but he knew of him and how valuable he was to the Count. On the other hand, Alessandro had heard many good things about Frank and he was immensely impressed by what he had heard.

The two men shook hands warmly in greeting and drove towards the wealthy Basiglio, a commune or municipality in the province of Milan in the region of Lombardy, to Count Luigi Boggia's opulent apartment in the village Cascina Vione. Once they had reached their destination, the Count kissed Frank on both cheeks and they hugged each other in sincere greeting.

In the following days, all three had much to discuss regarding their trip to Antwerp. The Society had decided that Frank was to fly to Milan, meet up with the Count and Signor Longo, and they would all drive from Milan to Bern, Switzerland, through Luxembourg, before reaching Brussels and onward to their destination of Antwerp, the Diamond centre of the world. Once in Antwerp, the men would be the guests of Maurice Englert, a Jewish jeweller who was also an Associate of the Society. Maurice, a slim, smartly dressed gentlemen, wearing his Jewish features with pride, his bald pate accentuating his small green eyes and aquiline nose, lived in the Jewish Quarter and rented a small office in the Diamond Centre. Maurice was also a polyglot and spoke several languages fluently; this was one of his many talents.

As far as the authorities were concerned, the visiting gentlemen were in Antwerp to hold an old friends' reunion with Maurice, since all had worked together years before in

New York and had not seen each other in a very long time. It had been arranged for them to stay with Maurice at his large five-bedroomed home for the entire length of their visit, giving them sufficient time to survey the Diamond Centre's surroundings for themselves. Maurice knew the area like the back of his hand. He had lived there for several years and knew the daily comings and goings of the many diamond merchants, he being one of them.

It was arranged that Verna, Maurice's beloved wife, would go away to visit her sister in Brussels, knowing she would be in the way once her husband's visitors had arrived. Verna knew very little about her husband's visitors, only what he had told her. Apparently, Maurice had known these men from his years spent in New York long before she and Maurice had met. The one thing she did know was that her husband and his visitors had all been good friends and, over the passing years, had remained so. In actual fact, Maurice had never met any of his visitors before. Of course, the Society had made sure all four Associates were fully briefed on the full background of each other. Maurice was fully aware that Count Luigi Boggia and Frank were master thieves, even now in their latter years. They were highly talented in their individual fields and, with regard to Alessandro, he was probably one of the best drivers in the whole of Europe, controlling his car in the same way a proficient rider controlled his horse. Very few other people could outdrive Alessandro Longo.

Maurice, after greeting his visitors warmly, showed them to their respective bedrooms. He had decided to put on a traditional Belgium meal, consisting of mussels and eel in green sauce for his guests. In the unfortunate event that one of them might have a fish allergy, he had also made a classic French dish transformed with a delicate Belgian touch.

Dinner was a great success, and the men swallowed it down with excellent wines. For the remainder of the evening, the business of why these men were together here in Antwerp was discussed, maps pored over, ideas, suggestions and concerns listened to, and talked through; the expertise of the four experts coming to fruition.

Frank looked up from the large walnut table, covered with photographs of vaults, which lay two floors beneath the Antwerp Diamond Centre, his dancing brown eyes sparkled with excitement as he uttered huskily, "If this goes wrong, we are finished."

The following Sunday, as a weak sun fought its way through the cloudy early morning dawn over a sleepy Antwerp, Count Luigi Boggia, Alessandro and Frank drove speedily back through Luxembourg, Bern and at last into Italy with millions of dollars' worth of gems. They were assured of their safety until first thing Monday morning when the special guards would routinely check the vaults beneath the Diamond Centre and realise there had been a massive heist carried out over the weekend. Only then would all hell break loose. The plan had been executed perfectly; no alarms, no police and practically no problems. Frank and the Count secretly congratulated themselves in the knowledge they were probably the best diamond thieves in the entire world. Maurice had already burned any incriminating evidence at his home. Although Antwerp provided a wealth of opportunity and a good place to fence hot property, it had been decided by the Society that all gems, consisting of loose diamonds, jewellery and gold, should be taken back into Italy. They had specialised Associates ready and waiting to deal flawlessly with this very hot merchandise for them, expertly dismantling diamond necklaces and bracelets, and selling their individual gems for cash throughout the world at a very high profit.

As Alessandro sped expertly towards Italy, Frank whistled and exclaimed, "I would say at a guess, we have at least $350 million worth of gems."

The Count laughed, slapping his friend on the back, and replied, "Siamo ancora i migliori del mondo, amico mio." *(We are still the best in the world, my friend.)*

Early on Monday morning, Frank was on the first flight out of Malpensa International Airport, Milan, flying direct to New York's JFK Airport. On the long flight home, as Frank closed his tired eyes, his mind, as always, was full of Belinda and how much he would love to be with her now that the special job had been executed with great success for the Society.

Approximately five hours after Frank flew out of Malpensa for New York, the whole world was buzzing and talking about the Antwerp Diamond Centre heist which apparently, as correctly anticipated, was only discovered after guards had checked the vault first thing on Monday morning. When news of the heist reached the airborne plane carrying one Frank Lanzo, everyone on board started to discuss this breaking news. Everyone had an opinion of how this could have happened because the vault was believed to be impenetrable. There were supposedly layers and layers of security, a magnetic field, infra-red heat detectors, and many other sensors to protect the millions of dollars' worth of gems, jewellery and gold in the largest Diamond Trading Centre of the world. It was reported that the foot-thick steel door of the vault was ajar when the guards arrived early to carry out their usual checks. It was further reported that the specialised Diamond Police could not explain exactly how the heist was pulled off.

Frank joined in the excitable discussions with other passengers, agreeing with most of them, while all along he wanted to laugh out loud at some of their ridiculous assumptions of how the thieves had managed to mastermind this amazingly perfect robbery.

As soon as the plane landed at JFK Airport, Frank was one of the first passengers to disembark. A white Lincoln limousine, property of the Society, was waiting for him as he walked out of the large glass swing doors into the sunlight of a warm spring day. As Frank settled into the back seat of the limousine, he adjusted his wristwatch to New York time. While the driver drove smoothly through the busy streets towards the headquarters of the Society, Frank laid his aching head back on his seat, closed his tired eyes and allowed his weary mind to picture Belinda.

During the following week, the whole world talked of nothing but the Antwerp diamond heist. It was the breaking news on all TV and radio channels. There had been no arrests as yet, even though the famous Diamond Police had interviewed hundreds of diamond traders in and around Hoveniersstraat, the diamond district's main street. Maurice had been one of them. For over four hours, he was cross examined aggressively by the Diamond Police and was only allowed to leave when they were satisfied with his answers to their many questions. Maurice, together with several other diamond traders in Antwerp, was advised not to leave the country. Verna, Maurice's wife, arrived back from her visit to her sister in Brussels, full of questions regarding the diamond heist.

"What did your visiting friends think about this robbery, Maurice?" she asked her husband.

"Oh, they left early Sunday morning and were back in Italy before the heist was even discovered," replied Maurice, not daring to look at his wife directly in the eye, knowing she had an uncanny way of reading his every thought. "The Count called on behalf of Alessandro and himself, saying how shocked they were to hear about it, and Frank telephoned me from New York later on Monday evening. He says it must have been the work of the world's most talented master thieves," Maurice added, opening his newspaper and keeping his eyes down.

"Yes, that is the general opinion, quite unbelievable," agreed Verna, walking out of the room, deep in thought. As she reached the door, she turned to face her stressed husband, adding, "It feels quite uncomfortable having the world's eyes focused on our little city."

The Society called for a special meeting honouring Count Luigi Boggia, Frank, Alessandro and Maurice. This was to be held in New York as soon as the Diamond Police in Antwerp lifted the travel ban on certain diamond traders. The four elitists were to be honoured for their outstanding services to the Society; this, in turn, would make each one of them extremely rich indeed.

Chapter 34
Karma Chameleon

C lose to the end of April, a beautiful bouquet arrived at the Top Drawer Agency. The attractive delivery man requested a signature, and Freddie was more than happy to oblige, signing in his usual flamboyant manner, which caused the delivery man to rush out of the door as quickly as possible. Neither Dawn nor Belinda had arrived yet so Freddie excitedly placed the bouquet on Belinda's desk, searching the flowers for a card. There was in fact a small golden envelope attached to the outside of the elaborate silver paper surrounding the most gorgeous flowers, with the name 'Belinda' written on it. Of course, these must be from Frank, presumed Freddie, and he felt happy and jealous of her.

Dawn arrived, hurrying into the agency. She stopped in her tracks as her wide eyes caught the beautiful bouquet sitting patiently on Belinda's desk.

"How lovely! Lucky Belinda. I wonder who sent them?" she uttered, smiling at Freddie and winking.

"Yes, I wonder," replied Freddie, winking back at her. Almost immediately, as if on cue, the door opened and Belinda walked in, pulling off her jacket. Reacting exactly like Dawn had before her, Belinda stopped in her tracks, eyes shining with anticipation.

Rushing to the bouquet, she turned to her two close friends and, pointing to herself, enquired, "For me?"

"Of course for you, darling," answered Freddie, turning his eyes towards the heavens, then added, "Who on earth would send me flowers?"

The two ladies, seeing Freddie's antics, burst out laughing, and as Freddie joined in, little Queenie chased his fluffy white tail around and around in circles, loving to see his beloved master so happy.

Slowly and lovingly, Belinda took the small white card from the inside of the golden envelope and read Frank's handwritten message. 'Bellissimi fiori per la mia bella amore.' *(Beautiful flowers for my beautiful love.)* She was watched closely by Dawn and Freddie, who were mesmerised when large tears flowed from Belinda's eyes, as if they had come from the very depth of her soul.

Days later, Belinda received a text message from Frank, telling her he hoped he would be back in London very soon and how much he missed her lovely face and body. Replying to his message, she thanked him for the beautiful flowers he had so kindly sent her, and told him they were still as fresh as new, just like her deep love for him was after all this time.

In the first week of a very pleasant and sunny May, Jane Baxter, Top Drawer Agency's original Marilyn Monroe, arrived at the agency looking drawn and red-eyed. Dawn and Belinda greeted her warmly, which caused her to suddenly break down and sob her heart out. Trying to compose herself so she could speak to them, Jane found she could not; the words appeared to be stuck deep in her throat, as if she could not bear to say them. The two agents looked at each other, both knowing instantly the reason for this very sad outpouring of grief from Jane. They were, of course, correct. Jane's darling mother, Brenda, a fighter to the end, had passed away two days earlier. Leaving Dawn cradling the sobbing girl, Belinda, tears in her eyes, walked slowly into the kitchenette to make them all tea.

Freddie arrived at the Great Room entrance of the Grosvenor House Hotel in Park Lane for the AIDS gala half an hour early. He had gone to great pains to make sure he was dressed as flamboyantly as possible, wearing his gold lamé three-piece suit, the one he'd had specially tailored for his first appearance as Liberace. Teamed with this, Freddie wore a black frilly silk shirt, which complemented the gold lamé suit perfectly.

"Wow, Freddie, you look almost as sensational as I do," came the throaty amused voice of Kevin as he and Wayne strolled up quickly towards Freddie.

"Glad you approve, Kevin. Don't you remember it? I wore it for the German photo shoot last year," answered Freddie, twisting around slowly to show off his flashy attire.

"Oh yes, of course, and it really makes a statement; I love it," giggled Kevin, turning on his multi-coloured six-inch stilettos and striding through the entrance of the plush Grosvenor House Hotel, hurriedly followed by Wayne and a slightly nervous Freddie.

At their arrival, everybody turned, mouths ajar, not quite believing their own eyes as they took in the apparition before them. Kevin, the Boy, strode through the large glass swing doors, his blue tartan bondage trousers joined by a leather buckled belt between his legs, in true Boy George fashion. The frilly cream shirt worn beneath a black, mock fur waist jacket complemented his glowing skin, but it was the hat that was the star attraction, almost upstaging its wearer! Consisting of emerald green sequins, its purple chiffon scarf flowed dramatically from it. The make-up, applied expertly on Kevin's handsome face, would have put the real Boy George to shame.

After successfully passing Freddie off as his personal dresser, the three were shown to the large changing area, set aside for the waiters, waitresses, members of the band and all performers, including tribute acts and the table magicians. The opulence of the ballroom, with the most amazing chandeliers, encrusted with thousands of crystal stones, sparkled brighter than Kevin's blue eyes. There were at least one hundred tables, dressed to perfection with red coloured tablecloths, together with matching giant bows strategically placed on each golden coloured chair, to delight the many guests for this AIDS gala.

Looking across the room with delight, Kevin uttered huskily, as his eyes took in every small detail, "You know, ladies, I have worked this joint many, many times, and yet it never fails to thrill me, especially this ballroom."

Porcelain crockery, together with golden coloured cutlery, blended gently on the red tablecloths; even the champagne buckets were coloured gold. The centrepiece on each table consisted of a beautiful heart-shaped flower arrangement made up of tiny cream rose buds. Wayne nodded in agreement with Kevin, although he too had seen this ballroom many times before. Freddie, having never been to the Grosvenor House Hotel, could not take his glowing eyes off the beautiful chandeliers, hanging like stately centurions over the equally spectacular ballroom.

The evening proved to be a great success, with all proceeds going towards the British AIDS Foundation. Kevin, as Boy George, and the George Michael tribute act were amazing on stage during their individual performances. Kevin ended his set with the very famous *Karma Chameleon*. Intoxicated, excited guests jumped to their feet and clapped enthusiastically along to the music while Kevin strutted across the entire stage as he played to his adoring audience. Freddie and Wayne watched his performance from the side of the stage, Freddie completely in awe of this phenomenon.

During the course of the evening, Freddie found Wayne was a very quiet but charming young man, possessed of a dry sense of humour. While the show thrilled the crowds, Freddie and Wayne remained in the changing area, chatting with one of the table magicians who showed them some of his amazing tricks. Although Wayne was not only the bodyguard but also Kevin's live-in lover, Freddie noticed, more than once, that whenever an attractive girl passed by, Wayne's eyes lit up as he looked them up and down with interest. Not the normal behaviour of a homosexual man, mused Freddie.

After their performances, the two tribute acts were required to mix and mingle with the many guests for the following few hours, this being part of their contracts. Kevin took the clients to one side and explained he would only mix and mingle if his bodyguard was by his side the whole time, purely for his protection.

"After all," Kevin continued with all his devilish charm, "one can't always be sure that all guests will be on their best behaviour, especially as most of them are drinking alcohol and we have had trouble with intoxicated revellers many times before."

Whatever the Boy wants, the Boy gets, so it was quickly agreed by the client that Wayne and Freddie were allowed to stay close to Kevin as he sauntered about in the midst of the noisy crowds, many requesting that he pose with them for photographs. Freddie thoroughly enjoyed watching Kevin as he played to the guests with all his usual bombastic gusto and charm, smiling, strutting and preening himself, a perfect imitation of the peacock. One or two guests insisted Freddie be in the photographs with them, as well as Boy George and George Michael, because they all agreed that Freddie looked amazing in his gold lamé suit. As the cameras flashed, a group of young men asked Freddie which lookalike he was supposed to be but, feeling embarrassed that they did not notice his resemblance to Liberace, he told them that he was not a lookalike but the dresser to the Boy George tribute act.

At the end of a very successful evening, Kevin was feeling frivolous and happy-go-lucky. Freddie found Kevin's many mood swings quite exhausting, although exhilarating at the same time. Wayne, on the other hand, knew the problems that could arise when accompanying the Boy out in the big bad world, especially in the huge cosmopolitan city that was London.

"Hey, ladies, the night is still young! Let's take a wander down Carnaby Street or Soho, have some fun with the tourists," suggested Kevin, devilment creeping into his voice.

"Good idea, Boy, I am definitely game," replied Paul, looking more like George Michael than George Michael.

"Me too," giggled Freddie, excitement building in his stomach.

"Okay with you, Wayne?" asked Kevin, turning to look at his lover and adding, "It will round off the evening nicely. We will not make it too late, seeing as we have to drive to Birmingham in the morning."

Freddie, never missing a trick, noticed that Wayne's face took on a worried expression as he quietly agreed. "Okay, Kevin, but not for long. I have to do the driving, remember?"

Kevin gave Wayne a quick hug and the four young men walked off into the night.

Carnaby Street, the heart of Swinging Sixties London, was packed with people, as always. This street, made famous by The Beatles and Mary Quant many years before, was still one of London's biggest tourist attractions. Its cheerful pedestrianised area in north Soho lay just behind the curving Regent Street, and the side streets nearby were crammed with many small boutiques. Kevin and the others walked through the narrow passage of Carnaby Street leading into Kingly Court, where many shops and restaurants, some with an outside dining area, offered to make your visit very memorable indeed. Wayne fell quickly into place beside Kevin, and Freddie did likewise beside Paul.

Before they had reached the most crowded spot in Kingly Court, a man rushed out of the crowds and tried to punch Kevin in the face. Like lightning, Wayne did a karate chop on the unknown assailant, stopping the blow before it had a chance to connect with his lover. Unfortunately, this drunken troublemaker was not alone and two other men rushed to join their friend. Wayne was having trouble as one of the men grabbed him from behind and held his arms down while the drunken man punched him in the stomach. Kevin darted quickly out of harm's way as Paul and Freddie jumped in to assist Wayne, who by this time was lying outstretched on the cold pavement while one of the assailants proceeded to kick him. Paul, as George Michael, standing tall and strong framed, summoned all his strength to shove the man away from Wayne, which caused the man to lose his footing and topple over, hitting his head hard on the pavement close to where Wayne lay.

Nobody was more surprised than Freddie, as a string of expletives escaped from his mouth, then he began to give a good kicking to the drunken man who tried to run away from the scene. But being intoxicated and unsteady on his feet, the man fell flat on his startled face, and try as he may, he could not get up again.

Taking off his stilettos, Kevin ran to Wayne, crying as he gently shook him and tapped his ashen face, trying desperately to revive his best friend and lover. Wayne's eyes were closed and he was rasping for breath, which caused Kevin to panic. Tears gushed down his terrified looking face as he noticed Wayne appeared to be unconscious.

Somebody must have called the police because within minutes they arrived, six of them, tall and burly, taking complete control of the situation. Kevin, Paul and Freddie were handcuffed by one of the policemen; three others were kneeling down to check Wayne and two of the troublemakers, who were all lying unconscious on the ground. The third troublemaker had managed to lose himself in the crowds of people and escape. The remaining two policemen hurriedly moved the crowds of people along and away from the scene, telling them that the entertainment was now over and that there was nothing more for them to see.

Within minutes, an ambulance arrived and Wayne, together with the two unconscious assailants, were taken speedily to University College Hospital, where all three were kept in overnight for observation.

After the police had finished taking statements from Kevin, Paul and Freddie, they spoke to several witnesses in the watching crowd. A young man came forward who had videoed the whole incident, proving that Wayne had only tried to protect Kevin and the other men had started the fight. After a strong caution, Kevin, Paul and Freddie were told to attend the police station the following morning to give their written statements.

After the crowds had dispersed and the police had left the crime scene, Kevin drove to the University College Hospital in Euston Road, accompanied by Paul and Freddie. Enquiring about Wayne as soon as they reached the hospital's reception desk, they were told that Wayne was as comfortable as could be expected, but would be kept in overnight for observation.

Paul had a badly bruised right fist and Freddie had damaged his big toe on his right foot through kicking one of the drunken troublemakers. Poor Freddie, his gold lamé Liberace suit was completely ruined, split down the back of the jacket and ripped on the left leg of the trousers.

Within the hour, they were eventually sent for X-rays. Kevin sat alone, sipping black coffee and waiting for Paul and Freddie so they could all go home for some badly needed rest. Suddenly realising it would be impossible for him to travel to Birmingham in the morning without Wayne because he himself was in no fit state to drive either, Kevin knew Dawn and Belinda would be furious with him when they learned he could not honour his contract with their clients in the Midlands. But he felt sure they would understand if he explained to them how unwell he was feeling and for him to travel anywhere would be an impossibility. Hopefully, they could secure the other Boy George tribute on their books to take his place. Admittedly, it was very short notice and although the other Boy George was nowhere as good as he was, it would be far more professional for a second choice lookalike to turn up than none at all.

When Paul and Freddie came out of the X-ray unit and walked towards him, Freddie suddenly realised that Kevin was the only one who came out of this fracas without a single scratch.

Just as Kevin thought, Dawn hit the roof when she heard he had developed a very bad migraine and a sore throat during the night and would have to cancel his lookalike job in Birmingham that day.

"For God's sake," screeched Dawn down the telephone at him. "Who do you think can rush up to Birmingham at a moment's notice to cover you?"

Kevin, making his voice sound as husky as possible, suggested she contact the other Boy George lookalike on her books. "If you call him now, there will be plenty of time before he has to leave for Birmingham, and he can either drive up or catch the train. They leave from Euston every hour." He apologised again for causing her such stress so early in the morning.

"Okay, Kevin. I am sorry to sound so angry but this took me completely by surprise," said Dawn, calming down after considering his solution to her problem. "Go back to bed and rest. I will call Stuart now and hope he is available to take your place," she added.

Before she put the receiver down, Dawn asked him how Freddie enjoyed the gala and Kevin assured her Freddie thoroughly enjoyed himself. Slowly strolling back to his bed, Kevin was very sure that both Paul and Freddie would substantiate his story. As he had explained to them the night before, it would be bad for business if the agency were to find out that their number one Boy George tribute act and lookalike was not able to fulfil his contract because he did not have the confidence to portray Boy George in public without his bodyguard to defend him.

A relieved Dawn managed to contact Stuart, her number two Boy George lookalike, and luckily he was able to stand in for Kevin, driving up to Birmingham and fulfilling the signed contract for the agency. Neither Paul nor Freddie mentioned anything to Dawn or Belinda about what had happened the night before, and confirmed they were aware that Kevin was feeling unwell by the end of the previous evening.

"Oh, yes, the Boy was definitely coming down with something nasty by the end of the night. He mentioned to me that his throat was beginning to feel very sore," Freddie explained to them when he and Queenie eventually arrived at the agency later that morning.

Kevin had sent text messages to Paul and Freddie, letting them know that thankfully, Wayne had been discharged from University College Hospital and was on his way home. Apart from having to take it easy for a couple of weeks, Kevin was relieved his bodyguard and lover would be fine.

Chapter 35
Deception and Death

As May wafted into London, bringing the promise of warm, sunny days, alongside a multitude of coloured flowers and dry dusky evenings, Belinda noticed a missed text message on her mobile phone. It was from Frank. Eagerly, fingers shaking with excitement, she tapped the phone's screen to open the waiting message. A warm glow filled her senses as she read his words, telling her he would be back in London within the next two weeks and wanted to meet her again at the Rainbow Blue Edwardian Hotel, where they were together on his last visit. This was, unfortunately, to be another quick business trip, and he would only have one day and night to spend with her, and he hoped she would not be too upset that they would only have a short time together yet again.

Immediately replying to his text, Belinda assured her lover she would gladly go to the ends of the earth for just one hour in his arms.

The following weekend, Belinda spent time with her sister, Sandra, and her brother-in-law, Tony, who lived in Kew Green. They were the proud owners of a beautiful four-bedroomed Georgian house backing on to a pond with unusual plants and trees surrounding the affluent area. Being

Italian, Tony fussed about making sure they all had a fun time and cooked wonderful Italian dishes for their pleasure. Belinda adored staying with them, finding she relaxed easily.

Sandra was fully aware of her sister's affair with Frank, and occasionally cautioned Belinda to be very careful.

"After all, darling," she said, "you really have no idea whether this man is married or living with a partner. He can tell you exactly what he wants you to know, and you have no option but to believe him."

Although she did not want to hear these words, Belinda knew her sister was right and she was only looking out for her. The sisters were very close, having only one year's age difference between them. They always had a strong sisterly bond, and Sandra knew only too well how sensitive and vulnerable her younger sibling was. The fact that Belinda knew very little about her lover seriously worried Sandra.

"Why don't you tell Matt you have a lookalike job in New York and go check out Mr Frank Lanzo once and for all? You should find out the truth, Belinda," Sandra suggested at dinner one evening.

"Yes, you are quite right. I would like to know where I stand with him after all this time. Admittedly, he may be telling me the truth about how he lives with his son in an apartment opposite Central Park, but I do worry because he has never asked me to visit him there," replied Belinda, sipping her wine.

"Maybe Sandra is right after all, Belinda," said Tony gently. "Perhaps you should try to find out exactly where you stand with this person. You know we would hate to see you get hurt," he added, pouring more wine into their glasses.

"Maybe you could take one of your friends with you, just in case," suggested Sandra, offering Belinda vegetables from a white porcelain dish.

"You know, I might just do that. Tanya was only saying last week that she would love to visit New York. I will call her tomorrow and see what she thinks about the idea," replied Belinda, taking more carrots from the dish. "One problem though: I have no idea at all exactly where in New York he lives. I know it is opposite Central Park, but that is all," she added, looking down at her dinner plate forlornly.

"Well, when you are with him again and he is sleeping, take a look in his wallet," said Sandra, grinning at her sister.

Laughing at his wife's suggestion, Tony asked, "And what do you know about this sort of thing? You have been watching too much television, my darling," he said, rubbing his wife's back affectionately while Sandra giggled.

"No, I think that is a good idea actually," said Belinda, thoughts running wildly through her mind.

"You must be very careful though, darling, and make sure he is out cold," warned Sandra thoughtfully.

"Oh, don't worry, I shall make doubly sure," replied Belinda, grinning. "Frank is invariably tired with the continuous jet lag of flying so often, and besides, he sleeps like a babe in arms after our sex sessions," she continued in a mock whisper, causing Tony to almost choke on his wine and Sandra to burst out laughing at her sister's directness.

Tanya was very interested when Belinda approached her regarding a three-day trip to the Big Apple. Because

Tanya had two lookalike jobs provisionally booked during the month of May, she told Belinda she could possibly go sometime in June, if that was suitable. As Belinda had a lookalike job coming up at the beginning of June herself, the two friends decided on the middle of June to visit New York. When Belinda spoke to Matt about her potential lookalike job in New York, he said he would love to go with her but would be far too busy with the Derby in June. Matt told Belinda he was not happy for her to go alone but she assured him that the New York client was well known to Top Drawer Agency and a couple of the other lookalikes were booked on the same job so he need not worry. How she hated lying to Matt, but she appeased herself that part of her story was in fact true, that she and Tanya would be going to New York, and therefore she would not be alone.

When Frank flew in for his quick business trip, Belinda found herself gazing into those wonderful dancing brown eyes, as always, seeming to mock her. Feeling the hot blush on her cheeks as he gently pulled her into the hotel room and into his strong arms, her legs went weak, and if he had not scooped her up and held her close to him, Belinda would have collapsed with sheer excitement.

Quickly, he undid the buttons on her chiffon blouse and using just one hand, expertly undid her white lacy brassiere, releasing her panting breasts as she stepped out of her cotton trousers, which he had deftly pulled down and dropped to the floor. There she stood, naked apart from her white crotch-less panties, which he had purposely left on her. Throwing back her head in sheer ecstasy, Belinda let out a deep moan as Frank began to rub the tip of her nipples with his thumb, making them stand up with passion. His manhood was hard. She could feel it pressing against her stomach, causing her to breath heavy with desire for him. Urgently, they fell on the large bed.

Exhausted from their eager, passionate lovemaking, Frank fell asleep almost instantly with Belinda lying beside him, and started to snore loudly, disturbing the quietness of the night. Moving slowly and sliding off the king-sized bed, Belinda tiptoed into the bathroom. Frank's heavy rhythmic snoring could be heard as she quietly closed the bathroom door. Finishing in the bathroom, and after making sure Frank was in a deep sleep, Belinda made her way stealthily to his jacket, which was strewn across the gold brocade armchair. Although Belinda hated being sneaky, especially towards Frank, she knew she had no alternative. Besides, she owed it to herself to find out just how truthful he had been with her regarding his private life. Part of her was fearful to learn the truth, in case she found out something that would break her heart, but at the same time she knew she had to do this.

Frank's dark blue passport was in the breast pocket of his tan jacket. Gently lifting it out, Belinda looked on the photo page: no address. Gingerly, she tiptoed across the room and, at the open closet, found Frank's medium-sized black leather trolley case. There was a wine-coloured tag tied to the handle with a white card inside, which gave the address of the hotel. With hands slightly shaking, Belinda pulled the card out of the tag and turning it over, stood staring at an address on Fifth Avenue, New York.

Moving deftly towards the large walnut desk, she quickly wrote the address down on the little notepad that was laying on the desk. Slipping the note into her handbag, she crept gently back onto the bed and wrapped her arms around the man she adored, who continued to sleep soundly.

With hot tears filling her eyes, Belinda whispered into the dark silence of the room, "Forgive me, darling, but I have to be sure about you, otherwise I will go crazy."

Flaming June arrived in London as if in mockery under a dull heavy grey cloud, suppressing the excitement Belinda was feeling at the prospect of visiting New York and surprising her lover. Tanya, having never been to the United States of America before, was as excited as her friend, especially at the prospect of all the shopping she would be doing once there.

Poor Belinda could not conjure up the courage to ask the hawk-eyed commissionaire, who resembled a snooty peacock, as he paraded in front of the exquisite building just off Fifth Avenue on 58th Street, one block from the entrance of Central Park, as to whether or not Mr Frank Lanzo was in. Instead, having spotted a coffee shop situated below the building, she explained to Tanya she would definitely try to muster up enough courage to ask the commissionaire once she had another strong cup of coffee.

"Belinda, darling," soothed Tanya, "this is the very reason why we came to New York. I know you are fearful of what you might find out about Frank, but think positive, darling. You really do need to know whether or not he has been truthful with you. Let's have another coffee and see how you feel."

Nodding her head and agreeing with her friend, Belinda ordered two more skinny lattes, one with an extra shot of espresso to steady her nerves. As the friends chatted, Tanya, glancing out of the coffee shop window, almost choked, coughing loudly as the hot, frothy liquid slid down her throat, causing her to splatter. Immediately jumping up in alarm, Belinda began to tap her friend gently but firmly on her back to stop her from choking, handing her friend a handful of napkins from the silver holder on the marble table. Turning to see what all the commotion was about, a couple of the other customers stared at the two women disapprovingly for interrupting their sleepy early morning coffee. As Tanya endeavoured to recover from her unexpected coughing fit, Belinda's eyes followed her friend's shocked stare out of the window, and immediately her legs felt like they would collapse from under her. Strolling leisurely on the opposite side of the street was Frank.

As they watched, he threw his strong head back and he appeared to laugh at something the very attractive woman had said as she walked by his side, an arm possessively linked through his as the sunlight turned her blonde hair halo-like, shimmering over her elegant head.

"Oh, my God, Belinda, I am so sorry," murmured Tanya, protectively throwing her arms around Belinda's quivering shoulders as she sobbed silently trying to catch her breath, which she felt had been kicked out of her by the image she had just witnessed. Truly, for the first time in her life, Belinda now knew what it meant to have her whole world fall apart around her, leaving all her dreams shattered and laying at her feet.

"Darling, she could be just a friend," offered Tanya quickly, not really believing this for one moment. Turning her sad tear-filled eyes to her friend, Belinda just shook her aching head.

Trying desperately to compose herself, she answered in a very remorseful voice, "No, they looked much more than just friends. You saw that for yourself. Thank you for trying to protect my feelings, but my female intuition tells me differently. I came here to find out the truth, and that is exactly what I have found."

A strong feeling of dismay and sadness enveloped Tanya. Knowing how very much Belinda adored Frank, she was also aware that Frank had been the only man to win her dear friend's heart in all the years she had known Belinda. Although the feeling of desperation remained heavy in her mind and soul, Belinda did her best to be as good company as possible for the few remaining days of their stay in New York. Tanya herself tried listlessly to cheer her friend up but knew there was nothing she or anyone else could do to mend Belinda's shattered heart and reasoned that if Frank really loved Belinda as he claimed he did, he would have made sure the lady on his arm had been no one other but Belinda.

The friends rushed around the big city, making sure they ticked everything off their list of things to see. Visiting every reputable store, spending hours looking around the rails and rails of fashionable clothes and shoes. Sombrely, amongst the crowds of visitors, they lay flowers at Ground Zero, becoming aware of the poignancy surrounding the site and were mesmerised inside the American Museum of Natural History.

They spent a wonderful evening at the Radio City Music Hall where the stage was soaked with five hundred gallons of simulated rain for every single performance of *Singing In The Rain*. Tanya and Belinda adored the show so much and chatted excitedly about what they had experienced as they made their way back to the hotel for their last night in the

Big Apple. Frank had never, for one second, left Belinda's mind, and it was a relief to be returning home the following morning, wanting to be as far away from him as possible. Way down in her deepest soul, Belinda knew she would never get over this man, but she had to try for the sake of her sanity.

The sun shone for their arrival at London, and the next morning after arriving home, Belinda slept in late. Matt had left early for his drive to Soho because Saturday was his busiest day of the week. Before he left the house, gently waking Belinda, he told her he would take her out for dinner that evening so they could catch up with each other.

"I will book dinner at Valentina in Clapham Junction. I know you like it there," he called back over his shoulder.

Responding sleepily, Belinda replied, "Okay, that sounds lovely."

Then she tried to go back to sleep to forget the misery that was now consuming her life.

Dawn and Freddie listened quietly as Belinda confided to them she had finished her relationship with Frank, explaining to them what she and Tanya had witnessed when they arrived at the apartment building where he lived in New York.

Jumping up and walking swiftly to Belinda, Dawn put her arms around her exclaiming, "Oh, darling, I am so sorry, but you must look at this as a blessing in disguise. Can you imagine if you gave everything up for this man and this happened afterwards?"

A half sob escaped Belinda's throat as she fought back the tears threatening to spill.

"I know you won't want to hear this now, darling," said Freddie, striding to his heartbroken friend and giving her a hug, "but you are better off without him. He is nothing but a player, and it is better for you to find this out sooner rather than later."

Wiping her tear-stained face, Belinda nodded her head in agreement and assured them she would not burden anyone with her misery, but Dawn and Freddie insisted they would always be there for her and if she ever needed to talk. Freddie suggested Belinda have a drink with him after work in one of the many wine bars in the area, hoping this would help lift her spirits a little.

A concerned Tanya called at least once a day during the following week to see how Belinda was coping and to encourage her friend to forget Frank now they had seen for themselves what kind of a man he really was. These three friends were the only ones who knew what had happened in New York and they had all been very kind and understanding during this tragic time. Slowly, digging deep within herself, Belinda managed to carry on with her life, trying desperately to show her usual happy face to Matt. After all, he knew her so well and she did not want him to suspect anything was wrong which, of course, he would have done if he were to see her so sad and miserable.

Almost three weeks after Belinda and Tanya returned from New York, Belinda received a text from Frank, telling her that he would be in London shortly and saying how much he missed and longed for her. With sadness in her eyes, she silently showed the message to Freddie, who immediately deleted it from her mobile phone.

"How dare he?" retorted Freddie, his voice rising in anger. "You really must ignore him. Hopefully, eventually, he will get the message. Remember, he is a player and he will, one way or another, smash your heart into a thousand pieces."

With eyes downcast, Belinda nodded her head in agreement at Freddie.

"Good girl, I am proud of you, darling. This is his loss and I suspect one day he will realise just what he has lost," added Freddie, busily filling the kettle for tea. He was himself having relationship problems with Dodgy Rodger. Lately they seemed to be arguing about almost everything and anything. Dodgy Rodger, who worked five days a week, expected his dinner on the table or at least in the oven when he arrived home after a hard day. Although Freddie worked only three days in the agency, often he stayed late to help out when they were extra busy. Just lately, Dodgy Rodger had been complaining about the state of the house, calling Freddie 'Miss Havisham', liking him to the character in Charles Dickens' *Great Expectations*. Although this really angered Freddie, he found himself checking the corners for cobwebs. Freddie accused Dodgy Rodger of not pulling his weight; after all, he himself could not be expected to do all the chores in the home, hold down a job and have enough energy to have sex every night with such a demanding lover! Becoming increasingly angry at the thought of Dodgy Rodger's selfishness, Freddie tutted to himself as he poured two hot cups of tea for himself and Belinda.

It was two days later, shortly after everyone had arrived for work. They were all busy when the silence was rudely shattered.

"Oh no! Oh, my God!" screamed Dawn as she dropped the telephone receiver from her shaking hands after receiving the first call of the day. Freddie and Belinda jumped at the unexpected piercing scream that tore through their secret thoughts.

Fear gripped Belinda's throat when she noticed how shaky and ashen Dawn had become and, getting up from her chair, she rushed to her friend and asked, with some urgency, "Dawn, what is it? What on earth has happened, darling?" She was dreading to hear the answer.

As Freddie also rushed to console Dawn, little Queenie, sensing tragedy, ran after his master, whimpering. Putting her arms around Dawn, Belinda looked at Freddie and pointed to the receiver lying now on the desk. Freddie picked it up and enquired who was on the other end of the phone. Dawn appeared to be in shock so Belinda cradled her in her arms, gently soothing her.

Fear gripped Belinda's heart when she heard Freddie gasping as he held the receiver to his ear, his face now also turning ashen. Looking up at him, Belinda left Dawn and slowly walked towards Freddie, who held the receiver out to her so that she could speak to the person on the other end of the telephone. Taking the receiver, not wanting to hear what she was about to learn, Belinda spoke to the unknown caller. For a split second, she felt as though she would faint, the tragic words reaching her ears made her head spin. The caller was in fact a sobbing Rick, the disgruntled partner of Jane, the agency's second top Marilyn Monroe lookalike.

Her head spinning with shock; Belinda could barely make out his words of apology for being the bearer of such tragic news. Through his sobs and croaky voice, Rick was trying to explain to Belinda what had happened, but his words were confused and muddled with his misery and his explanation was going completely over her head. Numbness had attacked Belinda's mind and she was faintly aware of her voice asking Rick for his contact number because none of them were capable of thinking or speaking coherently at the moment. Freddie moved quickly to her and gently took the receiver out of her hand and explained to Rick that Dawn and Belinda were in complete shock due to the tragic news. They were unable to discuss anything right now but they would want to know the arrangements for the funeral of their dear friend, Jane. Rick told Freddie that Jane, who was at a low ebb in her life, had swallowed a whole bottle of sleeping pills, downed with water, after learning that Rick had found someone else and was leaving her.

It appeared that the tragedy of her darling mother passing away only a short time before had left Jane deeply depressed and now, losing the only man she ever loved, proved too much for her to bear. Rick was blabbering on about how he blamed himself for what had happened but he could not help falling in love with the other woman. In his defence, he explained he had broken the news to Jane as gently as he possibly could. Jane, he told Freddie, seemed to accept the situation of their break-up but he knew now that he had misread how she had really felt.

At the end of the call, Freddie laid the receiver on its cradle and put his lean, strong arms around Dawn and Belinda as they sobbed quietly together for their tragic friend.

Chapter 36
Dark Side of Fantasy

Twice in one hour, Belinda received text messages from Frank, relaying how very concerned and worried he was because she had not answered his earlier messages. Knowing this was quite out of character for her, he hoped everything was good on the other side of the pond. Immediately deleting both texts, Belinda took her black linen jacket off its hanger and put it on over her ivory-coloured lace blouse. London had been enjoying warm weather for several weeks now, making life for Belinda a little more bearable.

It was the day she and Dawn had been dreading: Jane's cremation. Freddie, together with Dawn and Belinda, travelled by black taxi to the crematorium in Golders Green. As the taxi pulled into the crematorium's grounds, the three mourners were not at all surprised to see so many people gathered outside the little chapel where Jane's Celebration of Life Service was to be held. Many of the crowd wore bright colours, and this made Freddie feel less conspicuous of his bright yellow waistcoat. Belinda noticed many of the lookalikes were present; some friends of Jane's and some wanting to pay their respects for a fellow artiste. Rick, looking extremely pale and gaunt, accompanied by some of his friends and his sister, walked sadly up to Dawn and Belinda, thanking them for attending. His new love had been wisely kept away.

"Dawn, Belinda," came the unmistakeable voice of Marina Greenslade, hurrying through the throng of bodies towards them. "Darlings, so glad to see you albeit on such a sad occasion. Come, let me take your arms," she beckoned, before kissing both in turn and nodding politely to Freddie.

As the congregation were ushered into the chapel for the service and while still busily finding their seats, a slight commotion could be heard outside. As all eyes turned towards the back of the chapel, a photographer moved quickly in, walking backwards taking photographs of whoever was about to enter. Neither Belinda nor Dawn were surprised as a woman walked into the chapel very slowly and deliberately, dressed immaculately in a short, tight black skirt suit, tottering on six-inch black stilettos, large sunglasses covering her eyes, and a black chiffon scarf over her beautifully coiffured blonde hair. Kay Carney had made her dramatic entrance, press in tow, at the cremation of her rival. Dawn, Belinda and Freddie glanced at one another knowingly.

As Kay was given a seat by the gentlemanly Jack Novak, the photographer flashed his camera several times in her direction. Kay looked demurely straight ahead as if she had not noticed him. The photographer next flashed his camera at Marina Greenslade, sitting between Dawn and Belinda, then twice at the seated congregation before he turned to discreetly nod at Kay as he took his leave.

It was a very beautiful, heartfelt farewell for a beautiful young person, and many of the women and a few of the men in the congregation wept openly or quietly into their handkerchiefs. Afterwards, making her way cautiously across to where Dawn, Belinda and Marina Greenslade were standing, Louise Rickman, the agency's second most sought-after Queen Elizabeth II lookalike, expressed her sadness for Jane. Louise had always been wary of Marina Greenslade because Marina had made no secret of the fact she disliked Louise Rickman, aware that Louise coveted her crown. This infuriated Marina because her rival was always so sweet to her face.

"Sorry to meet you again in such sad circumstances," said Louise quietly, as she reached them, not glancing in Marina's direction.

"Yes, Louise, we are all devastated," replied Dawn sadly, wiping a large tear from her eyes.

Belinda weakly smiled at Louise, sensing how embarrassingly frosty the atmosphere had become between her and Marina.

"I must say that the stunt Kay Carney pulled with the press was appalling," remarked Louise, continuing to ignore Marina Greenslade.

"I suppose that put your nose out of joint, Ms Rickman, because you didn't think of doing it yourself," snapped Marina, looking Louise straight in the eye.

"Excuse me, madam!" came the speedy reply from the thin lips of Louise as she blushed and turned to face Marina, who quipped, "Yes, I shall excuse you, scurry along now."

Dawn and Belinda were taken aback at Marina's rudeness. Thankfully, as if on cue, Lady Denise Ava came rushing up to Dawn and Belinda, blowing her nose gently into a large white handkerchief. As she reached them, she dramatically slung an arm around each of them and sobbed quietly. Dawn and Belinda hugged her in turn, for they knew how close she and Jane were. When the Lady finally composed herself, she huskily told the others she was still in shock by what had happened to her dear friend.

"You know, the lookalike business is like one big happy family, and even though some members might not know each other personally, having possibly never worked together, they still feel the loss when something bad happens to one of them," said Dawn knowingly, more or less to herself as she wiped another tear from her eyes.

One of the evening newspapers carried a photograph of Kay Carney at her friend Jane's cremation. The headline read: *Marilyn Monroe weeps at Marilyn Monroe's cremation*. Beside the photograph of Kay, was the photograph taken in the pew of Dawn, Belinda and Marina with the caption '*HM attends Marilyn Monroe's farewell service*'. The newspaper article told the sad story of Jane's suicide and how she and Kay Carney were good friends, even though the truth was they were hated rivals. When Dawn and Belinda read the article that evening, they could not believe Kay had told the press that she and Jane had been close. It was common knowledge in the lookalike world that neither of them had ever spoken to each other, and it was a well-known fact that they were bitter rivals for the Marilyn Monroe lookalike crown.

A heavy cloud hung thickly over the Top Drawer Agency in the days following Jane's cremation. Belinda became more and more depressed with life without Frank, Freddie's relationship with Dodgy Rodger was indeed now dodgy, and Dawn mourned the passing of Jane as if she had lost a child.

"Do you know what that awful man Dodgy Rodger said about darling Queenie last night?" asked Freddie as he handed each of them their morning tea. They glanced up at him questioningly. "Well, I confronted him about why he hardly ever took Queenie for his walkies when I am busy cooking. Do you know what he said?" he asked again, his eyes wide, looking from one to the other.

"Do tell us," encouraged Belinda, trying hard to keep a straight face.

"He had the audacity to say he could not possibly be seen out with a rat on stilts," replied poor Freddie, half-whispering as if it was too awful to repeat.

At these words, Belinda and Dawn burst out laughing.

"It's not funny, ladies. Poor little Queenie. I was mortified," retorted Freddie, picking Queenie up and kissing him on his little velvet nose.

"Sorry, Freddie," said Belinda, feigning an apology. "I am sure Dodgy Rodger did not really mean what he said."

"That's okay, ladies. At least I got you both laughing for the first time in ages," giggled Freddie, putting Queenie gently down and walking across to the ornate mirror to admire his reflection.

Suddenly, Belinda's mobile phone, which was on silent, danced on her desk, notifying her of an incoming call. Picking up the phone and checking the name of the caller, she immediately cut the call off as her eyes shone and her cheeks turned a deep shade of pink.

Never one to miss a trick, Freddie knew instantaneously who the caller was and he winked encouragingly at Belinda through the mirror. Although wanting desperately to speak to Frank to tell him what she and Tanya had witnessed in New York, Belinda decided to ignore him, certain he would just lie to her again and she would be drawn back into his web of deceit until such time he grew tired of her.

Within a few minutes, the mobile phone rang for a second time, but Belinda did not check the name of the caller; she knew in her heart it was Frank again. Dawn glanced at Belinda, raising an eyebrow questioningly at her, and Belinda responded by nodding her head to her friend, sadly smiling.

"Good girl," mouthed Dawn, and carried on checking the incoming emails.

Chapter 37
Love Conquers All

Frank was due to fly back to London at the beginning of the following month but his heart was heavy, having had no success in contacting Belinda. What on earth could have happened, he wondered? Why was she not taking his calls or answering his text messages? These thoughts kept going around in his head. Did she finally feel she'd had enough of their cloak and dagger love affair? He knew so well how she hated being unfaithful to her husband, although he also knew Matt was having fun behind Belinda's back. Frank was aware that Belinda suspected her husband of cheating on her, and Frank so wanted to tell her he knew for certain that Matt was having an affair, but for obvious reasons he could not confirm her suspicions.

Matt and James were extremely busy with the running of the betting shops. The Derby and Oaks races were imminent, making an already thriving business all the more hectic. Apart from this, the bets were coming in thick and fast for the Gold Cup.

The partners were expecting Gene to arrive any day. James was sure Gene's relationship was still flourishing with Belinda since Matt had mentioned to him that Belinda had recently been in New York, where she was booked on a lookalike job for the agency.

"New York, eh?" asked James, his devious brain working overtime. "Anywhere near Gene Capalti's home?" he asked.

"No idea," replied Matt, busily taking £50 and £20 notes from the tills. "It wouldn't make any difference even if it were on the same street as Gene's place anyway, would it?" Matt replied quickly, frowning as he glanced at James. "Neither know each other and Belinda is not even aware of Gene's existence. Have you forgotten we are sworn to secrecy?" he added, closing the last till and waiting for an answer from the younger man.

"Of course I haven't forgotten," replied James, a little flustered now. "It is just a little weird when you think they may have passed each other several times on the streets of New York, not realising how much they have in common," he said, flashing one of his endearing smiles at Matt, who shook his head in fake dismay at his younger partner's imagination.

Later that afternoon, Matt received a telephone call from Gene, informing him that he was flying into London the following Monday. Gene required someone to collect him at the airport and James was happy to do so when Monday came around, picking him up from Heathrow in his other car, a red Alfa Romeo Giulietta Spider.

On the way back through the busy streets of west London heading for Soho, they stopped for coffee en route. While they sat at a small table in a stylish Italian restaurant, drinking their coffee and chatting about the horse racing scene and other current topics, Gene asked how Matt was. Seizing the opportunity, James told the American that Matt was keeping very well and that his wife, Belinda, had been in New York a couple of weeks ago on a lookalike job. James cunningly watched for Gene's reaction to what he had just been told, but apart from the slightest flicker of his eyes, there was nothing.

"Oh, really?" exclaimed Gene, trying to hide his interest. "Where did she stay in New York?"

James, finishing his double shot coffee latte, replied, "Oh! I have no idea, but apparently she had quite a prestigious job by all accounts, both herself and another lookalike."

Although outwardly showing no emotion at all by James' revelation, inside Gene felt like a claw had gripped his heart and a blinding panic began to overwhelm him. Belinda in New York and not contacting him; fear filled his mind. What on earth made her turn against him like this?

Gene spent the whole of the following day at the Soho shop overseeing that all accounts and audits were in order. At the end of the day, Gene, together with Matt and James, had dinner at an authentic Sicilian restaurant, a little gem hidden in the midst of a busy Covent Garden. They all agreed the place was probably one of the best they had eaten at in London, which was a real compliment for the Sicilian restaurant because all of these gentlemen had frequented many five-star restaurants in their time.

After paying the bill, Gene told the others he would not be at the betting shop the following day because he had to attend a meeting for the Society, but he would be back with them the following morning to complete his commitments before he flew back to New York that evening.

"The BBC are coming in today, Belinda," announced Dawn as she rushed into the agency office, a little late.

Looking up and smiling, Belinda said, "That is good news. All publicity very welcomed indeed."

"Yes, too true, darling," agreed Dawn, hanging up her pale yellow jacket on the curved coat stand.

"Would you like to be interviewed, or would you prefer it if I do it?" she asked Belinda.

"Oh, you do it, Dawn. After all, you are the senior partner and you come across extremely professional on the television," replied Belinda, not feeling at her brightest.

"Thank you, darling. Yes, I do rather enjoy bragging about our agency," replied, Dawn glancing in the ornate mirror and smoothing her hair down.

At that moment, Freddie wafted into the office, little Queenie trotting beside him on his blue studded leash.

"Morning, ladies. How are we today?" asked Freddie, flashing his boyish smile.

"The Beeb is coming in today, Freddie, to speak to Dawn about the agency," said Belinda, bending down and petting Queenie, who, as always, rolled onto his back, hoping to have his furry little tummy rubbed.

"Oh! Wonderful, all publicity very welcome, I'm sure," exclaimed Freddie, helping himself to a cup of coffee.

"That is exactly what I said," smiled Belinda, returning to her desk to continue opening a pile of letters.

"Belinda, you and I, and, of course Queenie, can take a long lunch break and leave Dawn to it," suggested Freddie, raising his eyes questioningly at Dawn.

"Yes, that is fine," agreed Dawn. "They will be here around noon. I am quite happy to do the interview alone, but please stay if you would prefer to take part," she offered to Belinda.

"No, seriously, I will be ready for some fresh air and a stroll in the beautiful sunshine," said Belinda. "As long as you are happy to be interviewed alone," she added as an afterthought.

Dawn smiled at her friend and partner. "Oh, I will be fine. After all, I have been interviewed for television many times!" She giggled. "You have a nice lunch break with Freddie."

At precisely five minutes to noon, the BBC arrived with their cameras, interviewer and crew. In his usual flamboyant way, Freddie escorted them into Dawn's office.

"Good luck, Dawn, see you later," called Belinda as they left the agency together for their long lunch break.

The weather was unusually clement and the sun was warm and inviting so Belinda and Freddie decided to have a light lunch at the new Greek restaurant two streets away, which recently opened to rave reviews. They sat at one of the royal blue and gold painted tables with matching chairs placed outside the restaurant, enjoying the warmth of the sun, where little Queenie could lay at his beloved master's feet. The friends thoroughly enjoyed their lunch, swallowed down with a glass of Merlot. Finding that she felt less sad now because the wine made its way to her senses, Belinda began to feel strangely optimistic but she knew only too well that once the effects of the wine had worn off, her deep sadness would return two-fold, and yet still she needed the comfort of one little glass to drown her sorrows.

After paying the bill, they strolled slowly back to the agency with little Queenie keeping in step with them as he glanced up at Freddie for reassurance every few yards.

As the large brown oak door of the Top Drawer Agency came into view, Belinda was laughing at something Freddie had said to her. With the sun shining directly into her eyes, Frank noticed, not for the first time, they were the colour of deep emerald, so beautiful.

He was standing on the top step, dressed impeccably in a light brown three-piece suit, the sunshine catching his greying hair. Belinda stopped in shock and began to shake inside as she saw him.

Completely alarmed and not knowing what on earth was wrong with her, Freddie nervously enquired, "What is it, Belinda?"

But before she could answer her friend, Frank came slowly down the steps and walked up to his estranged love. They stood in silence gazing at each other, which immediately answered Freddie's question. So, this was the famous Frank Lanzo, he thought, now feeling a little like a gooseberry as the couple continued to stare at each other without saying a word.

"Belinda, darling, would you like me to stay?" Freddie asked protectively.

"No, no, Freddie, thank you," she replied, not taking her eyes off Frank. "Please tell Dawn I will be up in a few minutes."

Glancing briefly at Frank, Freddie turned with his usual flamboyant manner and trotted up the steps, disappearing through the agency door, little Queenie at his heel.

"I have barely five minutes to spare. I need to get back to work," said Belinda curtly, her voice hardly audible. Frank reached out to her but she backed away, keeping her eyes downcast, not daring to look at him, although she had noticed he had lost the glint in his own eyes.

"Darling, what is wrong with you? Why do you act like this?" were the first words from the lips of the man she adored.

As tears filled her eyes, she looked directly at Frank, anger rising up inside her.

"Let's just say, I hate game players. People having affairs because they truly love each other is one thing, but game players, they are detestable," she whispered, her tear-filled eyes downcast again.

"Game players?" asked Frank alarmed. "What has that got to do with me?" As she turned to walk away from him, Frank caught her left arm gently. "Darling, please tell me what this is all about. I swear to you, I have no idea at all," he pleaded, looking into her eyes imploringly.

Seeing the audacity of his fake innocence, Belinda blurted out everything that had happened. How she searched in the hotel room for his address in New York. How she had lied to Matt, telling him she had a lookalike job in New York and lastly, and most importantly, how she and Tanya had seen him with a blonde-haired woman on the day they arrived at his apartment building to surprise him. Frank's head was spinning, taking him a little time to register exactly what she was telling him.

"Why would you not ask me for my address instead of sneakily searching for it?" It was the first question of many that Frank asked her in the following minutes. Answering them all truthfully, Belinda began to walk up the steps to the agency's door.

"Belinda, I am saddened to learn you do not trust me at all. This hurts me so badly; you have no idea," said Frank, his voice rising and tinged with anguish.

Slowly and sadly turning to him, she answered, "The blonde woman, Frank. That is why I no longer trust you and cannot continue this affair."

Letting out a sound of relief, Frank ran up the few steps and took her in his arms.

"Il mio amore. *(My love.)* She is my young sister, Danielle!" Hugging her close to him and laughing out loud, Frank's eyes began to dance again as he explained. "I told you I had a sister quite a few years younger than I, don't you remember?"

Suddenly, Belinda started to blush, for she did remember Frank telling her about his family and he had mentioned at the time that he had a sister much younger than himself, whom he adored. Looking up into those dancing eyes, which were mocking her once again, Belinda nodded her head in embarrassment.

"So, you see, my darling, you have wounded me deeply for nothing," whispered Frank huskily as he brought his mouth down to hers and covered them in a long sensual kiss, not caring what the passing world thought about this display of emotion.

Running quickly into the agency, Belinda told Freddie that she would be going with Frank for the rest of the afternoon and asked if he would please explain to Dawn, who was still being interviewed by the BBC. When she quickly explained to Freddie about Frank's sister, he was extremely happy for her.

"Go! Have a lovely time! I can see you two are besotted with each other. The agency will be here tomorrow, don't you worry," fussed Freddie like an old mother hen. Eyes shining with emotion, Freddie added, "I am so happy for you, Belinda, darling. Now go; I will explain to Dawn."

Blowing Freddie a kiss, Belinda next called Matt and told him she would be late home because she was going to meet her friend Eileen for dinner. Matt reminded her to be careful when driving home later in the dark and she assured him she would be.

Frank had once again booked in at the Sherlock Holmes Hotel near Regent's Park on this trip, and now he and Belinda sat close together in the back of a black London taxi, speeding towards their destination. They felt deliriously excited at the prospect of the sensual lovemaking they would soon share, made all the more exciting after the anguish suffered by both of them during the last few weeks through a silly presumptive misunderstanding.

Taking the lift to the third floor of the hotel where Frank's room was located, behind closed doors the lovers rushed into each other's arms. Frank kissed Belinda fervently as if his whole life depended on it. Belinda's legs went weak, feeling as if they would give way from under her. All the sadness and desperate emotions of the last few weeks came flooding through their senses, highlighting their need for each other even more intensely than usual.

They were barely inside Frank's hotel room before clothes were swiftly pulled off until both were standing in their underwear. Sweeping Belinda up into his strong arms, Frank swiftly carried her to the bed and, placing her on her back, he fell gently on top of his lover, his mouth not leaving hers, their tongues meeting in passion.

Frank, his voice rasping, whispered quietly in his lover's ear, "Ti amo così tanto, mio tesoro." *(I love you so much, my darling.)*

He wrapped his tanned arms possessively around her glistening naked body as they both slumbered peacefully for some hours. When Belinda awoke, she felt ecstatically happy; her heart felt as if it would burst with love for this amazing man snoring quietly beside her. Bending over him, she put her lips lightly on his closed eyes and kissed them. Frank stirred and groaned as he woke up smiling and gently pulled her closer to him.

For the following hour, they chatted and discussed how empty and sad they both were during the weeks of silence between them. Frank told Belinda that he had a summer home at Spring Lake, New Jersey and hoped she would like to spend a week or two there with him either in September or October when he was planning to take a short break from his very high-powered but stressful job with the Society. Long ago, Belinda had resigned herself to the fact that it could be a few more years yet before Frank would be able to settle down and travel less with his job. He had explained to her many times that if she lived with him in New York, they would hardly see each other because he was rarely ever at home. After the weeks of silence between them, and remembering her deep despair of not seeing him at all, Belinda assured Frank she understood completely and would be very patient while looking forward to the day when they could be together for always; hopefully, she told him, before they reached their twilight years, causing Frank to laugh out loud.

Frank ordered a very sumptuous dinner to be served in his room. Because Belinda would not be staying the whole night with Frank this time, they agreed to stay in the hotel room until it was time for her to drive back home. They had so much to talk about and for the first time in their relationship, Belinda felt secure that Frank did in fact have deep feelings for her. Several times during the evening, she apologised for mistrusting him, explaining how she thought he had in fact been using her, but now, after learning about his sister being the blonde woman on his arm that fateful day in New York, she felt, without a shadow of a doubt, Frank did indeed love her.

Time was ticking by and passing quickly. There were barely a couple of hours left before Belinda had to leave, and they again spent these precious moments making sensual love.

Frank sadly told Belinda he was flying back to New York early the following morning, when in fact he would be concluding his audit at the Soho betting shop with Matt before an early evening flight out of the UK.

Just before midnight, Belinda and Frank kissed goodbye for the umpteenth time as he walked with her to her parked car. Climbing into the driver's seat, her eyes filled with hot tears as she looked up at Frank, who bent down to kiss her again through the open window.

"Drive safely, darling. Please text me as soon as you are home," whispered Frank, his lips against her cheek.

"Yes, darling, I promise," she replied, tears streaming down her face. Driving slowly away from her adored lover, Belinda heard his voice as he called out to her.

"You are my soulmate, Belinda, always remember that."

Back in his hotel room, Frank found it impossible to sleep, needing to stay awake for Belinda's text, assuring him she was home safe and sound. His heart was heavy and the feeling of loneliness returned two-fold to him now that his beloved Belinda had left. Yet he could still smell her. He promised himself he must find a way for them to be together for always as soon as possible, for without this woman in his life, Frank now realised he was only half a person.

Relaxing on the super king-sized bed, Frank switched on the television. An attractive brunette newsreader was relaying the latest regarding the investigation into the Antwerp diamond heist. Frank sat up with a start as he listened intently to what was being said. The Special Diamond Police were still completely puzzled as to how the heist had been accomplished so successfully, especially as the vault was thought to be impenetrable. Nonetheless, the newsreader was saying the police were continuing with their investigations for as long as it took for them to get a breakthrough. Frank's mind drifted back to the Society's gratitude and pleasure at how very professionally he and the others had masterminded and carried out the perfect heist.

Smiling to himself, Frank switched the television off and as he closed his tired eyes, images of Belinda flooded his mind, filling his dreams, thus missing her text, letting him know she had arrived home safely and that she adored him.

Chapter 38
All Good News

Dawn welcomed Belinda with a big hug and a wide smile when her partner arrived at the agency the following morning. Lowering her eyes and smiling like a little girl, Belinda affectionately allowed herself to be hugged by her good friend.

"Thank God this has all worked out happily. Your sadness was rubbing off on me," joked Dawn.

"Thank you, Dawn. I apologise for my misery the last couple of weeks," replied Belinda, switching on her computer.

"Freddie tells me the woman in question is his sister," said Dawn, pouring hot water into the coffee cups.

"Yes. Apparently she had been staying with him for a few days, and he did tell me when we first met that he had a younger sister," replied Belinda, taking one of the coffee cups from Dawn.

"Just goes to show how dangerous presumption can be," said Dawn, looking thoughtful.

"I totally agree. I have always been too presumptuous. Maybe this will teach me a lesson," answered Belinda, sipping the hot coffee. Enquiring about how the BBC interview went, Belinda was pleased to learn the documentary was to be shown in a primetime slot within the next few weeks.

"Thank God the lookalike business is still fascinating the world," exclaimed Dawn, blessing herself in mockery.

"Well, good morning, ladies," came the cheery voice of Freddie as he came rushing into the agency, Queenie in his arms. "I hope you are deliriously happy again, madam," he said, winking at Belinda.

"Yes, deliriously, thank you, darling," answered Belinda, winking back at him.

"Oh, I must tell you girls that Dodgy Rodger and I met a very cute young man called Rafael at the Two Brewers pub last night," announced Freddie, placing Queenie gently down.

"I have heard about that pub, Freddie; where is it exactly?" asked Dawn, looking up at him questioningly.

"It is south London's camp cabaret bar and is amazing," enthused Freddie.

"Oh yes, of course, I know it," said Dawn, nodding her head slowly.

"Hey, I hope you and Dodgy Rodger didn't fight over this young man," laughed Belinda, watching Freddie closely.

"Actually, he had so many piercings on his face and neck, we didn't know whether to kiss him or polish him," giggled Freddie, pouring himself a large cup of black coffee as the ladies laughed out loud. "Dodgy Rodger now refers to Rafael as Jingles, for obvious reasons," added Freddie, quite seriously.

"You make our day, Freddie," said Dawn, shaking her head, giggling.

"Yes, you certainly do, Freddie. What would we do without you?" echoed Belinda, smiling fondly at him.

Before lunch, Belinda received a text from Frank, explaining that he had fallen asleep the night before and missed her message letting him know she had arrived home safely. He promised that one day, hopefully sooner rather than later, they would be together for always, never to part again. Frank asked her again to please be patient. Tears filled her eyes as she read the last line of his text.

'Believe me, darling, my heart dies without you.'

The Society was pleased with the operation in the London betting shops. So far, between one and two million pounds of forged notes had been placed into the hands of the punters without anyone realising. That was a big profit for the Society, which Frank, Matt and James shared. After a sumptuous lunch at one of Soho's finest Italian restaurants, James offered to drive Gene back to the airport, although Matt had earlier told James he would be happy to do so himself. James, always ready to take a break from the betting shops, insisted that because he lived nearer the airport than Matt, he should drive Gene.

"Okay, if you are happy to do that," agreed Matt, glancing at James as he handed his credit card to the tall Italian-looking waiter.

"Yes, of course. I am more than happy to do so," replied James, smiling at his senior partner.

As James drove Gene through the crowded streets of a cloudy London, heading towards the airport, the men chatted happily. Although James was always extremely pleasant and respectful towards him, Gene could not squash a feeling of unease in the pit of his stomach regarding the junior partner who had been hand-picked by Matt. Always preferring the company of Matt out of the two men, Gene reasoned with his conscience this was probably due to the greater age gap between himself and James, but nevertheless his gut feeling had never let him down before, and he knew there must be a reason why he was wary of the charming James.

It did not go unnoticed by Gene that before they had reached the airport, James had mentioned Belinda several times in conversation. Perhaps, he reasoned, James had an attraction for Belinda; not only was she lovely, but she looked much younger than her years. He had noticed many younger men giving Belinda admiring glances whenever he was with her in public. Alighting from the car and bidding each other goodbye, Gene was relieved when James slapped him on the shoulder in a friendly manner, wished him a smooth flight home, and drove slowly away.

Completely out of character, Dawn whistled as she started to read an incoming fax. Pulling it off the machine, her searching eyes read the message as quickly as possible.

"Yes!" she shouted with glee. "Ladies and gentlemen, we have another big job, in Monte Carlo no less."

Freddie and Belinda looked up expectantly, all eyes hopeful. "Oh! Monte Carlo!" enthused Belinda. "May I go with the lookalikes as their chaperone please?" she asked, looking at Dawn, eyes gleaming with hopefulness.

Walking towards Belinda's desk, Dawn exclaimed, "Cinderella may go to the ball, but not as the chaperone; La Collins is on this client's list."

"Really? How fabulous!" squealed Belinda. "This is just what I need right now. Who else is on the list, Dawn?" she asked enthusiastically.

Handing Belinda the fax, Dawn went over to Camp Freddie and sadly shook her head at him, indicating that Liberace had not been selected this time.

"That is the luck of the draw, I suppose," murmured Freddy quietly to himself.

"That's show business, my friend; one day, you are in, the next day, you are out," exclaimed Dawn breezily, returning to her desk to start telephoning the chosen lookalikes for their availability.

A wave of excitement fluttered in Belinda's tummy at the prospect of spending two days and nights in the Hotel Eloquence, overlooking the Mediterranean. Checking the hotel online, Belinda read of its carefree elegance at the highest level, having been built in the early 1900s. It was an historic hotel, which offered not only luxury, but also an intimate and relaxed ambiance, right in the heart of Monte Carlo. Giggling to herself, she began to sing a few bars of the famous old-time music hall song, *The Man who Broke the Bank at Monte Carlo*.

When Belinda contacted Adam, he told her how good it would be to work with her again and thanked her and Dawn for putting him forward for this coveted job in Monte Carlo. Although fond of Adam, Belinda nevertheless felt uneasy at times when speaking with him, noticing he never failed to ask after Frank. The other lookalikes, apart from Tanya, of course, who were with her in Venice more than a year ago, had seemed to have forgotten she had met an American there, but not so Adam. It seemed to be of great interest to him whether or not she was still seeing Frank. Oh, she knew Adam was fond of her as a friend, but his questioning about Frank was beginning to aggravate her and she toyed with the idea of telling him the next time he asked that her affair with Frank had finally ran its course. Hopefully, that would put an end to his annoying interest in her love life once and for all.

The chosen lookalikes included Angelina Jolie, Brad Pitt, Helen Mirren, Robert De Niro, Joan Collins, Johnny Depp, Daniel Craig (007) and HM Queen Elizabeth II, and they were to attend the Golden Star Charity Gala held at the Hotel Eloquence. The client had requested that HM Queen Elizabeth II, Marina Greenslade, read a speech before dinner regarding the amazing work conducted by the Golden Star charity. All other lookalikes were expected to welcome guests and show them to their tables in the banqueting hall. After dinner, they were to mix and mingle, dance if necessary, and have photographs taken with the guests. The client also requested that all the ladies wore gold dresses, except HM Queen Elizabeth II, and the men were to wear dark suits and white shirts together with gold ties and matching handkerchiefs in their breast pockets. It was very exciting.

Chapter 39
Monte Carlo

Monte Carlo was even more beautiful than Belinda had imagined. After being shown to their elegant rooms to unpack, they were taken down to one of the little restaurants in the hotel, as eloquent as the hotel's name suggested. A round light oak table for ten was laid out for them, and everyone praised the red and gold cloths and napkins strategically placed beside the gold-coloured plates and cutlery.

Marina Greenslade mentioned quietly to Belinda that the crystal wine glasses were of top-grade quality and jokingly quipped, "Indeed, a table set for the Queen."

"Yes, indeed," agreed Belinda. "But, of course, they knew of your arrival, your Majesty," and the ladies laughed as Belinda feigned a mock curtsey to her friend.

The following day, once the lookalikes had transformed themselves into their characters, they were waiting patiently in Belinda's room when suddenly there was a knock at the door.

"Good evening, madam, would you all come this way, please? The Gala is about to begin."

As the group of Top Drawer lookalikes left Belinda's hotel room, each stealing a last glance at their reflections in the full-length mirror, Belinda smiled to herself as she closed the door and followed the others to the lift. Karen (Angelina Jolie) and Mark (Brad Pitt) were at the back of the group and the smile on Belinda's face froze as she caught a fleeting glimpse of Mark placing his hand on Karen's bottom and, in a very familiar way, squeeze a handful of her buttocks, causing Karen to squeal with laughter. Worry flooded Belinda's thoughts. For some time now, she had an idea there was something going on between them, which would be fine if they were both single, but they were not and Belinda knew only too well this would probably end in heartbreak. Of course, she had no room to talk because of her extramarital affair with Frank, but neither Frank nor she had young children to consider, as Karen and Mark had. Before entering the lift with the others, Belinda had decided she would mention this unsavoury situation to Dawn once back in the UK.

During the course of the glittering evening, the lookalikes were a great success, all portraying their characters amazingly. Although every one of them had worked in many wonderful venues during their careers, they all agreed this was one of the most beautiful and exquisite banqueting rooms they had ever worked in. The whole area was scattered with round tables, each covered with a gold-coloured cloth, surrounded by eight gold-coloured chairs with giant gold bows tied on the backs of them. The plates were white with gold trimmings and the cutlery was gold plated. The centrepiece on each table consisted of black and gold-coloured roses. The high ceiling was of a midnight blue with dozens of chandeliers sparkling like bunches of shining stars. The lookalikes welcomed the many affluent guests arriving at the entrance of the banqueting hall and showed them to their allocated tables. Many guests asked for photographs to be taken with their favourite lookalikes.

Just before dinner, the chairperson of the Golden Star charity made a heartfelt speech about how successful the charity had been during the last year and how the exuberant amount of money made had gone to help the war-torn areas of the world. Then, Marina Greenslade, looking and acting more like HM Queen Elizabeth II than the Queen herself, read a specifically devised speech regarding the forthcoming projects to be carried out by Golden Star charity.

After dinner, as Belinda began to mix and mingle with the guests, many stopping her to chat, a tall, very distinguished-looking gentleman walked elegantly up to her and requested her to dance with him. Accepting his offer at once, he led Belinda towards the dance floor, which had become very crowded. The band had begun a waltz and her distinguished dance partner gently put his arm around her slim waist and led her effortlessly around the dance floor to the music. Although he did not speak while they danced together, occasionally he looked down at her and smiled.

As the music came to an end, they both clapped, smiling at each other. He bowed and, in a cultured Italian accent, murmured, "Thank you so much. You are a wonderful dancer and even more lovely than Joan Collins."

Slightly blushing, Belinda thanked him for his compliment, adding it was he who was the wonderful dancer, she thought. Smiling graciously, his next words stunned her.

"You are too kind, Belinda." Shocked at the fact that he knew her name, Belinda looked up at him in bewilderment.

"I knew from the moment I saw you as the Joan Collins lookalike from the UK that you must be Belinda," he explained, a smile spreading across his classically handsome features.

"But how do you know of me?" asked Belinda, completely bewildered.

"Come, I will explain everything to you as I escort you back to your table," answered Count Luigi Boggia.

Belinda listened in awe as the Count relayed to her how his close friend Frank Lanzo had confided in him about a lovely English woman he had met in Venice last year who was a professional Joan Collins lookalike. A nervous laugh escaping from her dry throat; Belinda felt embarrassed, wondering exactly how much Frank had told this friend about their relationship. As they reached the table allocated to the lookalikes, which was empty now because the others were mixing and mingling with the guests, Count Luigi Boggia pulled out one of the gold-coloured chairs for Belinda, who smiled fleetingly as she sat down.

"I will ask you to give me the honour of dancing with you again, Belinda, if you are agreeable," he said, smiling down at her. Then slightly bowing and turning, he walked back across the room to his table where several beautiful people were waiting for him to join them. Feeling her cheeks flushing, Belinda was amazed at how small the world really was and wondered what Frank would think about it all. Checking her lipstick in a little gold compact, Belinda rose from her seat and began to mingle with the other guests; chatting to many people as she worked her way through the crowds, attracting the approving eyes of several gentlemen and women alike.

The evening proved to be immensely enjoyable for everyone. Belinda chatted about her role as a Joan Collins lookalike with the ladies, happily having photographs taken with whomever asked her. Several times during the course of the evening, she noticed Karen and Mark dancing extremely close together; Mark's hand brazenly resting on Karen's derrière. Suddenly, feeling anger rising inside her, but keeping a forced professional smile on her face, Belinda walked slowly and deliberately up to the couple and whispered quietly in Mark's ear. Moving apart quickly and making excuses for themselves, the pair immediately left the dance floor and walked in opposite directions.

Belinda could not get the Count out of her head, wanting desperately to speak with Frank, excited to tell him about the amazing coincidence of her meeting with his good friend. As the lookalikes were having a short break and chatting at the table, Count Luigi Boggia walked across to Belinda and asked her again if she would do him the honour of dancing with him again. Excusing herself to the others, she gingerly took his arm and allowed him to lead her onto the dance floor for another waltz. The others present at the table raised their eyes knowingly to each other and smiled secretly.

"What a charming gentleman," declared Marina Greenslade, her eyes watching the couple closely as they began to dance together, the Count smiling down at Belinda.

During the following dance, Count Luigi Boggia chatted to Belinda, explaining that he attended many charities all over the world. But more interestingly, Frank was due to attend this Golden Star gala with him until the Society had decided at the last minute to send Frank to southern California to chair a very important meeting. They both agreed that meeting each other here was an amazing coincidence.

As their second dance together came to an end, the Count kissed Belinda's hand while gazing into her eyes, and murmured, "It was wonderful meeting you, Belinda. I can now understand why Frank has at last fallen in love."

Blushing again and feeling like a schoolgirl under his gaze, Belinda, dropping her eyes shyly, whispered, "Thank you so much, it was wonderful meeting you also." Escorting her back to the lookalikes' table in silence, Count Luigi Boggia bowed and slowly kissed Belinda's hand as he locked his eyes with hers then turning, a flicker of a smile fleetingly touching his lips, he bowed to Marina Greenslade.

Staring after him in silence as he disappeared into the throng of the crowds, Marina, who was never at a loss for words, murmured quietly, "Well, well, Ms Collins. It looks like you have greatly impressed your very elegant and charming dance partner."

The remainder of the evening proved most enjoyable for all the lookalikes, but unfortunately time passed far too quickly.

"What wonderful jobs we have with the Top Drawer Agency," remarked Adam. "Not only do we get to attend these marvellous events in wonderful venues all around the world, but we get well paid for it too!" he added, winking at the others.

With adrenalin still racing through their veins, some of the lookalikes wanted to carry the evening on and were disappointed that the hotel bar had already closed. Lee (James Bond 007) suggested they had a last drink in one of their rooms. Belinda offered hers for the nightcap and everyone agreed.

"Where are Karen and Mark?" asked Belinda, looking around, only now noticing that the couple were not in the group.

"Karen told me she was very tired and wanted to go to bed," answered Julia (Helen Mirren).

"And Mark?" asked Belinda, her voice rising as her eyes looked around the foyer.

"Oh, he told me he was not feeling too good and went up to his room directly," explained Peter (Robert De Niro), taking his bow tie off and opening the top button of his ivory silk shirt.

"Really?" queried Belinda, before hastily adding, "Come on, it's my room for a night cap."

As they were having their last drink and chatting happily, Belinda suddenly asked Adam to check on Mark in his room to make sure he was feeling better. Turning to Julia, she asked her if she would check with Karen to see if she was okay. The two lookalikes agreed and left Belinda's room together. Marina Greenslade glanced at Belinda and raised an eyebrow questionably, to which Belinda just smiled. Within minutes, Julia and Adam arrived back, both with the same story to relay to Belinda.

"No answer from Karen's room," declared Julia.

"Same with Mark's room," said Adam.

Thanking them for their help, Belinda picked up the gold-coloured telephone on the dark mahogany desk and dialled reception. Asking for a pass key for both Karen and Mark's rooms, Belinda explained to the others that she would feel happier if she knew they were indeed okay, because as their agent she would find it difficult to sleep if she did not know for sure. The others agreed with her suggestion that she would check Karen's room again if one of the boys would kindly recheck Mark's room. Peter offered to do so and walked down to the floor below with Lee in tow.

"Make sure your gun is loaded, Mr Bond, in case we need it," quipped Peter in his finest Robert De Niro accent, and the two friends laughed out loud as they walked towards Mark's room.

On the floor above, Belinda explained to the others she would only be a few minutes and walked down the corridor until she reached Karen's door. A bellboy was waiting there and he handed her the room pass as she walked up to him. Taking a deep breath and stealthily swiping the key card in the lock, Belinda knew in her heart what she was about to discover. The bellboy, an embarrassed expression on his young face, lingered outside.

The sound of sex reached her ears before her eyes confirmed to her what she was hoping not to see. Even in the darkened room, Belinda could see the outline of the two of them entwined in each other's bodies, groaning loudly and breathing heavily. The full moon was shining strongly through the half-opened window and this, coupled with the light from the doorway, made it possible to see quite well inside the room. Mark, his small tight buttocks moving swiftly up and down masterfully, while Karen's long slender legs were raised to the ceiling, toes pointed like a ballet dancer. A large diamond ring on Karen's left hand caught the moonlight as its wearer squeezed Mark's buttocks. Karen let out a scream and Mark groaned deeply in his throat as Belinda's intrusion completely ruined his imminent ejaculation into his lover. Embarrassed beyond belief, Mark and Karen separated and pulled the white counterpane over themselves.

"I am so sorry I had to witness this unsavoury behaviour," whispered Belinda in a shaky voice. "When we get back to London, we will discuss this with Dawn. As you are aware, Dawn expects all her lookalikes to adhere to the agency's Code of Conduct."

Quickly turning, Belinda left Karen's room and closed the door quietly behind her.

Peter and Lee had returned to Belinda's room after having no success locating Mark.

"Well?" asked Marina Greenslade, inquisitively as Belinda entered the room.

"Oh, Karen and Mark are fine. They were on the veranda outside having a cigarette," replied Belinda but she could feel her eyes flicker under Marina's stony stare, who raised her eyebrows knowingly at her friend.

Before the plane touched down back in London, Belinda sent a text to Frank asking him to call her the following afternoon at the agency because she had something amazing to tell him. As she arrived back at the office, her mobile rang and she heard his deep warm voice come sensually down the airwaves, which made her blush deeply. Dawn and Freddie grinned at her, pretending not to notice her flushed face and shining eyes.

"Buon giorno il mio amore, spero che tu stia bene."
(Good day, my love, I hope you are well.)

Although not fluent in Italian, Belinda understood much of this wonderful musical language and she thanked her lover for his concern. While she relayed to Frank about her meeting with a very elegant and charming gentleman at the Golden Star Charity Gala in Monte Carlo, Frank interrupted her mid-sentence, surprised she had not mentioned to him before about her job at the gala. He told her he was due to attend the same gala but had been sent to southern California instead. Dawn and Freddie, both open-mouthed, kept their eyes on Belinda as they listened closely to what she was saying to her lover.

"Yes, I know you were meant to be there, Frank, because your friend Count Luigi Boggia told me," she answered, looking up and winking at her inquisitive friends. "Oh, by the way, the Count is a wonderful dancer," she teased, waiting for Frank's reaction.

"The Count? You met Count Luigi Boggia at the gala? That is a real coincidence. What a very small world," replied Frank, his voice taking on a strangeness Belinda had never heard before. "As you are already aware, Belinda, I was expecting to be in the Count's party at the gala and was quite disappointed when I was sent elsewhere by the Society," he said, his last few words uttered more to himself than to her. "The Count and I go back many years. We are close like brothers. How did you meet him?" Curiosity was getting the better of him.

"He asked me to dance, darling. Apparently he had a good idea who I was because you had apparently told him about a woman you met in Venice who was a Joan Collins lookalike from England, so when he saw me and the other lookalikes at the gala, he told me he instinctively knew I was the woman you spoke about to him," explained Belinda, noticing how Dawn and Freddie were hanging on to her every word.

"The wry old fox!" exclaimed Frank, suddenly laughing, and the sound of his laughter made Belinda tingle inside. Before saying their goodbyes, Frank told her he hoped to be back in London soon.

Lowering his voice, he whispered, "La mia anima e corpo lungo per te il, mio amore." *(My body and soul long for you, my love.)*

Chapter 40
Unexpected News

D awn was aghast after hearing what Belinda had to say about Karen and Mark's sexual encounter in Monte Carlo.

"The agency will not tolerate this kind of behaviour; Karen is married with a young child, for God's sake," hissed Dawn, her voice rising in anger. "Before we know it, her husband will be coming around here looking for Mark. Somehow these things always have a way of leaking out," she added, walking to the dark ebony coat hanger and taking her green crepe jacket from its peg. "I have to go to the bank, Belinda. Would you please call Karen and Mark to arrange a meeting with them here at the agency as soon as possible?" she said, closing the door behind her before waiting for Belinda's reply.

Alone now with Belinda, Freddie, always loving a bit of gossip, looked at her enquiringly.

"Sorry, Freddie," she told him gently. "I cannot tell you anything at the moment. Dawn is adamant we keep this between the two of us for the time being."

"Spoilsport," came Freddie's reply, but he knew Belinda would tell him all about it sooner or later. Besides, he already had a good idea what the pair had been up to in Monte Carlo, and sniggered as he sauntered into the kitchen to fill the kettle for tea.

The following day, Karen and Mark, looking sheepish, sat opposite their lady agents in Dawn's office. They were told in no uncertain terms by Dawn that as far as she and Belinda were concerned, they could do as they pleased with their lives, but not when they were booked on jobs with other lookalikes; then, insisted Dawn, they act within protocol.

"I really don't know how far this affair has gone and I really don't care. When just the two of you are working together, whatever you get up to is none of our business, but when you are working with other lookalikes, I expect – no, I demand – you to behave as responsible adults. If this fling of yours gets out, who knows what could happen," stressed Dawn, looking stonily from one to the other. Mark was profusely apologetic and Karen lowered her grey eyes to the floor and continued to look sheepish.

"You are our finest Angelina Jolie and Brad Pitt lookalikes, and you represent not only this agency but the UK as well. If you intend to carry on with your affair, please be extra discreet. I do not want to hear any more sordid stories about you in the future, you understand?" demanded Dawn, getting up from her chair and pouring herself a paper cup full of water from the cooler. Mark and Karen assured Dawn they understood perfectly and would make sure they were not a cause for concern to either her or Top Drawer Agency ever again.

Although life for Belinda was busy and full of adventure, she knew she would never be completely happy unless she could always be with Frank. Knowing only too well this was not possible for the foreseeable future, she resigned herself to waiting for his visits to London, making her mind up to take the time he could give her, rather than never seeing him at all. If she had her way, she would have asked Matt for a divorce, but Frank reasoned with her, yet again, that the time was not right and, as much as he hated it himself, they had to be patient until such time when they could be together for always.

"If there was anyone born to be a town crier, it most certainly would be Lady Denise Ava," remarked Belinda, smiling to herself after receiving a call from their Madonna lookalike.

Dawn looked up from her computer, curiosity getting the better of her. "More gossip?"

"I'm really not sure. She didn't have time to explain on the telephone, but she is coming in tomorrow to tell us all!" replied Belinda, wondering what had caused Denise to sound so excited.

"Oh good, I can't wait!" remarked Dawn sarcastically, raising her eyes to the ceiling. "What would we do without her?" she added giggling.

Laughing at Dawn's directness, Belinda answered, "Without her, we would have to buy newspapers!"

The following day, Freddie greeted Lady Denise Ava with his usual flamboyancy, kissing her on both cheeks. "Looking amazing as always, my Lady," he said, fussing around her. Everybody loved Freddie, including Denise, preening every time he referred to her as 'my Lady', momentarily forgetting that her father had bought her the title as a birthday present quite recently. Sometime before when Belinda had asked her why she wanted to have a title, Denise had looked coy but confided in Belinda that she thought it would help to meet and marry a titled English gentleman some day, which was her most coveted dream, to be accepted into English High Society.

Gracefully accepting the cup of coffee from Freddie, Denise made herself comfortable on the soft, cream sofa waiting for Dawn and Belinda to finish their individual telephone conversations. As soon as she had her agents' attention, she took out a copy of a well-known newspaper and placed it open on Dawn's desk so she could read the article.

Her eyes swiftly flickering down the page, Dawn looked up and exclaimed, "Oh, my God, what did I tell you? That girl was heading for trouble."

Denise spent the following half hour explaining to her agents everything she knew about the terrible incident that caused Kim (Tina Turner) to end up in an intensive care ward in St Thomas' Hospital. Dawn, Belinda and Freddie listened intently as Denise took centre stage and became not only the reporter, but also the storyteller again.

Apparently, on this particular day about a month ago, Kim had booked in a new client for her dominatrix business, an associate of one of her long-standing customers, who had verbally vouched for this latest addition to her long line of elite clientele. Apparently, when the new client arrived half an hour early for his appointment with Kim, she said he seemed jittery and she offered him a drink to relax. Accepting the drink from her, Kim noticed he never once looked her directly in the eye, but she put this down to shyness on his part. In actual fact, this seemed to be normal behaviour on most new clients' first visit. After discussing with Kim which services he wanted from her, she explained to him the price involved for what he had requested. Nodding his head in agreement, he pushed his fine, brown hair back from his forehead, and Kim noticed he was sweating, which seemed odd at the time because she always made sure her dungeon was well air-conditioned.

Apparently, Kim had removed her black velvet cloak, revealing her sexy dominatrix outfit, nipples peeping seductively through slits on the bodice of her red basque; her black lacy stockings showing the tops of her ebony plump thighs. The new client had removed most of his clothes and was standing, looking quite embarrassed, eyes cast down to the floor. His timid manner gave Kim extra confidence and she moved sensually towards him, wrapping her leather whip about his thin neck in a playful manner. Whipping him on his bottom, at first gently then becoming more aggressive, Kim apparently ordered him to get down on his hands and knees because, she explained to him, she would now punish him for being a naughty boy.

Slowly, he crouched down as he was told and began to breath heavily as she took her leather tawse and whipped him steadily in rhythm on his scrawny buttocks. Suddenly, from nowhere, Kim heard an unnatural sound coming from the throat of her new client. A sound that reminded her of the noise foxes make while having sex late at night, a horrible screaming noise that shot through your ears and into your brain, turning your blood cold. Like lightning, her feeble client was up on his feet and Kim noticed the pupils of his eyes had disappeared into his head, making him look like a blind man. Wrenching the whip from Kim's hand, he started to use it on her, lashing every part of her body. In a wild frenzy, still screaming, he kicked her then punched her in the face, blood spilling from her lips. Before she lost complete consciousness, somewhere far away at the back of Kim's shocked mind, she was faintly aware of a third person entering the dungeon, yelling and intervening in her nightmare.

Seeing the expressions of horror on her intrigued audience's faces when she had finished telling them about Kim, gave Denise a special satisfaction. She knew they could hardly believe what she was telling them.

"Goodness me!" exclaimed Dawn. "Poor girl, but who was it that came into the room?" she asked, eyes wide with disbelief.

"Yes, who saved her?" stammered Belinda, the colour drained from her face with shock at what she had heard.

"Well," said Denise. "Luckily, another of Kim's clients, who had an earlier appointment with her, was still upstairs taking a shower," she added, looking from Dawn to Belinda.

"Oh, thank goodness," uttered Belinda.

"Yes, quite," agreed Denise. "Thank goodness indeed! On his way down the stairs, he heard the wild screams, coupled with the commotion and without even thinking about it, he kicked the door to the dungeon almost off its hinges and the rest is history," Denise added, smiling broadly.

"So this new client, who the hell was he?" asked Freddie, taking the empty coffee cup from Denise's outstretched hand.

"Would you believe, he was a top-notch psychologist! He was definitely a weirdo but a very clever one apparently," replied Denise. "Kim's client, who had vouched for him, could not believe what had happened. As he told the police when questioned, the psychologist always appeared normal and gentlemanly," added Denise, folding her newspaper cutting and placing it back in her large green handbag.

"How is Kim now?" asked Belinda, walking towards the window and gazing out across the pale blue summer sky; the yellow sun was playing hide and seek behind the fluffy white clouds.

"On the mend now. But I don't think she will go back to her dominatrix career, not after this," said Denise knowingly.

Dawn looked up, her eyes cold as she said, "I am very sorry about what happened to Kim, very sorry indeed. But I am not sorry she no longer works for us. Trouble seems to follow that young woman wherever she goes, and Top Drawer Agency has a first-class reputation to uphold."

Belinda walked across to Denise and placed a hand on her shoulder. "We missed this story in the newspapers. Thank you for letting us know what happened. Please give our best wishes for a speedy recovery to Kim."

"Yes, yes, of course, thank you, Belinda. In fact, I am going to visit Kim at home tomorrow and will give her your message," replied Denise. "Oh, by the way, the weirdo is still in police custody, and word has it he will go down for a long time. This is one psychologist who desperately needs a psychologist," added Denise, shaking her head in disbelief.

Before kissing everyone goodbye, Queenie included, Denise signed a contract which Dawn had prepared for her regarding a week's work in Dublin. It would be an excellent job for her, together with several other tribute artistes of the same genre.

"Wonderful stuff. Let the good times roll!" exclaimed Denise, waving as she disappeared out of the door, a copy of her signed contract tucked safely inside her handbag.

During the next few months, the media occasionally mentioned the Antwerp diamond heist, keeping the public up to date on how the investigations of the Special Diamond Police were progressing. This case was far from closed.

Early on a particularly humid morning in New York, Frank switched on his television set as he ate a slice of toast with black coffee for breakfast. Don Levy, the resident presenter on *Good Morning New York*, was in the middle of reading the latest news.

"Now for the latest developments regarding the Antwerp diamond heist," came his distinctive voice through the television set, which made Frank almost choke on his coffee. Swiftly, he pressed the remote control to turn up the sound. Don Levy was saying something about an object being found at the scene of the robbery, which appeared to be completely out of place among the other gems that had been scattered about the floor, possibly dropped by the thieves in their rush to vacate the underground vaults. Forensics was looking at the possibility that this object had been the personal property of one of the gang who had dropped it by mistake.

A cold sweat broke out on Frank's brow as his mind flew back to Antwerp. All gang members knew not to wear any kind of jewellery or carry anything that could be dropped while executing the robbery for this very reason, but he would have never attempted to be part of the diamond heist without his good luck charm, which he carried with him at all times. Frank remembered feeling uneasy and sad about not being able to find his silver dollar, given to him by his beloved maternal grandfather, Cesare Finamore, on Frank's twenty-first birthday. Frank had treasured it, keeping it with him through all the years. He remembered missing it and searching for it when he, Count Luigi Boggia and Alessandro Longo were driving back to Italy from Antwerp after their mission had been accomplished. Frank mentioned his loss briefly to the Count, who assured him that even if he had dropped it, there were no initials or inscriptions on the dollar to incriminate him. It was only a silver dollar and could have been in one of the deposit boxes they had broken into.

"After all," reasoned the Count, "don't you remember? There were some jewels, gold and silver strewn across the floor, which we dropped."

Frank had reluctantly agreed, but nevertheless he could not shake off the feeling of uneasiness at losing his charm because without it, he felt his luck was no longer secure. Panicking slightly, Frank decided to call Count Luigi Boggia in Venice to see if he had seen the news. Relief flooded through him as the telephone was picked up at the other end almost immediately.

"Pronto," Count Luigi Boggia responded in his lyrical Italian voice down the line. After their usual warm brotherly greeting, Frank explained to the Count what he had seen on the New York news regarding an object that had been found and how he was very concerned it could be his lucky silver dollar.

"No, no, my friend, I was about to call you because Alessandro found your lucky charm down one of the back seats of the car. You must have dropped it there when we were on our way back to Italy. I remember you mentioning to us that you had mislaid it," added the Count reassuringly.

"Thank God! That is great news, Luigi. I was very worried there for a while. I will be pleased to get it back. Please keep it safe for me until we next meet," requested Frank, the stress leaving his face and voice.

The Count was fully aware Frank would not go anywhere without his lucky charm, but he reminded the American how easy it could have been to be caught out by such a trivial thing as sentimentality. Frank, of course, agreed with the Count's logic.

"By the way, Luigi," Frank said light-heartedly, "what is this I hear about you meeting Belinda?" He could hear the Count's quick intake of breath before he answered.

"Ah yes, the lovely Belinda, now I know why you are in love. Thank your lucky stars, Frank, that you saw her first. She is a very special woman, and as you are fully aware, I am a connoisseur of women. You must bring her to meet me again as soon as possible, my friend," he added.

"I will do no such thing, Luigi," laughed Frank, good-humouredly. "As you say, I saw her first. Occhi chiusi, amico mio." *(Eyes off, my friend.)*

Chapter 41
Charlie Chaplin

Luke Cohen, the greatest Charlie Chaplin lookalike, together with the agency's top Laurel and Hardy duo, was booked as part of the cabaret at a dinner-dance for a renowned golf club, which was situated in the beautiful countryside of Virginia Water on the southern edge of Windsor Great Park. Luke was a gentle young man, quietly spoken with the saddest, yet most beautiful, deep violet eyes, and black eyelashes the envy of every woman who saw them. Most people could not decide whether Luke was homosexual or heterosexual, and he loved to keep them guessing. Whenever Luke worked with one of the Marilyn Monroe lookalikes, he flirted outrageously with them, but he never took it any further. Luke arrived at his gigs alone and always left alone. Dawn adored Luke, having known him for several years now, and he had never caused her or the agency any concern; always the professional. There were several other Charlie Chaplin lookalikes on her books and most of them were successful, but Luke was almost the reincarnation of the genius actor. Dawn invariably sent Luke out as the little tramp for the highest price.

On this particular evening, the wonderful Laurel and Hardy lookalike duo had the whole ballroom in uproar during their twenty-minute skit, which was scheduled halfway through the evening. The audience gasped with wonderment as the famous comedy team drove on to the dance floor in a replica of the original duo's T-Model Ford, dating back to the 1940s. When the boisterous couple finished their performance, honking their hooter as they drove off the dance floor, Hardy flicking his neck tie at the guests in farewell and Laurel scratching his head in bewilderment, a roar of approval went up along with enthusiastic clapping of the audience's enjoyment. A short break followed where dessert was served to the guests, still laughing about the antics of the spectacular act. The talented duo, confident in the triumph of their performance, knew that Top Drawer Agency would receive several calls the following day from guests present this evening, eager to book the amazing act for their own forthcoming events.

As the waiters and waitresses quickly cleared away the dessert plates from the tables, the lights were dimmed and the orchestra quietly began playing the first few bars of a tune. You could hear a pin drop as a hush ascended on the ballroom. As the orchestra played, a spotlight picked out the figure of a little tramp, tottering towards the middle of the dance floor, his cane with its permanent curve held in his right hand, playing its part in the little tramp's iconic walk. On his black curly hair sat the trademark bowler hat, and in his left hand he carried a small, battered brown suitcase. Luke Cohen's twenty-minute silent sketch under the spotlight proved to be breathtakingly amazing. Again, there were tears in many of the guests' eyes, but this time with sadness, as they watched in wonder the performance unfold of the humbled little tramp-like figure, bringing to life the undisputed genius of Charlie Chaplin. With a flourish, the little tramp laid his battered suitcase on the highly polished floor and, sitting cross-legged beside it, took out a small white cloth on which he placed two cups and saucers. In the middle, he placed a vase of artificial roses. The poignancy of the piece touched the heart of every guest in the room as he lay a picnic for two, although he was quite alone, all the time smiling and flickering his beautiful eyelashes at an imaginary friend or lover. The soul-stirring tune of *Limelight* composed by Sir Charlie Chaplin accompanying the sketch, made it all the more heart-rending as the exquisitely talented Luke Cohen finished his tribute and tottered off the dance floor with the spotlight holding his every iconic step. There followed a full minute's silence before an outbreak of the loudest and longest applause filled the ballroom. Almost immediately, the orchestra struck up with *What Makes You Beautiful* as the tribute act for One Direction came on stage, led by the Harry Styles lookalike, cleverly changing the sombre atmosphere in the ballroom to one of fun and gaiety once again.

"Luke Cohen was a massive hit again last night," announced Dawn smugly as she replaced the receiver after taking a call from the impressed client. "I have a sneaky feeling Luke will go off to try his luck in Hollywood, and who could blame him? He is an amazing talent," she added, checking the computer for incoming emails.

"Yes, I think so too," agreed Belinda, turning on her computer. "He would be fantastic at Universal Studios. Charlie Chaplin is one of the biggest icons out there together with Marilyn Monroe. Hollywood's gain would be our loss, that's for sure," added Belinda, nodding her head.

Suddenly, the agency door swung open and Freddie sauntered in, Queenie tucked under his right arm.

Noticing he wasn't his normal jovial self this morning, Belinda, being concerned, asked, "Are you okay, Freddie?" She looked closely at him.

"Of course I am okay. Never been better, I don't think!" came Freddie's sarcastic answer, as he put Queenie down on the carpet, then he burst into tears, shocking Dawn and Belinda and causing little Queenie to whimper.

"Oh dear!" exclaimed Belinda, getting up from her chair and rushing towards Freddie, handing him paper tissues to dry his tears and blow his nose. "What on earth is wrong, Freddie?" she asked as Dawn walked across and patted Freddie on his shoulder, letting him know she understood.

Trying to compose himself and dabbing at his red swollen eyes, Freddie told the ladies how he had found Dodgy Rodger with another man in the bedroom of their flat.

The worse part, he explained to them, was the other man was Rafael, who they had met only recently and taken under their wing. "Remember, I told you about him, the one with so many piercings that Dodgy Rodger nicknamed him Jingles."

Freddie's sympathetic audience nodded their heads, confirming they remembered him telling them about the night they had met the young man. Freddie, now almost fully composed again, continued telling the ladies that Dodgy Rodger, Rafael and himself had dinner together the previous evening at the flat, and afterwards Freddie took Queenie out for his evening walkies. Dodgy Rodger had told Freddie he and Jingles would wash and dry the dishes while he was out with Queenie.

"As fate would have it," added Freddie, tears threatening to fall again from those beautiful blue eyes, "Queenie seemed uninterested in having a long walk, even though it was a lovely sultry evening, and after a little unsuccessful coaxing we had turned around and walked back to the flat. It couldn't have been more than twenty minutes since we had left, and yet those two," he almost spat the words out of his mouth, "were already at it in my bedroom!" His voice was building to a crescendo of indignation. Dawn and Belinda wrapped their arms around him as tears spilled onto his sad face.

"Freddie, darling, how many times have we tried to tell you that Dodgy Rodger was no good for you?" said Dawn, handing Freddie more paper tissues and a glass of cold water.

"Yes, Freddie, dodgy by name, dodgy by nature," chimed Belinda, patting a heartbroken Freddie on his heaving body as his sorrow flooded from his entire being.

"Please calm down now, darling. Little Queenie is really upset," encouraged Dawn, picking the little dog up and cradling him in her arms.

After much tea and sympathy, slowly Freddie returned to his usual optimistic self again and told the ladies he had physically thrown Jingles out of the flat and had given Dodgy Rodger notice to find alternative accommodation because he was no longer welcome.

"Once bitten, twice shy, that is my new motto of life, and believe me, girls, I will abide by it from now on," he bravely announced to Belinda and Dawn, who nodded their heads in agreement with him.

"Yes, indeed, that's the spirit," exclaimed Dawn. "There are plenty more fish in the sea, and none more fishy than Dodgy Rodger, I would say!"

This statement made Freddie and Belinda laugh hysterically, and the remainder of the day ran quite pleasantly and smoothly, although every so often, Freddie had to fight back the tears of sadness and regret.

It was Belinda's turn to lock up the agency, and as she turned out the lights and set the burglar alarm, a random thought flashed through her mind: "What a pity the world was full of fakes, in more ways than one."

Chapter 42
Web of Deceit

Matt decided to collect Gene on his next arrival at the airport himself when he was bringing in more fake money for the betting shops. On the way, Gene casually brought James' name into the conversation, asking Matt his opinion of the junior partner. Although Matt had been cheating on Belinda, Gene nevertheless appreciated Matt's honesty.

"Oh, he's okay really. A little too ambitious for my liking and a little too full of himself, but he will grow up soon enough," replied Matt generously, turning briefly to look at his passenger. "Any particular reason for asking?"

"No, none at all, Matt, just being my usual inquisitive self," replied Gene with a short laugh. "I have the same opinion of James myself. I guess he is still quite young," he added thoughtfully.

Matt could not help feeling a little concerned. He wanted and needed to keep Gene happy. As far as Matt was concerned, if Gene was happy with the way things were going on this side of the pond, then the Society was happy on the other side of the pond. Matt was astute enough to know that business had never been as good as it was now since the Society had become shareholders, and if James was aggravating Gene in any way whatsoever, no matter how trivial, Matt wanted to know so he could put a stop to it immediately.

"Listen, Gene, don't be evasive. If there is anything really bothering you about James, let me know and I'll deal with it pronto," said Matt, glancing quickly at the other man as his brand-new silver Mercedes-AMG GT pulled up outside the Soho betting shop. Gene turned and looked Matt straight in the eye.

"Hey, buddy, everything is good. Forget that I mentioned James. I will, of course, let you know if I want you to speak to him; like I said, I am far too inquisitive," replied Gene, smiling and releasing his seat belt.

No sooner had the two men entered the new elaborate entrance of the betting shop than James came rushing towards them, smiling broadly and holding out his hand to Gene, who smiled back at him, showing no sign whatsoever of the loathing he really felt inside for the junior partner. Ahead of Gene was two full days of work, dealing with every business aspect of the betting shops' turnover for the previous few months. Business was obviously very good, he mused to himself, noticing how Matt and James had changed their cars recently and knowing how much they had spent on them. Gene always enjoyed his visits to London, apart from the increasing risks he was taking when he carried larger and larger amounts of the fake American-made £20 notes into the country. Gene found the employers of all the betting shops polite and friendly towards him, and Matt and James invariably took him to lavish restaurants, many of which seemed to be springing up all over London. London, he realised, was arguably one of the world's most influential restaurant cities, home to a slew of bold-faced named chefs who were redefining food. Just like New York before her, London seemed to be the hub of the whole world these days, buzzing once again as it did in the 1960s.

On his second day at the Soho betting shop, Frank decided to take a quick break halfway through the morning as the weather was warm with the sun shimmering in a dark blue sky. Feeling an ache in his back and needing to stretch his legs, he called out to Matt that he was taking off for a short while to get some air. The pavements were crowded as usual with people of every nationality known to man, and he could hear occasionally his countrymen speaking loudly to each other as they walked past him on their way to their different destinations.

Gazing into the beautifully displayed window of jewellers, Frank was brought sharply out of his daydreams as he heard a voice close to his ear utter, "Well, well, I'll be damned. What a small world, Mr Lanzo? How nice to see you again."

Spinning around in surprise, Frank came face to face with Adam, whom he remembered from Venice the year before. Peering closely at his intruder to make sure his memory had served him correctly, Frank quickly reacted.

"Hey, there. Adam, isn't it?" he asked, accepting the outstretched hand from the young man in greeting.

"Spot on. Yes, it is, the one who caused all that trouble for everyone in Venice last year, remember?" replied Adam, his generous mouth turning into a big smile.

"No trouble once we found you," chuckled Frank.

"What are you doing in Soho?" asked Adam.

"Oh, I had a heavy business meeting this morning," Frank lied. "Just stretching my legs before making my way to the airport for an evening flight back home."

Adam was disappointed; he would have liked to spend time chatting with Frank because the American intrigued him for more than one reason. Adam was interested in Frank's past.

"Pity you have to leave so soon," said Adam, screwing his nose up with disappointment. "We could have had a nice catch up at dinner together; on me, of course," he added. "Oh well! Not to worry. Maybe next time you are in London?" he said, looking directly into Frank's eyes.

"Yes, of course. Why don't you give me your number so I can call next time I am here?" suggested Frank, purely out of politeness.

"By the way, I suppose you didn't get to see Belinda on this trip?" Adam asked, closely watching Frank's reaction.

Although this intrusion into his private life angered Frank immensely, he showed no sign of agitation whatsoever as he quickly retorted, "No, I suppose I didn't."

Frank then turned and strode away from Adam without taking his contact number. "So long, buddy boy," Frank called over this shoulder, and then he was gone.

A few days earlier, Frank had texted Belinda saying that he was looking forward to seeing her on Wednesday morning. He told her he would be flying into London for a few hours before flying to Paris that same evening in readiness for an important meeting scheduled for the following day. Belinda hated it when she and Frank could not spend the entire night together, making love and eventually giving way to sleep, wrapped in each other's arms. But she had promised him she would not complain about his job and agreed to meet him inside the entrance of Regent's Park on the first bench beside the pink rose gardens.

As he caught sight of her, his heart skipped a beat. Belinda was sitting alone on a bench, staring out across the glistening pond. As he walked towards the bench, the beautiful smell of the pink rose gardens enveloped him and filled his senses. Feeling his presence, as lovers do, Belinda turned towards the park entrance. There he was, the man she adored, the morning sun catching his greying hair and the summer wind doing its best to blow it out of place. Like a schoolgirl, she jumped up and ran the few yards between them, straight into his strong open arms.

"Frank," she whispered her voice shaky with emotion.

"Belinda, amore mio, come ho aspettato questo momento." (Belinda, my love, how I have waited for this moment.) He bought his head down to hers, his mouth found her waiting lips as they locked together, oblivious to the amused glances of the occasional passer-by.

When at last alone in Frank's hotel room, Belinda lay on the king-sized bed, desperately wanting her lover. His tongue wanted to savour every inch of her body. She was sweet to his taste and her feminine scent engulfed his senses. Every fibre of Belinda's body screamed for him. With his every thrust, her full breasts bounced before him, ever increasing his excitement. Lost in their passionate lovemaking, the sensual lovers exploded together in a trance like state of ecstasy. "I love you, Mr Lanzo," she whispered to Frank, who smiled and pulled her glistening body gently to him, wrapping his muscular arms around her pale shoulders.

Max Rushton, the UK's top Prince Harry lookalike, was spending his last few hours in Berlin, window shopping after a very successful photo shoot for a German television series that had taken place the previous day. Due to fly back to London in just a few hours' time, Max had decided to take a look at some of the very trendy shops situated close to his hotel.

Hard rock being his kind of music, he had found an excellent music store with plenty of choice. After selecting three CDs for his already large collection at home, Max was walking towards the cashier to pay for his purchases when his eye caught the cover of a DVD situated in the adult section. Curiosity gripping him, he stopped to take the DVD from the top shelf. On closer inspection of the picture on the black and red cover, featuring a man and woman in erotic positions, Max knew, without doubt, that he was looking at Kay Carney, the Top Drawer Agency's number one Marilyn Monroe lookalike. Max had worked with Kay on several occasions, and even though her face could not be seen completely on the DVD back cover, he knew her well enough to know without a shadow of a doubt that this was indeed Kay Carney. In shock from his discovery, Max purchased not only his chosen CDs but also the DVD, which was entitled Erotische Nacht mit Marilyn Monroe Doppel *(Erotic Night with Marilyn Monroe Double.)*

Max was shocked and found it difficult to believe that Kay had agreed to film what looked like a porn movie and if so, how did she think she would be able to keep it a secret, not only from the agency but from her family, friends and more importantly, her husband Charlie Cooper. Max was confused; this seemed out of character for Kay. It wasn't as if Kay needed the money; she was now not only the most sought-after lookalike in the UK and Europe, but the whole world.

The Top Drawer Agency had the previous week advertised for new lookalikes and tribute acts, so Dawn, Belinda and Freddie were inundated with hundreds of letters containing photographs and DVDs from all across the country with people wanting to become professional lookalikes.

"Honestly," giggled Freddie holding up a black and white photograph, "I do hate to be catty, but this bloke thinks he looks like Al Pacino! Poor man is delusional. He should have gone to Specsavers!"

Taking a closer look at the photograph and letting out a laugh, Belinda remarked, "Oh dear! I see what you mean, Freddie. Put him on the rejected pile, please."

Freddie replied, "Oh don't you worry, darling, I have already put him on it!"

Dawn was reasonably happy with the new lookalikes who were accepted by the agency; in particular, a very good Tina Turner tribute act, who had sent in a DVD of herself singing and gyrating exactly like the super star.

"This new girlie is every bit as good as Kim, if not better," she remarked, replacing the DVD in its cover.

"I just hope she will not prove to be as troublesome as Kim," she added as an afterthought, raising her eyes and glancing at Belinda.

"I doubt whether anybody could be that troublesome," replied Belinda. "But I do feel sorry for Kim. Ever since that terrible incident with the crazy client, which put her in hospital, the poor girl seems to have lost all her confidence; it's really sad."

Suddenly, Belinda's mobile phone rang, and it was Adam asking if they could talk. Politely explaining they were busy at the agency at the moment but she would call him back later, Belinda said goodbye. Offering to close the agency that evening, Belinda explained to Dawn and Freddie she had a couple of private telephone calls to make before her drive home. After they had left, she dialled Adam and was a little surprised when he answered immediately as if he had been waiting for her call. After the normal niceties, Adam wasted no further time in telling Belinda rather excitedly how he had bumped into Frank on Tuesday afternoon in London.

"Really?" she asked, surprise sounding in her voice. "You must be mistaken, Adam. Frank didn't arrive in London until Wednesday," she corrected a little meekly, but Adam was adamant that it was definitely Tuesday because he had gone to Soho to meet an old friend for a drink on the Tuesday, and besides, he explained, he was out of London himself on the Wednesday.

The blood drained from Belinda's face and neck as her confused mind tried to comprehend what Adam was saying to her, his voice seemingly coming from far away.

"You saw Frank in Soho?" she asked, trying to keep her voice steady, although her mind was racing wildly, trying to make some sense of what she was being told.

"Yes, Soho. Apparently he had just finished a depleting business meeting and was outside taking advantage of the sunrays. That was how we bumped into each other."

Belinda was confused; she distinctly remembered Frank telling her he had flown in early Wednesday morning and was in fact flying to Paris later that same evening. Was it possible he had been in London on the Tuesday and for some reason had kept it from her? But why would he do that? Belinda's mind could not answer her own questions, and she begun to feel increasingly confused and icy cold. Accepting now that Adam must have the day correct, Belinda knew she must call Frank and find out what all the secrecy was about and why he had indeed lied to her.

Unhappy at not being able to contact Frank on his mobile, Belinda sent him a text instead, briefly outlining what Adam had told her about him and Frank bumping into each other in Soho. Turning the lights out in the agency, she solemnly walked to her parked car and began the journey back home to south London, weaving her way expertly through the mayhem of the London traffic, her heart heavy with sadness.

As Belinda was closing the garage door, she tried once more to contact Frank. To her relief, this time he answered almost immediately. After their usual loving greeting to each other, Frank told her he had received her text and apologised immediately for his secrecy, explaining gently why he had not told her the truth about when he did actually arrive in London. Listening quietly as he explained he had no chance of spending time with her before Wednesday due to the fact he had to attend several important meetings and therefore thought it best not to tell her he was arriving in London earlier.

Letting out a sound of relief, Belinda asked quizzically, "By the way, what were you doing in Soho?"

Frank drew in a deep breath and replied, "As I have already told you, darling, I was attending important meetings for the Society."

"What a small world we live in," mused Belinda lightly. "Don't you remember I told you my husband works in Soho?"

Frank drew in another deep breath. "Oh, yes, of course, you did mention it some time ago. Isn't he a bookmaker or some such like?" asked Frank, feigning ignorance.

"Yes, he is," replied Belinda. "Well done, Mr Lanzo. You have an excellent memory," she added light-heartedly.

Max decided it was best to meet with Kay to show her the DVD he had found in Berlin, and as she arrived at The Grenadier Public House by taxi, she noticed Max was already waiting for her by the impressive entrance.

As Kay wiggled her way up to Max, all eyes were on her. "Hey, Marilyn, you are looking pretty good for a corpse," came the timely shout from a witty bystander in the crowd, which set everybody laughing. Giggling to herself at the fabulous uniqueness of the London sense of humour, Kay put her blonde head in the air, allowing the waiting Max to put his arms around her briefly before holding her at arm's length and whistling.

"As gorgeous as ever, Miss Monroe," he whispered in her ear.

"Why, thank you, Your Royal Highness," replied Kay coquettishly as she curtsied. Laughing, they hugged each other fondly as some of the crowd looked on mesmerised and held their mobile phones above their heads in the hope of snapping the fascinating image unfolding in front of them.

"I love this pub," remarked Kay as Max escorted her into The Grenadier, which had been built in 1720 as an officer's mess for the Foot Guards Regiment.

"Yes, I do too," enthused Max. "Did you know, it only became a pub around 1818, and rumour has it the Duke of Wellington used to pop in for refreshments," he added, finding a small space for them at the bar.

After ordering their drinks, Max and Kay were ushered to the dining area for dinner at the rear of the pub. The evening was quite delightful for the friends, and because they were having such a nice pleasant time, Max decided to wait until the end of the evening before telling Kay about the DVD, which was safely tucked in his light grey jacket pocket. After paying the bill, Max mentioned to Kay he had something to show her and hoped she would understand why he had not shown her earlier in the evening. Kay, although having had several glasses of wine, sobered up instantly. It was the look on Max's boyish face that made the alarms go off in her head; an intuitive feeling of doom descended on her and the corners of the smiling red lips uncharacteristically began to turn downward.

Caring as he did for his lovely friend, Max was gentle with Kay as he explained to her how he had found a DVD in a shop in Berlin a few days earlier. Taking it out of his jacket pocket and handing it to her, he whispered, "Hate to show you this, Kay, but I think you should know about it."

Instantly, Kay could feel her blood beginning to run cold as her searching eyes took in the cover and title.

Max let out a nervous cough as he murmured quietly to her, "It is you, isn't it, Kay?"

Lifting her eyes from the racy DVD cover and looking ashen, her voice hardly audible, she answered, "Oh, my God, Max, yes, it is me! Where on earth did you get this?"

Max ordered a double espresso for them both and explained to Kay exactly how he had come across the DVD.

"What on earth made you agree to do this, Kay?" asked Max, looking confused and worried, his eyes holding hers as if he would find the answer there.

Jumping to her own defence, with tears threatening to spill, Kay hissed under her breath, "I didn't agree to anything of the kind, Max. I am shocked you would think so little of me."

Quickly apologising to Kay, Max's brown eyes opened wide in disbelief at her following words. As the memory of her recent time in New York materialised before her, she uttered almost to herself, "I know exactly who did this to me, the bastard!"

Max stretched his left arm across the table and gently took hold of Kay's right hand. Seeing how upset she was, Max wished he had never seen the blasted DVD.

"Who was it, Kay? What happened?" he asked, concern showing on his face. "Please tell me, maybe I can help."

Looking Max straight in the eye, Kay told him of her suspicions about Paul Shay. When Kay finished telling Max her story, he knew she had fallen victim to one of the most affluent and terrible sex industries, which were prevalent in every city of the globe. Deciding not to reprimand Kay for her foolishness of trusting strangers in stranger cities, instead Max advised her to find a good solicitor in the UK and file an injunction against the DVD company in Germany to stop further sales.

"The one positive thing about all this is the fact they did not name you. It could be one of several women," encouraged Max, not believing for one moment what he was saying.

Kay was not fully convinced either but agreed she would speak to her solicitor first thing in the morning to find out exactly what course of action could be taken, if any, to having the DVD and original files confiscated.

"Obviously, he will want to see the DVD, Max, so I will make an appointment for us to see him together as soon as possible. Is that okay with you?" Kay asked, trying to keep calm about this awful situation she found herself in.

Max nodded his head in agreement. "Just give me a few days' notice."

Max was extremely concerned. He was aware the Top Drawer Agency would take a very poor view of the DVD and probably drop Kay from their books, no matter how brilliant she was. He also knew Kay would survive. She was indeed very popular with the agency's clients and had many private jobs from them. It seemed the whole world were hugely impressed with Kay Carney and often called her direct for bookings instead of first going through the agency. Kay was not alone; many of the lookalike and tribute acts resorted to this method of cutting out the 'middleman' without the agency's knowledge.

Chapter 43
Sad Turn of Events

"Excellent! A potential job has come in for an Elizabeth Taylor lookalike; Vicky will be pleased," announced Belinda as she read the incoming fax aloud to Dawn.

"Yes, but I hope she has kept to her promise about curbing her drinking habits. Be a darling, Belinda; when you call her, find out if she is sober these days," retorted Dawn, a worried look on her face.

Calling Vicky on her home number, Belinda waited for the telephone to be answered. As she was about to give up, there was a sharp click as the receiver was picked up and Vicky's soft voice answered. The two women chatted for a short while before Belinda explained to Vicky about the excellent job that had come in, requesting their top Elizabeth Taylor lookalike to attend a conference at the Dorchester Hotel, London in aid of the Betty Ford rehabilitation clinics. Having immediately faxed Vicky's promotional details and photographs to the client, Belinda was confident her friend would be accepted as always, because Vicky certainly had a strong resemblance to the iconic film star. Belinda chatted a little about what would be expected of Vicky from the client's point of view and relayed to her briefly the terms and conditions. Vicky, always anxious to make extra money, probably to feed her extravagant lifestyle, agreed immediately to take the job, if offered to her. Then she completely changed the subject and began talking about how fortunate she was in her life and how grateful she was to Lord Jesus, her Saviour, for all her blessings. Even Belinda was taken aback after hearing Vicky quoting from the Bible. Before the call ended, Belinda reminded Vicky about the 'No Alcohol' policy on all jobs relating to Top Drawer Agency.

Looking pensive as Belinda replaced the receiver, Dawn enquired, "Why the puzzled look, is anything wrong?"

Suddenly glancing up and meeting Dawn's eyes, she answered in a half-whisper, "You know, I strongly believe we have a born-again Christian Elizabeth Taylor on our books now rather than a boozy one!"

Letting out a short laugh in reaction, Dawn wittily responded, "Really? Well, let us pray with Jesus that dear Vicky will not be sliding down any more walls in a drunken heap!"

During August, Kay spent much time on lengthy telephone calls with Mr Barrington, her solicitor, who had decided they should go for an injunction to stop the German company selling further copies of the derogatory DVD.

Kay thanked Max for helping her.

"Actually, Max, would you mind terribly if I kept the DVD in case Mr Barrington asks me to bring it in again? That way, I will have it to hand?" asked Kay, looking up and meeting Max's eyes.

"No, of course not, Kay, that is a good idea actually," replied Max, taking the DVD out of the breast pocket of his leather bomber jacket and sliding it across the little round table towards Kay. She thanked him before placing it safely in her multi-coloured handbag.

"Keep me informed of what is going on, and if I can help in any other way, please let me know," said Max, waving down a black London taxi for Kay. Kissing each other goodbye, Max turned up the collar of his bomber jacket against the chilly night air then walked towards the tube station.

"Oh, my God!" exclaimed Belinda, cheeks burning with embarrassment as she apologised profusely before replacing the receiver after finishing the long telephone conversation with a very disgruntled representative for one of their clients. Freddie's deep blue eyes turned to her quizzically.

"That was none other than our new client who booked Vicky as Elizabeth Taylor for the Betty Ford convention," said Belinda, shaking her head and looking extremely worried.

"And?" asked Freddie impatiently, his voice becoming excitable.

"Dawn will go mad when she hears about this," continued Belinda, getting up from her desk and walking about agitatedly.

"Hear what?" asked Freddie.

"Vicky is back on the booze! That was the client's representative for the Betty Ford convention. They are insisting that Top Drawer Agency give a full refund to their company. Apparently, they were unable to use Vicky as the Elizabeth Taylor lookalike last night because she was drunk!" replied Belinda, a deep frown creasing her forehead.

Freddie walked into the kitchenette to boil the kettle for tea. "I thought you said she was sober last week when you spoke to her on the telephone?" he asked waiting for an answer.

"Yes, she was, Freddie, she was quite sober and full of the joys of spring because she said she had found Jesus," explained Belinda, continuing to look worried. "The clients are in a terrible rage, and who can blame them? I did my best to pacify them, but they are extremely angry. Apparently, halfway through the evening, Vicky was asked to give a little speech about the amazing work the Betty Ford clinics do to help people from all walks of life who have alcohol and drug addictions, but they said the whole convention were stunned when Vicky awkwardly climbed up to the podium, clearly under the influence of drink, and slurred her words as she gave her speech. To make matters worse, she was swaying from side and side and then, to the client's horror, Vicky began to tell the guests it was Jesus who had helped those poor unfortunate addicts, not the Betty Ford clinics, and they should all know that Jesus loved them and wanted them for sunbeams!" stressed Belinda, looking aghast as Freddie burst out laughing.

"Oh, my God!" he exclaimed. "Sorry, darling. I know Vicky's drinking is bad for business but I would have loved to have been there," he said, wiping tears of laughter from his eyes.

Although saddened and worried about the situation and knowing how Dawn would react when she found out about this awful situation, Belinda nevertheless could not help but imagine the funny side of Vicky's antics at the Betty Ford convention.

"How can I tell Dawn that Vicky is still drinking and sliding down walls but accompanied by Jesus now!" giggled Belinda, turning to Freddie who, on hearing this, almost choked on his hot cup of tea.

Kay sat quietly in her solicitor's chambers in Lincoln's Inn Fields, until Mr Barrington told her that their injunction had been accepted. Kay breathed a sigh of relief and on the steps of the renowned chambers on her way out, with autumn's pale sunlight in her eyes, Kay quickly took her mobile from her handbag and called Max to let him know the good news.

Arriving home in the early hours of the following morning, exhausted but exhilarated from her successful Marilyn Monroe job, Kay was surprised to see all the lights turned off in her luxury two-bedroomed flat in St. Katherine Docks. Kay complimented herself every day on how her amazing resemblance and portrayal of the famous American icon had given her the luxury lifestyle she now enjoyed. If she were to be truthful, she admitted that the only bane on her horizon these days was her husband, Charles Cooper. Kay was beginning to realise she had never really been in love with him, but that at the beginning it had only been the infatuation of a young girl towards an older man, a kind of Daddy figure really. Now in her mid-thirties, Kay had a roving eye, continuously searching for her soulmate, but never finding her one and only. Charles adored his lovely wife and had no intention of going anywhere. Once safely inside her home, Kay turned on several lights, wondering why Charles had turned them all off, something he never usually did. Hurrying into the dining room, she stopped short at the sight of her husband sitting in his favourite leather armchair, a bottle of beer held in his left hand as he stared ahead.

"Charlie, what are you doing sitting in the dark? Do you know it is two o'clock in the morning?" she asked, dropping her large handbag onto the stone-coloured carpet and walking towards him. Not receiving an answer from her husband, Kay was alarmed, noticing Charles had not even turned to look at her. Suddenly, her eye caught sight of something lying on the carpet by the side of his armchair. The cold hand of fear gripped her heart as Kay felt she would stop breathing, knowing instinctively it was the DVD of her with Paul Shay in New York. Panic flooding her mind, she stooped to retrieve the DVD, while her brain screamed, trying to fathom out how Charlie had found it. Kay distinctly remembered leaving it in the glove compartment of her new car, which was safely parked in the garage.

"Where the hell did you get this, Charlie?" she shouted, holding the DVD up in front of him.

Slowly turning his head and eyes towards her for the first time since she had arrived home, Charles took a swig of his beer and answered gruffly, "Where do you think I got it? In the glove compartment of your car, my darling wife, where you left it."

Kay could feel her temper rising as she snapped at him, "What were you doing in my car? It was locked in the garage."

Charles grinned sardonically at his fuming wife. "Looking for the road map, my sweet. Only I found much more than that, didn't I?"

Kay was feeling quite indignant and angry now. Every rung of the ladder they had climbed together was made possible by her perfect portrayal as the number one Marilyn Monroe lookalike. She had worked extremely hard to become the very best in the world. It was she who made most of the money, which allowed them to live a very lavish lifestyle.

"How did you get into the car? I had the key with me in my purse," she demanded, watching him closely, feeling slightly sick in the pit of her stomach, realising she had been found out.

"The spare key, of course, my darling," answered Charles. "I made a copy of both our car keys as a backup months ago, don't you remember? Your sordid little secret is out; you should have been more careful. Too late now, darling; I have seen quite enough of what you get up to when my back is turned," he added, walking across to the large window and looking down into the deserted marina of St. Katherine Docks.

For the first time in her life, Kay was stumped for words. Of course, there were none she could use to explain to Charlie what actually happened that fateful night in New York. He would never believe her. The fact remained that she'd had every intention of having a fling with Paul Shay behind her husband's back but, of course, without the video camera. Moving gingerly closer towards Charles, panic began to rise again in her stomach, as she said, "Look, Charlie, let me tell you exactly what happened."

But Charles raised his hand; he'd had enough heartache in his life already. Although he loved Kay dearly and could not bear the thought of a life without her, he knew this latest indiscretion of hers was the last straw. He could not stay married to her any longer and he certainly could never forgive her after seeing her in action with another man.

"Listen, Kay, there is nothing for you to explain; the DVD tells me everything I need to know. I shall leave first thing in the morning then file for divorce," he said, finishing his beer.

Kay, although in the past often wished her husband would leave, now froze at the prospect of not having him around to lean on. They had been together for so many years now, and besides, who would look out for her as well as Charlie did? Kay had always been overconfident that he would forgive her just about anything but now rushing to Charlie and throwing her arms around him, Kay begged her heartbroken husband to forgive her. Tears were pouring down her ashen face, but Charles gently pushed her away from him and shook his head, quietly whispering, his voice hoarse with emotion.

"No, sorry, I have had enough, Kay, you have overstepped the mark this time. This, I cannot forgive. I have to leave for my own sanity."

Slowly walking towards the door of the dining room, Charles, eyes now wet with tears, added gently to his distraught wife, "Think of the positive, Kay. You will never have to feel embarrassed again while walking beside me; people staring at us, the odd couple! You strutting through the streets, the vision of loveliness, and I, rushing along behind you, trying to keep up, although hardly managing to carry all your cases."

Kay let out a sob as Charlie turned his back and slowly walked away from her.

Kay spent the following weeks after Charles had walked out of their home and her life subdued and anti-social, refusing invitations from her many friends, acquaintances and admiring suitors. Although Kay had never been in love with her husband, she was fond of him and had grown to rely completely on him. Charles had not only been her husband, he was her driver, hairdresser, dog walker, housekeeper and, much more than this, her shoulder to cry on when her busy work schedule became unbearable. Outwardly, Kay was a happy-go-lucky kind of girl and loved all the attention lavished on her from the world as she strutted around looking like the reincarnation of the famous icon, but inwardly Kay was a frightened little girl who had left home at the tender age of fifteen when her mother, after divorcing Kay's father, married another man. When she first met Charles, Kay felt safe and secure with him and he, in turn, fell deeply in love with this much younger woman. The couple married as soon as Kay had reached the consenting age of sixteen, and for some time she was very happy. But after a few years, with all the attention she received from the opposite sex, her pretty head was turned and Kay began to look at other men, most of them younger than Charles Cooper.

Chapter 44
Mistaken Identity

Although James Swift had a lucrative career, he was becoming more and more dissatisfied with his life. Albeit an attractive young man with a certain charm, James could not hold on to any of his relationships. His natural blonde hair, crowning a handsomely boyish face, his tall, lean physique and fashionable dress sense helped make James a great success with the opposite sex. Since his university days, James was engaged no less than three times, but each of the relationships ended unhappily with all of the women ending the romance. There was something quite calculating about James. The eldest son of three brothers, feeling closer to his mother than his father, an auditor, who appeared to favour his two younger sons, James grew up desperately wanting to impress his aloof father, and became very competitive, always wanting to be the best and making sure that he was, which distanced him from his younger siblings. James was only truly satisfied when he found himself at the forefront of every situation. Although he liked Matt and was fully aware that he owed his good fortune to his senior partner, James was beginning to feel less and less satisfied with his own position as junior partner. Lately, this ruthless streak of his was getting dangerously out of control.

When Gene next arrived in London, James met him and insisted on buying Gene lunch on the way back to Soho, so they stopped at The Crown and Anchor pub in Chiswick, west London. James, always the perfect host, had decided in his conniving mind that this was a good opportunity to 'set the cat among the pigeons' and put his proposition to Gene, regarding the fact that he wanted to become a senior partner in the betting shops, making him an equal with Matt.

During lunch, James and Gene made polite small talk while James tried to muster up the courage to put forward his proposal to the American. Gene realised, not for the first time, he felt more and more uneasy when in James' company, especially when they were alone without Matt. An alarm bell seemed to go off in his stubborn Sicilian head; call it intuition, but when that happened Gene knew without a doubt there was something not quite right with the other person. After ordering coffee, James looked Gene insolently in the eye and made his proposal, explaining that he was a very ambitious sort of chap and now wanted to be made up to a senior partner position like Matt. The American's eyes narrowed as he made a point of eyeballing the younger man.

"You want to do what? Talk about bite the hand that feeds you!" spat Gene, shaking his head slowly from side to side while his brown eyes focused angrily on James.

"Can't blame a chap for trying; all's fair in love, war and business, I would say," quipped the younger man.

"Listen, you wise guy. Matt gave you a chance of a lifetime and you have never had it so good," came the harsh reply. "I will pretend this conversation never took place. You had better count yourself lucky, Mr Swift, that

I am willing to forget this whole nasty business," added Gene, swallowing down the last of his coffee. "I have seen dozens of guys just like you over the years. Even if you were given the role of an equal senior partner, you would soon be dissatisfied yet again, wanting more and more power, then you would start to make even more demands on the Society. You will never become senior partner, not now, not ever, and definitely not if I nor the Society have anything to do with it. Never! Do you hear me?"

James, sitting opposite the American, smiled deviously because he was now ready to drop the bombshell with the video on his smartphone of Gene and Belinda, taken in the Purple Sky Restaurant. Leaning across the table and confidently looking the seething American in the eye, James half-whispered, "Gene, old chap. Never say never!"

Gene quickly stood up from the table and demanded they leave the pub immediately, not wanting to spend another minute alone with this upstart.

James, ignoring the irritation and anger in Gene's voice, agreed. But as he opened the car door for his passenger, he smirked as he slowly remarked, "I think you will see things my way very soon. I have something, I am sure, that will make you change your mind, but it can wait until you are over your jet lag."

Gene focused his brown eyes on James' shining eyes and deliberately lowered his voice menacingly as he half-whispered, "Don't push your luck, dude. You have no idea who you are dealing with." Then, feigning tiredness, he decided to sit in the back of the car, as far away from the younger man as possible; allowing him to close his eyes and rest for the journey into the beating heart of a bustling London.

Matt, always pleased to see Gene, was genuine when he hugged him in welcome and friendship. Against all odds, Gene liked Matt as an almost perfect business colleague. It was a pity, he thought, that Matt had chosen James to be his prodigy, although he understood why Matt had decided on James out of all the other candidates. Matt had confided to Gene in confidence that he had sensed a dark side in James' character and knew he would be the type to go to any lengths to become successful and powerful in life and, of course, James was the exact type of person Matt had been looking for.

Due to the tight schedule Gene had on this trip, he was unable to see his beloved Belinda and it hurt him terribly not to let her know he was in her hometown. When he was due to leave London and fly to Berlin, Matt called him to say he had woken up with a very sore throat and was unwell that morning. He apologised that he would not be able to drive him to the airport but that James would take him instead.

The men sat side by side in James' Alfa Romeo on the way to the airport, both finding it tense while making polite conversation to pass away the time. James had decided this was his chance to approach Gene again and he smugly told him about the video on his phone. Turning briefly to glance at his passenger, James became aware of how the blood had drained from Gene's face and in that split second, he felt victorious. He could see the American's brain racing, desperately trying to make sense of what he had just been told.

"What the hell are you talking about, are you nuts?" yelled Gene, turning to face James who, conveniently for him, had to keep his eyes on the road ahead.

"There is no point you denying it, Gene," was James' smug reply. "I have several copies of the video but I am hugely curious to know where the two of you actually met. It is a well-known fact that Mrs Flynn never visits any of the betting offices," he added thoughtfully, turning briefly to meet Gene's eyes, which were full of fury.

"Please put my mind at rest, Gene. Did you meet Mrs Flynn before you met Matt or afterwards?" asked James, a smirk now playing at the corner of his slim lips. "This question has been running around in my head ever since I saw you lovebirds together."

Gene had decided to play safe and try to reason with James, reminding him that it was no secret Matt was leading a double life. He swore he and Belinda were just friends and nothing more. They had met by accident a few months ago in a coffee shop close to where she worked.

"It was pure coincidence. You must know, life has a way of placing people together. I guess you would call it fate," stressed Gene, his own words echoing in his ears sounding unconvincing, but hoping that James would buy his story.

"Of course, Gene, I know all about fate. But I also know that you and Belinda are far more than just good friends and as we are all aware, the camera never lies, my friend," came his impertinent reply. "By the way, does Belinda know about your friendship with the lovely Isabelle in Venice?"

Almost choking on hearing these words, deep inside Gene was seething with anger at James' audacity.

"Isabelle?" he yelled in disbelief. "How dare you! Isabelle is a good friend of mine, a work colleague, almost like a daughter, nothing more."

James tutted insolently and, smirking, replied, "Really? Funny way for a daughter to behave, entering your hotel room in the wee small hours! Believe me, I saw everything. Remember, our hotel rooms were on the same floor!"

Knowing he was in a tight spot, Gene nevertheless uttered solemnly, "You have a warped and dangerous imagination, dude. Enough of this crap."

James smiled slyly. "Whatever you say, Gene."

They drove on in silence, Gene, stony-faced now, realised that the younger man had obviously no idea exactly what the Code of Conduct really meant for all Associates of the Society.

Slowly lowering his hoarse voice, he said to James, "Listen to me, buddy boy, this smells a lot like blackmail but say one word of this to Matt and you will regret ever having been born. As soon as I am back in New York, I will speak to my superiors to see if, under the circumstances, they will agree for you to be promoted to the position of senior partner, alongside Matt. You will be informed on my next visit to London. Understand?"

James stopped the car at car drop-off and, having the audacity to grin boyishly at Gene, murmured, "Understood. No hard feelings, old chap. I look forward to a favourable outcome when we next meet, but remember, all is fair in love, war and business."

As Gene climbed quickly out of the car, not wanting to stay in this man's company a moment longer than was necessary, he turned slowly, smiling, his brown eyes dancing once again. "La prima legge della Mafia e la lealta, romperlo e si soffre le consequenza." *(The first law of the Mafia is loyalty, break it and you will suffer the consequences.)*

As James drove off, the following thought ran through his mind: I really must learn Italian.

The two men walked purposely in unison, falling into step with each other as people often do when they are used to walking together for several years, sort of knowing instinctively how to pace themselves. They passed quickly through customs at London Airport after flying in from Palermo, Sicily and walked towards a tall, lean chauffeur wearing a light grey uniform and dark glasses, who weakly smiled as he nodded to them in recognition. The shortest of the men was balding and thickset with an olive complexion; his dark black eyes missed nothing. He walked with the faintest suggestion of a limp. Antonio Tosato was one of the Society's most loyal and revered henchmen. Now in his late fifties, he had masterminded many perfect disappearances for his bosses.

His associate and colleague was much taller, slimmer and some ten years younger than Antonio; he too took in everything that was going on around him at a glance. Vincenzo de Luca had a classically beautiful face, dominated by a perfect Roman nose and light hazel eyes. As Antonio, Vincenzo was also one of the Society's most loyal and revered henchmen. Together, the pair were a formidable force. Antonio and Vincenzo enjoyed all the accolades bestowed on them as a special honour by the Society and they lived privileged lives accordingly. Their clothes, of the finest quality, were in the latest style; their shoes of the finest Nappa leather; their homes the envy of their neighbours and their families and loved ones, living the sweet life.

Without one word being spoken, the chauffeur ushered his special passengers towards the waiting limousine for the drive to their hotel. Due to their busy schedule, they were on a flying visit to London this time, and although eager to plan and carry out their new contract for their bosses, both men needed to sleep after their dawn start earlier that morning.

It had been a sunny yet chilly Friday, the sky already turning into twilight as the last punter left the Soho betting office. "Okay, James, that is everything," came Matt's voice as he moved from behind the large counter, a heavy bunch of keys gripped in his left hand. "Time to leave and go get that well deserved drink we have earned today," he added, partly to himself as his blue eyes flickered quickly around the shop, making sure everything was in order and ready for the following morning's rush of clients.

James, walking towards the door, turned to Matt and suggested he should leave his car and allow James to drive. "At the end of the evening, you could drop me off home, take my car to your place then pick me up in the morning for work. What do you think?" he asked.

"Excellent idea, James. No need to use both cars and besides, I only want one beer tonight; my throat is still not better from that nasty bug."

"Okay, let's go," said Matt enthusiastically, opening his mahogany leather briefcase and slipping the keys inside.

"Good chap," said James, slapping Matt playfully on his back. "In that case, my friend, I will get nicely plastered," he added, grinning boyishly.

"You will do nothing of the kind," retorted Matt to the younger man teasingly. "I need you bright-eyed and bushy-tailed tomorrow for our busiest day of the week," which set them laughing.

Green Man pub, a landmark of Putney Heath, south London dates as far back as 1700 and stands in an old duelling spot. After the many battles, the pub was often used for the contestants. Putney Heath is also notorious for its history of highwaymen, including the notorious Dick Turpin. James and Matt, heading towards Parkside at Wimbledon Common, had thoroughly enjoyed the Friday night atmosphere of Green Man, although Matt was good to his word and only drank one beer. It was threatening rain as Matt pulled into James' spacious driveway and, with some difficulty, helped the younger man out of the car and into the house. Managing to transfer a singing James onto the sofa, Matt put on the electric kettle in the adjacent kitchen and made them both coffee. After downing two cups, one after the other, James started to sober up a little as he began to yawn loudly. Laughing at his protégé, Matt tried several times to tell James he would pick him up early the following morning, before he walked towards James' front door.

Turning up the collar of his dark blue cashmere suit and holding a newspaper above his head to ward off the unexpected arrival of heavy rain, Matt left the house and walked quickly to James' parked Alfa Romeo, slid behind the steering wheel and started the engine, which purred like a kitten in response, causing a smile to appear on Matt's face. Remembering suddenly that he had forgotten to tell Belinda he was going for a drink with James that evening, he quickly tried to call her on his mobile phone but there was no answer. It was raining heavily now and as Matt checked the rear-view mirror, he failed to notice two shadowy figures walking swiftly towards James' house. On seeing the car's lights flash on, the shadowy figures stopped dead in their tracks and, turning around in unison, retraced their steps back in the direction they had come. As Matt pulled out of James' driveway, he also failed to notice a motorcycle, cleverly hidden about a hundred metres away, on which the shadowy figures, unrecognisable under their raincoats and hats, now quickly mounted.

Antonio and Vincenzo were about to fulfil their contract to break stealthily into James' home and make sure he would never blackmail anyone ever again, especially someone like Frank Lanzo. The henchmen had to quickly rethink their original plan now that James had decided to go out so late, thwarting their deadly intentions completely. Antonio and Vincenzo had only one thought in mind: how to honour the contract they had been entrusted with. Being professional killers, they instinctively knew they had no option now but to take James out while he was driving, making it look like an accident, which would be highly plausible on such a dark wet night.

"Grazie a Dio per il bel tempo britannico," *(Thank God for the great British weather)* uttered Antonio to Vincenzo, who sat behind him as the pillion rider. Vincenzo let out a low throaty laugh as he pulled a Ruger Super Redhawk, the ultimate Ruger wheel gun, from his raincoat pocket.

As Matt drove, he noticed how deserted the roads were and, anxious to get home as quickly as possible and confident in the fact he was an experienced driver, Matt put his foot down. Turning on the radio, he smiled to himself as Roy Orbison's distinctive voice came over the airwaves, singing *Pretty Woman*.

Matt tunefully sang along and was oblivious to the fact that a motorcycle was driving very close behind him. With the loud music completely filling his ears, together with the angry, heavy rain, Matt Flynn failed to hear the four shots that crackled like lightning, sinking bullets deep into the back tyres of James' Alfa Romeo. To his sudden shock and horror, Matt instantly lost control of the steering wheel as the car skidded drastically from one side of the wet road to the other. Trying desperately to do an emergency stop, fear gripping his heart and sweat pouring down his ashen face, almost blinding him, Matt slammed his right foot down hard on the brake, which caused the car to go into a twisting somersault, landing upside down on the slippery road, stopping only when the car smashed headlong into several large oak trees. The horrific screeching sound was followed by an enormous thud and the alarming sound of the horn going off as Matt's head smashed fatally against the steering wheel as smoke billowed up into the dark, wet and windy night.

The Kawasaki, which had overtaken James' Alfa Romeo after the riders had carried out their deadly deed, slowed down briefly to satisfy themselves that nobody could survive such an accident as this, and now picked up speed as it disappeared unnoticed. Looking over his shoulder, Antonio uttered, "Ora vai a ricattare il diavolo," *(Now, go blackmail the devil)* as Antonio and Vincenzo congratulated themselves on another successful contract.

Deep in a troubled sleep, Belinda thought she was dreaming when she heard, somewhere in her subconscious, loud banging on the front door. Rubbing her eyes as she slowly awakened, Belinda realised she had not been dreaming but there was in fact someone banging on her door. Startled and groggily opening her tired eyes, she quickly got out of bed. Panicking and rushing downstairs to the front door, calling out Matt's name as she descended the curved flight, Belinda presumed he had forgotten his door keys. Through the lacy net curtains in her dining room, she thought she could see flashing blue lights and called Matt's name again through the door, panic restricting her voice when he did not respond.

"Mrs Flynn, this is the police. Please open the door."

At these words, Belinda's heart froze as she tried several times to open the heavy oak door, eventually coming face to face with three police officers, one male and two female. The male officer began to talk to her but she could not comprehend what he was trying to say. One of the female officers stepped forward and put an arm around her shoulders, ushering Belinda back inside the house, out of the angry, wet night. Her mind screamed in disbelief as the officer's words started to cruelly sink in at last. Belinda was only aware of a strange, piercing noise, similar to the sound a wounded animal would make, but she did not realise it came from her. Belinda's mind could not, would not, accept what the police were trying to make her understand.

It must be a mistake; Matt was an excellent driver, and would never drink and drive, she heard herself saying in her husband's defence.

Chapter 45
Departures and Arrivals

The following weeks were a foggy blur for Belinda. Her sister Sandra stayed with her for the first week, after which, her other sisters, Christine and Carole, offered to stay, but Tanya had already insisted she would keep Belinda company during the week leading up to Matt's funeral. Although grief stricken at her loss, Belinda felt the strong bond of her family and friends' love surround her when she most needed it, helping her to come to terms with the tragedy. Matt had taken out a large life insurance plan, which would now be awarded to his grieving widow. Matt had also left a substantial amount of money to his wife, making Belinda's financial future very secure indeed, and of course there was the house.

Gene was deeply saddened after receiving a telephone call from James, telling him the tragic news of Matt's demise. Trying to conceal the hate he felt for James in his voice, Gene was thankful that James had no idea poor Matt had died in his place and it was no accident. The police were satisfied that the car had dangerously skidded due to the ferocious weather, causing Matt to lose control of the car as it turned over, completely wrecking most of the body work and burning out all of the tyres as it crashed into the unsuspecting large oak trees, viciously ripping them from their roots.

Frank was anxious to speak with Belinda but decided to wait a few days. His heart went out to her, for no matter what state her marriage had been in, he knew she would be devastated at losing Matt from her life. Frank knew, for obvious reasons, that he could not attend the funeral, making the excuse to the Society that he was to have surgery days before the date set for Matt's burial. The Society decided to send Sergie Belladoni in Frank's place to represent them and their many Associates.

James was aware of the excitement building up inside him when he thought about the prospect of becoming senior partner of all three betting offices now. With Matt's demise, James felt even more confident that Gene would pursue his proposal and the Society would officiate this. Although James' video of Belinda with Gene was no longer viable due to Matt's sudden and tragic death, there was the little gem remaining regarding the beautiful Isabelle and her soirée with Gene Capalti in Venice, while the American had already started his affair with Belinda Flynn. James knew only too well what lengths Gene would go to keep this information secret from Belinda.

After the moving and beautiful Roman Catholic Requiem Mass at St Mary's Church, Clapham Common, celebrating Matt Flynn's life, James introduced Sergie Belladoni to Belinda, explaining to her that Sergie was a regular customer of the Soho betting office and was also a friend of Matt's. Pale and red-eyed, Belinda held out her hand to Sergie, looking up and weakly smiling at the big American, thanking him for the most beautiful wreath for Matt and for his sincere commiserations. Sergie told

Belinda he had really liked Matt and counted him among his good friends.

Although Belinda was deeply in love with Frank, she felt very alone after losing her husband. They had been together for many years and were extremely fond of each other, in many ways. In fact, they were best friends. Not wishing to speak to Frank yet, Belinda asked Tanya to call him in New York to let him know about Matt's fatal accident. During her brief conversation with Frank, Tanya explained to him that Belinda was extremely distraught but she would call him herself in a few days' time. Frank feigned shock at Tanya's news and asked her to tell Belinda how shocked and saddened he was to hear this and that if there was anything, anything at all, he could do, to please let him know.

Almost immediately, James tried his utmost to step into Matt's shoes. As far as James was concerned, it was business as usual for all the betting shops. Sergie stayed in London for some time to support James in his new appointment as senior partner and to oversee the betting shops. Much to James' disappointment, the Society selected a junior partner from the inner ranks of their up-and-coming Associates.

"Another bloody Yank," hissed James under his breath when he had heard the news, but the reality of his promotion to senior partner made him deliriously happy, and he texted Gene, thanking him for his co-operation. Before sending the text, James added, 'You will be pleased to know your soirée with Isabelle has now been completely wiped from my mind.'

Gene's top lip curled with disgust when he received this impertinent text message but he was placated by the knowledge that James would have to pay for his treachery sooner or later, even though an innocent man had given him, for the time being, a stay of execution by being in the wrong place at the wrong time.

When Belinda woke on a dull, overcast Saturday morning, she had an overwhelming desire to speak to Frank. Slipping slowly out of her king-sized bed, she picked up her mobile and texted him, asking when it was convenient to call. Instantly, her mobile whistled loudly and, answering it with a racing heart, she heard the deep husky tones of her lover's voice. Frank assured her he would be in London again within the next couple of weeks.

The following week, as Belinda arrived at the agency, Freddie jumped up and, swanning towards her with outstretched arms, wrapped them protectively around his good friend, as little Queenie rolled over and scratched his back on the thick carpet, delighting that his master seemed happy.

"Belinda, how are you, my darling girl?" asked Freddie. "Are you sure you're ready to come back to work?"

Fondly hugging Freddie, Belinda knelt down to tickle little Queenie's furry tummy and, glancing up at her dear friend, she answered solemnly, "Yes, Freddie, it is far better for me to be back at work again now. I feel so much worse at home."

"Good girl, this place has been miserable without you. Fabulous to have you back, darling," replied Freddie, flitting into the kitchen to fill the electric kettle with water.

"Belinda, darling!" came Dawn's high-pitched voice as she rushed into the office and enveloped her friend in her arms. Dawn and Belinda spent the following hour chatting about Matt's tragic death. Eventually, they checked the provisionally booked lookalike and tribute act jobs that had come in while Belinda had been on bereavement leave from the agency.

"You know, Belinda, while you were away, I had to use Sonia Smith in your place for the Capital Radio event," said Dawn, looking up over her glasses. "Apparently, by all accounts, Sonia did quite well, although we all know she doesn't look as much like Joan Collins as you do, darling, but nevertheless the clients were pleased with her."

Smiling weakly at Dawn, Belinda replied, letting out a little giggle for the first time that day. "Well! At least Sonia had a chance to prove herself at long last, and we now have an accomplished replacement!"

Dawn was relieved to see Belinda was gradually getting back to her usual carefree self.

When Dawn heard not only from Belinda but also from the disgruntled client concerned about Vicky Sutton's behaviour at the Betty Ford convention, she was furious. Dawn always maintained that her lookalikes and tribute acts conducted themselves accordingly to what the agency name suggested, in a Top Drawer fashion.

"Belinda, darling, would you please call Vicky Sutton and ask her to come in as soon as possible. It is high time I read her the Riot Act once and for all," announced Dawn, her voice rising slightly with annoyance.

Much to Dawn and Belinda's surprise, when Vicky Sutton did eventually come into the agency, she did not give Dawn a chance to complain about her recent unacceptable behaviour at the Betty Ford convention. Hugging Belinda and sitting down in the vacant chair opposite Dawn, Vicky announced she was giving up lookalike work to become a full-time born-again Christian, something now very dear to her heart. Wanting to dedicate her whole life to her new-found beliefs, Vicky explained she would not have time to carry out her portrayal of the legendary Elizabeth Taylor any longer because she now felt this was a shallow way for her to live and that anything so frivolous did not belong in her new life. She explained that within the next few months, she hoped to travel to Africa, with other members of her new church, to preach the gospel of Christ. Looking shocked, Dawn and Belinda raised their eyebrows at each other and queried the safeness of Vicky going to Africa. Answering without hesitation, Vicky proudly explained that the Lord would protect her and she had never felt as happy and fulfilled as she did now that she had found Jesus. Before Vicky left the agency, she asked the ladies if they would allow her to pray over them for inner peace, particularly for Belinda after her tragic loss. The prayers brought tears to Belinda's sad eyes, and afterwards she quietly confided to Vicky that she had felt peace and acceptance seeping through her while Vicky prayed.

"I am happy for her but worried at the same time," said Dawn, a frown furrowing her forehead as soon as Vicky had left the agency.

"I feel exactly the same, Dawn, but we must hope she will be safe, as I am sure she will be, now that she has Jesus," replied Belinda, glancing through the computer, studying the latest photographs of the remaining Elizabeth Taylor lookalikes on Top Drawer Agency's books.

Gene, together with Joey Franzini, arrived in London and was relieved when Jason, one of the employees of the Soho betting office, was waiting to drive the Americans into London. Gene was impressed with Joey, who was carrying a large amount of fake money in his luggage as he passed through the nothing to declare lane with the coolness of a seasoned professional. Joey had been carefully chosen by the Society to fill the vacant position of junior partner in London. At thirty-three, the American was admired by his peers for his diplomacy. Joey always thought things through before acting on them, even when angry or feeling offended. Gene, together with the Society, was more than satisfied with their choice of Joey to work alongside James and oversee the betting offices when Gene and Sergie were unable to be in London.

When Gene ushered Joey into the Soho betting office, James was ready to welcome them with open arms, although he was still unhappy the Society had sent one of their Associates to fill the vacant position of junior partner. Joey Franzini, of average height and slim build, his face possessing a child-like beauty, with eyes of a light hazel, smiled as he stretched out his right arm and shook James' hand in welcome. The two young men seemed to hit it off immediately, which pleased Gene. This was exactly what the Society wanted to achieve: James' trust in Joey.

A little later, taking Joey to one side, Gene whispered, "You have an old head on young shoulders. Make sure you use it well."

Turning to face his mentor, whom Joey had great regard for, he winked at Gene and quietly replied, with a cynical smile on his lips, "Come sempre, il mio amico, come sempre." *(As always, my friend, as always.)*

Chapter 46
New Beginnings

He stood outside the door to her luxurious home in Clapham. The first time he had seen where she actually lived. As if by clockwork, the door was opened slowly and they were rooted to the spot, staring at each other, emotions overwhelming them both. It was he who made the first move, swiftly walking across the threshold, taking her in his arms and holding her tightly to his masculine chest, a tiny breathless sound escaping from her as she felt his hard-muscled body close to hers.

"Oh, amore mio, amore mio, quanto mi sei mancato," (*Oh, my love, my love, how I have missed you.*) croaked Frank's voice as his mouth pressed gently to her ear. Once inside the house, Frank took her into his arms and began to kiss her mouth, his need for her growing like a wild animal inside him. Somewhere in the far distance, he thought he heard her muttering, "No, No!" Expertly, he slipped her panties off. Unable to resist him and moaning in surrender, her legs opened in answer to his urgency for her. His lips savoured every inch of her body. There was a feeling of raw excitement rising from the pit of her stomach, overwhelming her. With feelings of guilt now completely forgotten, they became more and more erotic in their lovemaking. Finally, with all their passion spent, they fell into each other's arms, sticky, hot and wonderfully exhausted.

As Frank encircled his lover, he whispered quietly, "Voglio sempre il tuo corpo e la tua anima, mia cara." *(I will always want your body and soul, my darling.)*

After making sure everything was running smoothly with the betting shops and the fake money expertly distributed, Gene (Frank) flew back to New York. As far as Joey and James were concerned, Gene was fully satisfied they worked well together and were already showing signs of becoming a successful partnership. Although both young men claimed to be heterosexual and loved the ladies, they found they had a strong chemistry between them, bordering on infatuation for each other. Both found reasons and excuses to speak together as much as possible during the working day, discussing trivial matters of no real consequence to the running of the businesses. Of course, Joey was made aware of the bad blood between Gene and James. He was also aware that although the Society were extremely pleased with the smooth way James had slipped into the senior partner position, they were not impressed at the deterioration of James' relationship with Gene. The only thing Joey knew for sure was that he was highly attracted to James, a member of his own gender. This was a first for Joey, and it caused him anguish as he questioned his own sexual orientation.

"Another job for Freddie!" announced Dawn as she quickly ripped the fax off the machine, as a weak autumnal sun fought desperately to push itself through the grey London skies.

"Excellent, that is great news," responded Belinda, clapping her hands.

"They are promoting a new Steinway piano in their factory in Hamburg and want a Liberace lookalike for a television commercial," Dawn read aloud from the sheet.

"Great!" exclaimed Belinda. "Freddie will be over the moon about this."

And, sure enough, he was. "It has been a while since my last job, so I am very happy indeed," enthused Freddie, swanning around the office, collecting the used coffee cups. "Belinda, darling, will you be able to take Queenie while I'm away in Hamburg?" he asked, strutting into the little kitchenette and placing the used cups and saucers into the dishwasher.

"Yes, of course," answered Belinda. "You will only be gone for one day and night, and besides, Queenie will keep me company."

Although the morning passed smoothly, during their lunch break Belinda felt Freddie was acting rather sheepishly. Knowing him so well, she asked Freddie what was on his mind.

Freddie's answer caused Belinda to let out a low moan then mutter under her breath, "Oh no, not again."

Apparently, a few days earlier and purely by chance, Freddie had bumped into Claudio, the Italian Opera singer, and by all accounts, the ex-lovers were back together. Disliking Claudio immensely, Belinda recalled how, when he was last in Freddie's life, he had caused such heartache for poor sweet Freddie, who simply adored the Italian but unfortunately, Claudio was a real player, breaking Freddie's heart in the interim.

"Listen, Belinda," came Freddie's hoarse voice. "I know how and why you dislike Claudio but, I promise you, he has changed."

Letting out a sarcastic half-laugh, Belinda almost shouted, "Changed?" Then, calming down, she added quietly, "Freddie, darling, please grow up; people do not change, not people like Claudio. Surely you know a leopard never changes its spots!"

Freddie looked crestfallen as he searched his friend's face.

"This is exactly why I didn't mention any of this to you earlier, Belinda. I knew what your reaction would be, but I know Claudio has changed and we are going to make a go of it seriously this time, so please, please try to be happy for me," stressed Freddie as his arms flailed dramatically in the air.

"Okay, okay, darling," murmured Belinda, moving slowly towards Freddie and embracing him. "You know how we all love and care for you, but we remember how heartbroken you were when Claudio treated you so shabbily last time," she added gently, kissing him on the cheek.

"Yes, Belinda, my sweet, I know, and I appreciate your concern, but I am deeply in love and I would be so happy if you and Dawn could be happy for me too," answered Freddie, taking Belinda's hands in his and squeezing them affectionately.

At that precise moment, for some unknown reason, Matt's handsome face flashed into Belinda's mind and instantaneously she felt the tears rising to her eyes. Freddie sensed her sadness and pulled her into his wiry arms.

"Dearest Belinda, I love Claudio with the same passion you love Frank, and I pray you and I find lasting happiness with our loved ones."

On hearing these touching words and unable to control her tears any longer, Belinda allowed them to flow hot and fast down her sad face as her heart grieved for Matt and Frank.

During the following few weeks, James and Joey became almost inseparable. One chilly Saturday evening after the young men had been out drinking together, both the worse for wear and unsteady on their feet, they hailed a taxi to James' house in Wimbledon. Because of the lateness of the hour and the fact they had drunk heavily during the evening, they decided Joey should stay the night. Fumbling for the keys in his jacket pocket, James giggled as he tried unsuccessfully to slip one of the keys into the lock of his large wooden front door. Laughing out loud on seeing James' feeble efforts, Joey masterfully took the keys from James' hand and proceeded to unlock the front door himself.

"Yippee, at last! Well done, Joey! Come on in, welcome to my humble abode," uttered James as he staggered across the threshold of his tastefully furnished home, hanging on to Joey's jacket sleeve and dragging the American into the house with him, almost falling. "Come along, we will have a couple of nightcaps before we turn in for the night."

Wishing he had not drunk quite so much, Joey cautiously followed James into the large lounge and dropped heavily onto the sofa. James disappeared into the kitchen to pour them a brandy, but when he returned Joey had fallen asleep, sprawled out on the sofa with his strong slim legs resting on the floor.

"Charming!" murmured James. "Hey, Joey, be a good chap, come on, wake up! Let's find you a bedroom, you will be more comfortable," coaxed James, his voice becoming insistent as he shook Joey roughly.

Trying to open his heavy eyes, Joey smiled broadly as he saw James bending over him.

"There's a good chap," cajoled James as he handed him a brandy.

Yawning and stretching out his arms, Joey slowly sat up and accepted the glass of brandy and downed it down quickly.

"Okay, dude, I am deadbeat. Show me to my boudoir so I can get some beauty sleep," giggled Joey as he staggered while getting to his feet.

"Follow me, old chap," James replied.

The room was charming, thought Joey, as his eyes took in his surroundings fleetingly before falling backward onto the king-sized bed.

"Goodnight, dude," whispered Joey, more to himself than to James, who knelt beside Joey on the bed, and asked sexily, "What? No kiss for your new best friend, then?"

In his alcohol-fuelled brain, Joey giggled and tried unsuccessfully to raise his head from the softness of the pillow to give James a friendly peck on the cheek. What followed was so surreal to Joey, he almost felt as if he was dreaming. James had deftly brought his mouth down ardently on Joey's lips and there followed passionate homosexual lovemaking as James expertly took the lead to introducing

Joey into a world the American had never ventured before. What amazed and slightly shocked Joey was the fact that, although he had drunk too much that evening, he actually enjoyed the new adventure James was taking him on. There was a strong chemistry between them, and deep down Joey knew it was inevitable something sexual would happen.

Frank called Belinda several times during the following weeks but she was morose and sad when he explained to her the Society were sending him to Las Vegas during the Christmas holiday to settle a pending dispute worth several million dollars. Saying more than once that he missed her dreadfully and hoped he would be back in London early in the New Year, Frank heard the disappointment in her voice.

Although she understood Frank's commitment to his job, Belinda continued to wonder why he had never invited her to visit him in New York, especially now she was a free woman. As always, she would spend the Christmas holidays with her family and friends. There was a Lissenden Players show for her to produce and perform in on Christmas Eve and a lookalike job in Paris on New Year's Eve. All exciting distractions from her deep sadness and loneliness of being apart from her lover yet again for the holidays and, at the same time, missing Matt terribly.

Just before Christmas, while Belinda was getting ready to close the agency after a busy day dealing with last-minute requests for lookalikes, the telephone rang on Dawn's desk and glancing up, Belinda decided to ignore it because it was past six o'clock. Stubbornly and insistently, the telephone continued to ring. Belinda swiftly lifted the receiver.

"Good evening, this is Top Drawer Lookalike and Tributes Act Agency. Can I help you?"

"Good evening, could I please speak with Belinda Flynn?" came the deep tones of the caller. Belinda frowned to herself, not recognising the voice on the other end of the telephone. The speaker had a charming accent, but she could not quite distinguish from which country it belonged.

"Yes, this is Belinda Flynn speaking. Can I help you?" replied Belinda, wondering how the caller knew her name.

"Belinda, this is Count Luigi Boggia. Do you remember we met at the Golden Star Charity Gala in Monte Carlo? I am a good friend of Frank Lanzo," he added quickly.

Belinda laughed nervously before answering. "Yes, yes, of course."

"I am in London on business and thought it would be nice to contact you. I hope that is acceptable to you, Belinda?" enquired Count Luigi Boggia, his deep melodic voice dropping a little.

"Of course it is acceptable to me. I know you are a close friend of Frank's," she added quickly.

"I was wondering whether you would do me the honour of having dinner with me tomorrow evening before I fly back to Venice."

"Oh! Dinner tomorrow evening," repeated Belinda, trying to keep her voice calm as she accepted his very kind invitation.

"Excellent, my dear. Would it be convenient for me to collect you from your home, or would you prefer I came to the agency?" asked the Count graciously.

Her mind was racing, and for some reason she felt really excited. After giving Count Luigi Boggia her home address, he bid her "Buonasera." *(Good evening.)*

Belinda's mind went back to their first and only meeting in Monte Carlo; remembering what an extremely handsome and charming gentleman he was and also an amazingly graceful dancer.

The next morning, Dawn and Freddie were very impressed when Belinda told them about the Count's telephone call and how she would have dinner with him later that evening.

"I can't wait to tell Claudio about this," chirped Freddie excitedly. "He will be extremely jealous of you, darling, fraternising with a real Italian Count!"

At precisely 8 o'clock that evening, a dark blue Bentley pulled up outside Belinda's home. Pulling her cream net curtains back slightly to peer outside, Belinda was alarmed to see a tall, slim chauffeur alight from the Bentley and open one of the gleaming back doors. Not wanting to appear nosey and dropping the curtain instantly, Belinda rushed to collect her coat, in the interim missing the elegance of the tall handsome gentlemen as he slowly alighted from the shadow of the back seat of the Bentley and walked purposely towards her front door, the mischievous wind playing annoyingly with his dark hair, now greying at the temples.

Like most people who met him, Belinda was in awe of Count Luigi Boggia, and during dinner he was most attentive to her and interested to know about her early life in London and her career as a lookalike. Almost immediately, Belinda found herself relaxing as the Count's charm put her at ease. He proved to be a most interesting dinner companion, telling her many things about his life which completely intrigued her. It had been a long time since Belinda had had such a wonderful evening.

When the Count excused himself and left the table to take a call, Belinda's thoughts were of Frank, realising suddenly that he had never asked her about her childhood, about her family, or anything or anyone who was important to her, and yet, in only a few hours, Count Luigi Boggia had shown such interest in her life. Somehow, the Count's genuine interest endeared him to her.

Returning to their table within a few minutes, the Count smiled warmly at her and asked, "More pink champagne, Belinda?"

Nervously laughing, Belinda nodded her head and mouthed, "Thank you, Count Luigi."

Before she was aware of what was happening, the Count stretched across the round table and gently covered her left hand with his own and, looking directly at her, murmured, "You are so very welcome, my dear."

Smiling awkwardly, Belinda gently pulled her hand away, lowering her eyes with embarrassment. After all, she was deeply involved with Frank, the Count's closest friend, and she certainly did not want to endanger her passionate relationship with Frank nor for the Count to get the wrong end of the stick! Her champagne-fuelled imagination started to run away with her as she began to wonder whether the Count and Frank had devised this dinner date between them, to see if Belinda was indeed faithful to Frank.

The remainder of the evening slipped by quickly and all too soon it was time for the Count to escort Belinda home.

Close to midnight, the maître d' walked to the Count's table and whispered something in his ear.

"Many thanks, Henri. Please tell my chauffeur we will be with him directly," replied the Count, before turning to Belinda and explaining that his chauffeur had arrived to drive them home.

Sitting comfortably in the back of the Bentley as it headed towards Belinda's home, she asked the Count whether he would tell Frank they had dinner together.

"But of course, my dear. Frank and I are very close, like brothers in fact. We tell each other everything; well, almost everything," he said laughing. "It was an innocent dinner between friends, and I am sure Frank will thank me for entertaining you while I was in London," he added, squeezing Belinda's arm.

"I will call him in a few days and tell him what a wonderful evening I had," agreed Belinda, thanking the Count for his kind generosity.

As they reached Belinda's home, the Count escorted her to her door and, looking deeply into her bewildered eyes, he kissed her hand softly then waited until she was safely inside.

Chapter 47
Dark Clouds Gathering

The next morning, Belinda was feeling happier than she had done for some months as she went rushing through the horrendous London traffic to work.

"Well?" said Freddie, on her arrival. "Dawn and I are waiting!"

Laughing out loud, Belinda answered, "Oh, you are, are you?"

As she sat down at her desk, looking up at Freddie and Dawn, a slight blush touching her cheeks as her mind floated back to the previous evening, she told them, "It was wonderful. Count Luigi Boggia is an amazingly knowledgeable and charming man, and I have never met anyone quite like him before."

Noticing how Dawn and Freddie looked at each other, giving knowing glances, Belinda laughed, adding, "No, no, nothing like that, although he is quite a man and his class seeps through every fibre of him. The Count, as you know, is a good friend of Frank's, and he was just being friendly to me, nothing more," she continued quickly.

"But of course, darling," agreed Freddie, winking.

The rest of the day passed quickly but before it was time to finish for the day, a loud knock sounded on the agency door and a voice called out crisply. "Delivery."

Freddie was first to reach the door, with little Queenie growling annoyingly as a delivery man, dressed smartly in the green and gold uniform of one of London's grandest stores, stepped into the office, a most beautiful bouquet of flowers held carefully in his arms.

"Oh! Hello, can I help you?" asked Freddie, surveying the bouquet and the man interestingly.

"Special delivery for Mrs Belinda Flynn," announced the delivery man, glancing at the two ladies present.

"Oh! How wonderful," squealed Freddie excitedly, as if the flowers were for him.

The flowers for Belinda were, of course, from the Count.

Belinda did not have to contact Frank; he called her the following evening, relaying how the Count had telephoned him from Venice earlier that morning, mentioning his dinner with Belinda in London. Although Frank agreed with her it was a nice gesture on the Count's part, Belinda heard in his voice that Frank was not altogether happy.

"Frank, I assumed you would not mind if I accepted his invitation to dinner because he is your very close friend," said Belinda defensively. Frank assured her several times he did not mind and was happy she had such a lovely evening, but somehow Belinda was not convinced.

Christmas was not a happy time for Belinda. Missing Matt terribly and feeling the sadness and pain from both their families and friends was heartbreaking enough, but equally painful was the absence of her beloved Frank. As far as Belinda was concerned, it appeared that sadly he was in no hurry for them to be together as partners. How much easier it would be, she reasoned, if they had at least lived in the same city, but Belinda had no intentions of mentioning her concerns to Frank again.

By New Year's Eve, Belinda was flying to Paris with several other lookalike and tribute acts for a charity ball in aid of World Vision France, founded in 1950 and now present in ninety-eight countries, helping more than one hundred million people worldwide to fight against poverty through its humanitarian aid. The chosen lookalikes were booked to meet and greet the guests at the ball, professionally mixing and mingling among the throngs of jovial people. Flashing cameras everywhere, excitable tipsy men were vying to stand close to the ever-glamorous Joan Collins and the other beautiful lookalikes. Adam made his way to Belinda's side as she was being pestered by a young Frenchman, busy explaining to her in broken English that he had always preferred the more mature woman of the world. On seeing Adam approaching, Belinda made her apologies to the Frenchman and quickly pulled Adam onto the crowded dance floor.

"So, I do have my uses after all?" laughed Adam as he fell into step with Belinda.

"Of course you do, Adam. Believe me, your timing was perfect, saving me from that silly little boy," came

Belinda's quick reply, and they danced around the spacious floor laughing together. As always, Adam asked after Frank, interested to know where Frank was these days and whether or not she had seen him lately in London.

The same uncomfortable feeling flooded Belinda's senses, and again she wondered why Adam was so interested in Frank and his whereabouts. Deciding to play safe, Belinda told Adam that she had in fact not seen Frank for some time now and was not sure when she would be seeing him again. For the foreseeable future, she explained to Adam, Frank would be located in Las Vegas on business, and she had no idea when or where they would meet up again.

"Okay, but please give Frank my kindest regards when you do speak to him," said Adam, as the dance came to an end and he courteously escorted Belinda off the floor.

"Of course I will, Adam. Thank you for the dance," she replied, politely smiling.

But, deep down, Belinda knew Frank had no liking whatsoever for Adam.

After the hectic Christmas and New Year rush, January proved to be quieter than expected for the agency. Dawn encouraged Freddie to take advantage of this slow period and have a few days off, which he readily agreed to because Claudio was not due to perform in Milan for another week and this would give the lovers more precious time together. Dawn and Belinda were pleasantly surprised how well Freddie and Claudio were getting along this second time around.

"Fingers crossed it will last for them now," uttered Belinda.

As Frank arrived at his lover's home, the wind gallantly joined forces with the freezing rain to bring complete misery to the end of the working week for millions of commuters in a dark, damp and cold London.

With her heart jumping and a warm glow flooding her entire body at the sound of his knock, Belinda slowly opened her front door, immediately catching her breath as Frank, manly and attractive as ever, stood in front of her, his amazing brown eyes shining and dancing in the darkness of the night.

Remembering all her lover's likes and dislikes, Belinda had an ice bucket cradling a bottle of champagne – Gosset Grande Reserve Brut – ready and waiting for them to toast the New Year, albeit a little late.

After removing his cashmere overcoat and laying it on one of the plush armchairs, Frank moved swiftly to Belinda and, taking her trembling body in his arms, whispered in her ear, "Mia cara, ho fame di te." *(My darling, I've hungered for you.)*

Before Belinda could comprehend what he had said in Italian, Frank swooped her up in strong arms and took her to the bedroom. Placing her at the foot of the king-sized bed and without taking his eyes off her own, Frank slowly undressed Belinda, gently pulling the black silk jumper over her head. The love she felt for this man enveloped her soul, making her body tremble and their passion for each other ever more lustful. Gently pushing Belinda back onto the bed, Frank began to kiss her quivering body, his tongue finding every crevice of her until she cried out in ecstasy while climaxing.

They lay in each other's arms for a long while, peaceful and satisfied after their passionate pleasure. Every once in a while, Belinda gently kissed her lover's mouth and chest, feeling cherished in Frank's strong arms, encircling her hot, glowing body. Carefully slipping off the bed, so as not to disturb his sleep, Belinda picked up her robe and threw it around her pale shoulders as she tiptoed into the kitchen to make sure everything would be perfect for dinner.

After the lovers had enjoyed a meal of generous slices of salmon with a dot of horseradish atop a traditional oatcake, green beans and oven sautéed potatoes with red onion, garlic and rosemary, Frank kissed the palms of Belinda's hands several times, complimenting her on the wonderful meal. They shared a bottle of the finest Italian wine and chatted openly into the early hours, Frank curious to know every detail of Belinda's dinner date with Count Luigi Boggia. Being aware that Frank was indeed jealous of the fact that his closest friend had sought out her company when he was in London recently saddened Belinda, and she found her memories of the wonderful evening spent with the Count now dampened. However, later, lying content in each other's arms after making passionate love again, Belinda dreaded the dawn that would soon creep stealthily into the bedroom, signalling the break of day; the day that would take her lover away from her once again.

Chapter 48
The Noose Tightens

It was a week of surprise visits for the Top Drawer Agency as Kay Carney also came in the following day, looking more like Marilyn Monroe than Marilyn Monroe! As always, Dawn made a big fuss of her; after all, she was their most successful lookalike and tribute act, in higher demand than any other character on their books.

Belinda noticed that Kay had her lips pumped yet again but whoever her surgeon was, she mused, he was to be complimented; Kay's lips were just perfect now. Of course, like many people, Kay denied having surgery of any kind, but of course, this was show business and looking good was the order of the day.

Dawn was well aware Kay did not need to join another agency to keep her career going. She knew that once Kay had worked for a client anywhere in the world, she was from then on contacted by those clients direct, cutting out the agency which, of course, angered Dawn and Belinda. They had hoped Kay would have stayed completely loyal to them but by becoming her own manager, Kay was making much more money for every job. This girl was in high demand; once seen, never forgotten. The ladies also knew the few jobs Kay still accepted from them was purely out of friendship, but for the most part Kay was running her own career. And she was going from strength to strength; making quite a name for herself as the number one Marilyn Monroe lookalike worldwide.

Kay revealed she was now divorced from Charles and was enjoying being a single girl again. Eventually strutting towards the agency door, in true Monroe style, Kay turned, flashing her new, extremely pure white, veneered teeth at them, and announced, "Oh, by the way, I am off to France next Friday for four months. I am under contract to portray Marilyn in Paris at the Fake Faces Tribute Shows, so ladies, unfortunately I will not be available for quite a while."

Noticing with a slight satisfaction the shocked expressions on their faces at her last-minute announcement, Kay raised her right hand to her luscious newly pumped lips and blew them a kiss, as only Marilyn and Kay could do.

Meanwhile in Soho, James and Joey were thoroughly enjoying each other's company. Joey found James a very confident and clever mentor, and made sure he took on board everything James was teaching him about the gambling business in the UK.

"Remember, the key to delegation is identifying the strengths of your team and capitalising on them," James stressed to Joey.

Although usually an insensitive man, James found he was missing Matt, but he was very pleased with Joey and had a special feeling for the young American. Unfortunately for James, there was a very greedy side to his character and it was this greed that drove him to line his pockets with a little of the Society's vast amounts of money. A thousand here or there would surely not be missed, he reasoned, then, smirking, complimented himself on the fact that the so-called best in the business, Gene Capalti, the Society's top Capitano, had failed to uncover any discrepancy on his last trip to London. James had a viable alibi ready in case Gene had found something amiss, but now he would keep that particular alibi for another time, if or when he might be in need of it. Being subtly sagacious by nature, James had decided not to let Joey in on his little secret. Always aware that Joey was, after all, an Associate of the Society, James decided it would be less risky to trust nobody, not even his lover.

Relaxing while reading his mail, which had been pushed through his letter box earlier that day, Adam's head sprung up as he heard an updated news account on the television about the famous diamond heist in Antwerp. The previous morning, he had travelled to Leeds in the north of England by National Rail first class, courtesy of the client who had booked him for a lookalike job for that evening. Resembling the handsome Johnny Depp had its highs, mused Adam. Apart from making plenty of money portraying the actor, he found he was in great demand with the ladies, which pleased him immensely.

Ever since his childhood, Adam had always been a bit of a sleuth and, for some unknown reason, he suspected Frank of knowing something about the Belgium diamond heist. Although always listening intently to his very reliable inner intuition, Adam knew his suspicions were partly due to the fact that he was still being kept in the loop by the Polizia di

Stato in Venice regarding the massive and unsolved diamond heist, which had taken place there many years before.

Frank's next trip to London was to be very quick, flying in early morning and leaving later that same day. This, of course, meant he would not have time to see Belinda. So as not to upset her, Frank decided not to mention his imminent arrival. After disclosing to the Society his suspicions of the last audit at the Soho betting office, Frank was informed that it had been arranged for Sergie to accompany him to London, enabling the Society's top Capitanos to work together to try to find any further discrepancies. Frank knew that if there was any deception on James' part, or indeed on any member of his team, he and Sergie would undoubtedly find it. After all, he reminded himself smugly, they were not known as Capitani d'elite within the Society for nothing.

During the following week, Frank telephoned Belinda, explaining to her as gently as possible that the Society would not be sending him back to London for quite some time. Hating himself for lying to her, Frank nevertheless decided this was the only action he could take under the circumstances.

A deep sadness descended on Belinda after hearing from Frank. The following morning, busy in the agency, a concerned Dawn glanced at her friend's face, which was full of misery, and her warm heart went out to her.

"Belinda, sweetheart, you must be used to this by now. You know Frank's job sends him here, there and everywhere. I hate to see you so unhappy, darling," she said gently, placing her hand on Belinda's shoulder in an effort to comfort her dear friend.

Large, sad eyes looked up at Dawn as hot tears spilled and rolled down Belinda's face as she sobbed uncontrollably. In deep despair, Belinda allowed herself to be hugged and rocked in Dawn's arms.

Although Joey was a man of honour and a fully initiated member of the Society, it had been unanimously decided he would remain ignorant regarding the outstanding contract on the head of James Swift. Gene had stressed to the Society that he had seen real proof in London which made him suspect James and Joey had become more than just good friends, and because he believed that the heart could rule the head where emotions were concerned, Frank had recommended that Joey be kept in the dark for the time being.

Welcomed by the good old British weather living up to its infamous reputation, Frank and Sergie arrived in London to be met by Joey's smiling face. Slapping him on the back in friendly greeting, Gene was relieved to see that James was not there. Frank took this opportunity to remind Joey and Sergie that he was known only as Gene Capalti here in London, and not Frank Lanzo.

It was Sergie who discovered the first discrepancy during the audit. Whistling and tapping Frank on the arm, he handed across the audit sheet he was scrutinising and sat back smugly smiling, waiting for Frank's reaction.

"Complmenti, Sergio. Abbiamo il bastardo questa volta!" *(Well done, Sergie. We have the bastard this time!)* Gene said, with satisfaction.

After a short, satisfying lunch, ordered and delivered from one of the many local Italian restaurants dotted around the vibrant Soho area, the Capitanos, James and Joey held a meeting to discuss the completed audit. As far as James and Joey were informed, everything was in order and all accounts and ledgers were accurate. Frank and Sergie glanced at James as this false information was announced to the young partners. The slightest glimpse of relief flashed fleetingly across his eyes, but Frank and Sergie had caught this and looked at each other with satisfaction.

"Pity you boys are flying out immediately," remarked James, slowly getting up from his chair and stretching his long, lean legs. "Joey and I are going to Gaucho in Piccadilly this evening and we know you would both appreciate this terrific Argentine restaurant," James said, glancing at the Americans and shrugging his athletic shoulders.

"Not to worry, guys," replied Gene. "We'll make sure we visit there next time."

Receiving several calls from Frank during the following weeks, expressing his undying love for her, Belinda, although missing her lover desperately, found that by keeping herself busy, the pain of being separated from him was a little less unbearable. It was now nearing the last Sunday of March, which meant the UK's clocks went forward one hour for the start of daylight saving. There was always a feeling of relief in the air when this date arrived in the Gregorian calendar; the longer evenings magically uplifting everybody's spirits in anticipation of the imminent spring and summer months to come and, more importantly, longer daylight hours.

❧

James and Joey were in the office when Joey's mobile rang and, surprised to hear Frank's unmistakable voice, he immediately excused himself from his colleague and stepped outside of the betting office to pick up a better reception. Frank came straight to the point and informed Joey Franzini his presence was required at a meeting in New York. Joey was informed his tickets had been taken care of and he was to fly on Thursday morning, allowing him sufficient time to make himself ready for the meeting scheduled to take place the following Sunday.

"But, Frank, we are in the middle of the busiest racing season here," objected Joey, the colour rising to his handsome face in annoyance.

"Listen to me, Joey. You will be gone for barely one week. James has plenty of staff at his disposal and will hardly miss you. This is an important meeting and you have to be there," replied Frank. "What has gotten into you? Don't ever question the Society again. Capisce?"

Before Joey could reply, Frank had already cut the connection, leaving nothing but the dialling tone ringing loudly in Joey's ear.

"I wonder what this meeting is all about. Have you any idea, Joey?" queried James, looking thoughtful after receiving a text message from Gene (Frank), informing him his junior partner was requested to be in attendance at the meeting and was scheduled to fly out in a few days.

"No idea whatsoever. Was just given my orders," replied Joey, a look of bewilderment in his eyes. "And orders are orders," he added quietly.

James gave his lover one of his beguiling smiles and reassuringly replied, "They certainly are, Joey, but even though you will be gone for only one week, I will miss you."

Unbeknown to Joey, as he flew out of the airport on his return to New York, Sergie had literally crossed him in the air and arrived to stay at the Sherlock Holmes Hotel where he was going to keep a low profile until such time when he would be alerted by the Society of his further orders.

The two men walked purposely in unison, falling into step with each other. Antonio Tosato and Vincenzo de Luca made their way slowly down the steps from the plane, which had just landed from John F. Kennedy Airport, New York. They knew exactly what was expected of them from the Society and they had made a pledge that this time, there would be no slip-ups; no mistaken identity. This contract must be carried out with perfect precision imminently.

James locked up the Soho betting office after all of his staff had left, and feeling quite lonely and missing Joey, he decided to drive straight home to Wimbledon and have a quiet evening. Mrs Smedley, his housekeeper, had telephoned to say she had left a homemade meat pie in the oven for him. Pulling into his spacious driveway as the sky turned murky black, James did not notice a small dark van parked nearby. Alighting from his car and locking it, he took his front door keys out of his jacket pocket and let himself in, happy at last to be able to have a few drinks and unwind. Walking past the ebony coat stand and casually throwing his grey tweed jacket over an armchair, James headed towards the kitchen to turn on the oven and warm Mrs Smedley's meat pie. Pouring himself a large glass of red wine, James did not expect to receive a knock on his front door.

Tutting and frowning to himself before taking a large mouthful of the comforting wine, he sauntered towards the front door calling out, "Yes, who is it?"

"Special delivery, sir," came a man's voice through the heavy oak door.

"At this time of the evening?" queried James, a puzzled look sweeping across his face.

"Yes, sir, we deliver up to 10 o'clock Monday to Saturday," replied the anonymous voice, the accent of which James could not decipher.

Opening the door, but keeping the heavy gold safety chain on, James peered through the gap at the stranger outside, dressed in a dark green delivery man's uniform with cap, holding a long narrow parcel and a signing machine.

"Mr James Swift?" asked the man, shifting his weight from one foot to the other.

"Yes," answered James. "But I am not expecting anything through the post," he added quickly, glancing at the parcel.

"Well, sir, these flowers are addressed to you. I am only the delivery man doing my job and I'd appreciate it if you signed for them," was the man's sullen reply.

"Flowers? From whom?" he asked, beginning to think this was a joke of some kind.

"I have no idea but there is a card attached to the box," offered the man, pointing to the lid of the long box and peering at James through the gap in the door.

"Okay, pass me the card, would you? There's a good chap," requested James, and the delivery man took the card off the box and pushed it through the gap in the door. After reading the message on the card, James let out an amused laugh as he slipped the heavy gold chain off the catch and opened the door to accept the box of flowers. They had apparently been ordered by Joey before he flew out of London.

"Okay, where would you like my signature?" asked James obligingly, a smile playing at the corners of his mouth as he took the box of flowers from the delivery man.

"Right here, sir," was the answer, but before James took the pen to sign, he was pushed back into the house and punched squarely in the face.

In total shock and before James could comprehend what was happening, a second delivery man come rushing in through the front door, kicking it closed behind him as he blurted out, "Va bene, Vinny, finiamo questa." *(Okay, Vinny, let's finish this.)*

The last thought to pass through James Swift's stunned mind as the succinylcholine (SUX) injection stopped his heart, silencing him forever was, 'I really must learn Italian.'

The next morning, as arranged James' golfing friend Martin Dennis arrived to pick him up for their booked game at the Wimbledon Golf Club. As he walked towards James' front door, Martin suddenly felt the nagging easterly wind, which belied the bright cloudless morning. Checking the time on his wristwatch, he pressed his finger on the brass doorbell. Receiving no response from within, Martin, a man of little patience, pressed the doorbell again. No answer! Noticing the heavy brass knocker, Martin banged several times on the oak door, bent down and shouted for James through the large letter box. Still no response. Becoming irritable and feeling again the sharpness of the easterly wind, Martin suddenly became concerned. Although he was aware his friend liked to have a few drinks in the evening, James had given him his word he would not be drinking heavily on Saturday and he would be ready and waiting for Martin to pick him up early for their game of golf. Ringing the bell yet again and repeatedly banging loudly on the door knocker, Martin then called another golfer friend who would by now be waiting for him and James at the golf club. After telling his friend his concerns for James, they agreed he should call the police.

Within fifteen minutes, a police car had pulled up outside James' house and tried to arouse a response from James, also knocking loudly on the door and calling, "James Swift," several times through the letterbox. No answer!

The body was stiff and lifeless, rigor mortis having expertly accomplishing its job. James' eyes were wide open and the expression in them told the onlooker he had been severely shocked by something, or someone, just before his death. The body had discoloured, but other than that the police were uncertain whether foul play had occurred or whether James might have had a sudden heart attack or fatal stroke. There was no evidence to suggest anybody had been in the house with him. Antonio and Vincenzo, being such elite henchmen, had made sure there were no telltale signs left behind, turning off James' oven containing Mrs Smedley's meat pie and taking with them the box of flowers and card, falsely signed in Joey's handwriting.

As they climbed into the waiting van, Antonio muttered satisfactorily, "Infine, abbiamo messo a tacere il bastardo ricattatore e ladro." *(Finally, we have silenced the blackmailing, thieving bastard.)*

As the tragic scene behind James' front door began to sink into Martin's mind, he started to shake, his face became ashen and he kept muttering to himself. After a few minutes, a second police car arrived at the scene. Martin, after being treated for his shock, was driven home by two police officers, while a third followed closely behind driving Martin's car, the scheduled game of golf now completely forgotten.

Chapter 49
Venice Sparkle

In New York, Joey swallowed the last drop of his espresso coffee and, grabbing his navy leather jacket off the armchair in his five-star hotel room, hurriedly let himself out of the door. A few minutes earlier, he had received a call from another Associate, Frankie Mazzarini, informing the young man that he was parked downstairs ready to drive Joey uptown for his meeting with the Society. Sitting back in the passenger seat beside Frankie, Joey took in the familiar sights of his native New York, but his thoughts were full of James and how much he loved him. Putting his foot down and driving a shade over the speed limit, Frankie kept silent until they reached their destination.

"Seguimi, Joey," *(Follow me, Joey)* said Frankie as he led Joey up the steps of the Society's headquarters.

As they walked through the swing doors into the impressive foyer, several Associates nodded to them in recognition. The room was smaller than Joey had imagined it would be for a Society meeting. On entering, the first person he saw was Frank, who smiled at Joey, a look of concern in his troubled eyes. Several of the Society's hierarchy sat together on a long, rectangular, highly polished table and Joey was ushered to an empty chair. He felt all eyes on him, which in turn started to make Joey feel desperately hot under the collar and very uncomfortable. He turned his head slightly to glance at Frank but Frank did not meet his gaze. It was a meeting of unusually short duration, and by the end Joey was devastated by what he had heard. Suddenly, Frank was now standing beside him and talking soothingly to him, but Joey could not comprehend what Frank was saying. Feeling light-headed, as if he were floating around in a foggy dream, Joey could not believe that he would never see or be with James ever again.

Back in London, Sergie arrived at the Soho betting office early on the Monday morning, being in possession of a set of keys given to him on one of his earlier visits to London. Gene had telephoned Sergie an hour before while Sergie was having breakfast in his hotel room, informing him that Joey would be back in London in approximately ten days. The Society had now decided Joey should attend James' funeral or cremation, otherwise employees of the betting offices and their customers might find it strange the junior partner was not in attendance, especially as they had been such good friends. Frank told Sergie that Joey had put in a request not to return to his position in London now that James was no longer there but the Society had rejected his request and ordered him to take a couple of weeks' bereavement leave and then return to London to work alongside Sergie for the foreseeable future. Joey knew only too well that contracts were contracts and once the Society had put them in place, there was no slipping out of them, no matter what.

The weeks passed and London was experiencing an unusually warm and sunny spring. Joey had slowly but sadly settled back into his life and position in a bustling London, his mind continuously dwelling on his past relationship with James whom, he knew deep in his heart of hearts, he would never forget or stop loving. Sergie was a fun guy and working with him was the best tonic for Joey. Whenever an astute Sergie noticed Joey becoming depressed, he sprung an idea out of the blue, always something magical and different for them to do. Since living and working in London, Joey had, through James, met with several of James' friends and many of these now rallied round to cheer Joey. To the Society's satisfaction, under the gaze of Sergie the London betting offices were continuing to flourish, as was Joey.

Gene (Frank) had flown in briefly once or twice since James' funeral, carrying large amounts of fake money with him but he had never mentioned these visits to Belinda because he had not stayed long enough to spend time with her. This saddened him deeply, and as time seemed to flash by quickly, Frank became aware that life was indeed short. He had at last decided to ask Belinda to live with him in New York. Fully aware that Belinda had a full life in London and would be loathed to leave her family and friends, Frank nevertheless had made up his mind to ask her. If Belinda decided she would rather live in London and visit him in New York as often as possible, he would be happy to accept that arrangement also. Knowing only too well he would always be in love with Belinda, Frank was ready at last to commit the rest of his life to her, however long or short.

"Venice?" queried Frank, looking askance at the telephone during a call received in his New York office from one of his superiors. The puzzled frown was still farrowing his brow as he made his way out of the door and down the lavish decor of the elegant spacious corridor towards the caller's office. The warm neutral shades of cream and dark brown of the extravagant decor within never failed to please Frank's dancing eyes. A brief meeting with one of the Society's hierarchy explained exactly why his presence was required yet again in Venice. Of course, the knowledge that he would be working closely with Count Luigi Boggia helped quash the irritation he felt of having to fly again to the Italian city of love. His troubled mind took him back some months ago to his encounter with Signor Gabrini, the security manager at Marco Polo Airport, and he knew he would have to make sure his fingerprints disappeared temporarily yet again.

Returning to his own plush office, Frank decided to call Belinda and tell her that once he had finished his commitments in Venice, he would fly to London for a couple of days so they could be together. After the lovers had chatted for some time, he finished the call by saying, "Belinda, I have something I must ask you when next we meet." Then, proclaiming his undying love for her, the line went dead.

Belinda was feeling happier than she had done for a very long time. Although still missing Matt, she had begun to realise that Frank was deeply in love with her as she was with him. What, she wondered, was he wanting to ask her? Smiling secretly, her heart started to beat quickly with excitable anticipation.

Feeling less edgy about being back in Venice, now that Frank had spoken at length with Count Luigi Boggia, he walked confidently towards the familiar foreign arrival desk of Marco Polo Airport. Luckily for Frank, the stony-faced female clerk was not on the desk, but instead a middle-aged man with a swarthy complexion was dealing with all the foreign passengers. Handing his American passport and visa documents to the clerk, Frank breathed a sigh of relief as he was waved through. Quickly making his way towards the baggage carousel and deep in thought, he did not hear at first his name being called out on the loudspeaker system, and continued to retrieve his luggage.

Suddenly, he stopped walking, for the first time taking in everything going on around him because he felt as if he had somehow entered a surreal world. His confused mind was racing as he tried desperately to make sense of the situation unfolding. At least a dozen police officers were walking straight towards Frank, pointing their sub-machine guns directly at him, their eyes never leaving his colourless face. The voice, rudely cutting through his confusion, sounded familiar.

"Signor Lanzo, we have reason to suspect that you have tried to smuggle stolen goods into Venice. Please come this way," ordered Pietro Gabrini, Manager of Airport Security.

Frank felt like he was about to explode as he turned abruptly to defend himself against such ridiculous accusations. His reaction caused the police officers to crowd around him in their endeavour to protect Pietro Gabrini. Frank's head was spinning and he was vaguely aware of people, both passengers and airport staff alike, standing around watching him.

"Signor Lanzo, please come with us quietly. It will be better for you in the long run," insisted the security manager smugly, turning away from Frank as he instructed the police officers to frogmarch the American to the same office where, some months earlier, he had detained Frank to retake his fingerprints.

Once again, Frank found himself sitting on the hard, wooden chair as the same fair-haired young man, from his previous encounter with the security manager's team, was busy going through Frank's dark brown leather suitcase.

Pietro Gabrini came straight to the point.

"We have been carrying out random checks on passengers' luggage for a long time, Signor Lanzo, and today is no exception. Unfortunately for you, Signor, diamonds worth millions of dollars were found in a secret compartment of your suitcase."

The sparkling gems caught the light in all their glory as the security manager held them up in front of his detainee. Trying to make sense of what Pietro Gabrini was telling him, Frank, with a look of utter disbelief in his eyes, began fervently denying ever having seen these diamonds before. Perspiring heavily, he was aware of his voice catching in his dry throat when he demanded they call his employers, Count Luigi Boggia and the American Embassy. For the first time that day, it dawned on Frank that he had been set up by the Venetian Airport Security Team. The only thing keeping Frank's spirits up was the fact that he had made sure his fingerprints had temporarily disappeared before flying out of New York.

While the Security Team waited for Count Luigi Boggia and a representative from the American Embassy to arrive at the airport, Frank was treated to a meal for one of the most famous and ancient regional specialities of Venice, risi e bisi; consisting of soup and thick risotto made of fresh peas and risotto. Although Frank was worried sick, he had not eaten for some hours and ate the tasty Italian meal.

The American Embassy's representative and Count Luigi Boggia spent considerable time discussing with the Manager of Airport Security and the police. The Count pulled out all stops for his dear friend's release, but to no avail. Pietro Gabrini had such a tight case against Frank Lanzo that his superiors agreed he was permitted to detain the American for anything up to one month while the Security Team investigated the smuggled diamonds.

Count Luigi Boggia was allowed to speak with an ashen-faced Frank. Resting his hand on the American's slumped shoulders, he said in a half-whisper, "I have already alerted the Society, my friend. They will be flying their best lawyers into Venice immediately. Please think positive; you know the United States and Italy are close allies."

Frank, the dancing eyes now vacant of any emotion, replied in a low, barely audible voice, "Luigi, if I am detained for a full month, my fingerprints will undoubtedly grow back again. If that happens, you know as well as I do that I will be finished for good!"

Count Luigi Boggia tried with difficulty not to look alarmed, completely forgetting there a possibility of Frank's fingerprints being held on file ever since the diamond heist in Venice many years before. Feigning a smile, the Count replied, "Frank, my dear friend, we will get you out of here long before then."

As he turned slowly to leave the security manager's office, the Count stopped briefly glancing at Frank and added encouragingly, "Devi pensare positive il mio amico, positivo." *(You have to think positive, my friend, positive.)*

Belinda's newly felt happiness seemed to uplift the hearts of Dawn, Freddie and, in turn, little Queenie. Confiding to her dear friends everything Frank had said to her when he had called from New York, Dawn and Freddie were indeed happy that, at last, Frank was ready to commit to Belinda, and hopefully make an honest woman of her.

It was an unusually quiet day at the Top Drawer Agency. Freddie had left with little Queenie and Dawn had gone to attend a dental appointment. Earlier, Dawn had become concerned after hearing the breaking news that Angelina Jolie and Brad Pitt had decided to end their turbulent marriage. With the separation of the iconic couple, this would mean a loss of work, not only for the lookalikes but also for the agency, although it was possible they could work separately in the future.

"The one positive thing about all this," said Dawn quietly to Belinda, "is hopefully Karen and Mark's little affair will eventually fizzle out!"

Alone now in the agency while browsing through newly received photographs of wannabe President Trump lookalikes, Belinda's mobile began to shrill. Quickly answering the call, Belinda became flustered as the unmistakeable heavily accented voice of Count Luigi Boggia reached her ears.

"Ciao, Belinda. I have just arrived in London on business and wondered whether you would permit me, yet again, to take you to dinner this evening?"

Before Belinda could reply to the Count, he quickly continued, his voice faltering.

"I have some very unfortunate news to tell you, my dear, but I cannot do this on the telephone, as I am sure you will understand."

Coming soon!

The Unravelling Crime Thriller Conclusion
Set in the World of Lookalikes

Double Deception II

Duplicity

Where one falsehood leads to another